STEALING INFINITY

ALSO BY ALYSON NOËL

ALYSON NOËL

STEALING INFINITY

Entangled Publishing, LLC
10940 S Parker Road
Suite 327
Parker, CO 80134
rights@entangledpublishing.com

Entangled Teen is an imprint of Entangled Publishing, LLC.

Visit our website at www.entangledpublishing.com.

Edited by Stacy Abrams
Cover design by Bree Archer
Cover images by
EduardHarkonen/Gettyimages,
wacomka/Gettyimages,
paulfleet/Depositphotos,
remuhin/Shutterstock, and abzee/Shutterstock
Interior design by Toni Kerr

ISBN 9-781-64937-150-8
Ebook ISBN 9-781-64937-155-3

Manufactured in the United States of America

First Edition June 2022

10 9 8 7 6 5 4 3 2 1

entangled teen
an imprint of Entangled Publishing LLC

For Elizabeth Bewley,
so many years and so many reasons.

At Entangled, we want our readers to be well-informed. If you would like to know if this book contains any elements that might be of concern for you, please check the back of the book for details.

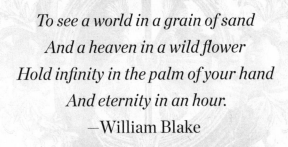

To see a world in a grain of sand
And a heaven in a wild flower
Hold infinity in the palm of your hand
And eternity in an hour.
—William Blake

Dear Reader,

At some point in the story that follows we're going to delve into a bit of numerology (not a spoiler, I swear!). And, since I figured some of you might not be familiar with this ancient divination tool, I thought I'd include a little primer right here, so you can add up your birthday and see how numerology applies to you.

Of course, if you prefer not to do any math, (which I totally get!) feel free to skip ahead. It honestly won't make the slightest bit of difference in your reading experience.

If you do choose to calculate, find me on Instagram @alyson_noel and let me know if your number rang true for you!

(Full disclosure: I'm an eight!)

Numerology: How to Calculate and Understand the Meaning Behind Your Numerology Life Path Number

Much like your sun sign in astrology, your Life Path Number reflects your strengths, weaknesses, interests, talents, goals, dreams, and the overall tone of your life experience and life's mission.

To calculate this number, add your full birth date (month, day, entire year) together, then keep calculating until you reach a single digit number, except for the numbers 11, 22 and 33, which are Master Numbers.

For example:
Birth date: May 24, 2004, or 5/24/2004
$$5 + 2 + 4 + 2 + 0 + 0 + 4 = 17$$

If your result is a double digit number, (again, except for 11, 22, and 33), add the two numbers together and reduce it to a single digit.
$$1 + 7 = 8$$
The Life Path Number for this birth date is **8**.

Okay, so, now that you know your number, what the heck does it mean?

Number 1 (10/1, 19/1): If you're a one, you are all about taking action. You're confident, independent, a bit of an innovator, and you carry some big-time natural leadership vibes. You're the one in your group who gets it started and sees that it's done.

Number 2 (11/2, 20/2): Twos are naturals when it comes to anything to do with relationships, cooperation, and bringing harmony where and when it's needed. If you're a two, you are sensitive to energies and are known for enhanced intuition, which makes you the go-to for friends seeking advice.

Number 3 (12/3, 21/3): Threes are big on communicating. Whether it's via speaking, writing, drawing, dancing, composing, whatever. If you're a three, you take great joy in expressing yourself, and your creations are known for inspiring others.

Number 4 (13/4, 22/4, 31/4): Fours like to take a more practical approach. They're logical, orderly, with strong earth-centered energy. If you're a four, you probably have a calming vibe and often serve as a grounding influence on others. You're the one your friends can rely on.

Number 5 (14/5, 23/5, 32/5): Fives practically live for freedom and adventure. If you're a five, you most likely have an appetite for learning, and a deep curiosity for just about, well, everything. Fives are natural life-long learners who love to travel.

Number 6 (15/6, 24/6, 33/6): If you're a six, chances are you're the go-to for anyone searching for help, healing, nurturing, or just a willing ear or shoulder to lean on. Animals and humans are equally drawn to your innate, protective, soulful energy.

Number 7 (16/7, 25/7, 34/7): Sevens are the investigators, the analysts, the ones who delve deeply to get to the root of the matter. If you're a seven, for you it's all about the research, because you know better than anyone that the details are the true key to understanding.

Number 8 (17/8, 26/8, 35/8): Eight is a power player. If you're an eight, you probably like listing your goals so you can cross them off once you've achieved them. Your hard work often leads to the sort of status, wealth, and success you've always dreamed of.

Number 9 (18/9, 27/9, 36/9): Nines are the old souls of the group. They tend to be selfless humanitarians who are more interested in serving the greater good than themselves. If you're a nine, you see the bigger picture of life, and people are drawn to you for the wisdom you offer.

Master Number 11 (11/2): Elevens, like twos, are all about communication and connection, except the eleven energy is intensified to a whole other level. If you're an eleven, you're artistic, creative, and your intuitive abilities are often the by-product of your own extreme life experiences.

Master Number 22 (22/4): The Master Number twenty-two, is the ramped up version of a four, with the addition of enhanced creative abilities. They're the architects who make their visions happen. If you're a twenty-two, you're probably a master at taking your hardships and spinning them into gold.

Master Number 33 (33/6): With the nurturing vibe of a six, and double the communication skills of a three, thirty-threes are masterful teachers and inspired visionaries. If you're a thirty-three, both friends and strangers are drawn to the deeply healing presence you carry.

FACT:

The Antikythera Mechanism: An ancient Greek hand-powered orrery lost at sea for over 2,000 years, is thought to be the oldest example of an analogue computer, used to predict astronomical positions and eclipses decades in advance. Many of the mechanism's pieces are still missing—including the wooden box it was housed in, the knobs used to turn the missing metal gearwheels, a collection of stones that stood in for the sun, moon, various planets, rotating dials, and more. Many of its hidden inscriptions have yet to be translated.

The Mystery Schools of Egypt: These ancient societies held and protected wisdom within the confines of the temple walls. Such secrets were passed down within the priesthood but forbidden to the ordinary man.

Tarot: The earliest surviving tarot deck, known as the Visconti-Sforza tarocchi deck, is said to date back to fifteenth-century Northern Italy, when it was commissioned by the Duke of Milan, Francesco Visconti. The twenty-two Major Arcana cards depict an allegorical pictorial processional of a youth who symbolically dies and is ultimately reborn. Though originally used as a parlor game, widespread use of the tarot for divination began to take off in the late sixteenth and early seventeenth centuries.

Henricus Martellus: In 1491, the German cartographer created a world map that depicted Europe and the Mediterranean that is thought to be the map Christopher Columbus relied on during his voyage across the Atlantic. Modern technology has recently uncovered previous illegible and hidden texts within the map.

All the artwork mentioned in this novel is real.

PROLOGUE

The Timekeeper

BASILIQUE ROYALE DE SAINT-DENIS, FRANCE

1741

I wake to a void of darkness and the tip of a cold, sharp dagger jabbing into my bound wrists.

"Get up," a voice shouts. "The sooner it's done, the sooner I'm gone." With a single flick of the blade, the rope that binds my hands falls away.

I grunt, flex my fingers, as a pair of rough hands forces me to my feet. The sudden movement causes a jolt of nausea to lurch through me so violently, I double over in agony and empty my belly.

"Good God!" my captor cries. Ripping the blindfold from my face, he smacks me hard across the back of my head. "Now look what you've done!"

A searing pain shoots through my skull, but at least the fog of sedation is beginning to lift. Swaying unsteadily, I focus on the vomit covering my captor's polished black boots.

New boots, not yet broken in. The boots of either the young, the vain, or the wildly inexperienced. When I meet my captor's gaze, I realize I'm looking at a match for all three. The blue eyes that stare back belong to a boy no more than fourteen.

Back home, he'd be considered a child, sheltered by parents

and governed by laws meant to keep him safe from exactly the sort of people he undoubtedly works for.

But here…

I glance around, trying to distinguish where I am. Though there's no question as to why I was taken.

Two boys had grabbed me off the street and stuck a needle into my arm. Just before I blacked out, I saw one of them bore the mark, or at least the beginnings of the symbol, but still, he offered no help. And though only one boy stands before me now, that doesn't mean the other isn't off lurking somewhere.

"What year is it?" I ask, the spike of dread in my unused voice echoing through the ancient, cavernous space. *Something feels off. Something's not right about this place.*

"1741," the boy spits.

So it is true. A slow chill creeps down my spine, my breath grows shallow and weak. I heard this was possible—traveling backward through time. And now that I've done it, it seems a shame I won't live long enough to tell anyone.

"You don't have to do this," I say. "You're being used. Sent on a coward's mission. You—"

"Silence!" The boy flashes his dagger, clearly eager to use it. Though he won't be willing to use it just yet. Not until he gets what he came for.

After that, escape is unlikely.

Though I've spent a lifetime training for this very moment, I'm still surprised to find that just beyond the regret lies a quiet acceptance of the doom that awaits me. *Is this how my ancestors felt when confronted with a Timekeeper's fate?*

I watch the boy unfurl a roll of old parchment and point to a faded sketch of a skeleton holding a vertebra.

My god. I inhale a quick breath, instantly recognizing the map as the one that once belonged to Columbus. Though the symbol was added a full century after the explorer had used it to cross the Atlantic. *How in the hell did he get ahold of that?*

"The Death card," the boy says, those blue eyes glinting as he seizes my shoulder and drives me toward a single crypt against the far wall.

Of course—we're in the Royal Necropolis. Where the French royals were buried for centuries. The boy, and whoever employed him, has misinterpreted the tarot and played right into the Order of the Timekeepers' hands. *The treasure is safe. And, for now, at least, it'll remain that way.*

"The Antikythera Mechanism is nearly complete. Only one piece to go." The boy's grin is smug, but the claim is a lie. The Antikythera will never be complete. The Timekeepers date back to the great Mystery Schools of Egypt—we understand the true workings of time and have dedicated our lives to protecting the very pieces this boy wants.

"You've solved all the clues," I say, "so don't let me stop you from winning this game."

It's a challenge the boy can't meet. The missing pieces are enchanted so that only the worthy can retrieve them. This boy clearly doesn't fit the criteria.

"Grunt work's on you." The boy glares. "Or I can always bring the girl back to finish the job…"

A sudden coldness seizes my core. I've gone to great lengths to keep her a secret. Hell, the other Timekeepers don't even know about my daughter. *So how does he?*

"It's time for you and your brothers to give up the pieces and return the Antikythera to humanity—*where it belongs!*" the boy snaps.

There are so many dangerous lies contained in that statement, but for me, one thing rises above the rest. "She's a child!" I shout.

"Not for long. We can either travel forward and find her in the future or wait it out. Now's when you get to decide if you'll spare her that fate."

Can they travel forward? I'm doubtful. Though there's clearly nothing to stop them from waiting it out.

"I'll get it." My voice shakes. "Just—leave her out of it." I squint at King Dagobert's tomb and the three carved panels above that tell the story of the Hermit John.

The early tarot portrayed the Hermit card—also referred to as Time—as an old man carrying an hourglass. Modern decks switched that hourglass to a lantern. Once again, the boy and his employer have played right into our hands. But still, two things are clear.

The boy has no intention of letting me live.

And my daughter is no longer safe.

Though…if I can delay long enough, the window for travel might close, leaving this boy trapped in a time and place he doesn't belong.

Not exactly a happy ending, but it's the best I can manage.

I get to work, prolonging the struggle to move the slab. But the boy grows impatient, pushes me aside, and shoves the lid to the ground where it breaks into chunks. "It's not there!" he cries, punching his dagger to my neck.

"It's *enchanted*," I remind him, my jaw clenched. "Isn't that why you brought me here?"

To the ordinary eye, the crypt is nearly empty. But a Timekeeper's sight is far from ordinary. When I look inside, the years quickly unravel to reveal the spot where, centuries before, one of my brothers stashed the gleaming gold decoy.

I reach past a pile of decaying cloth and old bones, close my fingers around it, and set about infusing the golden ball with an energetic message that can be unlocked only by my girl. Though I'd already started the lessons she'll need if they ever do find her, I realize now that I moved too slowly. Took too long. Foolishly believed I had an abundance of the one thing there's never enough of—the one thing that can neither be purchased nor conquered.

Time.

And yet, this boy and whoever employs him are determined to do just that. For them, the golden ball is a step toward ultimate power.

For me, it's my last chance to finish what I've barely begun.

When the boy does find my daughter—and he will—I can only hope it will lead to her uncovering this object.

"What the hell are you doing?" The boy makes a grab for the piece, but I ram past him and race for the exit.

There is so much to tell her about her Timekeeper legacy—how to manage the Unraveling, her gift for seeing through time. A gift that only recently surfaced.

She'd been terrified when it happened. And though I was glad I'd been there to help, I deeply regret never getting the chance to show her how to control it, much less explain how one day soon, she'll need to use it against our adversaries.

But now it's too late for any of that. The most I can leave her is a glimpse of the face of this young, blue-eyed enemy.

I've made it only a handful of steps when the tip of the blade slices through the air and plunges straight into my back.

The pain is immediate, slamming me to the ground, as the boy comes up from behind, pulls the blade free, and snatches the golden ball from my grip.

"Were you fool enough to think you'd get away, old man?" With a scathing grin, the boy stands over me, raises the bloodied dagger, and plunges it deep into my heart.

In an instant, my vision narrows, the world begins to fade. With a gaze clouded by pain, I look into the boy's eyes and say, "Are you fool enough to believe you're holding the real one?"

With my last ragged breath, I watch the color drain from the boy's face, then close my eyes and fall into nothingness.

1

Natasha
A Southern California high school
Present day

"God, I hate this place."

Mason shakes his head and mashes a plastic fork into a clump of avocado, quinoa, sweet potato, and some silky white block I'm guessing is tofu. I recognize it as one of the more popular Buddha bowls he must have picked up from the vegan café where we work. But to me, it looks like the adult version of baby food.

"I mean, what messed-up twist of fate landed me here?" He sweeps an elegant brown arm past the suburban hellscape of boring cinderblock walls to the hot-lunch station of our school's cafeteria, his collection of silver bangles clattering softly, before pausing on the tables reserved for the popular kids. The same tables where I used to sit, back when I was another girl, living another life. "I'm ninety-nine percent certain I was switched at birth, and now I'm trapped in someone else's dystopian nightmare."

I pick at my bag of vending machine chips, remembering how I used to play the "switched at birth" game, too, until my mom unearthed my birth certificate and waved it proudly before me. *"See?"* she said, face flushed with triumph as she dragged a chipped nail across her name and my dad's just below it. *"Like it or not, we made you."*

I shut myself in my room and cried all afternoon.

"Just take me away. Anywhere but here." Mason abandons his lunch and stretches leisurely across the bench. With an arm draped over his face, I'm left with a view of perfectly drawn red lips, reminding me of an actress in a black-and-white movie badly in need of some smelling salts. "So bored," he groans. "Draw me a picture with words."

"We're in Paris," I say, not missing a beat. It's one of our favorite games. "We have the very best table at the chicest sidewalk café, and we death stare anyone who dares to dress better than us. Which is basically no one, since I'm wearing a silk slip dress with a faux-fur stole and jeweled biker boots, and you're practically swimming in an elaborately embroidered tunic, vegan suede leggings, and five-inch blue velvet mules."

"And what are we eating?" he prompts, licking his lips.

Since I'm not exactly a foodie like him, I stick with the basics. "I'm idly picking at a chocolate croissant while you nurse a dairy-free but remarkably creamy café au lait that somehow never goes cold no matter how long we linger."

"Do you ever miss it?" He sits up so abruptly, it yanks me right out of Paris.

"Miss what?" I ask.

"You know, being part of all that?" He sweeps a hand over his shaved head and nods toward the place where I used to sit—before I ended up next to the recycle bin.

"No," I say, quick to turn away so he won't see the lie on my face. While I don't miss the table or the people who sit there, I do miss the person I used to be—the one who cared about my grades, the one who dreamed of a brighter future beyond these beige hallways.

I'm about to add something more when Mason groans and starts gathering his things. "All hail the queen," he says, and I look up to see Elodie approaching. "I can't believe you're still hanging with her."

I watch as Elodie makes her way across the cafeteria. Like a celebrity on a red carpet, so many people clamor for her attention, the trip takes much longer than it should.

"She's fun." I shrug. "And she has access to some pretty amazing things. VIP guest lists, courtside seats to the—"

"To the Lakers?" Mason shoots me a razor-sharp look. "Since when do you give a shit about sports?"

"I'm just saying...maybe you should give her a chance."

Mason shakes his head. "Trust me, I know a bad vibe when I see it, and that girl is trouble." He slings his knock-off designer bag over his shoulder, wanting to be gone before she can reach us.

"Sometimes trouble is fun." I laugh, needing to lighten the mood. But the way Mason scowls, it clearly doesn't work.

"Magic always comes with a price," he says.

"Are you seriously quoting Rumpelstiltskin?"

"Just stating the facts. Someday all this *fun* is going to catch up with you. If it hasn't already."

"And now you sound like my mom," I grumble, but then I remember how he met my actual mom the one time he showed up at my house unannounced. "Well...like someone's mom."

"It's not too late." His earnest brown eyes meet mine. "You can still turn it around, get your grades back on track. So why are you acting like the choice isn't yours, like you're not the one who writes your own story?"

He's right, of course. But what he doesn't understand is that I'm nothing like him.

Mason lives with his grandma, and what she lacks in money, she makes up for in her determination to help him succeed.

His grades count toward his future—they'll pave the way to a brighter life in a much better place.

I could be valedictorian and it wouldn't change a thing. I can't go off to college because I can't leave my mom. She's completely dependent on me.

As Elodie closes in, she sings out my name—"*Natashaaaaaa.*"

I really need her to stop calling me that. Natasha is the before picture of my life. The name given by a mom who dreamed of her baby girl's shiny future.

Nat is who I became after my dad ran off and never came back, leaving my mom too depleted to bother with the extra syllables.

Mason mumbles something about texting me later, then bolts before I can try to convince him to stay. It's the deal we agreed on. He'll (mostly) stop talking trash about her if I stop bugging him to give her a chance.

I know I *should* follow him before it's too late, but I find myself turning toward Elodie instead. And when she waves, and I watch her face break into a grin, I secretly smile to myself, pretending not to notice all the envious looks directed my way as the coolest girl in school again sings out my name.

2

"*Na—ta—sha!*" Elodie drags out each syllable. Her face flushed, eyes lit, she stands before me in all her teenage dream glory.

"*Elodie Blue,*" I reply, trying to match her tone, only I'm way off-key. Still, it sounds like a stage name, totally false. Her mom must have been an even bigger dreamer than mine.

Better at it, too, considering how her dream came true.

I lower my gaze past the prominent cheekbones and the sort of perfect pillowy lips people pay good money for, and onto what actually interests me—her clothes. One of the perks of hanging out with her: fashionable by association.

My mom used to joke (back when she still joked) that I went straight from reading Dr. Seuss to devouring *Vogue*. I love high fashion, design, art, artifice. Just because I can't afford it doesn't mean I don't fantasize about the day when a pair of thousand-dollar heels and the perfect shade of lipstick will transport me into a whole new existence.

Elodie catches me looking. "You can borrow it anytime. Say the word and it's yours."

The weird thing is, I know she means it. Elodie acquires as quickly as she discards. Though sometimes I wonder just how much longer before she grows bored of me and drops me as easily as the silk duster she's offering.

She starts to slip it from her shoulders, but I wave it away.

On her tall, willowy, runway-ready frame, the slouchy piece she's paired with a white ribbed tank top and faded jeans looks breezy and effortless. On my five-foot-three inches (in heels), it would look like I went to school in my bathrobe.

She loops her arm through mine and leads me out of the caf, past the row of lockers sporting a fresh coat of paint that fails to hide the most recent graffiti scandal. "Check it out—" Elodie taps a ring-stacked finger against the locker as we pass. "If you look closely, you can still see the word 'dick.'"

I roll my eyes and start to speed up, until Elodie catches hold of my sleeve. "What's the hurry?" she says. "You're not actually going to class?"

At first glance, with her fairy-tale blond hair, creamy white skin, pert little nose, valentine of a mouth, and flashing blue eyes, Elodie resembles an earnest cartoon princess. But I know from experience that Mason is right—she's exactly the sort of "bad influence" your parents warn you about.

"If I ditch, I fail." Seconds after I've said it, the final bell trills, sending the rest of the stragglers dashing for their classrooms, leaving just Elodie, me, and a deserted school hallway.

"Correction." She grins. "You're already failing, and now you're getting a tardy as well. Also, we both know you're not working today, so come." Another tug on my sleeve. "I know a club where we're guaranteed free admission—probably even free drinks if you're willing to ditch that bulky hoodie."

"Seriously—a club?" I check the time. "At one thirty?" My voice pitches high, making me sound as outraged as my mom when the phone rings while she's watching TV.

"That's what makes it exclusive." Elodie laughs. "Maybe this will convince you?"

She hands me her cell so I can squint at a picture of a boy with features so perfectly sculpted, I'm sure it's thanks to some serious filter abuse. Still, there's a slight hitch in my breath as

I linger on his sweep of dark hair and those navy-blue eyes. For some reason, he strikes me as familiar, but that's probably because he reminds me of the kind of boy I once knew in my former popular-table life.

"His name is Brax." She snatches the phone away and flings it into her bag. "He wants to meet you."

"Um, yeah. Super believable, El." I shake my head. "You're telling me that guy—that face-tuned pixel jaw—" I motion toward her bag as though he lives there with the tubes of lip gloss and breath mints. "Wants to meet *me*?"

"You up for it?" She smiles excitedly.

Even though I recognize the con, given the choice between the disapproving glare of my history teacher and some sketchy afternoon club with a boy whose face is too good to be true... there's really no contest.

Textbook history is basically the memorization of places, dates, and highly sanitized tales of old white men accomplishing heroic feats. It's an unrelatable bore of a class that's better used for napping.

Still, she doesn't even give me a chance to respond. She just bolts down the hall, yelling, "Race you!"

I remain fixed in place, watching Elodie sprint through the quad as she heads for the gate as though the usual school rules don't apply to her.

I wish I could explain my connection to her, or why I keep ignoring Mason's advice. All I know is that for the last few years, he's pretty much been my only true friend—and up until she came along, it felt like enough.

But then one random Wednesday, Elodie Blue showed up at our school and from that moment on, everything changed.

I remember watching in awe as she made her way across campus. She was so confident, so effortlessly cool. In other words, the exact opposite of me. And I have to admit, I was totally starstruck.

Of course, Mason disliked her from the start, claiming he could see right through her shiny facade to the layers of moldering rot. I think he even referred to her as a future cult leader, Instagram model, and crooked politician, all rolled into one.

But for me, Elodie was like the living, breathing embodiment of everything I aspired toward but could never manage to be.

Within days, the whole school was obsessed. And yet, despite the number of kids who'd be willing to risk their perfect GPAs to play hooky with her, she chose me.

Maybe it's because she knew I was already so far along on my own downward spiral that she couldn't be blamed for jeopardizing my future.

Maybe it really is like she's said, that I'm smarter than most, prettier than I think, and not afraid to take a few risks.

At the time, I brushed it off and mumbled some botched version of a Janis Joplin quote about freedom and having nothing to lose.

None of that was true, of course. When you have as little as I do, you can't afford to lose a single thing.

"C'mon!" Elodie cries, her voice competing with the one in my head warning me to go to class and get my life back on track.

If I don't follow that voice, I'll be solely to blame for whatever comes next.

With my heart about to explode in my chest, I ignore the voice and pick up my pace.

A blast of thunder cracks overhead as a bank of clouds bursts open and unleashes a downpour.

Immediately, I duck my chin and yank up my hood.

Elodie, of course, does just the opposite.

Tossing her head back, she flings her arms wide as though she loves getting drenched. Next thing I know, the gate screeches open, and Elodie makes a run for her car.

With my feet splashing behind her, I race to catch up.

3

"I thought we were going to a club." I glance between Elodie and the parking attendant who's simultaneously holding the passenger door and motioning toward the curb as though he doesn't think I can find it on my own. Elodie is the only person I know who will give it her all in spin class, only to valet park at the mall.

Without a word, she grabs me by the arm and drags me into some big, glitzy department store with gleaming white marble floors and the kind of aspirational price tags that are way out of my orbit.

"So I'm guessing the club is hidden in some sort of password-protected dressing room?" I release myself from her grip. "Or maybe a secret basement beneath the MAC counter?"

"Look—" Elodie turns on me so quickly, the toes of my Chucks bump against hers. "I don't know how to say this politely so I'm just going to say it." She places her hands on her hips and inhales a theatrical breath. "You need a new look."

I blink. She's right—that wasn't the least bit polite.

"I'm not trying to be mean, but for someone who's supposedly so into fashion, it's strange how you don't even try to look cute." Her finger traces a line from my ratty hoodie, to my baggy jeans, down to my worn Converse sneakers. "It's like you're purposely trying to sabotage yourself. And honestly, Natasha, I just want to help."

I breathe my own version of a theatrical sigh and shove right past her, pausing before a display of designer sunglasses that cost nearly a quarter of the monthly mortgage my dad stuck us with. But I try a pair anyway, just for kicks.

"Rumor has it you used to put in an effort. But I'm not sure I believe it."

"Understandable," I say. "I mean, why would you?" I switch the glasses for a pair with exaggerated square frames and lean toward the mirror. At first, I chose them as a joke, but now I'm thinking I like them. I slide them off and check the price.

Maybe in another life, with another bank account.

"But then I saw a yearbook from when you were a freshman."

I reach for another pair, mirrored and round. They don't fit my face, but they do hide my eyes, buying me enough time to prepare for what's next.

I know exactly where this is going. The one person who's never seen the Natasha version of me is now fully caught up with what the rest of the senior class has known all along—my freshman and senior years appear to belong to two different people.

"Not only were you smokin', but you were also voted ninth grade homecoming princess, class president, and you were rocking the honor roll."

I gape at her, fuming. It's not like my A-list past was a secret, but why the hell is Elodie checking up on me?

"I mean, it's a pretty dramatic shift, and I'm curious how it happened." She reaches for my wrist. There's genuine concern in her gaze, but the story of my downfall is not up for discussion.

"*Nothing* happened," I say.

Elodie's blue eyes fix on mine, searching for the truth she's sure I'm holding back. The smoking gun—the single, cataclysmic event that kick-started my descent. But the thing is, it was nothing like that.

I mean, it's not like anyone *died.*

It's not like my life imploded overnight.

It was more of a gradual decline. A small series of events that caused poverty, depression, and hopelessness to roll through my house like a virus, spreading first to my mom and then to me.

For a while, I tried to keep up appearances. But it wasn't long before the divide between me and pretty much everyone else at my school caused me to fall further and further behind until there was no point in trying.

What looks like failure is just self-preservation. I save my energy for my after-school job because we need the money. And, since no one's paying me to take a history exam, it doesn't top my list of priorities.

Still, I'm disappointed in Elodie. She's supposed to be the one person who allows me to tune out from my regularly scheduled life so I can indulge in a little fantasy and fun. If she's looking to switch it up and act like my life coach, then maybe she should embrace her new role and take me back to school where I belong.

"Is this supposed to be an intervention?" I ask. "Because I'd rather go clubbing." I peel her fingers away from my arm and return the sunglasses to the slot where I found them. "I mean, you can't have it both ways, El. You're either my partner in crime or my guidance counselor."

"Fine." She snatches the square frames and calls for a salesperson. "But like it or not, you're getting a makeover. Because this"—she shakes a disapproving finger at my hoodie—"is not going to fly where we're going."

4

We're outside. My long brown hair, stripped of its usual frizzy ponytail, has been coaxed into soft waves that fall around my newly made-up face, while my dress exposes way more thigh than the shorts I wear in PE.

"I feel like *Pretty Woman*," I say, referring to my mom's all-time favorite movie, which is basically some old-school story about an escort who gets a makeover from a rich client when he plucks her off a street corner.

When my mom decided I was finally old enough to watch it with her, she spent the entire movie either grinning giddily or anxiously clutching a damp tissue to her lips like the ending might change from the previous hundred or so viewings. By the time the final credits rolled, I guess she thought my own untouched box of tissues meant I didn't understand, because she tried to explain.

"But look!" she cried, rewinding to the part where the sex worker and the corporate raider ride away in a limo. "She saves him right back!"

Which I guess, in her mind, made up for the fact that this woman had to change literally everything about herself to be good enough for some dude. Yeah, no thanks.

"It's a seriously badass makeover." Elodie shakes me away from my thoughts and back to the present. "And the best part is, you don't even have to blow me in return."

I tug at the hem and frown. Makeover ethics aside, it's been a long time since I allowed myself to actually try to look pretty, and the effect is simultaneously aspirational and disturbing.

Like, one part of me is thinking: *Yes, this is who you are meant to be!*

While the other side insists: *You are never going to get away with this.*

"Honestly?" I say. "I feel...kinda weird."

My arms hang awkwardly by my sides, like I've forgotten how to use them. Between the dress, the shoes, the sunglasses, the makeup, and the new bra that makes my breasts appear way bigger than they actually are, Elodie has made a major investment, and she doesn't even seem to care that I can never repay her.

"Thanks," I say. "Really." I mean, it's the right thing to do when someone spends a bundle on you and asks nothing in return.

She waves at my reflection in the window before us. I wave back at hers. Elodie didn't get a makeover, mostly because she didn't need one. She just swapped her tank top for a silk cami and her sneakers for strappy heels.

Still, it's the first time I've ever stood beside her and felt like an equal.

So I decide to seize the moment and act like one, too.

I cock my hip, shake my hair, and adopt a vacant expression, like a girl in a misogynistic music video. Elodie responds with a raised brow and tilted grin that can only be described as mischievous, if I used words like that.

"Ready to venture into the vast unknown?" She hooks her arm through mine.

I run my gaze up the length of the building—a block of mirrored panes stretching from the sidewalk to the bank of gray clouds overhead. It's the kind of place filled with people who followed all the rules and did all the right things, only to end up slack-faced and numb, trudging through the calendar in pursuit of the weekend.

"I ditched my hoodie for this?"

Elodie throws her head back and laughs, then marches me toward the building next door, which is notably shorter, darker, and the few windows it has are all painted black.

"Oh, and one more thing." She presses something hard and rectangular into my palm. "It's members only. Just follow my lead."

The plastic card bears a picture of me that I know I never posed for, mostly because I'm wearing a top I don't own.

"Either magic or Photoshop." Elodie winks. "You be the judge."

I stare at the ID again. Apparently, I'm approaching my one-year anniversary since becoming a member.

"Arcana?" I glance between the name of the club and her. For some reason, the word feels like it's tugging at my brain. But Elodie's already approaching the bouncer and flashing her card, so I bury the thought and follow along, whispering to myself, "What the hell is this place?"

5

"They want everything," Elodie says. "Your bag, your cell, all of it."

I glance between Elodie and the girl working the counter. "Not happening," I say. "My phone stays with me."

Elodie rolls her eyes. "Stop being such a drama queen. You'll get it back when it's over."

"When what's over?" I ask, still clutching my bag.

Exasperated by my not wanting to give all my stuff to a stranger in a very strange place, Elodie grabs my backpack and cell and plops them onto the desk. In exchange, I receive a glare from the attendant and a black rubber bracelet with a number attached.

"This place is totally off the grid," Elodie says. "It's like, pre-selfie, old school. That's what makes it so cool." She leads me down a flower-lined path that ends at a small shelter crafted entirely of tree limbs and twinkling fairy lights. Inside, a woman sits behind a table covered by a blue silk cloth. Going by the crystal ball to her right, and the smoldering smudge stick to her left, I'm guessing she's a psychic.

Or, you know, posing as one.

The woman flips her long red hair over her shoulder and gestures toward the purple velvet stool just opposite her. "Are you familiar with tarot?" she asks, handing me a deck of cards, her questioning brown eyes settling on mine.

Just like with the name of the club, at the mention of *tarot* it's like a wire gets tripped in my brain. After years of ignoring all thoughts of my dad—since he clearly doesn't think about me, I refuse to think about him—I'm startled by the series of images that suddenly sparks in my head. The vision is so clear, it's like I'm watching it unfold through a thin pane of glass.

I'm young, somewhere around nine, and my dad and I are hunched over an ancient tarot deck he's spread across the table before us. One by one, he works through the cards, explaining all the hidden secrets within those strange illustrations.

Though I don't understand most of what he says, I listen, transfixed, wanting to soak up as much as I can. But he makes it only to the final card in the Major Arcana, the World card, when my mom's car pulls into the drive, and he sweeps the deck out of sight. Seconds before she walks through the door, he turns to me with a finger raised to his lips…

It was the last time I ever laid eyes on those cards.

One of the last times I ever saw him.

A few days later, he walked out of my life and was never heard from again.

Arcana. Of course. The name of the club makes perfect sense.

The tarot is made up of seventy-eight cards, twenty-two that comprise the Major Arcana, and fifty-six that make up the Minor Arcana, the ones he never got a chance to reveal.

To the woman, I say, "It's a pictorial key to the universe—an allegorical journey of life." Then I shuffle the deck like an expert, the cards moving so fluidly, it feels like I've been at it for years.

When I return the deck to the reader, I watch as she fans the cards in a half circle before me. "Choose one," the woman says. "And use your left hand."

"The Hand of Fate." The phrase instinctively leaps off my tongue, and I know it's an echo of something my dad once said to me.

I choose a card and watch anxiously as the reader flips it over.

"Your life is about to change," she says, then, using the pointed tip of her nail, nudges the card closer to me. "From this day forward, nothing will ever be the same."

6

I lean closer, trying to get a better look at my card, when Elodie grabs my shoulder and gasps, "The Wheel of Fortune!"

Though the image on the card is different from the one in my father's deck, as I study the two-headed snakes coiled on each side, the golden wheel with the face of a clock that sits in the center, and the winged creature perched along the top, a sudden rush of chills crawls over my skin.

"It's a good card, right?" Elodie asks.

"Good…bad… Change is what you make of it." The reader sweeps the card back into the deck and motions for Elodie to take her turn.

Apparently Elodie's not headed for great change. She chooses an entirely different card. Then again, her life is pretty awesome as it is, so that's probably a relief.

"Two of Cups." She grins as we walk deeper into the space. "A new love is coming my way. Or, at least for tonight. Shame you're going to miss it." She laughs.

I turn toward her, a wave of panic rolling through me. "Wait—what?"

"This is where we separate," she says, as though that was the plan all along. If it was, she clearly forgot to tell me.

"But we came here together!" I whine, my cheeks filling with heat when I hear just how pathetic and needy I sound.

The last thing I want is to be left on my own. But Elodie's

already turned toward a guy who's wearing a vintage suit. He's handing out masks, and she asks him for two.

"Relax," she says, returning to me. "It's just a club—it's meant to be fun. Besides, this way, it'll be a lot more hilarious when we meet up later and swap stories. But for now…" She hands me a black velvet mask. "Just go through the door that's marked with your card."

"But what if I get lost and can't find you? I don't even have my—" I was about to remind her that I don't have my phone, but before I can get to it, she's already gone.

I stare in the direction she went. Then take a nervous look all around.

This place is weird. And even though it's weird in kind of an interesting way, wandering around on my own is not at all what I thought I was in for when I agreed to ditch school.

Screw Arcana.

Screw Elodie.

I need to find my way back to the exit, reclaim my cell, and book a ride home. It's obviously the safest, smartest way out of this mess.

But just as I'm about to head out, a nagging voice pipes up in my head.

Why not give it a chance?

What if that tarot reader is actually onto something?

I mean, I know it's ridiculous, and while I've never given a shit about things like omens or signs or when Mercury goes into retrograde, my card did promise big change.

And it's not like my life is so great I can risk staying the same.

With a sigh of surrender, I slip on the mask. Mumbling, "To the Wheel of Fortune!" in a half-hearted attempt to rally myself.

Then I pull in a slow, shaky breath, find the door with my card, and step inside a whole new world.

7

Though the shriek of wind sounding from unseen speakers and the moonlit glow radiating from the black painted ceiling give the impression of being outdoors, it's clear that I'm not.

It's just a big, empty, unsettling space that I quickly make my way through.

When I reach the end, there's a narrow doorway that leads to another room, also painted black. Except this one features a long dirt path cut down the center, with a forest of fake pine trees bordering each side.

I follow along, my heels crunching over the gravel, when I notice an old doll lying abandoned on the side of the trail. Her dress is filthy, her hair trashed, and if I didn't know better, I'd swear her dull, vacant gaze actually follows me as I pass.

It's not until the way forks to the right that I recognize the doll as my favorite childhood toy.

Okaaay…

I run my hands over my arms to ward off a shiver and hurry toward a door that I'm hoping will lead me to the sort of exclusive underground club Elodie promised. Though honestly, I'm beginning to doubt it even exists. Because it's really starting to look like Elodie is having a bit of fun at my expense.

And then I see the doll again.

And again.

An entire chain of vacant-faced dolls, all of them leading to a single grave at the end.

Whoever designed this is fully committed to their vision. But still...what kind of creep show is this?

I stop before a fresh mound of dirt, strangely feeling more curious than scared. There's a headstone there, with an angel perched at the top. One of her hands clutches a pocket watch, the other points toward the sky.

Engraved on the stone is my name, my birthdate, and the day of my death...

Today.

8

I stare at my grave.

And while I guess I'm expected to scream or something, instead I find myself laughing so hard, tears fall from my eyes.

This is exactly the sort of prank Elodie would dream up. And I'm willing to bet she's laughing right along with me from some hidden place.

"What do you suppose she died of?"

I look up to find a tall, broad-shouldered boy standing in front of me. His jaw is sharp, his mouth generous, and his nose has a bit of a bend in the center that makes me guess it might've been broken. His dark wavy hair falls midway down his neck, and though his eyes are covered by a royal blue mask, his vintage suit hails straight out of the Victorian era.

I glance between him and my supposed grave. "I, uh…I'm pretty sure she died of boredom."

He regards me for a long, cool moment, his mouth tipping ever so slightly but stopping well before it reaches anything close to a grin. "I'm Braxton," he says.

"You're the boy from the phone," I blurt, my cheeks flaming with embarrassment the second it's out.

"Sorry?" He bends his head toward me as his lips tip up at the sides.

"Nothing," I say, with a quick wave of my hand. "Just…your friend's with Elodie, right?"

My eyes graze over him. *You're the beautiful one. The one who seemed so familiar. The one who supposedly wanted to meet me. And you're even hotter in person. No filter required.*

While I have no idea how he's reacting behind the mask, I'm relieved to see his grin grow significantly wider.

"Sure," he says. "I'll answer to that. *The boy from the phone*, Braxton, even Brax—they all work."

His voice bears a hint of the sort of clipped British accent that makes me think of posh boarding schools, fox hunts, and every dashing hero from my favorite gothic novels. And it leaves me wanting to know more, to *hear* more. But then I notice he's waiting, and I realize it's my turn to introduce myself.

"I'm the dead girl," I say, nodding toward my grave.

He tilts his head in study. "I have to admit, I've never seen anyone react the way you did."

"How do people usually respond to news of their premature death?" My tone is more flirtatious than usual. I blame it on the mask.

"Let's just say you're my first laugh."

Though I can't quite make out his eyes, I can feel the weight of his unwavering gaze settled on me. And while I'm sure I've never met this boy before—mainly because nothing about him is the slightest bit forgettable—there's something so familiar about the way he fills up the space, the way the atmosphere shifted the moment he arrived. Like there's an invisible current thrumming between us, and it leaves me feeling so trippy, so out of balance, I rush to fill up the silence in hopes he won't notice just how unnerved he's made me.

"So, what exactly is this place?" I say. "I mean, I was expecting a club, but so far it's more like some kind of super-stylized haunted house."

Braxton shoots a quick look over his shoulder, then turns back to me. "It really is a club," he says, voice barely a whisper.

"But I'm not supposed to be here. You're supposed to find your own way."

"Then why'd you go off script?" I ask, aware of the way my breath hitches as I watch him run a hand across his jaw as though deciding what to do next.

He shrugs. "Guess I got curious," he says.

Then, without another word, he leads me out of the graveyard and into a much stranger place.

9

"This is what Arcana is really about." Braxton ushers me inside a massive room that makes me think of the Palace of Versailles…if it had been decorated by Salvador Dalí.

The dance floor is crowded with couples, all of them swaying to the song sung by a torch singer wearing a long beaded gown and a mask with golden antlers.

The walls display a collection of oddities. Everything from antique clocks with hands that spin backward, to gold framed portraits where all the subjects, women included, sport curlicue mustaches. And just above, perched along the top like a crown, is a long row of taxidermy hunting trophies—each head dripping with tiaras, elaborate wigs, and piles of glimmering jewelry.

"Not to worry," Braxton says when he catches me looking. "They're fakes. No animals were harmed for the sake of aesthetics."

All around us, people are laughing, dancing, while waiters wander with drink trays expertly balanced on their palms, the boys in slinky black dresses, the girls in tuxedos.

It's exactly the right amount of strange. A visual feast for the eyes. And a million times better than school. It's probably the coolest place Elodie has ever taken me. It's too bad she isn't here enjoying it, too.

I survey the sea of masks, wondering if Elodie is somewhere among them, as Braxton waves over a beautiful boy in a black strapless gown, plucks the last two drinks from his tray, and hands one to me. The glass is cut crystal, its contents a pale shimmering green.

"It's called The Green Fairy." Braxton clinks his rim against mine. "To new beginnings," he says, his voice rising over the noise.

I watch him drain his glass, but I don't drink from mine. I mean, he's cute. And, at least on the surface anyway, he's harmless enough. But I'm not about to toss back some weird drink I don't recognize.

"Why do they call it that—The Green Fairy?" I ask, swirling the contents and watching the sparkling liquid swirl up and down the sides.

"Aren't you going to try it?" Braxton motions toward my glass.

I shake my head, about to offer it to him, when the singer switches to a familiar song—the same one Elodie and I sang on our way to the mall. The rain had paused, so she cranked up the volume and lowered the car's top. As I tilted my face to the sky, I imagined we were riding the wind to some distant horizon. The memory leaves me so floaty and light, I tip onto my toes, about to take flight.

"You okay?" Braxton asks, but the words are muffled, like he's drifted a thousand miles away.

All around me, the music grows louder, causing my ears to buzz, my breath to grow quicker, as my vision tunnels in and out of focus, while the bodies on the dance floor slither and blur.

Braxton leans toward me with a look of concern. "Natasha," he says. "You all right?"

I want to ask him why the whole room is shimmering and swirling. And how is it possible the animal heads are all laughing, as the oil painted faces tumble out of their frames. But I can't put a voice to any of that. All I can do is watch in horror as the collection of clocks melt and drip down the walls.

From somewhere far away I hear a voice say, *What the hell did you give me?*

It's a moment before I realize it's mine.

"I didn't give you anything." Braxton motions toward my glass. It's still full. But my fingers are shaking so badly, the tumbler crashes to the floor.

"Looks like Elodie was right about you," Braxton says, but I have no idea what the words actually mean.

The song has slipped deep into my brain, and now everything is distorted, including me.

Braxton's masked face looms before me. And despite the ground giving way beneath my feet, despite the ceiling and walls curling toward me, I still manage to gasp, "What the hell is happening?"

Last thing I remember, before I black out, is the feel of Braxton's arms breaking my fall.

"Oh darling," he says. "I'm afraid you're about to find out."

10

When I come to, I'm at my desk.

It's not until I see Mr. Jansen at the chalkboard that I realize I'm in English class.

What the—

Flashes from the night before appear in random bursts in my head. Like pieces of a puzzle, some fit easily together, while the rest are more like a dream—*guys in slinky black gowns, a moose wearing a tiara, something about a green fairy, a song like a lullaby for my mind—*

None of it makes any sense.

And worse, no matter how hard I try, I can't unearth a single memory of how I ended up here.

Frantically, I look all around, then glance down at myself, only to find I'm wearing my hoodie over the dress Elodie bought me when we went shopping.

Shopping.

It's one of the few things I remember, and I cling to the image of the two of us crammed inside that dressing room like the life raft it is.

When I look at my feet, I see the heels Elodie bought me have been swapped for my sneakers. Though my backpack and cell phone are missing.

A stream of images races through my mind…*Arcana—that strange underground club with the tarot cards, my gravestone, a boy in a blue velvet mask… Did I forget to get my stuff from the bag check girl?*

Or did something else happen?

Something so bad, my mind blocked it out?

My heart starts to pound, my leg to shake. And when I glance up, I see my teacher is staring right at me. So I stitch my lips closed, force myself to keep it together, and focus on the test sheet in front of me.

With a shaky hand, I sprint through the questions—checking random boxes, scribbling nonsensical words. Then the second I'm done, I leave it on his desk and bolt from the room.

As the door closes behind me, I hear him call out my name, but I can deal with that later. Right now, there's no time to waste.

I need to find my phone.

Need to text Elodie so she can explain what the hell happened to me.

The chilled morning air strikes at my cheeks as I rush toward my locker, hoping to find my bag and my cell stashed inside. My fingers twitch as I work the dial, mentally reciting the combination as I race against the beat of heavy footsteps thudding in the near distance.

C'mon, c'mon! I kick the locker below mine and curse my clumsy fingers for falling just short of the final digit, forcing me to start over.

"Natasha?"

Furiously, I spin the dial. The only person who calls me that is Elodie, and that wasn't her voice.

"Natasha Clarke?"

The footsteps grow more determined, and they're no longer alone.

"Step away, Natasha."

My heart runs a riot in my chest, my breath growing choppy and quick.

But I won't look.

Can't look.

If I can just get inside this damn locker, then—

A heavy hand clamps down on my shoulder and spins me around. It's Mr. Morris, the school principal. I recognize the red-faced man beside him as the school's security guard.

"Natasha, I'm going to have to ask you to step aside," Mr. Morris says.

"But why? What's—"

Before I can finish, the guard slips some tool from his pocket—a cross between a Slim Jim and a crowbar—and cracks my locker wide open.

The principal sighs.

The guard grunts.

And I stare in disbelief at a pile of brand-new designer clothes, shoes, and sunglasses that definitely isn't mine.

"Come with me." Mr. Morris gestures for me to follow as the guard clears out my locker.

"I don't understand," I say, my voice so shallow and empty, I feel like a ghost of myself.

11

Turns out, the worst part of the perp walk isn't getting the side-eye from the front office staff and the suck-up crew of students who choose to ignore a perfectly decent list of electives so they can work alongside administrators.

The worst part is seeing the exhausted slope of my mom's shoulders, the drag of her mouth and disappointed blunt of her gaze when she watches me getting hauled into Mr. Morris's office.

After my dad left, it was like our roles got reversed. My mom found a low-paying job where she showed up on time and acted like any other responsible adult. But the second she got home every night, she morphed into this fragile childlike state, looking to me to fill the void of my dad's absence.

I started handing over most of the money I earned from babysitting gigs, and later, my after-school job.

I did whatever I could to offer the kind of emotional support *I* was so desperately in need of.

Because of it, she's grown so dependent on me, she no longer acts like a parent.

And I can tell by the way she sighs when I enter the room that she views this whole mess as an act against her. I'm just another disappointment to add to the pile.

I take the seat next to her and fold in my body until I'm as small and inconspicuous as possible. With my shoulders hunched and legs tightly crossed, I wrap my arms around my middle and stare at the toe of my sneaker, waiting for the lecture to start.

"We received a credible report that you were hiding stolen merchandise in your locker. I'm sorry to see it confirmed. Is there anything you'd like to say for yourself?" Mr. Morris leans back in his chair, pretending there's a chance for me to explain this away, that he hasn't already made up his mind about me.

Between my abysmal academic performance and my mom's frayed blouse and nicotine-stamped fingers desperately shaking in need of another, he's drawn his own conclusions about the type of family I come from.

The father is gone. The mother is struggling. The daughter's given up.

And while he's not wrong about us, he is wrong about me. I may be willing to break a few rules, but I didn't steal any of that stuff.

Though I did recognize it as the pile of castoffs from yesterday's shopping trip. It's everything Elodie and I decided against.

Mr. Morris steeples his fingers and waits for me to defend myself.

What I say is, "Where's Elodie?"

For the first time, my mom looks directly at me. "Who?" Her eyes narrow until they've nearly vanished.

"Elodie Blue. Where is she?" Too late, I realize how ridiculous I must sound.

The steeple collapses. Mr. Morris leans forward, hands flat on his desk. "About the stolen merchandise. Do you have anything to say for yourself, the evidence we uncovered?"

Evidence?

That's when he turns his computer screen around and plays the surveillance video of me stashing a pile of stolen goods in my locker. With my dress bunched up near my crotch and my eyes heavy with smudged black eyeliner, this is not a good look.

According to Principal Morris, a crime has been committed and I'm their prime suspect. And while I know exactly who's behind it—I mean, who else could it be, but the very person who insisted on taking me shopping—I also know no one will believe me.

Elodie Blue has emerged as the star of this school.

While I've spent the last few years teaching people to expect the very worst.

"I really need to talk to Elodie," I say, my voice again betraying my urgency, but I'm too desperate to care.

Principal Morris sighs. Splays his fingers across his desk and confirms what I've already guessed: I'm in serious trouble.

I'm escorted outside, the principal on my left, a cop on my right. A crowd of students begins to gather.

Someone calls out my name, and I jerk my head around, needing it to be Elodie so she can say something, anything, to get me out of this mess.

Only my gaze lands on Mason's. He looks shocked, scared, and heartbroken all at once.

What happened? he mouths, but the cop yanks hard on my arm, harder than necessary, and hauls me away.

Before I'm shoved into the back of a squad car, I turn to my mom. "I'm sorry," I whisper. "But I didn't do it. I need you to believe me." I cling to her, searching for some unnamable thing she's too defeated to give.

"I'd hoped for more," she says, her bony frame pulling away, leaving me to wonder if she's talking about her life or mine.

12

There are worse things than jail.

I mean, nothing I've ever experienced, but there are definitely worse things than being photographed, fingerprinted, and frisked by a female cop with abnormally strong fingers. Every single day, people deal with tons of legit atrocities that make what happened to me pale in comparison.

But the worst part is knowing I brought it upon myself. There was a voice in my head that warned me not to follow Elodie past the school gates, and yet I went ahead and flipped it the bird.

"You're lucky," they tell me. "You're still a minor. Once you turn eighteen, the consequences become serious."

Well, my mom's disappointment feels pretty serious.

Getting expelled from school feels very serious.

The court fees I'm facing feel really, really serious.

The thought of going to juvie is unthinkably serious.

I haven't even made a dent in my list of *serious* when someone calls out my name.

"You Natasha Clarke?"

I nod, having no idea what to expect.

"You're free to leave."

"Seriously?"

The guard bends a brow, unlocks my cell, and arcs her arm toward the door. "Must be nice to have rich friends."

I have no idea what she's talking about.

After stopping by the desk to claim my hoodie, I head outside, where I pause on the sidewalk and tip my face toward a ragged scrap of cloud left blistered and singed by the noonday sun.

Freedom never felt so good, or so warm.

When I snap my eyes open, I'm looking at an idling shiny black Mercedes. The rear window lowers to reveal a boy in the back seat. My backpack dangles from his fingers.

Braxton.

Oh, hell no.

Without thinking, I make a grab for it, but he's quicker than me, and he yanks it clear out of reach.

"What the hell?" I cry. Refusing to give up so easily, I come at him again.

"Whoa!" He holds out a hand to stop me. "You might want to turn it down a notch. In case you haven't noticed, we have an audience." He jerks his head toward two cops paused beside their squad cars, both focused on me, and not in a good way.

"What do you want?" I whisper.

"C'mon," he says. "Let's go for a ride." He clears a space by moving aside.

I glance over my shoulder to see the cops slipping into their vehicles and driving away. Then I peer inside the Mercedes, trying to see who's behind the wheel, but the windows are blacked out and there's a privacy panel between the front and back seats.

"There's not enough ice cream and puppies in the world," I tell him. "Just give me my backpack already."

"You're not going to make this easy, are you?"

I cross my arms and frown. "Why the hell would I?"

Asshole.

Breathing an exaggerated sigh, he climbs out of the car and

taps the roof twice. A second later, it's gone, leaving just the two of us.

"You've had a rough night, Natasha," he says. "I'm sure you must be exhausted."

"What the hell did you do to me?" I take what's meant to be a menacing step forward. Though, unlike me, Braxton remains so completely at ease, I can't help but wonder if I should've taken a chance and made a big scene while those cops were still there.

Braxton raises both hands, clutching my backpack in one of them. "Whatever you're thinking, it's not what you're thinking. You fainted, that's all."

"Fainted?" My laugh is sharp. "Despite the costume you wore, this isn't actually the eighteen hundreds. Women don't just have fainting spells anymore."

The corners of his mouth tense. In a tight voice, he says, "I promise you'll get your bag. But first, let me buy you some breakfast. There's a diner up the road—they serve pancakes all day." He gestures vaguely in that direction, but I keep my gaze fixed firmly on him.

"I have another idea," I say. "How about I march back inside the station and tell them everything I remember from last night, along with everything I suspect. You do know I'm a minor, right?"

"I'm well aware." His tone is weary. "Thing is, you're not going to tell them anything. Mainly because you've been released into my custody. I'm the one who bailed you out. I'm the one who's going to clear your name and get your record expunged."

None of this makes any sense. From the moment I snuck out of school, I felt like I've entered an alternate world. At the most, Braxton's a year or two older than me. Why would they release me into his custody?

Not to mention—*where the hell is Elodie?*

What I say is, "What's really going on here? And don't try to lie. You fucked my whole life. The least you can do is tell me the truth."

I guess he wasn't expecting that because, for the briefest moment, he loses a grip on his cool. I can see it in the tightening of his lips, the twinge in his jaw. But it's his hands that really give it away. The second he starts to fidget with his gold signet ring, I take it as a sign that I've gotten to him.

When he notices me looking, he shoves both hands in his pockets. "I'm happy to answer your questions," he says, the words laced with the slight hint of a proper British accent. "Perhaps over some scrambled eggs, or a short stack?"

I open my mouth, about to totally lose it on him, when my stomach betrays me by howling with hunger, and I realize it's been almost twenty-four hours since my last meal.

"So much for the *I'm not hungry* excuse," he says, back to being an asshole again.

He offers his arm, but I shove right past him.

Making a show of rolling my eyes, I head for the diner.

13

"Nothing like a sticky plastic menu featuring mouthwatering pictures of food." He taps a finger against a photo of two fried eggs and a sausage arranged to make a smiley face.

I stare pointedly at my backpack, which so far has stayed on his side of the booth.

When the waitress comes by, I order coffee, juice, scrambled eggs, and pancakes. He wants only coffee.

"You know, you could've just handed over the backpack and stopped by a Starbucks on your way to…" I make a looping gesture with my hand. "Wherever it is you spend your day."

"And miss this sparkling conversation? Not a chance."

I frown and toss a glance out the window. There's a man stumbling around, talking to someone known only to him. He's so immersed in his invisible world, he's completely unaware of the number of people veering out of their way to avoid him.

When my food arrives, I dig in. I've never been one of those girls who's dainty with food or apologizes for having to eat to stay alive. I'm making a second pass with the syrup when Braxton says, "I'm sorry."

I continue eating. Refusing to so much as acknowledge him. He knows what I want, and now it's just a game of waiting until he gives in.

"I— Can you look at me, please?"

I take another bite, finish chewing, then say, "Can you take off your sunglasses? It's really unnerving how you're always hiding your eyes behind something."

"This is only the second time we've met. I'm not sure the word *always* applies."

I shake my head and continue to eat and stare out the window. The old man is now picking through a trash can. My heart breaks for him.

Braxton's sunglasses drop onto the table, and I glance up to find a seriously remarkable pair of blue eyes the color of gathering storms and wind-whipped seas splashing up against the sky.

He removes his knit hat and runs a hand through his hair.

I slide my gaze over him, then force a bored shrug, wanting him to think I'm left completely unimpressed by the final reveal.

"First, I want to assure you that nothing untoward happened last night."

"*Untoward?* Seriously?" I roll my eyes, stab a wedge of pancake, and angle it into my mouth.

"For one thing, you didn't drink. And even if you had, it was only water with green food coloring. Also, I have proof."

He's got my attention now.

"I'm a little off protocol here, but…"

He hands over my bag and, after a quick inventory, I determine it's all there, with the addition of a large white envelope I've never seen before. The front has a picture of the Wheel of Fortune tarot card I pulled from the deck.

"How does this prove anything?" I ask.

Braxton nods toward the envelope. "It's exactly like I told you. You've been released to me—or rather, to Arthur Blackstone, though I work as his proxy."

I peer at Braxton, remembering how the jailer mentioned a rich friend. At the time, it was so weird, I chose to ignore it. But now, even though he's given me zero reasons to trust him, there's a part of me that wonders if Braxton might actually be telling the truth. Or at least about this.

Still, I don't even try to hide my skepticism when I say, "Seriously. Arthur Blackstone?"

Braxton nods as though that's all the confirmation I need. But it's not. Not by a long shot.

"You mean the legendary, art collecting, tech trillionaire who just after claiming the top spot on the World's Wealthiest list went totally off the grid and hasn't been seen or heard from in years? *That* Arthur Blackstone?"

Again, Braxton nods.

"And this"—I wave the envelope before him—"is supposed to provide some kind of proof that not only is the great man still alive, but that he actually gives such a big shit about me that he sent you on a mission to deliver this personally?"

He drums his fingers against the base of his mug. "You should probably open it," he says.

I drop the envelope onto the table. "And you should probably just tell me what's really going on here."

Braxton pauses to sip from his coffee. It's the equivalent of a slow, monotonous drumroll, only it doesn't work. I'd just as soon finish my breakfast and leave without ever knowing what he's about to reveal.

Replacing his mug on the table, he says, "You've been accepted into Gray Wolf Academy." He waits, like he's expecting me to be grateful or something.

"Yeah, no thanks." I stab another forkful of buttermilk pancake and lift it to my mouth. Taking great satisfaction in the way Braxton stares at me in shock.

"Why would you say that when you don't know the first thing about it?" he asks.

I chew thoughtfully, as though I'm giving the question my full consideration. Dabbing my lips with a paper napkin, I say,

"Because I'm not interested." I slide the envelope toward him and watch as he blinks in confusion. Like I'm the one who's wandered off script and he's not sure how to get the scene back on track. "Sounds like a school for nerds."

He stares at me, incredulous, speechless. I decide I like him better that way.

"Well, okay then," he finally says. "While the choice is ultimately yours, before you make the sort of decision that can't be undone, would you at least hear me out?"

"And if I don't?" I place my fork on my plate, curl my napkin into a ball, and drop it there, too. "If I just get up from this table, walk right out of here, and pretend I never heard of you, Arthur, or your ridiculous Wolf academy—then what?"

Not missing a beat, he says, "Then you'd be exercising your right to free will." His navy-blue gaze sweeps over mine. "But, as you've so recently learned, there are consequences to your choices. And if you walk out now, you risk missing out on the kind of opportunity that can change your whole life. Not to mention, your mum already said yes."

14

"You spoke to my *mom*?" My voice screeches so high, some of the other diners turn away from their pancakes to stare disapprovingly at us. Still, it's pretty much the last thing I expected to hear.

"Arthur did." Braxton lifts his chin and narrows his gaze in the self-satisfied way of a boxer who just delivered the knockout punch. "She signed the papers. Your copy's inside."

He nudges the envelope back toward me, but no way am I going anywhere near it.

"Mr. Blackstone knows what it's like to come from humble beginnings, and so he started the academy to help other kids who are facing similar challenges. Natasha, you're bright, sharp, witty, pretty, and most importantly, you're not afraid to take a few risks. Arthur recognizes your potential and wants to help you live up to whatever dream you have for yourself. Your current problems will disappear. The past will be erased, as though it never existed. The only thing required is your attendance."

Sharp, witty, pretty, and most importantly, you're not afraid to take a few risks. It reminds me of how Elodie once chose to describe me, but I'm not sure I'd agree.

Risk-taking involves careful, calculated thinking.

My life choices would best be described as impulsive, self-defeating, and wildly reckless.

Still, what I say is, "If this wolf school is so great, then why go to all the trouble of drugging me and framing me so I'll agree?"

Braxton doesn't even flinch when he says, "First of all, if we had approached you with an offer, chances are you would've said no. You don't really strike me as the type to willingly choose a path that'll benefit you. And second, no one drugged you. Can we move past that already?"

"Maybe I didn't drink," I say. "But I know for a fact I didn't faint. *Something* happened at Arcana. Something you're purposely keeping from me. And what I really want to know is what's Elodie's part in all this?" I study Braxton's face, haunted by a vague recollection of him saying Elodie was right about me seconds before I blacked out. He also called me *darling*, but I'd rather not think about that. "Whether you admit it or not, I know you two are working together."

Braxton fidgets with the gold signet ring on his middle finger. And, since it's the second time he's done that when I veered too close to the truth, it's all the proof I need to know I'm on the right track.

When he finally looks at me, he says, "Thing is, Natasha, from the moment you agreed to ditch school, you were a willing participant. Way I see it, you're not really in a position to turn down an offer like this."

When he ends with a shrug, it's all I can do not to toss whatever's left of my coffee at his ridiculously handsome, smug face.

"Look—" I lean toward him. "I don't know who you are or why you've decided to go after me, but I do know this whole thing disappears if I can find a way to prove I was framed. And I *will* prove it."

Braxton leans back, idly stretching his arm across the vinyl banquette. "If you ask me," he says, "your life was a mess way before you were busted for theft." His gaze lights on mine, and just like that, the tenuous balance of power shifts yet again.

Clearly, he's right. But I'm also right about him and Elodie plotting against me. My proof: he didn't so much as blink, much less try to deny it.

"Does it really matter how you arrived when I'm offering you the chance of a lifetime? Natasha, this is the moment you get to decide between death or rebirth. The choice is entirely yours."

Choice.

It reminds me of how he found me laughing at my own tombstone. The clothes, the club, the tarot card, the drink, all of it was leading me here.

And now that I'm here, I guess it can't hurt to at least take a look at whatever it is that he's offering.

I mean, it's not like my life can get any worse.

I tear into the envelope to find an official-looking document tucked inside. But, since it's written in the sort of language only law school grads understand, I skip ahead to where my mom's signature hugs the very last line.

A sob builds in my chest as I trace the tight loops with my finger. The hollow feel of her arms, her look of despair as she said, *I'd hoped for better*, replays on an infinite loop in my head.

Maybe this is my chance to do better for her.

Or at least give her one less thing to worry about.

But still…can I really leave her?

I mean, who'll take care of her if I'm not around?

"I have a job," I say, but Braxton's already shaking his head. "Not anymore."

I stare at the paper, biting my lip as I struggle to keep it together. "If there's tuition, I can't—" I saved my best excuse for last, but Braxton cuts me off.

"Gray Wolf offers a full ride. Room, board, clothing, miscellaneous, it's all covered. In addition, Arthur will provide for your mom. He knows how important it is to maintain a stable family home."

"So it's a boarding school? Because I should warn you, I don't play lacrosse."

For the first time since we met, a ghost of a grin tugs at his lips. A second later, it's gone. "I don't think anyone will notice," he says.

I stare at the wreckage of my breakfast. There's a stubborn part of me that wants to lash out, rail against an unfair system and a bad friend I never should've trusted. But what would be the point?

Sure, I can go back to school, back to the life I've been living. But after years of dreaming of something better, shouldn't I at least take a chance?

Follow my own Wheel of Fortune?

I turn back toward Braxton. "What's expected of me? You know, in return for Arthur's generosity. What does *he* get out of all this?"

Braxton adopts a serious look that matches his tone. "Arthur gets the satisfaction of seeing you succeed beyond your wildest expectations."

I glance out the window again. The old man from before has moved on. Maybe it's time for me to move on as well.

"What happens now?" I ask, forcing the words past the lump in my throat. I can hardly believe I'm actually choosing this path.

He tosses a twenty onto the table. "We head for the airport."

I look past the window toward the curb.

The black Mercedes has returned.

15

I don't get in the car.

I'm not new.

"What are you doing?" Braxton calls from somewhere behind me.

I imagine his face is still astonishingly beautiful even in a state of outrage, but I don't turn around to confirm it.

What I'm doing is heading home. I need to see my mom. Need to know for sure that it wasn't a forgery, that she really did sign my life away to the world's richest recluse.

My sneakers pound hard against the pavement. It's getting warm, but that doesn't prevent me from lifting my hood and burying my hands deep in my pockets.

When I pass a building I recognize as Arcana, I veer toward it. Only to find the entry is shuttered and a For Lease sign hangs in the window. I squint at the black concrete box of a structure, wondering if I'm mistaken but sure that I'm not.

Then the bus rolls up and I break into a run, managing to catch it just before it pulls away from the curb. A lucky omen if there ever was one.

The bus lurches onto the street, causing me to teeter and reach for something to regain my footing.

"Watch yourself." A woman scowls, offended by the sight of my hand clutching the back of her seat. She holds her breath in her cheeks, waiting for me to move on.

I make my way down the aisle, find an empty seat, and rest my gaze outside my window. Preferring to lose myself in the view outside, so I won't have to think about the disquieting pitch and roll of my belly, or the five-alarm panic going off in my head. The one that screams, *What have you done? No, seriously, what the hell have you done? What is your life about to become?*

I shake the thought away and steer my focus to the crowds of people, bumping along the downtown sidewalks. All of them so hypnotized by their phones, they routinely bang into one another with barely a notice.

Once we hit the suburbs, it's a whole other story. Aside from the occasional jogger or dog walker, the sidewalks are mostly unused.

My mom and I live halfway up a hill, in the same house where my dad left us. Inside, it's like a time capsule; not a single thing has been replaced since the day he walked out. Mainly because we can't afford any upgrades. Over the years, the roof has begun to leak, electrical sockets no longer work, and in one of the bathrooms it takes an entire bucket of water to get the toilet to flush.

We really should sell and move on, but my mom insists on clinging to the dream of the life she once had. Moving from room to room like a shadow of her former self.

Mine is the next stop, so I pull the cable and make for the door. It's a few blocks to my house, and when I reach my street, I stop cold. There's a bunch of delivery trucks lined up outside, along with a team of men taking measurements, assessing the windows, the roof, the rain gutters, the bed of weeds that used to be a lawn.

In the driveway sits a brand-new luxury SUV. The woman standing next to it looks so happy that at first, I don't even recognize her.

Mom.

"It's all courtesy of Arthur Blackstone."

I take in the scene, not at all surprised to find Braxton has followed me.

"New roof, updated bathrooms and kitchen, new appliances, a new car, a generous monthly stipend…and that's just the beginning."

My vision blurs. I swipe at my cheeks with the back of my hand. I need to hear it for myself. Need her to look me in the eye when she explains why she chose an easier life over one spent with me.

I'm halfway across the street when Braxton's voice sounds from behind. "The choice is still yours. You can shred that document and pretend we never met. Your mom won't receive the monthly stipend, but Arthur will still cover your court costs and see that your record gets expunged. But what then? Do you really want to go back to the lives you both had? Or are you willing to take a chance on something brighter, better, for both of you?"

My chest squeezes too tight, catching and holding my breath like a butterfly caught in a net. I watch my mom run her hand across the molded curves of her shiny new car as though she just can't believe her good luck. Last time she looked so dreamy was at the end of that sex-worker-in-a-limo movie.

I want her to see me and beg me to stay. But she's surrounded by so much glimmer and promise, she doesn't even notice I'm here.

Your life is about to change. Nothing will ever be the same, the tarot reader told me.

Hoping with all my heart that it's true, I turn my back on the past, and slide inside the Mercedes.

16

It's my second time on a plane, though definitely my first time flying private.

So far, it's pretty much the opposite of my experience in coach class.

I make my way across the tarmac and up a short flight of steps where a pretty flight attendant greets me at the door and motions for me to sit anywhere.

There's a white leather chair by a window, and I sink onto its plush bucket seat, swivel toward the aisle, look at Braxton, and say, "How long is the flight?"

"Quite long. But exactly how long, depends on the winds." He claims the seat across from mine.

The flight attendant returns with a hot towel and a tray of champagne. I take the towel, run it over my face and hands, but decline the drink, asking for water instead. Braxton tips his flute toward me and takes a swill.

"Why would the wind make a difference?" I feel a little embarrassed to ask, but I really am curious.

He twists toward me. "When it comes to travel, the winds are everything. They're either driving against you and slowing you down or pushing from behind and speeding you along."

I nod, feeling even more ridiculous than before. If I'd taken the time to think it through, I could've figured that out on my own. For the millionth time, I wonder why, out of all the kids in my school—or hell, in the country—Arthur Blackstone chose me.

Braxton drains his champagne, looks at me, and says, "Wake me when we get there." Then, moving down the hall, he disappears behind a closed door.

"There's another bedroom if you'd like to rest," the flight attendant tells me. But even though I'm admittedly tired, there's no way I can sleep. I don't want to risk missing a thing.

I spend most of the flight checking out the plane (the bathroom is way nicer than mine at home); watching movies (there are hundreds to choose from); looking out the window (clouds, clouds, and more clouds); eating pretty much everything the flight attendant offers (cookies, warm nuts, a cheeseburger, and an ice-cream sundae—why not?); and staring at my phone as I research anything I can find on Arthur Blackstone (pretty much everything I already know and nothing I don't) and Gray Wolf Academy (not a single result—or at least nothing that fits, which makes no sense. What boarding school doesn't even have a website?).

Just after we land and are taxiing down the runway, Braxton appears, eyes squinted from sleep.

"Why's the academy a secret?" I ask.

He rubs a slow hand over his face, as though wiping away the remains of a dream.

"It's totally off the grid," I add. "There isn't even one mention of it on the internet."

He moves into the lounge (according to the flight attendant, that's what they call the section of the plane with the large screen TV, couches, and bucket seats), retrieves a sweater from his bag, and pulls it over his head.

"It's cold out there." He looks me over, settling on my legs for a moment before flushing slightly and averting his gaze. "Don't you have anything warmer?"

"It's not like I was allowed to pack," I remind him.

"Right. Sorry." He reaches back into his bag and pitches me a pair of sweatpants and the knit cap he wore earlier. When I start to pitch them right back, he says, "Trust me, you're going to need those."

"Trust *you*?" I shoot him an incredulous look. "You can't be serious." I toss the pants aside and crumple the hat into a ball I shove in the pocket of my hoodie. "Also, you still haven't answered my question."

He shrugs. "Clearly it's not a secret, Natasha. We're headed there now."

I start to tell him I prefer to go by Nat. But before I can put a voice to the words, the plane comes to a stop, the door springs open, and a flurry of biting-cold wind blows through the cabin.

Ugh, okay. Fine.

I tug on the sweatpants, pull the hat onto my head, sling my bag over my shoulder, and follow Braxton down the stairs and into a chauffeur-driven car idling on the tarmac.

17

"How's the wind out there on the water?" Braxton asks, peering out the back seat window. "Safe enough to cross?"

The driver's stony gaze finds the rearview mirror. Switching from Braxton to me and back again, he says, "It'll 'ave to be now, won' it?" His voice carries an accent I can't easily place. Irish? Scottish? Cockney? I've never traveled anywhere that would help me know the difference.

As he pulls onto a deserted two-lane road, the wind continues to gust, buffeting hard against the car, causing the wheels to vibrate, the windows to shake. When he finally parks before a small dock, I look at Braxton, dismayed. I guess I failed to make the connection between our destination and his earlier conversation about crossing the water.

"Please tell me you're joking," I say.

In a solemn voice and an expression to match, Braxton replies, "Wish I was."

Outside the car, the wind violently thrashes as I squint into the night, contemplating the choppy sea and the glint of rock in the distance.

"Gray Wolf Island." Braxton nods toward the faint glimmer of lights. "Arthur owns it, along with this dock, and pretty much everything else you see. One of the benefits of being at the forefront of the tech revolution." He slides the wool scarf from his neck and drapes it around mine, carefully looping it under my chin.

The act is so unexpected and kind, I feel the onset of tears, but I refuse to release them.

"Not to worry," he tells me. "The skipper knows these waters like he knows the winds."

I must look uncertain, because Braxton touches a finger to my chin and angles it toward him. "I'm sorry," he says, his gaze resting on mine. "About everything, all of it. I—"

The skipper clears his throat loudly from where he waits at the end of the dock.

I gaze past the beam of the lighthouse to the shadowy fortress sprawled across the top of the hill. It's the kind of place where a girl like me could easily disappear.

"You can't always control the circumstances you find yourself in," Braxton says. "But you can control how you choose to respond."

"Who are you quoting?" I ask, assuming he must've stolen it from a meme.

"Every wise person who's ever lived." His gaze meets mine. His lips pull into a close-mouthed grin. "It's going to be okay," he assures me, but it fails to land. My feet are glued to this small patch of earth, and my legs refuse to bend.

I can't do this.

If something were to go wrong, I'm not a skilled enough swimmer to survive those currents. If hypothermia doesn't finish me, drowning will.

And if by some miracle we were to cross safely, what then?

Am I stuck on that island forever?

Do I get to go home for holidays or the occasional long weekend?

Will I ever see my mom again?

"Natasha." Braxton draws me away from my thoughts and

offers his hand.

I remember the side-eyed burn of the office staff when I was perp walked out of there.

The disparaging glint in my principal's eyes when he decided I was no longer fit for his school.

Mason's look of dismay when he saw how far I'd let myself fall.

The greedy gleam of my mother's gaze as she tallied the worth of Arthur's donations.

Braxton's features soften, his lips softly parting.

When you can't go back, the only choice left is to move forward.

Ducking against the wind, I take hold of his hand and follow him down the dock to a waiting skiff, where the skipper hands me a rain slicker and a pair of tall rubber boots. Then I settle onto the bench and hope for the best.

The journey that follows is even worse than I imagined.

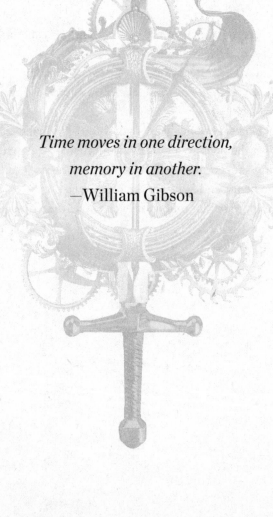

Time moves in one direction,
memory in another.
—William Gibson

18

U p close, the island is so much bigger than it first appeared. In the boat, with the water violently churning around us, I set my focus on the lighthouse like a dancer uses a spotting point to keep from tipping over. All I wanted was to survive the currents and reach the safety of that creamy, luminous glow that beckoned to us like a ghost.

Now that we've arrived, that same structure appears stark and severe, like a finger raised in warning, cautioning us to turn away, go back to where we came from before it's too late.

Only there's nothing to go back to. Not for me.

"What do you think?" Braxton asks once we're tucked inside a warm car, heading up a winding road, destined for the top.

I peer out my window at a barren landscape made entirely of dirt, rock, and not much else. I guess the winds are to blame for the absence of trees.

"'Isolated' is the first word that comes to mind." I turn to see the glare from a streetlamp slice through the window and split his face down the middle. One half illuminated, the other darkened in shadow.

Instinctively, I know it's the truest depiction I'll ever have of him.

A second later, it's over, the car's dim, and Braxton's tapping on an ultra-slim phone that looks to be a few generations newer than mine.

"It really is a fortress," I say, my breath quickening, my stomach clenching with nerves. As we round the final bend and the building pops into view, I can't help but gasp.

Crafted entirely of stone, the academy appears massive, unwelcoming, foreboding. When the front gate swings open, I rise off my seat, expecting to find it surrounded by a moat bursting with crocodiles or something.

"Does...Dracula live here?"

A ghost of a smile shades Braxton's lips. "First impressions are often deceiving," he says, slipping his phone into his pocket as the driver stops the car before a large iron door. "I think you'll be surprised by what's waiting inside. C'mon." We exit the car together and walk toward the entrance.

He presses his thumb against an electronic keypad and the door automatically opens. "This way."

Braxton gestures toward a dimly lit tunnel, but I remain rooted in place, trying to figure out why the phrase on the plaque overhead is so familiar.

"Panta Rhei." Braxton glances between the sign and me.

"What does it mean?" I ask, hoping for something that'll jog my memory.

"*Everything flows.*" He shrugs, as though that explains it. As though this boy has ever explained *anything* to me.

Before I can push him for more, he hurries me through the tunnel to a beautiful moonlit garden that's so unexpectedly lush, it takes a moment for my eyes to adjust.

Within the calm shelter of thick stone walls, we cross a mosaic-tiled path bordered by towering palms and lavish beds of evening primrose, their delicate yellow faces slanting toward a sky littered with stars.

"It reminds me of the Tarot Garden." I motion toward a glistening fountain bursting with water lilies and surrounded by whimsical sculptures of colorful six-headed snakes and other fantastical creatures.

"You've been to Italy?" Braxton turns in astonishment, and I realize it's the first time I've shared something from my life that truly surprised him. And I gotta be honest, it feels pretty good to have the upper hand. Even if it's trivial, it still counts as a win.

I wander toward a sculpture of a giant birdlike creature with a bright crescent moon standing in for a heart. "I did a paper on Niki de Saint Phalle for freshman year art class. She's one of my favorites."

Braxton relaxes, clearly relieved to confirm nothing slipped his due diligence. "This is one of many sculpture gardens," he says. "Arthur is a collector."

"Of art?" I run a tentative hand over the montage of shiny tile and grout.

"Of beauty." He walks ahead. "Come on," he says. "Time to meet the others."

19

B raxton leads me out of the courtyard and into a spacious entry with a plush velvet chaise that hangs from the ceiling and a crystal chandelier resting in the center of the white marble floor.

"An upside-down room?" I say, intrigued by the concept, but Braxton just shrugs and waves me down a long wood-planked hallway that reminds me of a lane at a posh bowling alley.

A chorus of voices drifts toward us. The closer we get, the louder they become. Growing in intensity, the shouts resonate, and though I can't quite make out the words, clearly someone is having a serious argument.

The instant Braxton strides through the doorway, the room falls silent. I stand awkwardly beside him, feeling totally out of my league. So far, Braxton was right—this place is nothing at all like I thought it would be.

I take in the odd assortment of wingback chairs swinging from thick silver chains and the strangers who occupy them. As I run my gaze over the collection of faces, they use the moment to scrutinize me as Braxton starts making introductions.

Oliver, Song, Jago, Finn—I try my best to keep them all straight.

Oliver is brown eyed with white skin and a quick, sure smile that instantly masks a residue of anger.

Song has lovely dark brown eyes and long black hair that

drapes around her shoulders like a shawl.

Jago is tall and lean, with warm brown skin and a deep topaz gaze. He greets me with a brisk nod as he swings back and forth in his purple velvet throne, watching me warily.

Finn is slim with a shock of straw-colored hair, a smattering of freckles sprawling over his nose, and a gleam in his sleepy green eyes that makes for a roguish elfin effect.

And as I stand here before them with Braxton's knit hat yanked past my ears, and the hem of my little black dress bunched around the sagging waist of his sweatpants, it's obvious there's been a mistake. Everything about this place is so beautiful, so curated, including the people—surely I'm not the only one who can see I don't fit.

I need to find a way out.

I don't care if my mom traded me in for a new SUV; there must be some kind of loophole—or even a way to escape—

Next thing I know, Braxton is nudging my shoulder, shaking me away from my thoughts, as he says, "And of course, you know Elodie."

20

I turn to see Elodie slink into the room, her gait languid and assured. She wears an orange strapless mini dress, sparkly blue ankle boots, and a tiara perched on her head as casually as she once wore a New York Yankees cap.

"Natasha," she says, her face pulling into a grin.

With a clenched jaw and a furious gaze, I watch as she comes to stand beside Braxton. The way she presses her shoulder to his reminds me of a dog pissing on a fire hydrant, marking its territory.

My teeth grind, my fingers curl into fists, as a flurry of accusations storms through my brain, but the hail of *How could you—how dare you—why me*—melts on my tongue the moment she steps forward to hug me.

"It's so good to see you," she says, her lips pressing somewhere north of my ear.

I remain fixed in place, stone-faced and silent. My only real consolation is that I don't hug her back.

Pretending not to notice, she says, "I knew from the start you wouldn't be easy."

I have no idea what that means. No idea what any of this means.

Why do the chairs hang like swings? Why is Elodie dressed like royalty? Why is everyone so unsettled by me? Why was I chosen to be here with them? But most of all, where the hell am I?

But while I may not have answers to any of those questions, I still have my suspicions.

"You framed me. Both of you, you set me up." My gaze jumps between Elodie and Braxton. But now that I've found my voice, it's left me feeling exhausted, silly, and small.

Braxton turns his focus to a large, bright canvas dominating the far wall.

Elodie dips her mouth open, about to explain, when another voice breaks in.

"I'm sure you have many questions."

I glance up to find the legend has joined us.

My first impression is that he's a big brick of a man, but a second glance tells me that's not at all true. It's more an expectation shaped by newspaper articles, magazine profiles, and pictures taken with a camera tilted skyward.

In person he's actually pretty average, with the sort of rangy body and coiled energy of a long-distance runner. His features are appealing with just enough character to keep from being bland. The chin is assertive, the jaw sharp, the nose slightly hawkish, while the lips, not too thin or too wide, are framed by a set of deep smile lines sunk like parentheses on each side.

In his faded jeans, designer loafers, and blue sweater, Arthur Blackstone gives off a casual, easy vibe I'd be tempted to believe—if it weren't for his eyes.

Dark and glinting, his gaze reminds me of something I learned about obsidian that one time Elodie dragged me into a shop that sold crystals.

"It's not a stone for amateurs," the salesperson told me as I reached for the shiny black rock. "It's powerful, merciless, allows nothing to remain hidden. It explodes the truth right into the open and can prove overwhelming to a beginner."

I immediately swapped it for a small, polished citrine instead. "A stone of abundance," Elodie claimed, which mostly drove the decision to buy the smallest, cheapest piece I could find and stash it inside my bra.

Sadly, the stone's magick didn't take.

Or maybe it did. Maybe it's how my mom got a fancy new ride and home renovation, and I ended up here.

But now, contemplating Arthur's gaze, I realize that, like obsidian, it's where his truth lies.

I also understand that where he's concerned, there will be no way to hide mine.

"Natasha, welcome." His voice is commanding, his handshake firm. "I apologize for the journey. But I'm afraid you can expect similar winds any time you venture past the academy walls."

"Is that all you apologize for? The weather?"

I force my gaze to meet his. *Let the truth telling begin.*

Braxton shifts uneasily. Elodie inhales a breath so sharp, it sucks the air right out of the room. Jago, Oliver, Finn, and Song lean forward in their seats, everyone waiting to see if I can get away with talking to Mr. Blackstone so disrespectfully.

I watch as his lips pinch at the corners, feel the sting of his gaze as it slices right through my display of bravado to the uncertain girl quaking beneath. After a few measured beats, Arthur says, "Tomorrow, your questions will be answered and your concerns addressed. For now, Elodie will show you to your room. I'm sure you're in need of some rest."

His tone is pleasantly nonnegotiable, and luckily for me, I'm smart enough to know when to quit. Besides, Arthur is right— I'm definitely in need of some rest. If for no other reason than a good night's sleep will help clear my head, so I can wake up tomorrow and start working on a plan for getting out of this mess.

21

Elodie leads me away.

And the second we've made it safely out of Arthur's hearing range, she says, "I know you're mad, but someday soon, you're going to thank me for bringing you here."

"You sure about that?" I stop in my tracks and stare hard at the wall, so angry, so close to the boiling point, it's a moment before I notice the painting in front of me.

It's of a woman standing in a graveyard, her back to a grove of tall, barren trees. Her golden red hair is long and thick, and she's dressed in a filmy black gown that reveals her bare breasts underneath. In one hand, she carries a skull with a crown. In the other, an hourglass with time dwindling down.

"*Vanitas*," Elodie says. "The painting. It's by Leon Frederic, a Dutch artist."

"Belgian," I correct, surprised by the mistake. Art class was where we first met, and what Elodie lacked in talent, she made up for in knowledge. Even our teacher was impressed. It's only when I see the smug tilt to her chin and the gleam in her gaze that I realize she was purposely baiting me.

Ugh, fine. Score one for Elodie.

"Can't we just leave the past behind and start over?" she asks.

A silent pause stretches between us, and I know she's waiting for me to go off the rails, to make a big scene. But I've said all that I will for today. My only goal right now is to prove just how little she knows about me.

"Whatever." She sighs. "You'll come around. They always do."

She turns and motions for me to follow, but we aren't in high school anymore, and last time I followed Elodie, it didn't turn out so well.

Still, I have to admit there's basically no chance of me finding my room on my own, so I reluctantly trail a few steps behind as she leads me down a series of hallways and up a few flights of stairs before finally stopping outside a glossy red door.

"If you need anything, Song is the purple door to your left," she says. "I would tell you where to find me, but I don't think you're interested."

I stare at my own door. It doesn't even have a handle, so I give it a push, but it refuses to budge.

"It's biometric." Elodie gestures toward the keypad. "Your thumb print opens it. It's already set up."

"Wait—what?" I turn toward her, only to find her expression as annoyingly sweet-faced and placid as ever. Still, the fact that I'm here pretty much proves Mason was right.

I never should've believed her.

I should've listened when he tried to warn me that she was ruthless and fake and that hanging out with her would lead to no good.

"You know, you're going to have to learn to trust me," she says. Her tone is gentle, but it still sets me on edge.

"Pretty sure we're way beyond that," I snap.

Her gaze runs the length of me before returning to mine. "You better hope you're wrong about that. Someday soon, your life may depend on it."

Without another word, she hurries down the hall, leaving me with a deeply seething anger and a long list of questions.

First among them: *how the hell did Arthur get ahold of my thumbprint?*

22

I'm not gonna lie, starting the day in a canopy bed with high thread count sheets, in a room so swanky it's more like a luxury suite than an academy dorm, feels like a dream.

And after making good use of the spa-style bathroom with the super-size shower stall and the impressive collection of pricey soaps, lotions, perfumes, shampoos, and conditioners not found in drugstores, I head into a huge walk-in closet that's crammed with so many designer dresses, shoes, and accessories, it barely all fits.

And the best part is, everything's in my size.

I wander over to a rack filled with the sort of fancy dresses normally reserved for fashion shoots or celebrities attending A-list parties—all of them with labels from the most coveted brands—Gucci, Balenciaga, Dior, Louis Vuitton. And as I begin to sort through them, I'm not at all embarrassed to admit I actually squeal with delight.

I pull a slinky black Valentino cocktail dress from the rack and shimmy it over my hips. Then I toss a silvery tweed Chanel jacket over my shoulders, slip on a pair of sky-high Louboutin pumps, sling a satin Prada evening bag over my arm, and strike a power pose before the full-length mirror that puts the Hadids and the Crawfords to shame.

This is literally every high fashion fantasy I ever had come to life, and I'm happy to say the reality does not disappoint.

And yet, as much as I'm enjoying this glitzy new version of

me, there's a nagging voice in my head that insists none of this grandeur is actually free.

I mean, maybe I'm just being cynical. Unappreciative. Overly suspicious of a trillionaire's startling display of generosity.

I tend to be wary and guarded by nature, so it's not like those traits are at all out of character.

But as I teeter on my five-inch heels across an expanse of soft woven rug to a large picture window overlooking the grounds, I can't shake the feeling that there's a lot more to this academy than I was originally told.

I raise a hand to the glass, only to be met by a shock of blistering cold. Remembering how the island looked when I arrived—a stark and desolate chunk of rock bounded by a wind-whipped sea—I'm guessing the near frigid temperature is normal for Gray Wolf. And as someone used to much warmer weather, the thought alone fills me with dread.

I pull my jacket tighter around me, push onto my toes, and peer down several stories below to see a cloaked figure moving through a labyrinth of hedges toward a glimmering crystal sphere that sits at its center.

Well, that's a bit...odd.

I squint, trying to get a better look at the scene, when from somewhere behind me the small bulbs on the crystal chandelier begin to crackle and wink as the floor beneath my feet starts to shake.

Great, just what I need—an earthquake. I can't believe I traveled all the way from California only to deal with them here at Gray Wolf, too.

I shake my head, turn away from the window, only to find my feet are suddenly locked in place and the entire room is falling away.

Oh no... Oh crap... Please let it be an actual earthquake... please.

Let it be—

The green-paneled walls and white coffered ceiling begin to crumble and fade. Which means no amount of pleading will change the fact that the weird thing that sometimes happened back when I was a kid—the thing I haven't experienced for nearly a decade—is now happening again.

The Unraveling.

The name my dad used for those terrible moments when reality tips on its side.

According to him, it's part of a lineage that's been passed down for centuries. And though he spoke about it only once, I distinctly remember him telling me there were two rules I needed to follow whenever I found myself caught in the middle of one.

One: No matter what, hold on, keep calm, and wait for the reveal.

Two: You must never, under any circumstances, tell your mother or anyone else about this weird thing that happens to you.

Of course, what sounds easy in theory is nearly impossible to put into practice. So when the entire room has fallen away, reducing my world to little more than the small patch of wood at my feet and the sound of my own wildly thudding heartbeat—I'm definitely not keeping calm.

And as I watch the cloaked figure reach the center of the maze, press a finger to the sphere, then vanish as though they never were—only to watch as that same person reappears a few seconds later—I'm barely holding on.

With unblinking eyes streaming with tears, I focus on the small brown object clutched in the cloaked figure's hand—an object that definitely wasn't there before. An object that I'm thinking might be a book, or maybe even...

From out of nowhere, a hand clamps down on my arm.

A familiar voice calls out my name.

The vision fades.

My room reassembles.

And I turn to find Braxton's face pressing toward mine.

23

"What the hell are you doing?" I cry.

In the same instant, Braxton asks if I'm okay.

But my voice is louder, angrier, and it demands to be heard.

"You can't just barge in! What if—" My mind whirls with a list of all the embarrassing things I could've been doing. Yet few of them are as bad as being caught in an Unraveling.

I mean, how am I supposed to explain why he's caught me standing frozen before my own window, tears streaming down my face, as I mumble, whimper, and hyperventilate?

I jerk free of Braxton's grip, flip the switch next to the hearth, and move to stand in front of the fire, where I make a show of warming my hands, hoping to mask the real cause of my jittery fingers.

"I knocked." Braxton's tone is less defensive than I would've expected. "Multiple times. And loudly, I might add. Natasha—" He makes to step toward me until he sees my sharp look of warning and wisely stays put. "Are you okay? Did something happen?"

His gaze is imploring, but I'm quick to turn away and stare into the flames. It's been so long since the last Unraveling, I assumed I'd outgrown them. Still, I'm not about to explain it to him. I can barely even explain it to myself.

"Is that how things work around here—if I don't answer on your timeline, you storm in?" My tone is harsh, but I have every right to be angry. "And how the hell did you even get in — is your thumbprint all-access? Is there no respect for anyone's privacy?"

He exhales a deep sigh. "I'm sorry," he says. "But, after repeated knocking, I decided to look in."

"And as you can see, I'm fine," I insist, though I don't dare meet his eyes for fear he'll see the lie.

Braxton regards me for a long, cool moment as though debating how to proceed. Deciding on a practical approach, he motions toward an elaborate silver tray heaping with fine china, freshly brewed coffee, and pastries.

"You're scheduled for lunch soon," he says, "but, since you missed breakfast, I thought this might tide you over." He busies himself filling two gold-rimmed cups, one of which he offers to me.

On the surface, the gesture is kind. But it's going to take a lot more than that for me to lower my guard. Still, I take the coffee, pluck a croissant from the basket, and settle onto a velvet settee. Seeing as how I'm now stuck on this rock for the foreseeable future, I may as well use the moment to learn what I can.

I don't waste any time; I get straight to the point.

"What exactly is this place?" I tear off a piece of croissant and plop it into my mouth, hoping to come off as just curious and not at all bothered by the sight of that disappearing person.

According to what little my dad told me, the Unraveling is kind of like how a psychic sees into the future. Only instead of the future, I get a glimpse of the past.

Which means at some point, a person in a red velvet robe disappeared, then reappeared in the maze down below.

Though what it might mean, and why I was chosen to see it, is anyone's guess.

Braxton sits stiffly in the silk-upholstered chair beside me. "What is it you really want to know?" he asks.

Without missing a beat, I say, "What's the price? What does Arthur want from me?"

Braxton doesn't so much as blink. And with his blue gaze resting on mine and his hands on his knees, he reminds me of a witness on court TV—nervous, sworn to tell the whole truth, but not yet decided whether he will.

He inhales a slow breath. On the exhale, he says, "This isn't about human trafficking or mail-order brides." Reaching for his coffee, he cradles the cup between his palms. "That's the first conclusion most people jump to, but it's nothing like that. Gray Wolf really is an academy, though I admit, it's not the usual kind. The classes here are more…hands-on. The lessons have real-life applications—and implications as well."

"Real-life implications like people vanishing into thin air?"

He tries to play it cool, but it's too late. I catch the startled look that flashes across his face.

"Down there." I motion toward the window. "In the maze."

His features darken and shift as though considering whatever comes next. "There's nothing down there, Natasha. Or at least, there's no maze."

24

I blink, expecting him to crack a smile, admit to the joke. When he does neither, I move over to the window.

"Look," I say, finger pressed to the pane. "Right there."

He stands behind me, breath wafting over my ear. "I am looking," he says.

I tip onto my toes, press closer to the glass, and gaze down at the same Tarot Garden I wandered through the night before. No sign of a maze anywhere.

"I—I don't understand…" I squint at the collection of colorful sculptures; it doesn't make any sense. In all the other Unravelings, it's only the people who weren't real—the surrounding landscape stayed unchanged.

Does that mean the maze existed before Arthur installed the Tarot Garden?

And if so, just how far back did that Unraveling go?

"Maybe this will answer some of your questions." Braxton leads me back to the settee, where he hands me an off-white tote bag with the academy name in a blocky black font stamped across the front, and a strange cross-like symbol marking the center. Inside I find a green sweatshirt with the exact same design.

GRAY WOLF ACADEMY

"You don't seriously expect me to wear this?" I run my thumb over the fabric. It's soft, but now that I have access to Gucci and Prada, I'm not about to go back to wearing a hoodie. To Braxton, I say, "I mean, have you seen inside my closet?" I toss the sweatshirt aside.

"Everyone wears one," he says.

"Even Elodie?" I shoot him a challenging look. And the second Braxton confirms it, I try to picture Elodie wearing something so ordinary.

"Only hers is…"

I turn to find Braxton contemplating his coffee, hesitating in a way that puts me on edge.

Well, even more on edge.

"Hers is what?" I prompt. "Covered in sequins? Designed by Hermès?"

"Hers is a different color," he says. "Most of them are. But only because everyone else has been here longer. And I'm sure that in no time, you'll catch up and—"

I drop my croissant, cross my legs at the knee, and lean toward him. "In case you haven't noticed," I say, "this little coffee klatch you've arranged isn't going nearly as well as you hoped."

Braxton sighs, runs a hand through his thick mop of movie-star hair. "What I'm trying to say is that all the students wear the academy sweatshirt. Which means you need to wear one, too."

"But *you're* not wearing one." I motion toward his black sweater, which, though I can't say for sure, appears to be cashmere.

"I'm not a student."

"What are you, then—a teacher?"

He shakes his head.

"A hall monitor?"

"Look," Braxton says, "I don't have a title, okay? I'm just

here to help."

"Oh, so that's what this is—*helping*."

Braxton's gaze meets mine, but whatever he's thinking, he keeps it hidden from me. Because, of course. "Look," he finally says again, setting down his cup. "If we can just stay on schedule, then—"

"Fine," I cut in. "But first, just answer my question. Who else wears green?"

With a weary sigh, Braxton closes his eyes, which is all the answer I need.

25

"So let me get this straight," I say. "Green equals newbie. And newbie equals me, and probably nobody else. Which means, by wearing this hideous sweatshirt, I basically have a Caution: Student Driver sign stuck to my back."

"It's nothing like that," Braxton says, but his voice, along with his energy, is starting to fade.

"Then exactly what is it? Has Arthur divided us into factions? Is this some sort of weird *Lord of the Flies* scenario, where the different colors battle for dominance?"

"Do you have an actual question?" Braxton says.

"Oh, I have loads of questions." I tap a finger against the strange image stamped on the front of the sweatshirt and the bag. "For starters—what's this?"

Braxton's face softens, as though I've thrown him a softball and he can let his guard down. "It's the symbol for the academy."

I stare back with dead eyes. He's lucky I didn't roll them. Does he really think I couldn't figure that out on my own?

"It's also the alchemical symbol for antimony. Lupus Metallorum—the wolf of the metals. It's a corrosive or biting agent that unites with all the known metals, except gold, in which it serves to purify."

"Okaaay…" I drag out the word. "What the hell does that have to do with the academy, or anything else, while we're at it?"

"The Gray Wolf is the penultimate stage in the making of

the philosopher's stone."

"The philosopher's stone." The statement hanging heavy between us. "So...this is a school for alchemy?"

"In a way..." Braxton leaves the statement unfinished and reaches for his coffee again.

"And which version of alchemy?" I ask. "Making lead into gold, the search for eternal life, or spiritual enlightenment? I mean, what exactly are we studying here?" My voice pitches unfortunately high.

Even though I sensed there was something very odd about this place, this has taken a turn I didn't expect.

"You're getting worked up over nothing," he says. "It's just a symbol—a metaphor—for the kind of personal transformation Arthur's students experience here." Braxton gestures toward the bag. "You'll find today's program inside. Though I'm afraid you're getting such a late start, most of it no longer applies. Still, you'll get some idea of what to expect."

I pull out the schedule, along with a green notebook that also features that strange alchemical symbol. For a place so off the grid, they're surprisingly big on branding.

Printed on a creamy, high-quality card stock with the Gray Wolf emblem embossed at the top, my name is printed below in a fancy black font:

Natasha Antoinette Clarke

Beneath that is a day of events so strange, I skim through it twice and it still doesn't make sense.

07:00 – 8:50: Breakfast in the Spring Room
09:00 – 09:15: Orientation
09:20 – 10:00: Tour of the academy

Even though it's way past the appointed hour, I hope the tour is still on, since, from what I saw of this place last night, I'll never find my way around on my own.

But here's where things take a turn:

10:05 – 11:00: Aptitude Test- Procurement

11:05 – 12:00: Aptitude Test- Equestrian

12:05 – 13:00: Lunch in the Spring Room

13:05 – 14:00: Aptitude Test- Swordcraft/Survival skills

14:05 – 15:00: Aptitude Test- Languages/Cultural norms

15:05 – 15:20: Break in the Summer Room

15:25 – 16:45: Introduction to the Fourth Dimensional Road

18:00 – 19:30: Dinner in the Winter Room

19:35 – 21:45: Personal Time in the Autumn Room

22:00: Lights Out

When I reach the end, I clear my throat. "Um, here's a question," I say. "What the fu—"

Before I can finish, Braxton's phone buzzes; he leaps from his seat and mumbles something about needing to speed things along. "When you're ready," he says, already on his way to the door, "I'll be downstairs."

"Wait—so you're seriously not going to explain why I'm scheduled to take a class in sword fighting and survival skills?"

He stares down at his feet for a long, tense beat. When his chin finally lifts, his gaze burns with something I might easily mistake for remorse, self-loathing, or shame, if I were foolish enough to think this guy was capable of feeling any of those things.

"I know you won't believe this," he says. "But I volunteered to give you the tour hoping that we could be friends." He rakes a hand through his hair and narrows those astonishing blue eyes that've probably won over plenty of hearts, just not mine. "I know it's all really intimidating, but if you can put aside some of your anger and give it a chance, you'll see—"

"And if I don't give it a chance?" I cut in. "What then? Will

Arthur let me leave?" I run my gaze over Braxton's face, trying to peer past the beautiful veneer he wears like a mask, to get to the truth he's unwilling to share.

When he does speak, his voice is grave, his body shifting uneasily. "Don't be so quick to choose that route," he says. "It may not lead where you think."

Before I can ask him to elaborate, he's out the door, leaving me with the hiss of flames in the hearth and the disquieting echo of his words.

26

Even though I'm seriously tempted to ignore Braxton's advice and head downstairs in my fancy dress and Louboutin heels—if for no other reason than to prove that I make my own rules—I'd also hate for Arthur to get the wrong idea and think I'm so superficial he's already won me over with a room full of luxury clothes.

Not to mention, these heels are seriously starting to kill.

So, when I do finally head out in my green Gray Wolf sweatshirt, dark denim jeans, and a brand new pair of sneakers, only to find Braxton at the bottom of the stairway, I must do a pretty good job of not hiding my frustration, because he's quick to say, "Look, I get that I'm the last person you want to see, but there's a lot of ground to cover, so we really should get started."

He tries to hurry me along, but I stubbornly stick to my own, more leisurely, pace, moving so slowly, my sneakers practically drag across the floor.

He frowns at my feet. "Don't you think this is a little childish?"

I come to a full stop, refusing to budge a single step farther. "What—you're afraid I'll be late for my Procurement exam?"

"Natasha—" He starts to move toward me, but I stop him with a hand raised in warning.

"It's Nat," I say, instinctively hugging myself at the waist. Then, realizing it probably makes me appear as scared and small as I feel, I force my arms to my sides.

He makes a point of looking from me to his watch. "I know you're upset," he says. "But if we could just get through this, then—"

I lean against the wall and hook a defiant hand on my hip. I'm testing his patience. I can see it in the tightening of his jaw, the quickening tap of his foot against the limestone floor. And when his gaze lands heavily on mine, even though it's partially obscured by the stray lock of hair falling over his brow, it's clear I'm successfully wearing him down.

Which would be great, except for the fact that I'm wearing myself down as well.

It's been years since I last let myself cry, but I get the distinct feeling that if I were alone in my room, with the shower running on high, that's exactly what I'd be doing.

"For the record," he says, voice barely a whisper, "on my first day, I was scared out of my wits, too. All of us were. It's perfectly normal to feel like you do."

The look he gives me is so gentle and kind, it's like I'm seeing him for the very first time. Not just as some unattainable hot guy—the enemy who stole my backpack along with my (admittedly crummy) life—but as a true flesh-and-blood person with maybe his own regrettable past.

The academy will reveal itself soon enough, but this may prove to be my one and only chance to really learn something about him.

"So you *were* a student once upon a time. How'd you end up at Gray Wolf?" I ask.

His gaze meets mine, and he doesn't even flinch when he says, "Theft. Just like you, I drew the Wheel of Fortune card, too."

My breath hitches. I take a moment to process. "Was Elodie responsible?" I ask, already convinced that she was.

How many people has she manipulated?

How many lives has she ruined?

I should've listened to Mason when he tried to warn me, but I was too caught up in the rush of hanging with her.

Elodie was exciting. Intoxicating. She did what she pleased—pushed every boundary, broke every rule—without any consequence.

My life was the opposite. I was walking a high wire with no net to catch me. And yet, whenever I was with Elodie, I fooled myself into believing I could live like her, too.

Braxton studies me for a prolonged beat, then abruptly turns away. "Come, Tasha," he says. "We have a lot of ground to cover."

"Nat," I correct him as I race to catch up. But he pretends not to hear.

The campus is surprisingly big, covering way more ground than I initially guessed. And as Braxton leads me through a never-ending labyrinth of halls, I can't help but admire how Arthur has managed to so seamlessly blend the opposite worlds of classic art and high tech.

We pause outside a formal, old-world-style library with polished wood paneled walls and an endless collection of books arranged on stacks of shelves that appear to soar as high as the sky.

"Actual books?" I turn to Braxton. "I would've expected a towering pile of ereaders."

"Arthur made his money in tech, but he prefers tangible things he can touch. Also, most of those books you see are rare editions. Now come."

Braxton leads me away from the library and over to a classroom that looks like it could double as an operating room from the future. Every single surface is so glossy and white, I'm forced to squint in order to take it all in.

"Is this where the lessons in swordcraft happen?" I glance

over my shoulder at Braxton, but he's waving at me to move on.

The next room is more like a theater. There's a large round stage in the center, with a few rows of comfortable-looking chairs arranged all around it.

"And this must be where the cast of the school play meets for rehearsal?" When Braxton ignores me, I say, "I thought you were here to answer my questions."

"Then ask me a real one," he says, moving farther down the hall.

"Is that an original Picasso?" I jab a thumb toward a painting I recognize from sophomore year art class.

"One of many." Braxton nods. "And the walls, in case you're wondering, are covered in the most expensive Venetian plaster money can buy."

Not wanting to appear too impressed, I run a hand along the big ticket wall and say, "And yet, it looks a lot like cement. Also, this place could definitely do with a window or two. I mean—" I accidentally bump my thumb against a biometric door pad, prompting a bark of an alarm to sound in protest. "Guess that room's off-limits." I let out a chirp of a laugh, hoping to cover how embarrassed I am, but Braxton barely notices.

"Think of Gray Wolf like a small city," he tells me. "It contains everything one might possibly need without ever having to venture outside."

"Is that because no one's *allowed* to venture outside?" I shoot him a sideways glance as I walk alongside him. Considering the remote island location and fortresslike walls, the suggestion can't be all that far off.

Braxton leads me around a corner that opens to yet another long hall. "You act like this is a prison," he says, our footsteps landing in unison.

"Well. Isn't it?"

"You can't be serious." He gives a quick breath of a laugh

and motions toward the gleaming marble floors, the gilt-framed old masters lining the walls, the abundance of crystal chandeliers hanging overhead, the intricate mural of glorious angels and terrifying demons engaged in the ancient battle of good versus evil depicted on the domed ceiling.

"Fine," I say. "So it's less a prison and more a luxury snow globe. Either way, there's no viable way to escape."

Braxton stops dead in his tracks, his mood looking like it's taken a serious turn. "This is your home now," he says, his authoritative tone clashing with the quick glance he shoots over his shoulder, as though worried someone might overhear. "As for your former home, you need to leave it behind. You can never go back there."

27

*Y*ou can never go back there.

Braxton's words repeat in my head.

"Never is a really long time," I finally manage to say, trying not to let on just how panicked he's made me. "And I really don't like feeling trapped."

Braxton regards me with a mix of sadness and regret. "You have to stop this," he says. "You have to find a way to adapt."

"Is that what you did?"

He presses his lips so hard, the edges turn white.

"And exactly how long did that take?" I ask. "How long before *you* gave up the fight?"

He closes his eyes and sighs. When he opens them, he says, "You assume I had a life worth fighting for." The words come softly, but they echo through me as though they were shouted.

I stare at my feet, overcome with embarrassment for acting like I knew the first thing about him. I, of all people, should have known better.

As I silently walk alongside him, Braxton points out the more important works of art while reeling off a list of academy facts.

The campus covers several square miles.

It houses just shy of one hundred people—a mix of students, instructors, and various support staff.

But it all blows right through me. My mind has traveled into the past, remembering how ashamed I used to feel that I could never reimburse Elodie for her showy displays of generosity. But now I know it wasn't at all what I thought. All that time she was bankrolled by Arthur, the two of them plotting against me.

"You feel guilty," I say, cutting into Braxton's monologue about the building's various architectural and technological features. Although I hadn't taken the time to properly examine the thought, I know that it's true. "You feel guilty for sending me here. That's why you're going out of your way with the coffee, croissants, the tour."

I remember how he apologized back on the dock, right before boarding the skiff I was sure would lead to my watery death. Clearly, he's conflicted about the part he played.

Braxton stops and stands before me, arms hanging loose by his sides, staring at me with a gaze that's surprisingly open, his eyes deep and blue as the sea.

"And I'm guessing I'm not the first person you've sent here," I add.

His mouth tugs at the sides. His jaw twitches ever so slightly. But more importantly, he starts to fidget with his signet ring—a sure sign that I'm onto something.

It's a game of emotional archeology, and I'm one trowel jab away from unearthing his truth.

"So, what I'm wondering is, why'd you go through with it? I mean, since you're the one who—"

"The one who what—decides?" His tone is harsher than I've come to expect, though the posh accent rings loud and clear. He swipes a hand through his hair, shoots a sharp glance down the hall before continuing. "I was sent to do a job, and I did it. You think you're the only one with a parent supported by Arthur?"

I swallow hard. My gaze holds steady on his, but inside, I feel jittery, tense.

"Fine." He sighs. "You want to know why you're here? Aside

from the fact that you *chose* to be here?" His gaze burns on mine. "It's because you were actively and willfully failing—both in school and in life. And, more importantly, you had no one around who was present enough to save you from yourself, despite how hard you tried to save *them*."

The stabbing truth of his words slices straight through my heart, leaving me wrecked, struggling for each shallow breath.

"Everyone here has a similar story," he says, adopting a much softer tone, "but we've learned to make the best of it, and I suggest you do the same."

There's a dull throb in my belly, a searing pain in my chest. And though I was right about Braxton feeling guilty, I'm no longer sure it was worth the price of confirming.

"We've got ourselves way behind schedule," he says. "So, what if I just give you a quick rundown of all the rooms you'll need to access the most?"

I follow along in subdued silence, silently admiring the strange juxtaposition between the ancient and modern—the works of old masters lining the walls, and the advanced technology where everything operates with a push of a button.

After showing me the two dining rooms and two break rooms, each of them labeled with their corresponding alchemical symbol over each door:

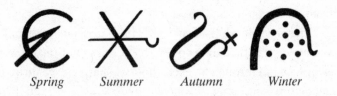

Spring   Summer   Autumn   Winter

Braxton turns to escort me to my first classroom, when his phone begins to buzz.

He looks from his screen to me and says, "Arthur is ready

to meet you in the Spring Room for lunch."

My stomach churns. That can't be good news. "But what if I'm not hungry?" I ask.

"I'm not sure that's the point."

I study Braxton's face, trying to glean what's really going on, but the curtain is drawn.

While I'm sure there are hundreds, maybe even hundreds of thousands, of people who would kill for a private audience with Arthur Blackstone, it's not like I have an app to pitch or a product to hawk, so I don't count myself among them.

"Come on," Braxton says. "Quickly." He starts to lead me toward the Spring Room, but it's not far, and I figure I'm capable of going alone.

"I got it," I tell him, needing to appear more confident than I feel. "Really, I'm good."

Braxton looks at me with concern. "It's going to be okay," he says. "I'm sure it's not what you think."

"I'm not sure what I think," I mumble to myself, and make my way down the hall.

28

When I enter the Spring Room, I'm surprised to find Arthur already seated at a table near the far corner.

I thought for sure he'd act like one of those high-powered executives who're always running a minimum of fifteen minutes behind, for the sole purpose of making everyone wait so they'll know who's in charge.

But as I rush toward him, my sneakers squealing so loudly I cringe at the sound, I realize that Arthur is onto a much better strategy. By him being the first to arrive, it leaves me feeling so flustered and off balance, I immediately start apologizing, and just like that I've lost any small bit of power I had.

His face pulls into the sort of enigmatic Mona Lisa smile I recognize from his *Time* "Person of the Year" magazine cover. According to what I was able to research on the plane, it was the last interview he ever gave. Shortly after, he disappeared from public life. Though I'm willing to bet he's been hiding out here the whole time.

The question is, why?

He leans forward, rests his forearms on the table. "I hope you don't mind," he says, "but I've taken the liberty of ordering for you."

Of course you did. I'm tempted to roll my eyes but settle for nodding instead. Unlike last night when I had to force myself to hold back every hateful thing I wanted to say, now, sitting alone with him in this large, empty dining room, the words just won't come.

"I'm sure you have lots of questions," he says. "Now's your chance to get some answers."

I swallow hard, gaze down at the white linen tablecloth, the gleaming silver flatware, the leaded crystal water goblet with the thinnest slice of lime floating on top. "Why is it called the Spring Room?" I ask, noting that while the décor is perfectly nice, there's nothing to distinguish it from the Winter, Summer, or Autumn Rooms.

With a look of bemusement, he waves a hand, and the next thing I know, the light warms like sunshine, the song of chirping birds sounds from every corner, a hologram of a sparkling river lined with cherry blossom trees twists along the tables, and a monarch butterfly lands on the tines of my salad fork.

The sight is so amazing, I audibly gasp.

"Go ahead, touch it," he says.

I glance from Arthur to the butterfly, then tentatively tap the top of its wing with the tip of my finger, only to feel a shimmer of vibration reverberate all the way up my arm to the top of my shoulder. A moment later, the butterfly flits toward a field of gleaming red tulips.

"How is that even possible?" I stare after the monarch.

Arthur's gaze narrows. "I'm sure you'll find much about Gray Wolf that skews toward the impossible." His fingers idly tease at the jeweled ring he wears on his right hand. Though, unlike Braxton, it's not a nervous tell. It's more like he wants me to notice it.

My hunch is confirmed when he catches me looking, and immediately slips it from his finger and offers it for closer inspection.

The band is gold and thick, with intricate carvings marked all around. The bezel has similar etchings and a dark glimmering ruby placed in the center.

"It belonged to Edward the Black Prince," he says.

"Why did they call him that?" I ask. It's not one of the questions I'd meant to ask. Then again, showing interest in Arthur's treasures is probably a better move than the kind I might normally make.

"Some say it's because of his distinctive black armor and jousting shield. Though there are other theories, of course."

I have no idea what he's hinting at. I've never had much interest in history. Though the irony is not lost on me that by choosing to ditch AP History so I could hang out with Elodie, I ended up here.

I return the ring, watching as he slides it onto his finger. "Looks like the sort of thing you might find in a museum." I reach for my water glass and take a sip, even though I'm not thirsty.

"Have you visited the Louvre?" Arthur asks.

I look up in surprise. Surely, he's well versed on the details of my completely unadventurous life. To him, I say, "I've made a few trips to the website."

His eyes glint with something unknowable as he pushes at the cuffs of his burgundy sweater, exposing a set of bare wrists. I'm surprised to see he's not wearing some big expensive watch. Then again, to a man like Arthur Blackstone, king of this castle if not planet Earth, time is his to command.

"Maybe someday you'll visit Paris and see the Louvre in person," he says.

I shrug. I mean, sure, I hope to visit a lot of faraway places someday. But from where I sit now, it's like dreaming of a trip to the moon.

"Maybe I can spearhead a Gray Wolf Academy field trip," I say, tacking an awkward snort onto the end that I instantly regret, until Arthur joins in with a surprisingly genuine, full-bodied laugh.

"Oh, I'm sure we can do much better than that," he says, continuing to chuckle softly to himself long after the joke has worn itself out.

And while it's nice to think I've managed to amuse him, and while seeing him laugh does help to humanize him, I can't help but worry that there's something more behind it. Because judging by the dark glint in his eyes, I get the terrible feeling that the real joke is on me.

29

The chef who serves us is French.

He's also short, round, and wears a white double-breasted chef coat, a royal-blue neckerchief, and a white chef's toque sunk so low on his head, I'm left with the impression of a set of bushy gray brows, a wide baguette of a nose, a thick curlicue mustache, and pretty much nothing else. He looks so much like a cartoon chef I once saw in a movie, I can't help but wonder if, like the butterfly, he's not actually real.

"Try not to get used to lunching like this," Arthur says. "It's not the normal menu."

Though I have no idea why he's going to such lengths to impress me, I give my full attention to the meal, and with every mouthwatering bite, I can't help but think how much Mason would love this.

Arthur raises his glass of wine. "I would offer to pour you some," he says. "But seeing as you still have a few classes ahead…"

"About that—" I set down my fork, determined to make Arthur understand that whatever's going on here, whatever this academy is about, I'm not a good fit. "I don't think I'm cut out for this—whatever *this* is."

"How so?" He swirls his glass, watching the wine splash up and down the sides before he takes a tentative sip, seems to enjoy it, and takes another.

"Well, after looking at my schedule and all those aptitude tests, I'm thinking maybe I should just save you the trouble and leave before you waste any more time or money on—"

"Do you honestly take me for a fool?"

For the first time since the food arrived, Arthur has stopped eating, stopped drinking, stopped fussing with his fork and knife, to concentrate fully on me. And the result makes me wish I hadn't said anything.

"Do you honestly think I'd go to all the expense of bringing you here if I thought you had nothing to offer in return?"

I gulp. My breath grows unnaturally thin. And before I can stop it, my mouth falls wide open and a whole heap of nonsense spills out. "No. Of course not. I only meant—"

Thankfully, Arthur stops me before it can get any worse. "Believe me, I've seen it all." He waves a hand that makes the cherry blossoms, the sparkling river, and the butterflies all disappear. Leaving nothing to distract from Arthur's weary gaze and the serious ferocity behind every word. "Do you know why I've managed to become so successful?"

I fidget with my napkin. He can't actually expect me to answer.

"It wasn't because I was a tech whiz, or child prodigy, or whatever story you may have heard. It's because I use my eyes for seeing."

My fingers still. I have no idea what that means. I mean, don't we all?

"I've been heralded as a futurist, a dreamer, an outlier, a genius…" With a turn of his wrist, he waves the accolades away like one might flick away a fly. "And it always reminds me of the quote by Schopenhauer: *Talent hits a target no one else can hit. Genius hits a target no one else can see.*"

I swallow past the lump in my throat. Press a hand to my belly and will it to calm.

"What truly separates me from everyone else isn't the score on my IQ test. What's lifted me above the horde is *vision*." He assesses me with a narrowed gaze. "Have you ever heard of the invisible-ships phenomenon?"

I shake my head, take a nervous sip of my water.

"It is said that when Captain James Cook arrived at the coast of Australia back in 1770, the natives completely ignored their arrival because the fact that they'd never seen a ship before left them literally unable to perceive the very ship that appeared off their shores. According to the captain's journal, not a single native looked up."

"Is that true?" My fingers seek the stem of my water glass. "Because honestly, it sounds pretty implausible. I mean, maybe the natives did see it and they were left unimpressed by the view. Sounds to me like Cook was annoyed they didn't all stop what they were doing to admire his ride. At best, it's petty. At worst, it's totally racist."

Arthur nods. "I've heard the same story attributed to Columbus in 1492, and Magellan in 1520. And from what I've seen, you're probably right. It's yet another grossly exaggerated myth used to serve their own narrative. Still, while the teaching is a mess, the message is solid—most people *do* surrender their sight early on. They allow themselves to see only what other people tell them is possible. But I've always been different. Since a young age, I've peered at the world through a deeply curious lens, and I routinely challenge myself to see far beyond the accepted societal perceptions. Thanks to my vast collection of art, my eye for beauty is world renowned. But what most people fail to understand is that my vision far surpasses anything they'd even dare to imagine. And it all begins here."

He leans back in his seat, lifts his wineglass to the room at large, then takes a slow, thoughtful sip, allowing me time to process his words.

But honestly, there's not enough time in the world.

"I—I'm afraid I don't understand," I stammer, cringing at my inability to grasp at his meaning. I feel like a bumpkin, even more like I don't belong in this place. I'm not used to having conversations like this or, hell, actually using more than one fork for my meals. Clearly, he can see that. So, why does he insist on keeping me here?

"Of course you don't understand," he says. "Everything here is new and unfamiliar, and your coping skills could use a little work. So, rather than allow yourself time to adjust, you've created an idealized version of your past and convinced yourself that it's true."

The steady set of his gaze, combined with the slight lift of his brow, tells me he will not be played. Not by me or anyone else.

"You've built up quite a misty-eyed story in your head," he continues, "but tell me—if I were to grant your wish and send you back home, what exactly would you be returning to? Go ahead, close your eyes, and tell me what you see."

I do as he says. I mean, I close my eyes, anyway. And even though I had no intention of examining my past (basically everything that occurred up until yesterday), a string of images still manages to scroll through my brain. Here's what I see:

I miss Mason.

I miss the version of my mom that died the day my dad left.

And that's pretty much it.

My eyes begin to sting. So I hold a few beats before I open them again. Arthur may see right through me, but I refuse to let him know how deeply he's gotten to me.

"Never forget that out of all the possible candidates, I chose you." His tone is more tempered now that he's clearly maneuvered me right where he wants me. "And because of it, you've been granted admission to a world you never thought possible, where you have access to everything you could ever want—including everything you never knew you wanted because your life outside was so small, it stunted your vision. Gray Wolf is not only a place of unparalleled luxury and beauty, but one where you'll transcend all your preconceived limits, and, in time, you will come to understand that the best thing about the past is that we get to pick and choose the parts that suit us and discard all the rest."

The most I can do is blink and breathe. It's a lot to take in, and I'm pretty sure Arthur prefers I not interrupt.

"You have something very special, Natasha. A very rare gift you're just now becoming aware of. And I'm going to help you hone and develop that gift into something truly remarkable."

My fingers pick nervously at the square of linen draped over my lap as I muster up the courage to ask, "And in return?"

My gaze tentatively meets his as he pauses to sip from his wine. It's the same question I asked Braxton. But after listening to Arthur, I'm convinced he's expecting to get a lot more out of this arrangement than the thrill of watching an underachiever reach their full potential.

"I mean, it's a pretty big promise, so you've got to be expecting something in return for all of your...generosity?"

I watch as Arthur lowers his glass to the table, placing it just to the right of his plate. His manner is so precise, so deliberate, it reminds me of the old saying: *How you do anything is how you do everything.* And I know that where Arthur's concerned, everything about this lunch has been orchestrated to bring us to this very moment. He's expertly steered me straight into this port, and I didn't even realize it until I was already docked.

Arthur pauses long enough to center that obsidian gaze upon mine.

"In return," he says, "you're going to help me fulfill my greatest ambition."

30

I sit silently before Arthur, wishing I'd never asked. This is a man who's accomplished more in one lifetime than pretty much anyone else on the planet. So, what could he possibly be aiming for next? And what could a high school loser like me actually offer—what part does he think I can play?

"And, uh…what exactly is that?" I say, unable to hide my unease. "What is your greatest ambition, if you don't mind my asking?"

In an instant, Arthur's hard and angular features soften as he focuses on some distant horizon visible only to him. "Soon," he says, leaning back in his seat. "Soon, you'll discover what Gray Wolf is really about. But not yet."

When he returns to me, he wears an expression gilded by so much unwavering faith in my abilities, I'm suddenly willing to do whatever it takes to meet the ridiculously high expectations he's set for me.

And yet, I'm also dreading the day I'll eventually prove myself to be nothing more than dreadfully ordinary.

Because if there's one thing I know for sure, it's that that day will come.

If I were to make a graph of my life lived so far, it would consist of a gradual (though seriously unimpressive) incline, followed by a sudden and dramatic decline, that ultimately levels off to a long, consistent flatline of the sort that only a miracle can revive.

Is Gray Wolf that miracle?

Arthur clearly thinks so.

As for me, I've never been one for harboring hope.

"For now," Arthur says, "why not just allow yourself to settle in and enjoy the process as it unfolds?"

I know the question was hypothetical, but in my head, the answer comes swiftly—*because what if I don't like what I discover?*

I look to Arthur, about to respond, when the lights start to blink on and off, and the ground begins to shake.

I freeze. *Please no, not another Unraveling.* Never has this happened twice in one day. Before I saw the person vanish in the maze, it'd been years since the last time reality cracked and I was forced to witness the real reason my dad left.

It was after school, and just after letting myself into the house, I headed for the pantry in search of a snack. When the fluorescent lights started to flicker, I didn't pay it any notice. It was only when the ground began to tremble and I heard two raised voices that I turned to find my parents standing next to the sink.

I called out to them, but they acted like I didn't exist. And though I was used to the sight of them arguing, I was struck by how much younger they looked—their bright, unlined faces still new at the fight.

I zeroed in on my mom's shaking hand and the pregnancy test pinched between her fingers. Her chin quivered, her shoulders shook, as my dad stood before her, face creased in anguish.

It took me a minute to realize I was the baby who'd made those lines appear on that stick. And my dad's look of torment was all the proof I needed to know I'd been unwanted from the very first moment he'd learned of my existence.

"Natasha." The sound of Arthur's voice yanks me out of the reverie. "Are you okay?"

I snap my eyes open to find my fingers gripping the edge of the table, while the room that surrounds me is unchanged.

"Gray Wolf is home to the world's most advanced technology." Arthur narrows his gaze in study. "It generates massive amounts of energy, which sometimes results in the sort of effects you just experienced. Eventually, you'll grow so used to it, you won't even notice."

I nod in embarrassment and mumble some excuse about not having slept well, but one look at his pointed gaze tells me he sees right through the lie.

Tossing his napkin onto his plate, he pushes away from the table. "Come," he says.

"Where to?"

Arthur regards me with a shaded look I can't read. "Looks like you're ready to jump ahead in your studies."

31

Arthur escorts me out of the Spring Room and past a crowd lingering in the hall.

It's the most people I've seen since I arrived, and while the majority are somewhere around my age, give or take a few years, it soon becomes clear that Braxton was right—everyone really is wearing a Gray Wolf sweatshirt, and mine is the only green one. Most of the others are blue.

So it really is like I thought: green equals newbie.

I pick out Song from among them; she's standing beside a boy I recognize as Finn. I give a little wave, they wave back, and as their eyes trail after us, I watch as Song tips onto her toes and whispers into Finn's ear.

The way they watch us, looking from me to Arthur, reminds me of how the popular kids used to react every time Elodie deigned to acknowledge me at school. Their eyes scouring over me, searching for clues, trying to solve the mystery of *what's so special about her?*

Now more than ever, I need an answer. Because just knowing that Arthur's betting on me to fulfill his biggest dream has left me feeling really uneasy.

Arthur leads me down a new set of hallways I haven't yet traveled, and when we reach the end of the corridor, he taps an earpiece I didn't even notice he was wearing, and says, "I have Natasha Clarke here. She's ready to jump ahead in her schedule."

Although he's not what anyone would consider especially tall or wide, when Arthur turns to face me, he commands such a large presence, it feels like he towers above me.

My belly begins to twitch. There's a tickle forming in the back of my throat. I want to tell him I'm not at all ready to jump ahead to anything, but sensing that won't go over so well, I eke out the words, "Um, actually, I go by Nat."

Arthur studies me for a long moment. And I could be mistaken, but I think there's a fleeting glimmer of compassion in those obsidian eyes—until it vanishes before it can truly take hold.

"No," he says, his tone unmistakably definitive. "Not anymore."

I give a sheepish nod and stare hard at the floor, all the while wondering if I can possibly live up to my mother's long-ago dream of the Natasha she once hoped for.

The door swings open.

Arthur leaves.

And as I step inside, I'm instantly struck by a single bright spotlight.

32

"Natasha?"

I squint. Nod. Lift a hand to ward off the glare and take a tentative step forward.

"Sorry about that," the voice says. The next moment, the light dims and I lower my hand to my side. "Why don't you come this way so I can properly introduce myself."

I move toward the front of the room, careful to avoid an intricate replica of a carriage, the kind you see in movies set in historical times, when the voice says, "Oh, don't mind the holograms. Feel free to walk right through them."

"That's a hologram?" I pause to gape at the apparition. "But it looks so real... So...3D." I reach out to touch it, but before I can make contact, it vanishes.

"That one's not quite ready. Soon, though."

I look up to find a man standing before me, holding a clear tablet as thin as a credit card. Like Braxton's phone, it's at least several generations beyond those sold in stores. With a series of quick taps, the room empties out, leaving two folding chairs, a potted plant in the corner, and little else.

"I'm Hawke." He tucks the tablet under his arm and offers a hand.

"Nat—Natasha," I say, hoping he didn't notice how I flubbed my own name.

"First day?" He turns and motions for me to follow.

"What gave it away, the green sweatshirt?" I frown at the hideous thing as I hurry to keep up.

"That, and the unmitigated look of sheer terror in your eyes." He takes the seat on the left and gestures for me to take the other one.

"How long have you been here?" I ask. As he taps and scrolls on his tablet, I use the moment to study him in a way I won't be able to once I truly have his attention.

His hair is the color of sand with a few blonder bits near the front. It's sort of wavy and long, as though it's been several months between cuts. And his white skin wears the sort of bronzed glow that has me wondering if somewhere around this cold and windy place there's access to a tanning bed, a spray tan booth, or both.

At first sight, I'm tempted to peg him as one of those hoodie-wearing, twentysomething tech bros straight out of Silicon Valley. Except he wears a faded blue denim button-down instead of a hoodie, and his accent sounds more East Coast than Northern California.

When he slides his tablet under his leg and settles on me, I note that his eyes are blue, but not the same stormy blue as Braxton's. Hawke's are much lighter in tone, and his smile is quick and easy, displaying a slight gap between his front teeth.

"How long have I been here?" He adopts a thoughtful expression, tips his chair back, and peers at the ceiling as though the answer is written among the rows of canned lights. "Are you familiar with Einstein's theory on time?"

I rub my lips together, worried the test has already begun.

"It's all relative." He grins, lowers the front legs of his chair, and enjoys a short burst of a laugh. "But, if you must know, my best guess would be seven years or so."

"Your best guess?" I can't help it—that's a really weird way to answer. Like, who doesn't know how long they've worked at a job or lived in a place?

"So, I take it you're skipping ahead to the good stuff?" He regards me through a tilted-head, narrow-eyed gaze.

I shrug. Slouch lower in my seat. Then, realizing what a sloppy impression that makes, I straighten my spine, cross my legs primly, and say, "To be honest, I have no idea what I'm doing here."

Hawke's gaze pores over me, really taking me in but giving no hint as to what sort of conclusion he's drawing. "Uh-huh. Uh-huh…" He reaches for his tablet again. "Let me ask you this—can you ride a horse?" He taps, scrolls, then waits for my reply.

Uhhh, what? I shake my head no.

"Any languages—good at accents?"

I glance between the tablet and him. "Um, two years of high school French?" My voice inadvertently lifts at the end, like I'm unsure and looking to him to confirm it. "Oh, and aside from a spot-on impression of the head cheerleader, no talent for accents." It was a little shot at levity, but it's met by dead silence, a few taps, and a long drawn-out scroll.

"What about acting abilities? Any roles in the school play—anything like that?"

Another no. *What are these questions?*

"Can you wield a sword? Ever take a fencing class?"

I gaze down at the floor. The room is cool, but I'm starting to sweat. "Um, *wield?*" I shrug, pull my shoulders in tighter, horrified by how quickly I'm failing this test. And even though I thought I wanted to go home, after my lunch with Arthur, I'm no longer sure that's such a viable option. And if it is, then I'm no longer sure that I want to.

"How about solving puzzles, cryptology, that sort of thing?" His gaze is flat, his voice holding little hope.

My breath whooshes out of me. I offer a tight, pleading grin. It's a desperate attempt at a save, but Hawke regards me with that same bored expression.

"Well," he says, uncrossing his legs. "Guess that's how you ended up here. I'm your last chance."

I look at him with a startled gaze, but he just laughs.

"Not to worry," he tells me. "You're in good hands. You're about to learn everything you need to know from the master himself."

He returns to his tablet, and while he taps and scrolls, I can't help but think how smug that last comment was. I mean, seriously? This guy is truly full of himself.

"So, I'll leave you to it, then." He rises from his chair and starts to leave.

"Wait—what?" I glance between the newly vacated chair and him.

"Oh, and don't forget to take notes!" Without so much as a look in my direction, he's gone.

I'm just about to go after him when the lights dim and Albert Einstein, or at least an eerily realistic hologram of Einstein, pulls up the chair, leans in, and says, "So, Natasha, what do you say we begin at the beginning?"

33

At Gray Wolf, we dress for dinner.

I know this because of the note card stating as much that was slipped under my door.

Though just how far I'm supposed to go in this new *dress for dinner* world, I'm not sure.

Do I wear one of the formal gowns hanging at the far end of my closet?

Or do I go with one of the simpler, but still pretty, dresses hanging just beside them?

Should I choose a vintage look or something more modern?

My wardrobe is bursting with choices.

Not wanting to look like I'm trying too hard, I reach for a pretty but still understated navy-blue Dior dress, thinking the color might send a subliminal message that after spending the bulk of the afternoon in deep, one-on-one conversations with Einstein, Stephen Hawking, Michio Kaku, among other notable physicists, both living and dead, I'm ready to make the jump from team green to team blue.

But just as I'm reaching for the hanger, I notice the gorgeous emerald green slip dress hanging nearby. There's a faux fur stole just beside it and a pair of jeweled Jimmy Choo biker boots placed underneath.

My breath hitches. It's an exact replica of the outfit I described on my last day at school, when Mason and I played a round of Anywhere but Here.

But how could Arthur have known?

Did he hack the mic on my phone?

And if so, what else has he heard?

I trail a finger down the length of the dress. It's made of a heavy, high quality silk. No fast-fashion, polyester knockoffs here. Then I carry both dresses to the mirror and take turns holding each one against me, trying to determine if it's some kind of test, or even a dare, when there's a knock at my door.

"Hey, Natasha—it's Song." Her voice carries through the door. "I thought you might want to go down together. I know it's your first night, or your first dinner anyway, and—"

Still holding both dresses, I open the door.

"That one." Song points at the slip dress. "No contest."

"I take it you've been to the Winter Room?" Song walks alongside me, her delicate silver heels clicking against the stone tile floor.

With her minimal makeup and long black hair twisted into a loose bun, she wears a billowy, low-cut, tulle dress nearly the same shade of blue as the collection of aquamarine studs artfully arranged in each of her ears. From her neck hangs a beautiful crystal necklace, making for an effect that's so effortlessly glamorous, I worry that my last minute dash of red lipstick might've pushed my own look too far, even though Song did encourage it.

I fidget with the faux fur stole, run my tongue along my upper teeth, when Song stops, grasps my arm, and says, "Stop it. You look amazing."

I can feel my face flush. I'm embarrassed by how much I needed the reassurance. "Everything here is so different," I start. "Back home we never dressed up for meals. We never dressed up for anything, really."

Song shoots a worried look down the hall. Determining the coast is clear, her dark eyes then settle on mine. "The sooner you forget about home, the easier it'll be to adapt."

On the surface, it sounds like good advice, but I can't help but think there's a warning attached.

She holds my gaze, and when I nod in reply, she releases my arm, and we continue the walk.

"Can I ask you how long you've been here?" I say.

She stares straight ahead, her expression a perfect blank slate. "You could," she finally replies. "But I'm not sure what you'd gain from knowing."

It's a definite roadblock, but there's still one more thing I'm determined to ask. "Is—" I bite my lip, look all around, and in a lowered voice say, "Is there… I mean, are we being…watched?"

Song's expression goes blank. After we've walked a few minutes longer, she says, "Look, Natasha, I'd really like for us to be friends. If for no other reason than having friends is useful around here."

I stare back in return. I have no idea how to respond. *Um, thanks?*

"Everyone saw you today, having lunch with Arthur."

It's not like I hadn't noticed them looking, she and Finn included. But I'm also not sure why it matters. "Is that weird? I mean, I guess I assumed everyone gets a turn." I shrug like it was no big thing, but from the look on her face, that was the wrong way to play it.

"A word of advice?"

I can hardly breathe, but I'm still capable of nodding.

"Don't assume anything here, about anyone or anything. Understand?"

I swallow. Hold for the punch line. When it doesn't arrive, I say, "Well, that sounds ominous."

34

Song pauses just shy of the Winter Room entrance, allowing space for a group of laughing people to enter. "I was sincere about us being friends," she says after they've passed. "But I'm afraid Blues dine together. There's not a lot of mixing between the levels during mealtimes."

My heart sinks at the thought of eating alone. Even when I was demoted to sitting next to the recycle bin at my old school, I still had Mason for company.

She clasps my arm briefly. "Don't worry," she says, "it won't last forever. You'll make the leap soon enough."

"And if I don't?"

Her face turns serious. "If I were you, I wouldn't consider that an option. Oh, and just so you know, you're sitting at Braxton's table tonight."

An audible gasp escapes my lips. And though I'm not even sure why, and while I'm definitely in no mood to examine what it might mean, the worst part is, Song heard it.

"It's possible he's not nearly as bad as you think," she says, her gaze sliding over me. "Then again, it's also quite likely he's worse. Guess that's for you to determine." The grin that follows is sly, like she's in on a secret I've yet to unearth. "But Elodie, on the other hand…" She sneaks a glance past my shoulder before returning to me. "Be careful with her."

"Pretty sure I already learned that the hard way," I tell her.

"It's how I ended up here."

Song looks me over. "Not what I meant," she says. "I'm talking about her need to be Daddy's favorite. And by *Daddy*, I mean Arthur. Or at least that's how she thinks of him. And today, you threatened her spot as favorite daughter."

"Okaaay," I say. "But I'm not sure how that's my fault. I mean, it's not like I asked to join him for lun…" My voice fades when I see Song's attention drift away as she waves to someone inside the dining room.

When she turns back to me, she places a hand on my arm. "Look, I'm not trying to scare you, but what you did or didn't ask for probably won't matter to her. If anything, it'll just make it worse." Her hand falls back to her side, the edges of her lips tugging down into a sympathetic frown. "Just watch your back, that's all. And try not to fall into old patterns with her. Living here makes it hard to tell the difference between what's real and what's fake, and Elodie is a product of this place. She's spent most of her life here, and it shows. She's like the personification of the best and worst that Gray Wolf has to offer."

"For someone who claims they didn't mean to scare me, you're kind of freaking me out." I frown, my heart nearly doubling its pace. "I mean, lunch happened, and I'm not really sure what I'm supposed to do about that."

Song steals another glance inside the dining room, which makes me wonder if she's starting to regret ever bringing this up. When she turns back to me, she says, "If it were me, I'd count myself lucky that Arthur took an interest. Lunching with him is not standard practice. Or at least I never got one. And considering how he's the first and last word around here, you might consider milking that for all it's worth. Just try not to flaunt it, that's all. Deal with Elodie the same way you would any venomous snake — try not to agitate her, and do what you can to stay out of her way."

Before I can even drum up a reply, Song swings her hair over her shoulder and goes inside.

35

Snow drifts from the sky and blankets the floor.

Crystal chandeliers dip from the ceiling, flickering softly with candlelight.

A fire roars from a large hearth as a baby fawn skitters across a frozen pond, wobbling past rows of diners as his mother patiently waits on the other side.

And there, among all the tables heaping with fancy stemware, gleaming golden cutlery, and plates of fine china, sits Braxton.

Braxton—with his fancy dinner jacket, ridiculous face, and those astonishing blue eyes that latch onto mine, holding me hostage no matter how hard I try to break free.

And I really do try, but apparently my body has stopped taking orders from my brain. My feet keep crossing the room, carrying me closer to him, as my gaze remains fixed on his as though there's no other place I could possibly look.

When I reach the edge of the table, he rises from his seat. "Wow," he says. "You look ama—" He stops as though catching himself. His face reddening, he makes a stiff gesture toward my clothes. "What I mean is, that's a really nice choice, and…"

He's flustered, which comes as a relief. At least I'm not the only one left unsettled by this weird magnetic vibe that insists on thrumming between us.

I can feel a rush of heat rising to my face, so I'm quick to turn away and reach for my chair, only to find he's already there.

"Allow me," he says, sliding my chair back and ensuring I'm settled before returning to his.

I busy myself with unfastening my stole and draping it over the back of my seat. Only then do I determine myself ready to face him again. "I don't remember you being so chivalrous at the diner." I laugh, hoping it comes off as the joke I intended it to be, while also hoping he doesn't notice how my skittering pulse has left my voice sort of shaken and wobbly.

"That had more to do with the booth situation than a lack of manners." His gaze sweeps over my shoulders, dipping as low as my neckline, before veering away.

"Is it just us?" I ask. For some reason, when Song told me I'd be sitting at Braxton's table, I pictured something bigger, with at least a few other people. From what I can see, ours is the only two-top. "Did you volunteer for this, too?"

Braxton leans toward me, the sleeves of his midnight-blue dinner jacket framing either side of the elaborate gold place setting. "I thought you might like some company," he says. "But if it makes you uncomfortable, I can go…"

He waits for me to reply, but I take my time to decide. Partly because the thought of eating alone fills me with dread. But mostly because the more time I spend with Braxton, the harder it is for me to hate him, or at the very least, stay mad at him, and I'm not sure that's a good thing.

I mean, just because he has a perfectly chiseled face and a body that can really fill out a suit—just because he's admitted to feeling a certain measure of guilt over the part he played in luring me here—doesn't mean I should let my guard down.

An uneasy silence stretches between us. I tease it out a bit longer by lifting the cloth napkin from my plate, removing the golden ring shaped like a crown, and carefully spreading the square of starched linen over my lap. "I think I get what's going on here," I finally say, lifting my water goblet and surveying the crowd. "Arthur is purposely isolating me in hopes that it'll spark some of my long dormant ambition, so I'll do whatever it takes to make Blue."

In a subtle show of relief, Braxton relaxes into his seat. And I'm glad for the extra space; it makes it easier to breathe.

"You're not wrong," Braxton says. "But the question remains—will it work?"

I nod toward the hologram of the pond where that poor fawn is still struggling to cross. His hooves scrabbling clumsily across the ice, front legs comically crisscrossing, hind legs spreading too wide. "Probably." I shrug. "But, at the moment, I'm feeling a bit like Bambi over there."

Braxton glances past his shoulder, then back at me. "Not to worry. By the time the dessert course is finished, he'll have made it to the other side. He always does."

"So it's the same show every night?" That strikes me as odd, if not a little disappointing. I was sure Arthur was far too imaginative to settle for reruns.

Braxton shakes his head, causing a random dark curl to fall into his eyes. And as I watch him distractedly push it back to where it started, I'm struck by his utter lack of vanity or pretense.

I mean, obviously, he knows he's good-looking. But he doesn't dwell on his beauty or try to use it to gain an advantage. After the constant show of posturing and preening by the selfie-obsessed kids at my school, I'd forgotten how people normally act in the absence of ring lights and portrait mode.

"The tech team likes to switch it up," he says. "Though I have seen an earlier rendition of this one."

"Then you can't be sure this new version will also end happily."

Braxton reaches for his wine goblet. His fingers trace the beveled base. "Arthur doesn't invest in failures," he says, and though he doesn't outwardly shift in any discernable way, something in his demeanor is markedly changed. "He has no tolerance for either the ordinary or the mundane."

I take another look around. The space is designed to provide an atmosphere of elegance and opulence, and the students who occupy it are the cream of the crop. But if those students were once anything like me, and Braxton assured me they were, then they didn't start off that way. It was failure that landed them here.

"I guess Arthur really is an alchemist," I say. "He collects high school losers and spins us all into gold."

Braxton shrugs, takes a sip of his wine, but I can see the ghost of a grin behind the glass.

"And yet, there must be more to it?" I search Braxton's face, but he's fully committed to avoiding my gaze. "Because it's a lot of trouble to go to with no guarantee it'll work. I mean, failure happens. It's unavoidable. And it's not like Arthur's psychic or can see into the future and know how things will…"

My voice fades as my mind reels back in time to earlier today, when Einstein and Stephen Hawking taught me about the fourth dimension.

The two of them patiently explaining, in layman's terms, that the fourth dimension is one of time and space, and that all one needs to do is create a tunnel through that fourth dimension and the result is time travel.

And that tunnel is also known as a wormhole.

While I found it fascinating in theory, I was sure that's all it was—a high-minded theory floated before me in the world's strangest hands-on science class.

But now I'm no longer sure. I mean, that can't be what's happening here at Gray Wolf—can it?

And if so, is it somehow connected to the girl I watched disappear, then reappear from my window this morning?

Was that more than just the Unraveling?

36

"You okay?" Braxton reaches for my hand. The unexpected warmth jolts me away from my thoughts.

"Fine. I'm…fine." I free my hand from his and rest it on my lap, where he can't get to it.

"You don't seem fine. Here—" He slides my water glass closer, as though rehydrating will work to solve anything.

Still, I take a slow, measured sip, if for no other reason than it buys me enough time to get a grip on myself.

"Tasha," he says. "There are things I'm not supposed to discuss yet—"

He's on the verge of a major reveal. I can tell by the way he fidgets with his jeweled cuff links, the gold ring on his finger. But before he can start, a waiter appears with two tiny dishes he announces as tonight's amuse-bouche. By the time he's moved on, Braxton has settled back into his seat, and the moment has passed.

"What I meant is"—Braxton reaches for his fork—"all of us have failed here at some point. But no one is ever *sent home* for failing. That's not what matters at Gray Wolf."

"Then what does matter?" My breath stalls. The pieces of the puzzle are coming together, but I've got a terrible feeling about the image they're forming.

All around the edges of our table, brilliant dots of three-dimensional white light suddenly appear, forming into an

opaque wintry shield that blocks us from the rest of the room.
I look between the snow wall and Braxton, wondering if the
sudden onset of chills that prickle my skin is caused by the
suggestion of snow, or my suspicions that Braxton is somehow
responsible for putting it there—that he's intentionally shielding
us from everyone here.

When I meet his gaze, he regards me with a face so conflicted,
I know right away that whatever he's going to tell me, the real
answer resides in the part he holds silent.

"Did something happen?" He leans toward me, his fingers
now resting on my side of the table, the black silk lapels of his
jacket against the midnight blue fabric reminding me of the
night sky back home—streaked with smog and full of airplanes
that stand in for stars. "At your lunch with Arthur?"

I'm on the verge of telling him what Arthur said—about
how he's counting on me to fulfill his greatest ambition. But
just as I'm ready to put a voice to it, I realize how completely
ridiculous it would sound to actually say those words out loud.

I mean, no matter what Song said, Arthur probably gives
a version of that same pep talk to every fresh recruit in a bid
to help us feel special, chosen, so highly exceptional we were
hand-picked by the maestro himself. When really, it's just an
attempt to soothe some first day, fish out of water, new kid at
the academy jitters.

I steal another glance at Braxton, wondering if he was
foolish enough to fall for Arthur's bullshit speech, too.

"What?" Braxton says, catching me looking at him.

In an instant, my cheeks fill with heat, and I nervously reach
for the butter knife, angle it before me, and check my reflection,
only to regret the silly display of vanity and put it right back. I
need to get a grip on myself, get my imagination in check. And,
failing that, I need to just calm the hell down.

But knowing a thing and actually doing a thing are two

different skill sets. And before I can stop myself, I'm saying, "There's something very strange going on in this place." My gaze cuts between the blizzard and Braxton. Desperate to know the truth but terrified of having my suspicions confirmed.

"Tasha, what's this really about?" He leans so close, he's practically halfway across the table. And just like that, I've lost the upper hand. In his eyes, I'm reduced to a scared little girl in need of his comfort.

And I just can't tolerate that.

"It's nothing." I force a bit of cheer into my voice. "Lunch was fine. And after, I had a nice chat with Einstein. Turns out, he really is a genius. All in all, a good day."

Just after I say it, I realize that, despite all the troubling moments, it's true. Or at least it was better than most days back home.

Which makes me wonder if maybe I shouldn't be in such a big hurry to make an escape.

Maybe I should at least try to give Gray Wolf a chance.

I look up to see Braxton's lips part, about to reply, when Elodie slips through our curtain of snow.

37

Elodie stands beside our table wearing a strapless black dress that drips from her body like candle wax. And though I hate to admit it, she looks more stunning than I've ever seen her, and that's really saying something.

"Natasha," she says, her voice false and bright. "It's so good to see you again. And this whole look you put together—totally *adorbs*." She cocks her head, allowing a cascade of loose blond curls to tumble to her waist.

The smile I flash in return is as empty as her false show of flattery. In Elodie speak, *adorbs* is reserved solely for puppies and babies. For anything over age two, it's an insult.

"I saw the snow shield and thought I'd come over. So, tell me, what's the big secret?" She glances between us, lips pushed into a pout. Back home, Elodie always got what she wanted, but I've yet to see any evidence her charms work as well here.

"What do you want, El?" Braxton's tone is more reasonable than the words might imply, but there's enough of an edge to prompt her to snake her fingers onto his shoulder and give it a squeeze.

"Oh, you know. Just checking in on my friends." She squeezes again, and from the way her knuckles blanch, it's much harder this time.

Elodie's on edge. Which is something I never imagined I'd see.

And to make it even weirder, I'm pretty sure she's on edge because of me.

Well, because of Braxton and me.

Not that there *is* a Braxton and me.

And not that I would ever want there to be—because *no*.

But still, it's really starting to look like Elodie's worried there might be.

Which means if what Song said about Elodie needing to be Arthur's favorite is true, then seeing me sitting here with Braxton must feel like a double slam to the heart—tangible proof that I've invaded yet another one of her territories. And even though that couldn't be further from the truth, after everything she's put me through, I'm in no rush to explain anything to her.

"We still meeting up later?" she asks.

I watch Braxton shift in a way that effectively hides half his face, making it impossible to discern if the flicker of displeasure in his gaze was a trick of the light or the reveal of a much deeper truth.

"Oh—sorry, Natasha!" She flutters her lashes at me. "I don't mean to exclude you; it's just Brax and I usually hang out with the Blues after dinner and sadly, Greens aren't allowed. You do understand, though, right? I mean, it's not like you'll be on your own forever. I'm sure it's just a matter of time before you're one of us, too."

More than anything, I want to snap back with the sort of biting reply that'll make her slink away in shame, or something along those lines.

But my brain hasn't caught up with my tongue. So when my mouth pops open to really let her have it…absolutely nothing comes out.

"Awkward" doesn't even begin to describe it.

"Humiliated" is a much better word.

And, of course, Elodie clocks it.

She leans toward me, and just when I'm sure she's about to call me out and say something cutting, her face softens. "Mine is the pink door, at the very end of the hall," she says. "You know, in case you decide you want to talk." Her lips press together, a few silent beats pass, before she adds, "Look, I know you don't believe me, but I really am sorry about how all this went down."

I study her expression. On the surface, she seems so sincere it makes me wonder if I should at least try to give her the benefit of the doubt and believe her.

I mean, maybe she wasn't fluttering her lashes—maybe her voice wasn't really dripping with saccharine. Maybe that's just how Elodie looks—how she talks—and I've become so paranoid, I can't see anything clearly anymore.

But just as I'm about to talk myself into giving her a chance, I'm reminded of what Song said about how with both Elodie and Gray Wolf, it's difficult to tell the difference between what's real and what's fake.

I definitely shouldn't trust her. I'm a fool for even considering it.

And yet, there's an undeniable part of me that wants to believe she really is sorry and that we really were friends.

But that's probably because it's a lot easier for me to believe her than to face the reality that I was just another target, and a ridiculously easy one at that. Just another pathetic girl so desperate to break free from the prison of her life, she was willing to pay any price.

It's funny how when I look at Elodie now, I can so clearly see all the things Mason warned me about. But that sort of hindsight is basically the definition of too little, too late.

"I really do hope we can get past this," she says, cutting into my thoughts. "We're a family here at Gray Wolf. And, with any luck, you're going to be here with us for a very long time."

Without another word, I watch Elodie leave as quickly and

gracefully as she arrived.

"You okay?" Braxton asks, once she's gone. His troubled gaze fixed on mine.

"What did she mean?" I ask, staring at the spot where she stood. "Why am *I* in need of luck? I'm getting mixed messages here. I thought I was pretty much stuck in this place whether I like it or not?"

I turn to Braxton just in time to catch the fleeting shadow of discomfort that crosses his face. And I'm just about to press him to explain when the waiter appears by my side and goes about the business of swapping out one course and replacing it with another.

By the time he's gone, Braxton's moved on. Lifting his fork, he just smiles and says, "*Bon appétit.*"

38

"Well, it's official—you survived your first dinner at Gray Wolf," Braxton says as the remains of the dessert course are whisked away. "What should we do for an encore?"

A quick glance around the room confirms the snow has stopped, the fawn has crossed the pond to be reunited with his mother, and the crowd of diners is spilling out the door and into the hall. "Aren't we required to hang out in Autumn?" I ask. "I'm pretty sure I saw that on the schedule you gave me."

"I'm not sure I'd call it a requirement," he says. "Besides, you're with me, and I happen to have a smidgen of clout around here."

"A smidgen. How impressive." I grin.

He's loosened up. I don't know if it's the glass of red wine he drank with dinner or the fact that I've loosened up, too, having decided sometime between the amuse-bouche and the main course that it's better to make an ally than an enemy.

He rises from his seat and comes to stand beside me.

"I think I could get used to this sort of chivalry. Opening doors, pulling out chairs—makes me feel like I'm in a Jane Austen movie." I smooth a hand down the front of my dress as Braxton starts to drape my stole over my shoulders. "It's too warm," I tell him, prepared to just carry it, when he drapes it over his shoulders instead.

"What do you think?" he asks, tilting his head.

My eyes graze over him, moving from his mop of dark hair, to that ridiculous face, to his perfectly cut suit, to the faux fur stole with the jeweled clip arranged to hang down the front, and though I hate to admit it, my heart actually skips a few beats.

"I think you look quite dashing," I tell him. "In a modern, regal sort of way."

"Exactly the look I was after." He guides me out the door and down a long hallway. It's the opposite direction of where everyone else is heading.

"Where are we going?" I ask, the lug soles of my boots softly thudding against the stone floor.

"I figure you'll have plenty of chances to hang out in the Autumn Room with your friends, so—"

"Only I don't have any friends," I say. "Not here, anyway."

He sighs. "When you're the only Green, it can feel kind of lonely, I know."

That's when it occurs to me that Braxton isn't just being nice, or chivalrous, or making up for a boatload of guilt, but that he's actually—

"I don't need a babysitter!" I stop dead in my tracks, hoping it's too dim for him to see the flush of embarrassment staining my cheeks.

He shoots me a quizzical look, swipes a hand through his hair. "Well, that's a relief," he says. "Considering how I'm barely a year older than you, that would be weird."

I stand before him, feeling like I really am in a Jane Austen movie, only I'm cast as the socially awkward cousin who's suffered a fit of hysteria that'll haunt her forever. And, since I didn't have any wine at dinner, I have nothing to blame but my own paranoia.

"I'm going to give you a choice." He steps closer. "I can escort you back to your room and we can call it a night…"

We're standing just inches apart, and though I'm embarrassed to admit it, I've already ruled that one out.

"Or I can show you to a small gallery full of interesting works of art."

I take a moment to consider. Tempting, but I'll need to hear more.

"Or I can take you to a sculpture garden that's available only to those with a smidgen of clout." He tips his head to the side and raises his brow.

"And this garden, it's outside?" Suddenly, I realize I've gone an entire day surrounded by digitized nature but haven't taken so much as a single breath of fresh air.

Braxton grins, offers his arm, and sweeps me down a series of hallways until we reach a small door at the end. "There are four flights, and the staircase is pretty narrow so, after you," he says.

It's one of those winding staircases with no guardrail, so I'm forced to press a hand to the wall to keep from falling. By the time I reach the top and open the door, I can't tell if I'm breathless from the climb, or the startling sight that awaits me.

39

I step onto the terrace, lift my face to the sky, and inhale a wisp of chilled night air with a top note of fresh blossoms and sea brine.

Above me, the heavens glitter with stars, more than I've ever seen in my life.

Before me lies an enchanting walled garden so abundantly lush, it's like I've wandered right into a painting.

"Is this—" I approach a vine of jasmine woven around a wrought iron trellis, no longer able to tell what's real and what's a hologram.

Braxton reaches past me, pinches off a single white bloom, and lifts it to my nose. In an instant, I'm overcome by its heady aroma.

"Arthur has been able to replicate all of this, right down to the scent. But I guess I'm a purist, because for me, nothing compares to the real thing. Which explains why the Moon Garden is one of my favorite spots in all of Gray Wolf."

He arcs his arm wide, so I turn in a slow circle and survey the space. Nearly every inch of it appears to be in bloom, but the only parts I can clearly make out are the ones that the moon shines on.

"It's truly spectacular under the glow of a full moon," he says. "Arthur wanted to add artificial light so it could be enjoyed every night of the year, but I managed to talk him out of it."

"You have that much sway over him?"

"Hardly," he says, the word carrying an edge.

I turn my focus to a marble sculpture in the distance, and I'm reminded of something I once read. "Leonardo da Vinci said: *A painter should begin every canvas with a wash of black, because all things in nature are dark, except where exposed by the light*."

"Leonardo is a genius," Braxton says as he moves toward the far wall and peers through a lookout. When I join him, a twist of wind strikes at my cheeks as the same turbulent waters that carried me here crash against a bed of jagged rocks far beneath our feet.

"Was." For some reason, I feel the need to correct him. "He's been dead for more than five centuries."

Braxton faces me then, his gaze as stormy as the waters below. "I've been here nearly eight years," he says, voice thick with urgency. "I come from a nowhere town an hour outside of London, but I was living in a dump near Boston when Arthur found me."

"That explains the accent," I say, tacking a nervous laugh onto the end that only increases the gnawing unease in my belly. I'm not sure why I felt the need to interrupt him, other than it's starting to seem like this confession of his might lead to a place I'm not quite ready to visit.

But Braxton will not be deterred. "Don't be fooled by my Queen's English," he says, cracking a mere hint of a grin that fades before it can really take hold. "I'm not nearly as posh as I sound. My home life was shit, I was getting in fights—the usual spiral. And then, through a series of events much like your own, I ended up here."

"Why are you telling me—" I start, but he lifts a finger, and the words die on my tongue.

"When I saw you laughing before your grave, I was intrigued.

I broke protocol then, just as I'm breaking it now. You want to know what really happened back at Arcana?"

I nod, unable to speak, my ears filling with the sound of my pulse pounding as violently as the sea.

"You were hypnotized."

In an instant, I'm laughing. But when I see the look on Braxton's face, I fall silent.

"Hypnosis is real. It's science. And while there are those who might debate that, it's certainly *not* magic. In your case, it was simply a matter of bypassing your conscious mind to get to your unconscious and put you into a trance state. And yet, there's nothing simple about it. It doesn't always work, but it worked rather quickly on you."

I remember the strange room, the song like a lullaby, the clocks with the hands spinning backward before dripping down the walls like a Salvador Dalí painting...

And then I lost all sense of...

Time.

"It was the clocks." My voice is a strangled whisper, my heart beginning to race. "This—" I gesture widely. "This whole place... it's about time...or stopping time...or manipulating time...or..."

I gaze at Braxton with what I'm sure are wide, frightened eyes. I'm so close. My toes curled over the edge of the precipice. I can see it on his face.

Yet I can't bring myself to say it.

Can't utter the actual words.

Because if it turns out to be true, if he confirms my worst suspicions, then what?

40

B raxton looms before me, but my breath is coming so quickly, he falls in and out of focus.

"Leonardo *is* a genius," he says, voice barely a whisper in this windless tomb of a garden. "All of time is equally existent."

I press my palm against the rough stone wall, my fingertips seeking the sharp bits, using the quick stab of pain to steady myself.

I am here.

This is happening.

And there's no escaping it.

Braxton takes a breath. "As Einstein himself stated: *The distinction between past, present, and future is only an illusion, even if a stubborn one.*"

"And Arthur has found a way to shatter that illusion?" My voice pitches high, like a glass breaking in a silent room. Though it's soon consumed by a clap of waves far below.

Braxton lifts my fur stole from his shoulders and gently places it around me. I guess I was so stunned by the revelation, I hadn't noticed how badly I was shivering.

His fingers work the jeweled clasp. His face presses near. Up close, those high, chiseled cheekbones, that slight bend in his nose, and that bottomless gaze are even more appealing than they were from a distance. The shivering has stopped, but with Braxton so close, I can't be sure it's solely because of the stole.

"And Arcana? Is that a real place, or—"

"The building is real. You walked right past it after you left the diner. But it's not a real club, if that's what you're asking. Other than the tarot reader and a few other things, it was mostly a hologram, a construct. Your destiny was put into motion long before you arrived. Arcana was the final test, to see how you reacted to your surroundings."

"So because I laughed at my grave, I ended up here?"

"Arthur loved it."

"He was watching?"

"You're a big investment. He wouldn't just take Elodie's word for it."

"Why are you telling me all this?" I ask, sensing the reveal won't be risk-free.

"Because I owe you that much." He lifts a hand to my hair, tucks a few windswept strands back behind my ear. His fingers leaving a trail of warm sparks in their wake that leaves my knees wobbly and sets my pulse racing.

"But why me?" I ask. "I mean, plenty of kids are overlooked by their parents and failing at life."

He flinches at the echo of his words. "I'm sorry for being so blunt," he starts.

"Blunt I can deal with," I say. "It's the secrets that bother me."

Braxton's gaze turns inward, like he's grappling with something known only to him. Coming to some sort of surrender, his eyes find mine and he says, "The selection process begins with a list of a few dozen prospects."

"And how does that work?"

He rakes a hand through his hair, shifts his weight between his feet. His discomfort is clear, but he seems to push beyond it. "Arthur has developed an algorithm that involves birth certificates, divorce records, zip codes, tax returns, school transcripts, social media accounts—"

"I don't even have any social media accounts," I cut in. "I

mean, I do, but I never actually post anything."

"Exactly." He nods. "Anyone with a sizable following is immediately eliminated from consideration."

"Because Arthur's interested only in those whose absence will go unnoticed—who no one will miss," I whisper, my insides twisting at the bitter taste of the truth in my mouth.

"Once it's been narrowed to less than a handful," Braxton continues, "Arthur embeds one of us in the school so we can get a better feel for whether or not the prospect will fit in at the academy. If it's not a match, we move on to the next on the list. If it *is* a match…"

He makes a vague gesture toward me—the living, breathing example of what happens next.

"I'm sorry for bringing you to Gray Wolf," he says. "I'm sorry for all of it. But while I could pretend I didn't have a choice, in the end, you and I both had a choice. And we made the same one."

I'm about to deny it, to list all the ways he's wrong, when he lifts a hand as if he begs to be heard. I bite back the words.

"Technically, we both could've walked away. But in the end, we chose a better life for a parent, and a different life for us."

I close my eyes and breathe in the night. There's no point in disputing a truth that's so plain to see. I obviously chose the route that landed me here.

When I open my eyes again, he's tucking the jasmine blossom behind my ear. "Leonardo is right," he says. "About darkness and light. All the blooms in this garden instinctively turn toward brightness. It's a lesson for all of us." His gaze, like his words, cuts right through me. "It's not all bad here, Tasha. In some ways—most ways, really—it's spectacular. So much better than you can even imagine."

"And the dark parts? The not-so-spectacular parts—like being trapped here, unable to leave?"

"You can leave," he says. "You just can't go home."

41

My gaze wanders the garden. Like a metaphor for Gray Wolf, it's so easy to be distracted by the glittery bits, you overlook all the shadowy secrets hidden within.

"Eventually," Braxton says, "you'll learn to adjust your vision—stop looking back through the filtered lens of nostalgia and appreciate where you currently are."

"Find a way to adapt." I return my gaze to his.

"You would've learned all this soon enough. But I figured you deserve to know what you're in for."

"But why didn't you just tell me the truth this morning when I asked? What changed?"

He inhales a deep breath. On the exhale he says, "Me. Hopefully I'm still capable of that."

I don't know if it's the trail of wind that whispers around us or just being near this devastatingly beautiful boy, but as the moment stretches, I realize Braxton isn't the enemy I first thought he was.

He's merely looking to me for forgiveness, so that he might begin the long work of forgiving himself.

"Just to be clear," I say, finally having mustered the courage to nail down the one truth I've sidestepped until now. "This is an academy for…" I swallow past the lump in my throat, force the words from my tongue. "Time travelers?"

There. It's out. And there is no going back.

"I know it sounds inconceivable," he says. "But that's exactly what we do here. Of course, not everyone takes part. Being young is only part of the equation."

"Why would age matter?"

"Adolescence is a relatively new social invention. And considering how life used to happen at an accelerated rate—married at fourteen, dead by forty—being young helps you blend in. But Tripping requires much more than that, and only a few have what it takes. That's what the aptitude tests are for."

"Tripping?"

"It's what we call it when we travel through time."

"I'm not sure I understand. I'm not sure I understand anything you just said."

"Not to worry," he says. "You will."

"Does that mean you're not going to explain?"

"Just know that everything here—the classes, the fancy clothes, the music, even the wine that's served with dinner—it's all designed to help you become accustomed to the way life used to be lived—long before the advent of drinking laws, cell phones, and Taylor Swift."

"But why? I mean, what would it matter what music I listen to, or whether or not I drink wine with dinner?"

"Because time traveling comes with great risk." Braxton barely speaks above a whisper. "Which is why it's imperative to fit in as seamlessly as you can. You need to know how to handle yourself when you dance, drink, mingle, and blend with whatever time and place you find yourself in. Just try to keep that in mind when you're asked to participate in some of the more archaic protocols around here."

"Such as…" I lean toward him, but Braxton's shaking his head.

"I think that's enough for tonight. I've already shared more than I should."

"Will there be repercussions?" I ask. "For bringing me here to this Moon Garden—maybe from Elodie?" I cringe as I say it, but when he meets my gaze, there's not a trace of the usual dread that comes with trying to explain a murky relationship status. "And what did she mean when she said that bit about with any luck I'll be here for a long time? I mean, didn't you just say I can't go home?"

Braxton's face takes on a pained expression. The corners of his eyes pinch, his jaw clenches, his teeth grind. "Don't listen to her," he says.

"And…" There's something left unsaid, and I'm determined to hear it, whatever it is.

"Just try not to get on her bad side." He shrugs, clearly hoping to be done with it. But when he reaches for that gold signet ring and gives it a quick twist, I know there's plenty more still left to uncover.

42

A sudden silence falls between us. I break it when I say, "And which side are you on?"

Braxton scrubs a hand across his jaw as a wash of something dull and shadowy sweeps over his gaze. By the time I recognize it as remorse, he's pressing closer, breathing the name only he calls me. A name that's really starting to grow on me.

"Tasha," he says, "Darling, I…" The tip of his fingers graze against my arm, leaving a trail of sparks prickling over my skin as he traces a path from the faux fur stole at my neck all the way down to the slim circle of gold at my wrist.

Beneath the glow of the moon and smattering of stars glimmering overhead, his face shines raw and earnest before me. His gaze searching, questioning. His lips conflicted yet parting anyway…

Driven by the quickening in my chest, the tingling sensation stirring deep in my belly, I find myself instinctively pressing toward him. The fingers of my left hand entwining with his. Those on my right, curling at the base of his neck, adrift in his soft tousle of hair.

There's a disapproving voice in my head that's bent on reminding me how I don't really know this boy—that I need to take a step back and pull myself together before I do something I'll only regret.

The voice isn't wrong, but I ignore it. Because the urge to

kiss Braxton's beautiful mouth, the need to feel the brush of his lips against mine, is so primal and strong, it won't be denied.

"You feel it, too." Gazing at me through a thick sweep of lashes, he flexes his fingers and flattens his palm until we're lifeline to lifeline. "This energy between us. It's so familiar. I can see it in your eyes—it's not just me."

Stripped of all the masks he normally wears—academy tour guide, bringer of coffee, elegant dining companion—the vulnerable version of Braxton stands bared before me, revealing a boy who's so sure of the invisible lure drawing us together, he's willing to name it, claim it, as a tangible force that cannot be ignored.

This energy between us.

I swallow past the lump in my throat, knowing I can't lie about the attraction I've felt since the moment I saw him.

Can't deny how, for a fleeting moment, I wondered if I might actually know him.

Can't pretend this flicker of sparks now blazing within is nothing more than a conditioned response to the sort of devastating good looks Braxton is lucky enough to possess.

For the last year, I've sworn off moments like this—making out with random guys I barely know in a quest to feel seen, needed, desired, and chosen—only to end up with a blur of fleeting false pleasures that left me reeling with shame.

But the sound of my name dripping from Braxton's tongue, with the hard *T* at the front and the velvety *A* at the end, leaves no doubt that the long list of reasons for why this kiss shouldn't happen won't make the slightest bit of difference.

Because this boy, on this night, in this glorious moonlit garden, feels specifically designed for guilty pleasures like this.

And when his fingers lace with mine, his gaze holds the question I think I'm finally ready to answer.

Attraction is a hard thing to articulate, and impossible to

fake. It's either there, or it's not. And this energy pulsating between us, well, it's about as real as it gets.

It's just a kiss. Just one silly kiss. So why wait? Let it happen already!

With less than a whisper between his lips and mine, I tip onto my toes and lean closer to him. "I feel it, too," I say, my mouth instinctively slanting toward his.

Out of nowhere, a terrible sound echoes and we spring apart like two teens whose parents just caught them necking in the basement.

Only there are no parents.

No basement.

And who the heck even uses words like "necking" anymore?

Braxton squints as though waking from a dream, then fumbles for his pocket when the noise sounds again.

Only this time, I realize it's not so horrible.

In fact, it's actually pretty. Though it is really loud.

He shakes his head, pulls a small tablet-like device from his jacket, and silences the sound. "Mozart, 'The Magic Flute,'" he says. "It's the ten-minute warning."

I pull my stole tighter around me. I have no idea what is happening. But when I reach for Braxton, he moves away so quickly, my hand flops awkwardly back to my side.

"I'll bring you to your room," he says, his voice oddly formal considering what nearly happened between us just a few seconds earlier. And I can't help but wonder if he's glad for the interruption. Like maybe he's already regretting bringing me here, never mind how close we just came to a full-blown make out.

"Arthur goes pretty easy on us on the weekends," he says, shaking me away from my thoughts and back to the completely mortifying present. "But on school nights, he likes to keep to a schedule."

Oh sure, blame it on Arthur. I frown at Braxton's back as he heads for the door. I mean, fine, maybe it makes sense on the surface. But it also seems like a really convenient way to escape a potentially sticky situation.

One that's pretty much entirely of his making.

One that he's clearly having second thoughts about.

The trip back is quicker than expected, mostly because Braxton is practically running as I huff alongside him. By the time we reach the hall that leads to my room, I'm so out of breath, and so confused by his silence, I tell him I can take it from there.

"Thanks," I say, standing awkwardly before him. "For—"

I wasn't going to say anything that might get him into trouble, but I guess he doesn't realize that, because he's quick to cut in. "I think it's best if we keep what happened between us."

I'm not sure exactly which part he's referring to—the part where he told me I'm trapped in a posh boarding school for time travelers or the almost kiss...or both.

What I do know is just before I turn away, I catch a glimpse of Elodie darting out of view.

43

Last night, I dreamed of Arcana.

Blurred images of a torch singer wearing a crown of golden antlers, boys in slinky black gowns, and time dripping like tears down ornately paneled walls unfurled like a ribbon before me.

It's the same dream I've been having since the day I lived it. Only this time, I was aware of Braxton gently lifting my limp body into his arms before carrying me out of the room to where Elodie waited.

"Told you," she said.

Before Braxton had a chance to respond, I woke to the world around me still dark and the sound of someone urgently pounding on my door.

Only, once I was awake, I realized it was actually the sound of footsteps running down the hall.

I threw the covers aside and leaped from my bed. With my ear pressed to the door, I listened to the beat of an insistent fist thumping on wood, followed by a rush of urgent whispers.

When I tipped onto my toes to gaze through the peephole, I saw the noise was coming from Oliver's room across the hall. Finn stood inside the entry, hair disheveled, a silk robe draped loosely around him, as Oliver, looking equally tousled, soon came to join him. Tossing an arm around his shoulder, Oliver pressed a kiss to Finn's cheek and pulled him in close to his chest, while Song, her face red, probably from crying, hurried inside, leaving me staring into a dim, empty hallway.

I backed away from the door, my skin tingling with chills, stomach tangled in knots, then immediately scolded myself.

I'm in a boarding school. Which means there's probably no shortage of drama, rivalries, cliques, and intrigue. Kind of like whatever was going on, or possibly was even still going on, between Braxton and Elodie.

Just because I'm not part of their inner circle doesn't make it sinister.

And yet, as I climbed back into my canopy bed and settled onto a pile of pillows, I made myself two promises:

One: Like I did at my old school, I'll keep to myself and steer clear of anything having to do with social politics or romantic entanglements.

Two: As far as Braxton's concerned, the almost-kiss in the Moon Garden is as far as we'll go. Which, considering how quickly he turned off the heat, that clearly won't be an issue.

But then I remembered all the stuff that happened just before Mozart intruded. The scorch in Braxton's gaze, the whisper of his voice when he said *This energy between us...* And I seriously began to doubt my ability to stick to my list.

The rest of the night, I slept fitfully. So when the first fingers of dawn reach around the edge of my drapes, I spring out of bed, rush to the window, and press a palm against the thick leaded pane.

I'm not sure what I expect to see. Maybe the maze returned, and the sight of a cloaked figure vanishing and reappearing.

What I get is a bird's-eye view of fat droplets of rain rolling down the collection of statues in the Tarot Garden. And for one fleeting moment, I have the wildest thought:

What if those statues are real, and the ones in Italy are fake?

44

After dressing for the day in a fresh Gray Wolf Academy sweatshirt I pull from a stack I found in a drawer (all of them disappointingly green), a pair of faded jeans, and running shoes, I open my door to find a boy standing outside, fingers curled into a fist that's headed straight for my face.

"Whoa—sorry!" He stops himself mid-punch. "I was just about to knock. Your door, not your nose. Still, how's that for timing?" He lowers his arm to his side and grins in a way that lights up his whole face. "Not my best move, considering we've met only briefly. But I wanted to introduce myself personally. I'm Jago."

My eyes graze over him. He's tall and lean, with a head of thick brown curls and eyes the color of topaz. I shoot a curious look at the package clasped in his hand.

"Found this sitting outside your door." He hands me the bag. "I'm guessing it's your slab."

"Slab?"

He laughs. "Officially known as the Gray Wolf Academy Tablet. More commonly referred to as the slab. But don't let Arthur hear you call it that. Or basically anyone else who's not wearing a sweatshirt."

"What is it?" I pull it free from its box and toss the packaging on the small table nearby.

"Think of it as your lifeline. It holds the day's schedule,

everyone's name and room number. The inspirational quote of the day. A GPS system to help you find your way around. It's all in there. There's also a text function that allows us to message one another."

I give it a dubious look. It's barely bigger than a tarot card. "Can't I just download an app on my phone and use that instead?"

"Your phone doesn't work here." His lips fall as flat as his gaze.

"Well, if I could get my hands on a charger, then—"

"Trust me, your phone's as good as dead. The slab is your newest addiction. It holds everything you need—or rather, everything they think you need. Though be warned, your days of going live on the social feed of your choice are long over."

"Looks like I missed my chance." I shrug. "I never did anything worthy of an audience."

"Same." He laughs.

I meet Jago's gaze. If his eyes are anything to go by, he's so much warmer than he was the night I arrived. And so far, he's the friendliest out of everyone I've met. That includes Braxton who, last night in the Moon Garden aside, veers much closer to the moon than the sun.

"You going down for breakfast?" Jago asks. When I nod, he says, "If you're up for company, we can head that way now."

I close the door behind me and walk alongside him. We're halfway down the hall when I say, "Why is your sweatshirt yellow?"

He shoots me a sly sideways grin. "Because I'm on my way to blue, baby!" He pumps his fist in the air, which strikes me as funny, though a little out of place in such a refined atmosphere. Then, eyeing my own green sweatshirt, he says, "Don't worry, you'll get there. Probably sooner than you think."

I give a half-hearted shrug. "I hope you're right," I groan. "I mean, I know it's been only a day, but I'm already sick of being left out."

Only, just after I say it, I realize it's not entirely true. I've probably spent more time with Braxton than I have on my own. Still, after I nearly lost my mind in the Moon Garden last night, getting so swept away by his smart English accent and his ridiculous pretty face, that situation is starting to feel like a bit of a landmine.

"Listen—" Jago starts. After running a quick glance up and down the hall, he tips his lips toward my ear. "A word of advice that no one gave me?"

I lean closer, desperate for anything he can tell me about how to find my way here.

"There's nothing normal about this academy. You're going to see some really weird stuff here at Gray Wolf, but if you're smart, you'll choose your battles wisely, because there's no use fighting a match that's completely rigged against you."

I swallow hard, nod for him to continue.

"That said, don't ever lose sight of your value. And never allow yourself to forget that they need us more than we need them. Because the more they invest in you, the more reluctant they are to lose you."

"*Lose* me?" My stomach clenches, my mouth goes dry. I have no idea what that means, but Jago pulls away so quickly, it's clear he's not about to explain.

45

J ago stands before me, his handsome face showing absolutely no trace of the ominous tone from just a moment before.

"Now," he says, switching to a more formal stance and offering his arm. "Shall we?"

I glance between his crooked elbow and him. It's such an outdated gesture, I'm not sure what to make of it.

"Um…what are you doing?" I ask.

"One of those rules I mentioned," he says. "Things like comportment, carriage, and manners—they matter here."

I bite down on my lip and continue to stare. *Is this one of those archaic protocols Braxton warned me about? Because there's no way in hell I'm agreeing to take part in such an outdated, misogynistic social ritual.*

To Jago, I just shake my head and continue down the hall. "No offense," I say. "But I really don't need a big, strong man to show me how it's done. I'm perfectly capable of walking on my own."

Jago laughs and follows along. "Look, I get it," he says. "On the surface, it's ridiculous. But there's a purpose to everything in this place. And it won't be much longer before it all starts to make sense."

He gestures toward some of the other students who've entered the hall—all of them walking arm in arm. Boy/girl, girl/girl, boy/boy—it's like I've wandered onto the set of a historical film where everyone is in character except me.

"This is absurd." I frown. "Not to mention outrageous, clownish, totally and completely ludicrous…"

Jago flashes me a patient grin, the kind a teacher might give to a student who just isn't getting it. "Remember when I told you about the rules that aren't worth the fight? This is one of them. But don't get the wrong idea—while linking arms is expected, other displays of romantic affection are strictly prohibited during school hours."

I blow out a frustrated breath and, with a great show of reluctance, hook my arm with his. Still, I can't help but say, "What could possibly be the point?"

I gaze up at Jago and, since he's got a good eight inches on me, I'm practically craning my neck just to meet his gaze. And for the first time, it really hits me—with his nicely sculpted face, eyelashes practically longer than Elodie's, and gorgeous golden brown skin, Jago isn't just handsome, he's actually breathtaking. And when he speaks, his voice is low and deep with just the trace of an accent that sounds vaguely Spanish.

"Think of Arthur as a curator of the past," Jago says as we continue down the staircase, our arms linked. "He picks what he wants and discards all the rest."

"He said something similar at lun—" Remembering that my lunch with Arthur is not something granted to everyone, I'm quick to cut myself off.

"I know about your lunch," Jago says. "Everyone does. But you're smart not to flaunt it. Gray Wolf is way more competitive than you might think."

"But what exactly are we competing for?" I ask. "Are we on some sort of grading scale I don't know about?"

"Look," he says, "it's not that long ago that I was new, too. So I'm going to tell you something else no one told me."

I walk silently alongside him, hoping the reveal isn't nearly as ominous as the last one.

"One, forget your past. You've been given a chance to start over, so try to make the best of it. Also, don't go asking other people how long they've been here or where they come from."

I can feel my cheeks flush. I've pretty much done that with everyone.

"None of it matters anymore. And we've all worked hard to move on."

"Okay," I say. "Anything else?"

We've reached the entry to the Spring Room, and he steers me aside to let others pass.

"And two…" He removes the slab from my grip and presses my thumb between his and the screen. "This is how you turn it on, wake it up, and turn it off. The rest is intuitive; you'll figure it out. Also, whatever you do, don't lose it. They'll find it, of course, but it makes a bad impression."

"Does it come with a charger?" I ask, thinking that I didn't see one in the box.

"No need," Jago says. "As long as you remain on the island, it stays charged." He removes his hand from mine, but his topaz gaze continues to linger. He dips his head, about to say something more, when he suddenly stops, and I turn to find Braxton standing behind me.

"Sorry to interrupt," Braxton says, his gaze darting sharply between Jago and me.

"Just trying to help a Green find her way." Jago grins, flashes his palms. Then, directing a sly wink at me, he ducks inside the Spring Room.

I'm about to follow when Braxton says, "There's been a change of plans."

I glance longingly toward the place where breakfast, and the possibility of making new friends, awaits, and heave a loud sigh, not even trying to hide my annoyance. "What's this about?" I ask.

Offering his arm, Braxton says, "Ever been to Paris?"

46

When I refuse the offer of his arm, Braxton reaches for my hand, but I'm quick to pull away from that, too.

"Is something wrong?" The space between his brows pinches with concern. As though he has no recollection of how we ended last night.

But, since I'm not about to humiliate myself by reminding him how he totally blew me off after we nearly kissed, I just say, "It's—"

He looks at me.

"I'm perfectly capable of walking on my own, that's all."

With a brisk nod, he sets off.

"Also, I'm hungry," I call after him as I race to catch up. "Am I supposed to skip breakfast?"

"There'll be coffee and pastries where we're going."

"You mean in Paris? Because I'm not sure I can hold out that long."

He stops abruptly, his rubber soles skidding against the stone floor. "You want to be a Blue?" His gaze locks on mine.

I nod. I mean, I'm not exactly sure what that entails, but it's gotta be a lot less lonely than being a Green.

"Then now's your chance to jump the line."

"Seriously?" I stare imploring at Braxton's back. He's on the move again, and it's all I can do to keep up.

After making a series of rights, he pauses before a single

black door. "All you have to do is prove yourself," he says. "Show Arthur he was right about you."

"But right about what, exactly?" I ask. "Because I have no idea why he chose me, or what he actually sees in me…"

When I notice the way Braxton's blue eyes burn on mine, like they did in the Moon Garden last night, my voice falters, my breath backs up in my chest, and I force myself to look just about anywhere else.

I have no idea how to respond to this guy. Have no way of knowing what his intentions are when one minute he's hot, and the next he's ice-cold. All I know for sure is that I need to be a lot more careful where he's concerned. I need to protect myself, safeguard my heart. Because if there's one thing my past has taught me, I'm the only one who will.

Braxton starts to move toward me, but when he catches the wary look on my face, he's quick to fall back into place. And I breath an inner sigh of relief. The last thing I need is to give him any reason to think that near miss of a kiss actually meant anything.

Or worse, that it might happen again.

"Don't worry about it," Braxton says, pulling me away from my thoughts. And at first, I think he's referring to us, but then I realize I was the only one thinking about us. Braxton is still talking about Arthur. "All you have to do is be yourself and try your best."

Braxton turns away and presses his right thumb to the keypad. A buzzer sounds, the door swings open, and I follow him into one of the rooms I saw yesterday—the one with a circular stage in the center and theater-style chairs arranged all around it.

Since the other students are at breakfast, it's just me, Braxton, Hawke, Arthur, and another person Braxton introduces as Keane.

My first impression of Keane is how far my gaze needs to

travel before it meets his. He must be at least a foot taller than me, possibly more. And if his biceps are anything to go by, this is a guy who does not miss a workout. He has gleaming dark skin, medium-length hair styled in multiple twists, and beautiful dark eyes that taper ever so slightly at the sides. When his lips pull into a grin and he presses his palms together in greeting, I awkwardly do a version of the same.

Before I can lapse into my usual routine of asking him where he came from or how long he's been at Gray Wolf, I'm directed to a table loaded with coffee and pastries, as the rest of the group speaks privately. After I've inhaled a muffin and finished a latte, Braxton motions me over, but it's Hawke who explains what I'm in for.

"I'm assuming you took notes on yesterday's lecture?"

I self-consciously flick a crumb from the corner of my mouth and confirm that I did.

"Uh-huh, good. What we're going to do now is a simulation of sorts."

I stare at him blankly, and though I have no idea what that means, my stomach clenches as my palms start to grow clammy.

"You're going to make that trip down the fourth dimensional road, only virtually."

"A virtual wormhole?" My voice cracks, betraying my nervousness.

"We're jumping right in here," Hawke says. "Skipping the usual progression of modules. Think of this as a crash course, encompassing a series of lessons that usually span several weeks."

His tone is encouraging, but a quick glance at the others reveals Keane looks doubtful, Braxton hopeful, while Arthur is completely unreadable.

"Ignore them," Hawke whispers. "You'll do fine. You wouldn't even be here if Arthur didn't see something special in you."

I study Hawke, wondering if they're all in on the ruse, if

Arthur specifically tasked him with telling me that. "Yeah, well, joke's on him," I say. "Turns out, there's nothing all that special about me."

Hawke regards me for a long, steady beat. "You better hope that's not true," he says, his voice edged with an unmistakable warning.

47

Keane leads me behind a screen and into a room that houses a collection of what must amount to hundreds of gowns—all of them hanging from the sort of racks you'd expect to find in a dry cleaner from the future.

"Ace this test and you'll be wearing one of those in no time."

I glance between him and rows of fancy dresses that look more like costumes. "Is that a nod to *The Matrix* or *Alice in Wonderland*?" I gesture toward his T-shirt. It's black and fitted with a picture of a white rabbit with a pocket watch hanging from its neck.

Kean looks down with a grin. "Just a reminder," he says, shoulders casually lifting, his voice traced with the hint of a laugh.

"A reminder of…" I shoot him an expectant look, hoping he won't think I'm being too nosy.

"To not take myself too seriously," he says. "And to always remember, the best moments happen to those who are willing to take the trip down the rabbit hole."

I take a moment to consider his words.

"Just try to stay open to the journey," he says, "and you'll see some amazing things. I promise you that. But for now, Charlotte is going to help you get fitted."

Charlotte greets me with the sort of expectant wide grin that reaches all the way to her eyes and sends a flush of pink sprawling across a complexion so white, it practically blends into her thick mane of oatmeal-colored strands. She has a laid-back demeanor that instantly puts me at ease, and if I had to pick one word to describe her, I'd choose "cozy." She's just one of those people who radiates a caring, nurturing, maternal vibe.

And for one fleeting moment, the sight of her makes me miss my own mom so much it sends a shuddering breath up my throat. Until I realize that what I *actually* miss is the long ago version of my mom—the one who tucked me into bed, wiped away tears, and on nights when the sky was clear, would sit with me out back so we could marvel at the everchanging faces of the moon.

The mom I used to have, before my dad left.

I shake away the thought and focus on Charlotte. She's dressed in a crisp white blouse worn under a plain gray smock that visibly strains against the abundant mound of her chest, and as she dips into a curtsy the soles of her sensible white sneakers squeak so loudly, she bursts into an infectious fit of giggles that gets me laughing as well.

"I shall help you," she says, her accent so thick and notably French, I find myself wondering how she found her way to the island. But remembering Jago's warning against asking those sorts of questions, I settle for dressing in silence.

She helps me into a stretchy black one-piece, then escorts me onto the stage where I stand awkwardly before the four of them, having no idea what I'm supposed to do.

"Pull her hair back," Hawke says. "Nothing fancy. A simple ponytail will do."

As Charlotte loops a rubber band around my hair, Keane asks, "How're you feeling?"

"Good," I say. "I mean, I'm not really sure what—"

"Turn around," Keane instructs, so I do, only to find a table with a series of objects arranged across the top.

A deck of cards.

An elaborate gold frame.

A bejeweled leather sheath.

And…a riding crop?

I glance between my audience and the objects displayed before me, unsure how I'm supposed to proceed.

"We'll go in order," Hawke tells me. "Starting from the left."

I reach for the deck of cards and hold them facedown on my palm.

"Choose one," Hawke says.

I cast a dubious look at the cards. Last time I did this, it didn't turn out so well. The thought of doing it again sets my insides into a twist.

"Sooner the better," he says, making a rolling motion with his hand.

A hazy memory of my dad slips into my head, but before it can fully take root, I shake it away. From the moment I stepped inside Arcana, it was like a circuit got tripped in my brain. And now, after years of blocking his memory, nearly every strange thing I encounter reminds me of him.

Focusing on the cards, I shuffle the deck, cut three times, then pluck the one from the top. "Well, at least it's not the Wheel of Fortune," I say, unsure whether to be relieved or worried. Realizing they're waiting for the reveal, I wave it before them.

"The Magician." Hawke nods in approval. "Now look at the card and tell us what you see. Whatever pops into your head."

This deck is newer, more modern than the deck my dad showed me, and some of the symbols are changed. I'm about to tell them as much, but for some reason those words just won't come. Though thankfully, other words do.

"He's Major Arcana. The first card on the journey, right after the Fool, which is numbered zero. He's highly creative, an inventor…" My voice fades, my belly's gone queasy, and for some unknown reason, I'm starting to sweat.

"*And…*" Hawke prompts.

"And, uh…" My hand is shaking, so I take a steadying breath and start again. "There's an infinity symbol over his head, and, well, you know what that means. Also, his right hand points skyward. Oh, and it holds a wand. The left hand points toward the ground. The pose is meant as an *as above so below* sort of thing. He's got all his tools assembled and he's ready to combine spirit and matter and…and transcend this known realm." A lump builds in my throat and I force the words past. "Also, he's ruled by Mercury, which is also an alchemical symbol."

"Anything else?"

I rub my lips together and stare at the card so hard, my vision actually blurs. As a one card, the Magician is related to the Wheel of Fortune card, which is a ten, and since the cards are connected to numerology, in which $1 + 0$ reverts to 1, they're connected.

Although I choose not to share any of that.

"Natasha—is that all?" Arthur barks, pulling me away from my thoughts.

I lift my gaze to his, suck in a quick breath, and say, "The card is you."

48

Before me, Arthur's gaze darkens, but his lips tip up at the sides.

Hawke takes a few notes on his tablet, then says, "Uh-huh. Good. Now move on to the next."

I stare at the gold frame, wondering what this is about. I know he said I'm jumping way ahead in the program, but I don't remember seeing any mention of tarot card analysis on my class schedule. Though I did see swordcraft and equestrian, and those objects are included in the lineup.

"When you're ready," Keane prompts.

I reach for the frame, and the second my finger taps the edge, the stage disappears, and I find myself standing smack in the middle of a museum.

It takes me a second to realize it's the Louvre.

Is this what Braxton meant when he hinted at a trip to Paris? Because while I know I haven't left Gray Wolf, it's like my senses have been hijacked and transported me to a new time and place.

I'm surrounded by glorious paintings as a large crowd of tourists wanders about. When a small child breaks free of his mother and runs into me, I'm shocked to find myself fumbling backward to keep from falling, even though there is no child. No museum.

Not a single bit of this is real.

And yet, the effect is so visceral, I smell the floral perfume worn by the woman standing beside me—catch the scent of a recently smoked cigar clinging to a man's corduroy jacket. I can hear the shuffle of feet, the murmur of voices.

And suddenly it dawns on me: *this is how they created Arcana*.

From somewhere outside the illusion, Hawke says, "Now move toward the crowd."

A sign on the wall tells me I'm in Denon Alley. And though the name rings familiar, I'm not sure why until I catch sight of the *Mona Lisa* hanging on the far wall.

"Tell me everything that comes to mind," Hawke says. "No holding back."

"It's one of the most famous paintings in this museum," I say, the words spilling out in a rush. "One of the most famous pieces in the world. Though it wasn't until after it was stolen by a Louvre employee back in 1911 that the world finally took notice."

"And how do you know all this?" Keane asks.

I move through the virtual crowd to get a better look. "I don't know," I say, which is true. I don't know how I know most of the things I've shared so far. "I guess I learned about it in art class, maybe?"

"You don't sound like you're sure," he says.

"I feel sure that it's true."

"Anything else?"

"Some people find it disappointing," I say. "Because it gets so much hype, seeing how small it is in person feels like a letdown."

"But what do *you* see, Natasha? What does your first glance reveal?"

I peer closer, startled to find the virtual crowd has vanished, which allows me a clear view of the painting. "I, uh…" My tongue falls flat, the words fade from my mind, as I gape at the bizarre sight suddenly unfolding before my eyes.

"Natasha?"

It's Keane again. Or at least I think it is. But all I can do is stare as the last five centuries swiftly peel away, until I'm left gaping at a vision of the portrait stripped down to its original sketch, as a disembodied hand pops in from out of nowhere and adds the first brush stroke.

I shake my head. Inhale a quick breath. I need this mirage to fade, for the museum to snap back into place. If it weren't for the steady lights and solid floor, I'd swear I was caught in yet another Unraveling. But this…this is something else.

And I can't help but wonder if anyone else is watching this unfold.

"You okay?" Keane calls. The words are kind, but his tone hints at impatience.

"Yeah, um…" I clear my throat, press a hand to my belly to steady myself. "Just feeling a little… Anyway, I'm not sure what I can add when so many art historians…"

"We're not interested in academic critiques," Hawke says. "We want to know what *you* see."

With a tentative step, I move closer, watching as that disembodied hand continues to add layer after layer of paint. *Is this part of the hologram, or—*

"Natasha?"

"Um, the river—" With a shaky finger, I gesture toward the recently painted strip of blue positioned just behind her. "It symbolizes the passing of time."

"Is that academic theory or—"

"No," I say, the words coming quickly. "I mean, it is, but it also happens to be true. And…"

"Go on," Hawke prompts.

"Well, I feel like it's somehow connected to the saying: *You cannot enter the same river twice.*" The words replay in my head— the voice that speaks them belongs to my dad.

My dad? I squeeze my eyes shut. *What the hell is happening to me?*

"And who said that?" Hawke asks. "The quote, I mean. Where's it from?"

One long ago, long forgotten day, my dad whispered it to me, but it's only now lit a spark in my brain.

I open my eyes, try to shake the thought away. To Hawke, I say, "I'm not sure." A second later, time is restored, the painting's complete, and the crowd of tourists is back to jostling around me.

"That's okay," Hawke says. "Now, push through the crowd, all the way to the front. Is there anything else?"

I do as he says. With a bit of exaggerated stealth, I slink through the masses until the masterpiece is directly in front of me. "She's keeping a secret," I say. "Something to do with that river. Something to do with the true nature of time."

"*She's* keeping the secret?"

"No, the artist is. This isn't so much a portrait as a signpost — a message only for those who can read it."

"And you think you can read it?"

I lean forward, straining to see. "Not anymore." I shrug. "I — "

"That's okay," Keane says. "You did well. Now, I want you to reach out, and I want you to take it."

49

The second I grasp Keane's instruction, my entire body goes numb.

"You heard me," he says. "Take the painting, Natasha."

I swallow hard, remind myself that none of this is real, and yet I can't keep my hand from shaking as I force myself to reach out and grasp the edge of the frame. Just like the butterfly in the Spring Room, it feels real.

"Remember, it's fragile and irreplaceable," Keane says.

"But—it's just a hologram, right?" It's a question I have no choice but to ask. The room is so authentic, there's some major mind-fuckery at work here, and I'm honestly no longer sure.

"Remove it from the wall," Keane says. "Gently."

I can feel the crowd growing uneasy. People are staring, pointing, whispering to each other. Some are even backing away.

I close my eyes and push my breath in and out of my lungs. *It's a hologram. A construct.* The only negative outcome would be displeasing Arthur—and that's scary enough.

Focusing only on the task before me, I place both hands on the frame and, with a small thrust, I manage to lift the painting right off the wall as a wide grin spreads across my face.

I did it! I—

Next thing I know, a terrible alarm shrieks through the room as a swarm of uniformed guards come barreling toward me.

"What do you do, Natasha?" someone says. Keane? Arthur?

Hawke? Braxton? I can't tell. And I don't care.

Frantic, I look all around, my pulse throbbing so loudly, it rattles my ears. There's nowhere to go. Nowhere to run.

"What do you do, Natasha?"

Somewhere nearby, a child, is shrieking. A man points at me, yelling at the guards to hurry.

"What do you do, Natasha?"

My gaze darts wildly, searching for an opening, but there isn't one.

The alarm is getting louder. My body's dripping with sweat.

"Natasha, what do you do? Surrender?"

Yes! Exactly. I mean, what choice do I have?

I open my mouth, ready to wave my verbal white flag, when an emphatic *"NO!"* thunders out of me instead.

In an instant, a flashing green arrow appears before me, and I race toward it, only to watch in horror as a heavy iron gate begins to fall. Soon it will cut off my only chance for escape.

I'll never make it. I'll be trapped with an angry mob and even angrier guards.

The screech of grinding metal blares in my head as I pump my legs faster, determined to beat the gate and follow that green arrow all the way to the end, all the way to—

On my next step, my feet drop off the stage, and I find myself free-falling into an empty black space.

A pair of arms locks tightly around me.

A voice whispers in my ear, "Darling, well done."

A moment later, Braxton gently lowers me to the ground.

First thing I do when my feet touch the floor is look at my hands. But, of course, they're empty.

It was a construct. None of it was real. I was never in danger.

Though my hammering heart and trembling limbs need a little more time to adjust to the news.

"You did well," Keane says, flashing a grin that puts his

dimples on full display.

Hawke nods in agreement, but Arthur's face gives nothing away.

Then Keane holds up a tablet displaying a series of jagged lines that reminds me of a polygraph test. "You'll need to work on keeping your pulse stable, but considering how it's your first go…"

"You were *monitoring* me?" I ask, though I probably should've guessed when Charlotte fitted me into this catsuit.

He nods. "Anyway," he adds, "what do you say we take ten before we move on to the next one?"

"Next one?" I look to Braxton, a mix of excitement and apprehension building inside.

"Looks like you've earned a trip to Venice," he says.

50

For the trip to Venice, I'm fitted into an elaborate gown with a low square neckline, an extremely snug bodice, and an enormous skirt with so much volume, the fabric swishes all around when I move.

I run my hands over the soft silk damask and gaze at my reflection in the mirror, my eyes filling with the sight of my breasts rising like moons. Thanks to the corset, they're pushed so high, I'm worried they'll pop right out of the gown. Especially if I'm forced to run for my life like I was in the Paris construct. But Charlotte assures me there's no need for concern, then orders me to sit so I can try on the shoes.

The silk brocade pumps have small heels, no more than an inch, and a bright blue bow at the vamp that I'm tempted to remove.

"Is there another pair?" I squint toward the wall of shelves where she chose them from among hundreds. "I'm not exactly a fan of the bow."

I cringe a little when I say it, hoping it didn't come off as spoiled or high-maintenance. Because honestly, I'm not even sure why I'm making such a big thing about the shoes. I mean, I practically slept in my beat-up old Chucks. And besides, it's not like I'm actually going anywhere. This is more like an elaborate game of dress-up—or a rehearsal for a high-tech school play. And yet, no matter how hard I try to convince myself to chill, I continue to frown at that ribbon while my breath hectically saws in and out of my lungs. This may seem like make-believe, but I know I'm being tested every step of the way. And even though I aced the last one, that doesn't mean the same thing will happen this time around.

"They'll have to do for now," Charlotte says. "Later, if you make it, you'll be fitted for your own custom pair."

"*If* I make it?" I repeat, my heart now beating in triple-time as my voice rises to compete with the alarm bells going off in my head. But Charlotte ignores me and continues to hum softly.

Her hands move quickly as she gathers my hair off my neck, gives it a few twists, then pins it high on my head. She stands back, tells me to turn my head, first this way, then that. When she's satisfied, she instructs me to stand.

"Normally, I'd create something more elaborate. But for these purposes…" She shrugs, gives a little tug at the bodice of my dress, exposing another millimeter of my breasts, which feels like several millimeters too much already. "Sorry," she says. "But that's how it's meant to be worn. Chin up, now. You'll do fine." She runs her hands down the front of her own more modest attire.

This time, when I gaze at my reflection, I'm mostly happy with the result. Also, the dress is so long, it's not like you can even see the bows. Though I am stuck on the way she said *these purposes*. I mean, what exactly are *these purposes*, anyway? What is Arthur grooming me for—to snatch famous paintings off the walls of the Louvre? Because what works in a construct will fail in real life.

Or was that simply a test, meant to determine how far I'm willing to go, how much I'll risk?

And if so, did I pass?

"Everyone's in place." Charlotte bows her head and does that strange little curtsy. "Bonne chance," she whispers as I make my way out of the dressing room and onto the stage where Jago waits.

Dressed in a period costume of knee-length pants, tights, buckled shoes, a long velvet jacket that I think is referred to as a tailcoat, a cream-colored ruffled shirt, and a purple silk cravat looped around his neck, Jago bows before me.

"Mademoiselle," he says, his gaze roaming the length of my dress. "Might I say you look ravishing."

This time, when he offers an arm, I take it. I'm pretty sure this is part of the test, and I'm determined to surpass whatever expectation Arthur has set.

Jago leads me past a wooden staircase that leads to a wide platform, then over to the table that, in addition to a jeweled sheath and riding crop, holds two masks—one for me, one for him. He hands me a green mask that glitters with small jewels encrusted along the front, while he chooses a simpler design of shimmering black velvet. Once our masks are secured, I turn to find myself immersed in a magnificent ballroom.

"It's a masquerade ball!" I whisper, my gaze sweeping past a crowd of masked revelers dressed in elaborate costumes and gowns, while the faint strains of classical music play in the background.

"Not just any ball," Jago says. "You, my friend, are in the Palazzo Ducale, or Doge's Palace, whichever you prefer."

The Doge's Palace! I flip through the stack of postcard images in my brain, ultimately landing on the majestic gothic masterpiece located in St. Mark's Square.

"Inside these walls, one hundred and twenty Doges presided over the fate of Venice for nearly one thousand years," Jago says, leading me deeper into the elegant space.

"I've seen pictures of it only from the outside," I tell him, recalling the magnificent facade I once saw in a luxury travel magazine. "I'm not really familiar with the inside." I try to maintain my composure as I look around, but there's so much glittering opulence, it's like looking through a gold-tinted lens.

Jago laughs. "And you still aren't. It's merely a hologram. A good one, but it's definitely been altered to fit the requirements of this lesson."

He steers me past a collection of sculptures and paintings by the greatest Renaissance artists, beyond a beautiful golden staircase, and over to the dance floor. "You'll attend a lot of these," he says. "As a new Tripper, wearing a mask makes it easier to blend. You'll know you've really made it when you get to show your true face."

I'm about to pretend I have no idea what he's talking about when Jago tips his head toward me and, in a low voice, says, "I think we both know you've been told what really goes on here at Gray Wolf."

51

I look at Jago as though I can't believe he'd even suggest such a thing. "No one's told me anything," I lie, turning toward the virtual party in progress. "I was hoping *you'd* fill me in."

Jago lightly jabs his elbow into my waist. "Nice try," he says. Then, motioning toward the room, he adds, "Seeing as how this is part of your Languages and Cultural Norms exam, I'm thinking we should probably dance." At his suggestion, the music swells, and I guess he probably senses my hesitation, because he tips his lips to my ear and whispers, "Just follow my lead."

We join the others on the dance floor, and though I do my best to mimic their moves, I'm so notably awkward, tripping over my own two feet, I hear Keane say, "Braxton, mark her down for lessons in dance and comportment. Jago, move her on to the next part of the construct."

My shoulders sink. Whatever small bit of confidence I'd managed to gather blows right out of me.

Of course, I'm not cut out for this time. I'm barely cut out for my own time.

But Jago grabs hold of my hand and gives it a reassuring squeeze. "Ignore them," he says. "You're doing fine."

With my hand grasped in his, he leads me up that golden staircase, where I watch several couples push into empty rooms and dark corners. The sounds of muffled laughter and soft moans soon follow.

"What is this, some kind of hologram orgy?" I laugh nervously.

"Shhh," Jago whispers. "Stay in character. They can hear you."

By *they*, he's referring to our audience. And of course, he's right. It was an amateur move, and I vow to do better.

This is a construct. I repeat the words in my head like a mantra. *I'm on stage. None of this is real—it's all just—*

Next thing I know, Jago sweeps an arm around me, pushes me up against the nearest wall, and buries his face in my neck.

His skin is warm, and he smells really good. But even though he's undeniably beautiful and charming, and even though I'm well aware this is all strictly for show, I'm still kind of surprised to find that this staged version of making out with Jago isn't nearly as thrilling as almost making out with Braxton. Because with Jago, there's literally no attraction. But with Braxton...

"Don't move." Jago's lips brush against the lobe of my ear. "Now, lift your head slowly, and look past my shoulder. Only don't stare. Keep your lids half drawn, like you're so overwhelmed with passion, you can barely focus."

To the best of my ability, I do as he says, but I'm willing to bet I'm not fooling anyone.

"The woman with the black hair, wearing the gown covered in roses. Do you see her?"

I nod, slide my hand to his neck as part of the pretense.

"She's one of the Doge's courtesans."

"One of?"

"There are many, but that's not your concern. See that pin in her hair—the one shaped like a rose and made of rubies?"

"Yes." I breathe, but just barely. I know what's coming next. And even though I also know it's not real, my racing heart can't tell the difference anymore between make-believe and the truth.

"You're going to take it," Jago tells me, his hand pressing at my waist.

"But...*how?*" My voice rings so loudly, he covers my mouth with his. But it's not a kiss. Not even close. It's more a move to shut me up and save me from my sorry self.

He pulls back ever so slightly, though his hand still clutching my waist feels like a warning. With a gaze equally filled with doubt and encouragement, he releases his hold, pushes me away, and says, "I'm afraid this one is on you."

52

As I follow the woman in the rose-covered gown, I remember the long-ago weekend I spent at Mason's, the time his grandma was away. Since it was raining outside, we mostly hung out in his room watching *Breakfast at Tiffany's* on repeat, gorging ourselves on tubs of pistachio ice cream, bags of dark chocolates, and swigs from the bottle of cheap sparkling wine that gave us both headaches.

By the time the rain was spent, we were bored, moderately buzzed, and looking for fun. Deciding to recreate a scene from the movie, we walked over to one of those big discount stores — the kind with bright orange signs permanently parked in their windows, claiming Everything Must GO!

Inside, we made straight for the party aisle, where we slipped on a pair of masks — a masquerade one for me, and a Marilyn Monroe face for Mason. Then we dared each other to pocket something remarkably cheesy but truly spectacular, a symbol of our friendship we'd then give to each other.

We took off in separate directions, in search of that one perfect gift. My stomach queasy from too many sweets and an unsteady gait I blamed on the wine, I headed first for the floral and home section, thinking I'd pick up something fun for his room, until I realized that in order to go undetected, I'd have to think on a much smaller scale.

I found my way to cosmetics, but the makeup was so garish,

I went over to the jewelry department instead. After sorting through piles of bracelets, rings, and silver necklaces with colorful rhinestone pendants shaped like unicorns and parrots, I settled on a glittering tiara encrusted with crystals, then propped it onto my head and strode right out of the store with no one the wiser.

By the time I reached the designated corner, Mason was already there. I placed the tiara on him, he slid a pink princess crown ring onto my finger, and we laughed all the way back to his house. Neither of us felt the slightest bit guilty for what we had done.

And looking back now, I realize I feel only the slightest twinge of guilt. But even so, I'm quick to remind myself we were just a couple of bored kids looking for fun—the trinkets were cheap, and no one got hurt.

Though I do sometimes wonder what really made me go through with it.

Was it the wine? The sugar high?

Or am I just a natural-born criminal with a talent for theft?

And if so, is Arthur already aware of that?

Is that why he really decided to bring me here?

I follow the woman down a long hallway. When she stops to admire a painting, I figure it's showtime.

"*Saturn Devouring his Son*," I say, one hand motioning toward the canvas depicting the wild-eyed Roman god eating his own son, as the other hand sneaks into her hair, snatches the pin, and slips it into one of the many pockets hidden in the folds of my dress.

A standard *spotlight of attention* move I learned on a long-ago trip to a magic store. Simply by directing the focus toward the painting, I made sure my target didn't notice what my other hand was doing.

Remembering what Braxton said about the need to fit

in to whatever place and time I find myself, I say, "It's quite remarkable." My voice sounds so stilted, so unnatural, but I try again anyway. "And, I might add, quite gruesome, as well."

"It was never meant for public consumption." The woman speaks with an accent that's polished and clipped. "It's part of a collection referred to as the Black Paintings. The artist, Francisco de Goya, painted this on the plaster wall in his dining room. After his death, it was transferred to canvas. Imagine staring at this while you take all your meals." She shakes her head, forces an exaggerated shiver. "As for me, I much prefer the one just beside it." She gestures toward a portrait of two old men leaning over a globe, one praying, the other laughing. The sight of it sends a sudden rush of chills skittering over my flesh.

"Heraclitus," I breathe, unaware I've spoken out loud until the woman turns to face me.

"Along with Democritus," she says, and it's only then that I realize the masked woman is Elodie.

53

I stand before her, trying, but failing, not to gape. Between the black wig and posh accent, I had no idea I was talking to Elodie.

And, of course, unlike me, she's perfectly poised and at ease. And she definitely doesn't break out of character like I just did.

Then again, Elodie's a pro at games of deceit.

"Are you familiar with this work?" She nods toward the piece, the haughty tilt of her chin reminding me this is my game to fail.

My hand instantly flutters to the bodice of my dress, fingers nervously picking at a seam, as I force myself to stay calm, to return to the painting. Still, my voice cracks when I say, "A Dutch artist…I think?"

I THINK?

The second I hear myself say it, I'm dragged under by an emotional undertow of shame and defeat.

Why would I end with a question when I know for sure that I'm right?

Why did I leave it to her *to decide?*

And when will I ever learn that everything with Elodie is a power play, and that I seriously need to stop giving mine away?

Pushing past the roar of my own frantic heartbeat, I swallow hard, set my jaw, and vow to get this scene back on track whatever it takes.

"Yes," Elodie says, her lips twisting into a close-mouthed grin. "But what I meant was, are you familiar with the deeper meanings of the artist's intention?"

I smooth a hand down the voluminous skirts of my dress and glance between Elodie and the painting, sure that the plaque above the entry to Gray Wolf, Panta Rhei; the phrase I quoted about the river in the *Mona Lisa*, *you cannot enter the same river twice*; and this painting before me all lead back to that same ancient Greek philosopher.

But why—what could it possibly mean?

Elodie snaps her tongue against the roof of her mouth—her version of a ticking clock. I'm about to say something, anything, when Jago appears next to me and secures an arm at my waist.

"My dear," he says. "I've been searching everywhere for you." The look he gives me is unmistakably flirty, but I'm sure it's just the role he's playing. Still, there's no denying my relief when he tips his head toward Elodie and starts to whisk me away.

"You've secured the prize," he whispers to me. "But you've made a grave mistake by overstaying your visit."

Just when I think I'm free, Elodie shouts, "Hey—somebody stop her! She's a thief!"

In an instant, Jago releases me. "Good luck," he says, and quickly moves out of the way.

Frantically, I look all around, searching for a way out, as Elodie continues to scream a slew of accusations at me.

"You've got three choices," Keane hollers, but he fails to include what those might be.

At Elodie's urging, a crowd of men begins to gather, and as I watch them approach, my mind reels with all the ways I might find a way out of this mess.

I can flee.

I can surrender the jewel.

Or…

I race for the table where we got our masks and, without another thought, grab hold of the worn leather sheath.

"She's choosing to fight!" one of the instructors cries in disbelief.

54

With a shaky hand, I pull the sword free, only to discover it's so much longer, sharper, and heavier than I ever expected it to be.

Does that mean it's real?

Either way, I figure I'll just swing it around for a bit, enough to ward off the crowd, then maybe grab hold of the riding crop and...and then what? Gallop into a hologram sunset when I've never even been on a horse?

I can feel the weight of everyone watching me fail. And the worst part is, I've dug myself into a hole so deep, there's no foreseeable way to save myself.

Next thing I know, Elodie emerges from the crowd. When she stands before me, arms crossed at her chest, lips pushed into her infamous smirk, it's like the sword takes on a life of its own.

"*Jeee-sus!*" a voice cries. I think it might've been Keane, but there's no way to be sure. "Someone stop her before..."

I ignore the voice and make my advance. Elodie may have a mob at her back, but from what I can see, I'm the only one armed.

"I'd be careful with that if I were you." Her voice is tart, showing no signs of fear. "You have no idea how to use it."

"You sure about that?" With a quick flick of the wrist, I jab the tip to a tender patch of flesh just under her chin. "Looks pretty self-explanatory to me."

Her blue gaze narrows on mine. "You don't have the guts to go through with it," she says, but her jaw is clenched, as though she's actually a lot less sure of that.

I give another light jab, not enough to break the skin but certainly enough to make her second-guess everything she thinks she knows about me.

"None of this is real, you know. It's all just a construct." She speaks through gritted teeth.

I shoot a quick glance around the space before returning to her. "Yeah, no kidding."

She rolls her eyes, but I ignore it. For some reason, I'm more interested in the choker that circles her neck.

"What I mean is, *I'm* a construct," she says.

I stare at her in disbelief. *What sort of game is she playing?*

"Don't believe me?" she taunts. "Go ahead, give me the full Marie Antoinette and see what happens."

My gaze locks on hers.

"I mean, you hate me, right? For wrecking your life and bringing you here? So now's your chance to see if you can get rid of me for good."

Taking the bait, I twist the hilt ever so slightly, causing the tip to screw into her flesh as a tiny drop of blood drips from her chin.

Would a hologram blade cause a hologram person to bleed?

In Arthur's world, anything is possible.

"Is someone going to stop this?" a voice cries. Keane again? Hawke? I no longer care.

"And yet," Elodie says, "you have to admit this is way more fun than Mr. Osbourne's tedious AP History class."

I swallow. Fight to keep a steady hand.

Would a hologram know about Mr. Osbourne?

Probably.

Most likely.

But still…

"So, what's it going to be?" Elodie asks, as though she's just curious and not the least bit afraid of losing her head. And that's when I realize, this really is Elodie, and unfortunately, I've fallen right into her trap.

For someone as emotionally warped as her, the sheer joy she gets from watching me succumb to the darkest part of myself is well worth the risk of any injury I might choose to inflict.

In an instant, I lower the sword's edge to the hollow of her neck. The audible scrape of the tip sliding over her skin whispers between us as she inhales a sharp breath.

I slip the blade lower, knowing it's time to move on, to release us both from this ridiculous game, and yet, I can't shake the feeling that this is all a big ploy to distract me from the truth she doesn't want me to see.

Doesn't want me to see… The phrase repeats in my mind.

Vision.

It's what Arthur prizes above all else—the ability to see what hides in plain sight.

Genius hits a target no one else can see, he recently quoted to me.

Nothing in these constructs is an accident. According to Jago, it's been specifically altered to fit the requirements of this lesson. Which means everything is connected, but nothing is quite what it appears.

My gaze lingers on Elodie's neck, and for a fleeting moment, I see what no one else can. Though just to make sure, my mind flashes back to the painting of Heraclitus and Democritus, mentally scrolling for symbols. Both men are posed in a way that obscures their *necks*. And while Heraclitus's hands are folded in prayer, Democritus has one hand positioned on a golden piece that looks like a fleur-de-lis, while the other one *points directly toward it*. And, since the portrait clearly doesn't belong in a palace that's dedicated to celebrating Italian artists, I take it as a sign I can't afford to ignore.

My gaze locks on Elodie's, and with a single flick of the wrist, her black velvet choker drops onto my palm.

The sword crashes to the floor.

Elodie stumbles back, away from my grasp.

And as I turn to face the audience, I watch Arthur rise from his seat and hold out his hand.

From my pocket, I pull out the ruby rose I nicked from Elodie's hair and toss it to her.

Turning back to Arthur, I say, "I think this is the one you really wanted." Then I hand him the black velvet choker.

Arthur regards the small golden fleur-de-lis charm that hangs from the thin strip of cloth. "I asked for a ruby," he says.

"It's a locket," I tell him. "There's a hinge on the left."

He looks me over, his gaze brightening, but only briefly, before the latch unlocks to reveal the gleaming red ruby within.

I have a vague awareness of the audience gasping, but in this moment, I have eyes only for Arthur.

"You'll need to work on your social skills," he says. "Comportment, etiquette, diction—that sort of thing. And of course, you'll need riding instruction, along with lessons in swordcraft. Still, you impressed me. Which, I might add, is a rare occurrence."

A breathless moment passes between us, and I find myself caught between the undeniable thrill of winning his approval and the personal indignity of realizing the lengths I was willing to go to get it.

"For now," he continues. "Why don't you get changed, so Keane can take you out to the stables."

I'm on my way to the dressing room when Elodie calls out my name. "Hey—how'd you know about the ruby?" she asks.

When our eyes meet, I'm surprised to find that, for the

moment anyway, she's dropped the animosity and truly is curious.

"First one was too easy," I say.

I'm relieved when she simply nods and goes on her way, sparing me from sharing the real truth that, just when I started to question whether I was misreading the clues, I saw right through the golden charm to the gleaming jewel hidden within.

55

At six o'clock, I'm ready to head down for dinner, but before I go, I give myself a quick once-over in my dressing room mirror.

Today's triumph has left me feeling daring and bold, like I'm not one to be messed with. I matched my outfit to my mood with a black lace, off the shoulder, body skimming dress and a pair of hot pink sling-back heels with square crystal buckles on the straps.

At the last minute, I riffle through a pile of jewelry, looking for something similar to that pink princess crown ring Mason gave me, the one I wore until it literally fell off my finger. And even then, I took the two broken halves and tucked them away in a drawer, refusing to part with the memory.

I wonder where Mason is now—what he's doing, what he thinks of my absence.

Is he defending me from all the inevitable rumors?

Or is he fanning the flames, figuring it's what I deserve for leaving him to eat lunch alone?

Either way, I'm sure he's not happy with me for flaking on work, leaving him to deal with the mob of snooty spin-class moms lining up for their post-ride, gluten-free Buddha bowls until they can hire my replacement.

Between school, work, and Sundays spent poring through fashion magazines, touring art museums, or watching old movies, our lives used to be so intertwined, it's impossible to think I might never see him again—might never get a chance to explain that by choosing to hang out with Elodie, I didn't realize I was choosing a life without him.

My fingers reach for the counter, gripping hard at the edge as I chase away the thought. Braxton is right. This is my home now, and I need to stop clinging to a life that's no longer mine.

I gaze into the mirror, fluff my hair around my shoulders, and force a smile onto my face. If Mason could see me now…

He'd tell me to add a statement piece.

I lift a single earring from the pile of treasures. A jeweled dagger that, once inserted, looks like it's plunging straight through my earlobe. It's a bit edgy for this outfit, but I like it. It hints at the sort of rebellion I hope I can hang on to.

I pull my hair back, so the earring makes more of an impact, and I'm on my way out the door when Braxton messages me on my slab.

Braxton: See you at dinner. I have a few stops to make first, so please start without me.

Me:

Every reply I begin to type, I end up deleting. In the end, I don't send anything.

Truth is, I was hoping to spend time with the other students. I know I can't eat with the Blues, but what about Jago? Who do Yellows dine with? *Are* there other Yellows? According to Braxton, Gray Wolf is home to nearly one hundred people, but apparently none, besides him, are willing to eat at my table.

By the time I arrive, Jago's already there, wearing an over-the-top blue velvet suit that only someone as confident and good-looking as him could pull off. And from the looks of the champagne flowing freely among the Blues, they're celebrating.

Looks like someone jumped ahead on the color wheel.

When he spots me from his side of the room, he waves

happily, and I immediately feel like a jerk for begrudging his success.

I had a good day. Experienced my first real win in this place. And while that's worth feeling proud of, the fact is, if it wasn't for Jago's direction, I might not have done half as well as I did.

I force a grin to match his, return the wave, and head to the vacant table for two.

Tonight's wintry theme is all about ice. There are baby polar bear holograms scampering about, and the entire room is made to resemble pictures I once saw of the original ice hotel somewhere in Sweden. A faux fur blanket is draped across the back of my chair but, since the room isn't nearly as cold as it appears, I leave it lying there.

I'm finishing up my entrée of braised duck with a red wine reduction when Braxton arrives. "My apologies," he says, sliding onto his seat. "I wasn't sure if you'd be here."

"Where else would I be?" I lift my glass and use the moment to look him over. He's wearing a burgundy velvet dinner jacket with matching silk lapels, and he's paired it with an ivory ruffled silk shirt. Like Jago, it's the kind of thing that's hard to pull off, but he totally nails the look.

Then again, he'd probably look just as hot wrapped in a trash bag. Or nothing at all… A vision of what that might look like begins to bloom in my head, but I'm quick to shake it away before it can really take hold.

"You do know dinner isn't mandatory," he says. "You can order food up to your room. If you do it too often, you'll probably have to meet with a counselor, but every now and then is okay."

I set my glass on the table. Now there's something I didn't know. And if tomorrow night looks anything like this, I'm ordering in. Because eating alone in a room full of people who're so clearly enjoying themselves has left me feeling unbearably lonely.

"Did you get my message?" He butters a dinner roll, then gracefully pops a piece into his mouth.

For a moment, I consider pretending I didn't, but there's really no point. "Yes," I admit. "I did."

He looks away, trains his focus on his jeweled cuff links.

"And the only reason I didn't reply is…well, I thought it would be good for me to make other friends. You know, other than you. But there's no way to break through, and—" My voice falters, a wave of embarrassment rolls up my cheeks.

"Do you want to get out of here?" he asks. When his gaze meets mine, it's like a crack of warm sun reaching through a stretch of bruised sky.

Without even thinking, I'm up and out of my seat.

Next thing I know, my arm is in his as he leads me away.

56

"You did well today. Really," Braxton says as I walk alongside him.

After spending most of dinner conducting a mental review of the long list of things I need to improve (my equestrian skills at the top of the list), it's nice to hear. Still, I can't help venting some of my frustration when I say, "But there's so much to learn. So much to—"

Braxton steers me into an elevator I didn't even notice until the doors slide open before me.

"Where are we going?" I ask, watching the floor numbers race by at a pace way faster than it feels from inside.

"You'll see." He shoots me a cryptic, squinty-eyed gaze, and while I hate to admit it, that's all it takes to set my pulse racing.

When we arrive, we pass through a long and narrow hallway that leads to a single steel door at the end. Then I watch as he pushes his thumb to a keypad, and the door opens to a room so wondrous, it's like being suspended in moonlight.

"It's not a hologram," he says before I can ask. "It's all real."

The room is large, rectangular in shape, and made entirely of glass. And I mean *everything*—the floor, the ceiling, the walls, all of it—and through some miraculous feat of engineering, it soars straight out of the rock, with absolutely no sign of support. It literally hangs in midair, allowing for an uninterrupted view of the world beyond. And as I move across the crystal clear floor, it feels like I'm walking through space.

"How is this even possible?" I gaze past my shoes to the foam-tipped black waves of the turbulent sea crashing below, marveling at how only a whisper of glass keeps me from hurtling straight into a watery grave.

Cautiously, I make my way to the far wall, press my palms to the pane, and stare in wonder at a sky full of stars and a waxing moon that's slightly fuller than it was the night before.

No sign of the lighthouse, though. I must be looking at the dark side of the rock.

"This is amazing," I whisper. "I mean, I can't even fully wrap my head around how—"

Just then, a swell of classical music cuts into the space, filling the room.

And when I turn, I find Braxton standing before me, his jacket abandoned, his sleeves rolled up, and a shiny silver dagger gripped in his hand.

57

My heart freezes mid-beat as I stare at the weapon now in Braxton's possession.

A weapon he definitely wasn't holding just a moment before.

Though I tend to lean much more toward flight than fight, that doesn't stop my hands from instinctively curling into fists, or my fingernails from biting into my palms, as my mind frantically calculates the number of steps between the door and me.

"Um...what are you doing?" I ask, my voice ratcheting up a handful of octaves, as Braxton takes a step forward, his gaze burning on mine.

Is this a sexy gaze or something else?

What's the opposite of sexy? Threatening, menacing—

Before I can reach a conclusion, Braxton swings the dagger toward me and says, "Let the first lesson begin."

When he hands me the weapon, I let out an audible breath.

"For a first timer, you did okay with the sword," he says, shoulders casually lifting, as though he was left only marginally impressed by my earlier triumph over Elodie.

"Just okay?" I balk in a playful, exaggerated way, sure he's trying to bait me. But Braxton's expression remains sober and unsmiling, way too serious for a room and a night as beautiful as this.

"Do you want to learn, or do you want to be flattered?" He cocks his head to the side in study.

"Are the two mutually exclusive?" I counter, still determined to lighten the mood, but Braxton is so earnest, the joke crashes on impact.

"Make no mistake," he says, his voice carrying an edge as sharp as my blade. "Had Elodie been armed, things would've ended differently today."

Okay, now I'm really annoyed, and I don't even try to hide it. It's been a long time since I let myself try hard enough to excel at anything, and I'm not about to let Braxton dim the glow of my victory.

"It's only hubris if I fail," I snap. It's a quote from Julius Caesar, but I'm betting he won't know that. "Besides, not only did I succeed, but I'd even go so far as to say, I *exceeded* Arthur's expectations."

Braxton appraises me for a long, cool beat. "You're right," he finally says. "And while you should celebrate your wins, you also need to understand that when it comes to a sword fight, anger will get you only so far, and it's certainly no match for skill. Which is why you need to learn how to properly handle your weapon, in addition to keeping your ego in check."

The words land like a punch. And when his gaze locks on mine, I'm so riled up, I'm about to really let loose, when I realize that's exactly the sort of problematic, knee-jerk reaction he's referring to.

"Elodie triggers you," Braxton says in a voice that's steady, even, with no trace of judgment. He's merely stated a fact, and I can't even deny it. I've been nurturing my grudge against Elodie like most people watch over a baby, a puppy, or even a brand-new piercing—obsessively tending to it in a way that'll ensure its survival. "Arthur is all too aware of the dynamic between you. It's exactly why he chose her over Song, Finn, or anyone else he could've pitted you against."

"Are you saying I actually…*failed* the test?" I'm not sure if

I'm more horrified or embarrassed by the thought. What I do know is that the heat of shame instantly finds its way to my face.

"You didn't fail," Braxton says, quick to dismiss any doubt. "Arthur got what he wanted, and, in the end, that's what matters. But when you're on a Trip, you need to leave your grievances behind and concentrate on the task at hand. And, for the record," he says, "hubris didn't work out so well for your Roman emperor, did it? Wasn't it a brutal stabbing by a friend that ended Caesar's reign?"

Touché. I breathe a deep sigh and study the dagger, if for no other reason than it feels safer than looking at Braxton.

"In the construct, my blade was much bigger." I tighten my grip on the hilt, raise my weapon in front of me, and shred the air to invisible ribbons.

"True, but in the places and times you'll travel to, women don't carry large weapons. Which means you'll need to train with a smaller blade—the sort you can easily conceal under a gown."

I lower my weapon, needing a moment to process his words. "It's still hard to believe that it's real." I try to envision the sort of logistics involved, but the best I can come up with are random scenes from various time travel movies that rely on phone booths and sports cars to get the job done. And though I still have no idea how Arthur has managed it, I'm sure he's invented a far more elegant mode of transportation. "I mean, you talk about Tripping like it's normal, but I'm having a really hard time wrapping my head around the concept."

"I'm not sure you ever fully get used to it," Braxton says. "And yet, five years at Gray Wolf have taught me that the only real limits are those of imagination."

"And Arthur's imagination, along with his bank account, are limitless?"

"So it appears." Braxton grins in a way that doesn't quite reach his eyes. Then again, grinning doesn't come easily to someone like him.

"And when does Arthur plan on making the big reveal? I mean, just how long am I supposed to pretend I don't know what the constructs are for?"

"For most people, they're either a few months in before they flat-out ask, or a formal meeting is arranged where someone informs them what they've really been brought here to do."

"Okay, so that's most people. What about me?"

Braxton shrugs. "Arthur's got you on an accelerated schedule, so you can probably expect a meeting any day now. Thing is," he adds, "you won't be traveling anywhere until you master some skills."

I watch as he grabs a sword from a glass container by the door. I guess I was so entranced by the view, I failed to notice anything else.

I glance between the sword and him. "This hardly seems like a fair fight," I say, nodding toward the length of his blade, which is so much longer than mine.

"It's not meant to be," he says. "Mainly because it's a lesson." His gaze squares on mine in a way that sends a shiver racing straight down my spine.

"So, you're actually serious about teaching me? Here? In this all-glass room?" Another quick look around leaves me wondering if this might actually be a terrible idea.

I mean, just how thick are those panes, anyway?

Braxton positions himself before me, his stormy blue gaze locking onto mine as the sharpened edge of his weapon glints under the moonlit sky.

"Let's go," he says.

And before I have a chance to react, Braxton's blade is swinging straight for my neck.

58

In a moment of terror, I take a giant, clumsy leap back. The sound of my dagger as it slips from my fingers and clatters hard against the glass floor is in direct competition with the frantic thud of my wildly beating heart.

I stand before Braxton, unarmed and on the verge of hyperventilating.

To his credit, he doesn't take advantage and he doesn't laugh. He merely lowers his sword to his side, nods toward my weapon, and lets me regroup and get a grip on myself.

"I'm not going to hurt you," he says. "I probably should've opened with that, but I guess I assumed it went without saying."

"Unlike you, I can't afford to assume anything in this place." I force the words past a tongue that's gone dry, as my breath slowly steadies and my stomach gradually finds its way out of my throat and back to where it belongs.

"You'd be wise not to," Braxton says. "So, allow me to state now and for the record, that I would never, ever harm you in any way, whatsoever. Does that cover it—are we good?"

When his warm gaze lands on mine, I'm left even more shaken than I was when I thought for sure he was aiming to take off my head. I mean, how am I supposed to concentrate on anything when he looks at me like that—so heated, so intimate, so—

"But when you're out there Tripping," Braxton says, clearly

unaware of the effect he's having on me, which definitely comes as a relief, "and a weapon is drawn, you can be sure your opponent won't grant you the courtesy of going easy on you."

I nod. Swallow. Go to great lengths to avoid meeting his gaze.

"If you're ready, we'll start by shadowing. Just follow my lead."

I watch as he raises his blade, then I raise mine as well.

When he lowers his, I do the same.

"Good," he says. "Now, when I step back, you move toward me, and vice versa."

Though I try to mimic his postures with the same grace and ease, he moves with such natural elegance, I feel awkward and clumsy in comparison.

"Am I about to get an F in mime class?" I groan.

"Think of it like a dance," Braxton says, and that's when I realize he's moving in time with the music.

"Oh, I get it," I say. Aiming my blade toward his shoulder, I remember how Arthur told him to mark me down for lessons in dance, comportment, and just about everything else. "This is a dance/swordcraft two-for-one." I laugh, but again, Braxton is fully devoted to staying in serious mode.

"Focus," he whispers. "Stay in the moment, quiet your mind, and ignore all distractions. Then combine that focus with your intuition to see if you can anticipate my next move."

He lowers his blade and jabs it toward my ribs. And, since I didn't see it coming, I arc my body away, falter slightly on my heels, but then quickly recover and counter with the same.

Braxton repeats the move, giving me a chance to do better. Only this time, the top edge of my blade veers a little too close, and after skimming over his torso, it catches on a button and shreds a hole in his shirt.

"Omigod," I gasp. "I didn't mean—"

The button pings and bounces across the glass floor, but my eyes are locked on the place where the fabric is torn and Braxton's smooth, taut abs are exposed.

A ripple of heat courses through me, and I guess my gaze must linger just a little too long, because Braxton clears his throat, and says, "Let it go."

I can't tell if he's referring to the loss of the button, or the way he caught me open-mouthed gaping at his rock-hard torso. Either way, I force myself to look away.

"Stay with me," he coaches. "Be right here, right now. Just you and me. There's nobody else." His voice is so low and deep, the words hook right into me.

Just you and me… Nobody else repeats in my head like a song.

Braxton walks a slow circle around me, reducing my world to nothing more than the two of us in this all-glass room.

"Where are you," he says, voice barely audible over the music.

"Here," I reply, my breath hitching in my chest when my eyes latch onto his. A classical melody plays in the background, but all I can hear is the burning silence that sizzles between us.

I want to look away, but I can't.

My eyes plead with his to look away, but he won't.

And with the winter's night sky glimmering overhead and the turbulent sea crashing far below, we return to this strange and delicate ritual of advance and retreat until I've come to know the strength of his lunge as well as he's learned the force of my parry.

When the song changes, Braxton expertly steers me to the far side of the room. His moves grow so increasingly complex, it requires all my focus just to keep up. Which reminds me of the guided meditation app Mason once made me listen to, swearing it would help still my mind and "center myself." When all it really did was allow for a front-row seat to the parade of anxious thoughts that incessantly storm through my brain.

Apparently, that slim thread of memory is all it takes to drive me off course, because the next thing I know, my dagger clangs to the ground, I'm pinned against the glass wall, and the cold, sharp tip of Braxton's blade is pressing to the hollow of my throat.

59

"Rule number one," Braxton says. "Never lose track of your blade."

"And number two?" I ask, breath quickening as my gaze runs up the length of his forearm, landing on the faint outline of a circle tattoo near the crook that leaves me wanting to see more, to *know* more.

What kind of symbol could a boy like him deem so important he permanently inked it onto his body?

"If you're going to pull a weapon, not only do you have to be willing to use it, but you have to be willing to live with the consequences," he says, breaking me out of my reverie as my gaze returns to his.

"And are you willing to live with these consequences?" I ask, my voice thin and tight.

"Absolutely not." He lifts the tip from my skin. "Though, like I said before, I'm an anomaly. When you're out there Tripping, you're more likely to encounter someone who's far more mercenary. And what will you do then, when you were this easily disarmed?" He watches me with a thoughtful expression, as though he truly is curious to hear how I plan to con my way out of that kind of mess.

"Beg for my life?" I flutter my lashes and force what's meant to be a flirty smile. But it's been a while since I was that girl, and I'm so out of practice, it's an immediate fail.

Braxton cocks his head and studies me with great interest. "Do you really expect that to work—out there, in the real world where the stakes are literally life and death?"

I swallow, all too aware that he's yet to abandon his blade. "Not likely," I say. "But I'm hoping *you* might take mercy on a poor, inexperienced Green. After all, it's only my second day here. Also, might I remind you—you did give me your word."

Braxton's face softens. But his hold on his sword remains. "Your mind wandered," he says.

Feebly, I nod. There's no point denying it.

"I clocked it the second it happened. I literally watched your eyes glaze and turn inward. You can't afford that kind of mistake."

"I know, I—"

"You were time traveling," he says.

My gaze jerks back to his. I have no idea what he's talking about.

"The reason it's so hard to stay present is because the mind prefers to dwell either in thoughts of the future or memories of the past. Where were you?"

"Back home," I admit.

Braxton lowers the blade, returns it to its sheath. And though I never for a second believed that he'd use it, my shoulders go slack with relief.

"I know I'm supposed to leave the past behind, but it's one of those things that's easier in theory than practice. Also—" I pause, trying to decide whether to finish the thought, then plunging ahead, I hear myself say, "It's just—everything about this place feels like a game." I'm not even sure what I mean by the statement, but somehow, I can't shake the feeling of being a pawn on a chessboard of Arthur's design.

Also, I'm not entirely clear on Braxton's intentions. If this were merely about the lesson, then why did he insist on doing it here, in this magical space, instead of an ordinary room?

"I assure you this is no game," Braxton says, but I'm no longer sure if he's talking about life here at Gray Wolf, or the two of us suspended together, floating in space.

He stands before me, so close I can clearly make out the place where the streak of his nose hits a bit of a bend. It's the only discernable flaw on his otherwise perfect face, and I feel such an overwhelming surge of fondness for it, I lift a tentative hand and follow the slant with the tip of my finger.

When he closes his eyes and sighs in response, I try to envision this dashing, elegant boy ditching class, brawling in school hallways, and worse. It's impossible to imagine.

But when his lids flutter open, and his gaze latches onto mine, I catch a shadow of something dark and unknowable that hints at those troubled times.

And it's that mystery I lean into, determined to uncover what could've possibly happened to him.

Who was he fighting?

What was he rebelling against?

And why is he always so serious…so…guilt ridden?

What exactly has he done on Arthur's behalf?

Over the last two days, this boy has become my closest companion, and while he seems to know practically everything about me, I know virtually nothing about him.

"Don't ever mistake this for a game," he says, breaking into my thoughts, and again leaving it unclear just exactly what he means.

I'm about to ask him to explain, about to ask him so many things, when he tips his index finger to the underside of my chin and the questions instantly fade.

There's a hunger that burns deep in his eyes, and I know without question it's the same hunger he's seeing in mine.

A sudden mad flutter stirs in my chest, as a low-key quiver

trembles deep in my belly. And I know in this moment that despite the promise I made to myself to steer clear of moments like this, kissing Braxton was never *not* going to happen.

Still, I need to at least *try* to protest. Let him know that I'm fully aware of just how irrational this is. I mean, he may claim to know all about me, but the fact is, we just met. Clearly this attraction we feel is purely physical, and not based on anything substantial or real.

"Tasha," Braxton says, his voice a gruff, throaty whisper. "You okay?"

A jumble of thoughts swirls through my brain, but the only one I can manage to voice is, "Um, here's the thing…"

I swallow hard. Braxton squints.

"Just to be clear—I don't even know if I actually like you." With knees gone wobbly, I pitch onto my toes.

Braxton just nods. "Totally understandable."

"I mean, I'm much more inclined to hate you." My lips part ever so slightly as I check for his reaction, but Braxton doesn't look the least bit offended.

"It's not like I blame you," he says, the lilt of his accent fading on a sigh.

"And yet…" The tip of my tongue slides across the roof of my mouth as Braxton stands silently before me, breath held in his cheeks, eyes blazing with heat. "While I'm pretty sure this is a terrible, regrettable, lamentable idea…one of the worst I've probably ever had…"

His head moves toward mine as the tip of his finger trails up and over my chin, where it lingers at the base of my bottom lip. "Go on," he says.

"I, uh…" I swallow hard and force myself to continue. "Well, I can't help but think that maybe we should just…get it over with, you know? I mean, obviously, we're both curious, so why not finish what we started and kiss each other already so we can put it behind us."

My heart crashes hard in my chest, and I'm pretty sure my toes have gone numb.

"Is that what you want?" Braxton's finger begins a slow slide across the length of my lip. "To *get it over with*?"

I watch as his own lips curve into a grin, and it's such a rare sight, part of me wishes there was more time to admire it.

But the other part, the more insistent part, is already thinking of a much better use for that mouth.

"Yes," I say, wondering if he can hear the frantic rush of my pulse, see the way my skin flushes and glows. "But only so we can get it out of our systems and move on as just friends. A sort of…one and done, so that—"

Thankfully, Braxton doesn't let me finish. Because all I know is that the feel of his mouth crashing onto mine makes for the most glorious kiss I've ever known in my life.

60

It's a perfect fit, this kiss.

It's a movie kiss.

A *halfway through a romance novel* and *I've been waiting for this moment* kiss.

The kind of kiss that obliterates the pitiable memory of every kiss that ever came before.

As Braxton's lips move over mine, tasting, savoring, lingering, stealing my breath, my ability to think, I'm left dizzy, light on my feet, and hungry for more.

So much more.

But just as my fingers are sliding into his tousle of hair, Braxton is already pulling away.

"You okay?" he asks, his voice soft and breathless, his forehead pressed against mine. "Are you ready to put that behind us and just be friends?" His voice is light and teasing, but his gaze sears right through me, leaving no doubt that while he wants this to continue as much as I do, he'll agree to walk away if I insist on following through with our deal.

But thankfully, I'm well past that nonsense. Under a sky lit with stars and a wink of moon hanging high overhead, I tip onto my toes, thread my arms around Braxton's neck, and find his lips again.

This time, the kiss is softer, more tender. Unlike the mad rush of before, when we thought we had to cram it all in after agreeing to never do it again, we move slower, taking our time to get to know this side of each other.

Braxton pulls me closer. So close I'm burrowed deep inside his arms, my body straining against his, as his lips brush against mine. Playing, tasting, teasing, he kisses me so fully and deeply and well, I can feel the echo of every sweep of his tongue reverberating all the way down to my toes.

My tongue rolls with his, as his hands make a slow, torturous journey along the hollow of my waist to the undercurve of my breasts. There's a question in his fingers as they trace along the bend of my ribs, and I can hear the words as clearly as though he spoke them out loud: *is this going too far?*

Oh, it's definitely going too far.

Not to mention this is all moving way too fast.

But try telling that to my body when it's screaming for more, more, more.

More of the sweet heat of his kiss—the delicious shiver of his touch on my skin. This boy has sparked a craving in me—a deep-rooted longing for the sort of unspeakable, blushing things I've only read about in books or seen in movies. The sort of glorious, body-shattering thrills taken by other boys before him but never once offered to me.

"Tasha," he groans, and I open my eyes to find his beautiful face swimming before me. His eyes shadowed with secrets, lips shaped by desire. That bit of bend in his nose the only tangible truth he willingly offers.

It would be so easy to consent to this, to skip all the levels and claim this boy for my own.

But not yet.

Not so fast.

Braxton is an enigma, a walking storehouse of riddles, and I will take my time to explore all his mysteries.

For now, there's so much more kissing to do.

I close my fingers over his and, with a small jolt of regret, lead them back to my waist. But when he crashes his mouth onto mine once again, I'm instantly lost in the wonder of his embrace.

"Tasha…" he breathes, his lips pressing a woozy line of kisses down my throat, grazing the line of my collarbone, as I bury my face in his neck, inhaling the sweet spice of his scent. An expensive, rare, custom blend of vanilla, cocoa, and ginger made solely for him—or so I imagine.

"Tasha, I—"

My eyes slide open, and his gaze latches tight. He's on the verge of telling me something—something that's making his brow crease, his confidence waver—when music suddenly blasts from out of nowhere and slams us back to reality, just like it did the night before, except this piece is different.

With a weary sigh, Braxton releases me and reaches into his pocket to silence his slab. "Mozart," he says. "'Requiem.'"

"Let me guess." I tug on the hem of my dress and straighten the neckline. "It's ten to ten." When I raise my gaze to meet his, I find him looking at me, brow creased with concern.

"You okay?" he asks. "Because I need you to know, I didn't mean for any of that to happen."

"Oh really?" I make a wide gesture around a room that looks as though it was made for exactly the sort of things we just did.

A sudden flush fills Braxton's cheeks. "Hey, I'm not saying I'm sorry it happened." His mouth quirks at the side as he rubs a nervous hand across his jaw. "But I get that it's moved really fast. Or at least it has for you."

"Just me?" I ask, confused.

"I've had the advantage of knowing you longer." He shrugs. "It's my job to familiarize myself with our recruits, so I kinda had no choice but to get to know you. As soon as I read your file, I was intrigued to know more."

He stands before me, his top teeth sinking into his bottom

lip. He's made himself vulnerable, put it right out there, letting me know he liked me well before he even approached me at Arcana.

Which means he also liked me when I was giving him shit in the diner.

And later when I was giving him shit in my room.

And then even later when I was giving him even more shit during the tour of the school, and again when he sat across from me at dinner, and…

He's liked me this *entire* time. He let me dump all over him, which, granted, he totally deserved, but I…

While it's nice to know he fell for the paper version of me long before he actually met the real-life version of me, I'm starting to think my initial instincts were right—the two of us kissing was not my best plan. Because if my limited experience has taught me anything, it's that boyfriends burn out pretty fast, while a good friend is in it for the duration.

And more than anything, I could really use a good friend around here.

When I lift my face to his, determined to find a way to relay all of that, Mozart pipes up again. Braxton takes hold of my hand, and he hurries me out the door.

"I'm beginning to really hate Mozart," I say, rushing alongside him.

"Just wait until you meet him," Braxton replies, and even after I turn to study his face, it's impossible to tell if he's joking. We've just stepped into the elevator when he says, "Hey—where's your tablet?"

It takes me a moment to remember what I did with it. "I think I left it back in my room."

"Try not to do that," he says, his expression more serious than I would've expected. "If something were to happen, they could use it to find you."

"What could possibly happen here—in this gilded cage?" I race to keep up as the elevator doors slide open and he grasps my hand and leads me back to my room.

"Nothing," he says, his voice shaded, his accent lilting in a way that leaves me convinced he's holding something back. "Just a precaution, that's all."

When we reach the end of my hall, "Requiem" begins to play again. It's now ten o'clock. Soon the lights will go out.

"You should head back to your room," I say, realizing just after I've said it that I have no idea where that is. There's so much I don't know about him.

"Good night," he says, pressing a quick kiss to my cheek.

Then he races for his room and I make for mine.

I've just reached my door when the lights click off—and someone shoves a bag over my head.

61

"Scream and you're dead, understand?"

I blink through a void of black, immediately recognizing the voice as Elodie's, and I've no doubt she wants me to believe it.

But while Elodie is pretty much capable of anything, I seriously doubt she'd go so far as to kill me.

Or would she?

A jolt of terror blows through me, leaving me dizzy, unsteady on my feet, struggling to breathe. "What the fu—" My voice is a rasp, but before I can finish, Elodie yanks the bag so hard, it presses tight to my face, and I truly fear I might suffocate.

"Nod your head, Nat, so we know that you get it."

She grips my arm so harshly, I stifle a yelp and do as she says. In an instant, the bag loosens, and I frantically suck in a lungful of air.

"Don't make this harder than it has to be," she snaps.

Make what *harder? What the hell is going on?*

I inhale a series of short, shallow breaths, and with my heart about to explode in my chest, I force my brain to stay focused, as I struggle to fit all the pieces together.

For pretty much the first time ever, she called me *Nat.* I'm not sure if she's trying to appear friendly, or if she wants to remind me what a loser I was before I arrived on this rock. Considering she put a bag over my head, I'm leaning toward the latter.

Also, the fact that she said *we* means she's not alone.

This is verified when someone else starts tying my hands behind my back. Though who she might've roped into this—whatever *this* is—is anyone's guess.

Next thing I know, I'm on the move, as someone—I'm guessing it's still Elodie—drags me by the arm, and someone else pushes hard against me. And, despite my attempt to stay calm, that's when my anxiety really starts to spiral.

My stomach is churning, my body is covered in chills, while fat beads of sweat drip down my forehead and drip into my eyes. *Screw keeping my cool and playing along.* I need to find a way to stop this hazing, or abduction, or whatever the hell this is before it goes any further.

I try to resist, dig my heels in, and when that doesn't work, I make my whole body go limp, forcing them to work even harder to propel my dead weight. When someone else grabs hold of my right arm and starts hauling me forward, I realize there's at least one more in this party.

Great. That makes a minimum of three against one. The odds are definitely not in my favor.

"Where the hell are you taking me?" I struggle against them, try to catch a glimpse of the ground, hoping to maybe figure out some semblance of where I might be heading. But it's impossible to see much of anything.

"Shut up," Elodie snaps, squeezing my arm even harder. "I'll do the talking. But, if you must know, you're going on a little field trip, so stop being such a whiny little baby, and—"

A door bangs open. A blast of cold wind cuts through my skimpy lace dress and slices straight to my bones.

I recoil from the chill, try to fold my body forward, but it's no use. Next thing I know, I'm pushed deeper into the squall as the door slams shut behind me and another one opens in front of me.

"Get her inside the car and watch her head!" Elodie says, her voice barely audible against the howl of wind.

No. There's no way. I absolutely will not *get in the car. I won't—*

Next thing I know, I'm shoved into the back seat, scrunched into the middle with a body pressing against either side of me. And that's when I know what this is really about.

We're headed straight for the dock.

They're going to push me into those cold, violent waters and watch from the shore until the current drags me under…

They're going to force me into the skiff and watch as I battle the waves until I eventually capsize and drown…

I shake my head, cutting off the stream of horror-movie images scrolling across the screen in my brain.

I can't afford to panic. I need to stay focused, alert—ready to spring into action and make my escape the first chance I get.

"Where the hell are you taking me?" I shout, my voice pushing against the confines of the bag, my unseeing eyes staring into the dark. But when no one replies or acknowledges me in any way, I clamp my lips shut and set to work trying to loosen the rope that's binding my wrists.

After a never-ending drive around a series of bends and curves, the car stops, the engine dies, my hands are still bound, and I'm back outside, where the wind has its way with me once again.

"At least give her a blanket," someone says. And though it's hard to hear above the gust, when I replay the words in my head, I'm certain it was Jago.

Just then, a spray of water kicks up, leaving me partially drenched, and that's when I unleash the full extent of my fury. I have no intention of dying of hypothermia just because Elodie decided to get her revenge.

My hands may be tied. And yes, there's a bag over my head.

But I can still kick with the best of them.

"Ow!" Elodie cries as the pointed toe of my pump meets her shin. "You little fu—"

It's the last thing I remember before I black out.

62

When I come to, I'm in the lighthouse.

The freaking lighthouse.

The same one I saw beckoning from the skiff the night I arrived.

Except now that I'm inside, I realize it's a lighthouse only from the outside.

Inside, it's remarkably plush, decorated with piles of velvet cushions and soft faux fur blankets. The only light source comes from the flickering candelabras scattered about.

They're either planning on a night of serious debauchery, or about to conduct a séance.

And either way, I want out.

I sit up so abruptly, my head starts to spin. As I fight to catch my breath and will the constellation of stars swirling before my eyes to vanish, I realize that in addition to Elodie and Jago, Finn, Song, and Oliver have also come along—all of them looking at me with varying degrees of apprehension. Elodie is the only one who doesn't appear the least bit frightened.

"What the hell, Elodie?" I start to scramble to my feet, but I move too quickly, and frantically reach for the wall to steady myself.

"Oh, for the love of— Would you just sit down?" Elodie says, her voice bored but firm.

And as much as I hate to obey her, I dutifully sink back onto my cushion and spend the next few seconds tenderly examining my head, sure that she must've whacked me out there. How else could I have passed out?

"No one hit you." Elodie laughs. "You hyperventilated, which caused you to faint, which gave us no choice but to carry you up a bazillion flights of stairs. Which, again, was made extra difficult by the way you kicked the shit out of my shin."

She pushes up the leg of her Gray Wolf logo sweatpants to show me the lump. Through the flicker of candlelight, I can make out the swell of what is on its way to becoming a sizable knot, with a nasty bruise to go with it.

If nothing else, I take consolation in that.

To her, I say, "Maybe if you hadn't decided to abduct me in the first place, then—"

"Stop being so dramatic. No one's abducting anyone." Elodie rolls her eyes.

With my vision finally adjusted, I look to Song, Oliver, Finn, Jago, and say, "What's going on here? Is this some sort of hazing?"

In reply, every single one of them looks away.

Oliver moves closer to Finn and lays his head on his shoulder, confirming what I already guessed, the two of them are a couple.

Song huddles deeper into her puffy coat until she's just barely visible.

Jago, glorious Jago, lounges against a pile of velvet cushions and conducts a thorough inspection of his cuticles.

Which only goes to prove that this is all Elodie's doing.

"I'm out." This time when I stand, the room no longer sways. "Oh, and for your information, putting a bag over someone's head, binding their wrists, and throwing them into the back seat of a car, without their consent, is the definition of an abduction." I make for the exit as Elodie continues to lean against the wall, watching me through a flinty-eyed gaze.

"And just where the hell do you think you're going?" she says.

"Back." I reach for the doorknob.

"Oh, you're going back, all right."

A hard turn of the knob reveals the door is locked. And, since I don't have the key, and I'm not exactly desperate enough to jump from a window and risk plunging to my death on the rocks far below, there will be no immediate exit for me.

I stand before them, trying to appear more confident than I feel. "Is this because of Braxton?" I ask, watching as Elodie turns on me, every hair perfectly in place, but her face is a jeer.

"Yes, Nat. This is all about Brax. Because boys are clearly the biggest prize that someone could ever possibly hope for."

I can't help but cringe. When she puts it like that, I realize how archaic it sounded. Maybe Song was right, maybe it really is about Arthur.

She rolls her eyes and laughs, obviously enjoying my discomfort. "Clearly, there's a dire shortage of hot, straight, or fluid boys around here, but—"

"Hey!" Jago tosses a cushion at her, which Elodie effectively dodges.

"Oh, cool it," she tells him. "Play your cards right, and maybe someday I'll get around to you, too."

They both laugh, then Elodie turns back to me, and points at the cushion I abandoned in my attempt to flee. "For the last time, sit."

Left with no other choice, I do as she says.

"What's going to happen here is not about you." Her voice takes on a hard, brittle tone. "You're just not that special, despite what you think."

I don't say a word or react in any way. Better to appear cooperative and calm, while I work to uncover the weakest link in this chain. There's always that one person who's slightly less committed to the plan than all the others. And, in this case, I'm counting on Jago. Mostly because, after me, he's the newest student at the academy.

"You're about to be inducted into a long-standing, highly revered, rather sacred Gray Wolf Academy tradition that holds great importance."

I stifle a yawn. That's a whole lot of hyperbole, even for her.

"What we do here at Gray Wolf is the stuff of legend. But it also comes with great risk. In many cases, our lives depend on one another. Which means trust is essential."

"You've got to be kidding." I arc an arm wide, gesturing among them. "After what you all did to get me here—I don't trust a single one of you!"

"Well, we don't exactly trust you, either," Song says, her features arranged into a scowl. And I can't help but feel the sting of betrayal. Isn't this the same girl who warned me against Elodie and claimed she wanted to be friends? "But—" Song continues, sitting up straighter, her face peering out of her silver puffer, reminding me of a pearl nesting inside an oyster shell. "That doesn't mean we don't want to. Trust you, that is."

"Why?" I ask. "What difference could it possibly make?"

Song starts to reply when Jago cuts in. "Guys, she doesn't know." He shoots me a quick but meaningful look, then pushes away from the wall and leans forward. Bringing his knees to his chest, he folds his arms around them. "I told you, she's clueless."

"What don't I know?' I look from him, to Song, to Elodie, pretending to have no idea what they're talking about.

"About the time tr—" Finn starts, until Oliver places his hand over Finn's mouth and silences him.

"I thought for sure Braxton told you." Elodie peers at me, as though trying to peel back the many layers of my neutral expression in hopes of exposing the truth. "Or that you were at least smart enough to figure it out on your own."

She's baiting me, but I keep my lips clamped. Still, I can't help but wonder why Braxton saw fit to warn me about the time traveling, and yet failed to mention this charming, long-standing ritual.

Or are they only pretending this is some ancient tradition, when in fact, it's really a fresh new hell Elodie's invented solely for me?

Is this what Braxton meant when he warned me about getting on Elodie's bad side?

And what's Jago's game? Was that look meant to convey that he's secretly siding with me?

"Do you even want to be here, Nat?" Elodie brushes her hair over her shoulder and leans toward me. And the way she regards me, eyes wide and questioning, as though she's truly interested in hearing my reply, reminds me of the girl I knew back at school.

I can't allow myself to fall for that again. Because this is what Elodie does.

She makes you feel like you matter—like you really can be someone.

Like you're smarter, prettier, with infinite potential.

Like if you hang out with her long enough, you'll glitter like stardust, too.

"Do I want to be here? In this lighthouse?" I scowl. "No, El. I much prefer my own bed. Which is where I was headed before you shoved a bag over my head."

She continues to peer at me. Her gaze steady, even, giving nothing away. "At Gray Wolf, Natasha. Do you want to be here at the academy?"

Aside from the sizzle of flame meeting wax, and the gust of wind rattling the lighthouse windows, the room has fallen eerily silent.

"You do realize I wouldn't even be here if it wasn't for you. You set me up!" My voice screeches in a way that reveals my current state of anxiety, which only increases when I watch the way they all turn to one another, a silent message passing between them. "I mean, fine, maybe I made the ultimate choice to come to this island, but we both know it all started with you."

"No one's denying that," Elodie says, her face flickering in and out of view. "But now, I'm going to let you choose again. And this time, Nat, the choice is entirely yours."

63

The details of how they do whatever it is they're about to do are not for me to know.

I'm strictly a participant.

Though apparently, they're pretty serious about keeping the tradition alive, which means next time some unfortunate Green finds themselves here, I'll be the conductor. Under Elodie's guidance, of course.

Turns out, of all the Blues, Elodie's been here the longest. Having been recruited over a decade ago when she was just five years old and Arthur rescued her from an abusive children's home. He brought her to Gray Wolf to finish the usual schooling, along with a few other courses not normally taught.

To hear her tell it, Song was right. Elodie really does think of Arthur as her father, and she loves being a Blue. She could've taken a role as an instructor when she turned eighteen a few months back, but she's come to enjoy the perks of her position too much to ever consider giving it up. What those perks are remain a mystery. Though she does go on to reveal I'm only her second recruit.

"I'm sorry for the series of events that brought you here." She looks sincere, but then she's good at convincing people to believe in her, so I know better than to trust it. "And yet, I don't think you understand what a gift I've given you. I mean, here you have an all-inclusive trip to Oz with access to everything you've ever wanted, and in return, you act like an ungrateful twit. Even Song wasn't nearly as big of a pain as you've been."

I glance at Song, but her face betrays nothing.

"Why are you telling me this?" I ask, realizing it's the most she's ever revealed in our entire friendship. It's also the most she's ever spoken to me since I arrived. What I don't say is that in the story of Oz, it turned out the wizard was a fraud.

"Because you've ascended way faster than anyone expected. It took Jago months just to make Yellow. And though I have my suspicions for how you managed to rise so quickly—"

"Yeah, like a sudden, unexplained vacancy—" Song starts, but with a harsh look from Elodie, she's silenced. Which only hardens my resolve to follow up on that later.

"The point is, no one here believes you've done anything to earn it."

"Earn *what*, exactly?" I look among them. "I'm still a Green, so I don't know about this ascent you refer to—"

"You won't be a Green tomorrow. If you're still here, that is."

"What are you saying?"

It's then that Oliver speaks. "What would happen if tomorrow you were to take your first Trip?"

Remembering how Braxton told me about the time travel in confidence, I feign a look of confusion, like I have no idea what that could possibly mean. And honestly, I'm not sure I do. It still feels unbelievable to me.

"You'll understand when it happens," Oliver says. "But when you do go, you won't be alone. You'll be partnered with someone, and whoever that is—"

"Look," Finn interrupts him, and though it strikes me as kind of abrupt, if not rude, Oliver just sinks back against the wall and takes it in stride. "Thing is—no one here wants to Trip with a partner they can't trust, and according to Jago, you messed up today. A lot."

I look to Jago, wondering what the heck he told them. He merely shrugs, as though daring me to deny it.

"I scored the jewel." I glare hard at Elodie.

She nods. "And as impressive as that was, before you could even get to that part, you were incredibly sloppy and even tried to behead me."

"I think we both know I wasn't actually serious—" I start to defend myself, but Elodie won't hear it.

"Not to mention how we all just watched you hyperventilate. Over *nothing*, I might add."

"You seriously think that was noth—"

Again, she cuts me off. "Maybe your sloppy reactions aren't a big deal when you're here, but outside of Gray Wolf, in the places you're going, panicking can prove fatal. Which means you seriously need to learn some real skills and get your emotions in check."

"What are you even talking about?" I look from Elodie to the others, but they just stare back in stony silence. "I just got here," I remind them. "I mean, what do you even expect from me? Like, I'm supposed to know how to waltz? You've seen where I came from."

"What we expect is for you to try harder." Elodie's voice is as sharp as her gaze. "To stay in character. To blend in to whatever setting you find yourself in. To take the job seriously because it *is* serious. And more than anything, we expect you to help us get in and out without getting killed."

"Or worse, tossed in jail," Oliver adds.

"How is that worse?" Finn asks, his voice, like his face, full of dismay as he turns on Oliver.

"Have you even seen the jails? They're filled with rats, and you have to choose a corner to shit and piss in. I'll take the guillotine any—"

"Guys, please." Elodie frowns. With a dramatic roll of her

eyes and toss of her hair, she turns back to me. "You need to prove you're committed. That you're one hundred percent in, no looking back. Only then, will we agree to let you be an AAD."

"What the hell is an AAD?" My voice rings throughout the space, echoing back at me.

Song starts to reply, when Elodie stops her. "You haven't earned the right to know. You haven't earned any of this. But you're about to. Come on."

64

With Elodie leading the way, we head up another flight of stairs that ends at the highest point in the lighthouse. There are windows all around that must allow for an amazing three-sixty view during the day, but with a storm beginning to brew, it all looks the same—black sea meeting dark sky.

Jago stands directly before me. His nervous expression is not at all reassuring. Also, now that I know he was gossiping about me, providing a blow-by-blow account of my flawed performance today, he's clearly not the friend I hoped he would be.

Elodie stands beside Jago, while Song, Oliver, and Finn occupy three separate points along the wall.

"Don't worry," Elodie tells Jago. "She goes under really quickly." She shoots me an approving look, but I get the feeling it has less to do with me, and more to do with the fact that she recruited me.

Jago raises a hand and tells me to focus on the pocket watch that dangles from his finger. Its case is gold, with a pearlized face and slim black hands that spin backward, unspooling the hours already lived.

"Just to be clear," I say. "I'm not really *going* anywhere, right? This is all just theoretical?"

Elodie locks her gaze on mine, then signals to Jago, who begins to sing in a language I don't understand. Though I do recognize the tune as the one from Elodie's car. It's the same song the torch singer sang at Arcana. The same song that played whenever I hung out with Elodie.

"This isn't a real song," I say. "Or at least not one you can stream. You made it up! You—"

"You're so smart," Elodie coos. "Now, shh…"

While Jago continues to sing—his voice surprisingly melodious—Song, Oliver, and Finn unlatch the panels lined up beneath all the windows and begin flipping a series of switches that sets the room buzzing.

I have the fleeting thought that for an old lighthouse, it's surprisingly high tech. But then I find myself laughing for even thinking such a thing. Of course it's high tech. It belongs to Arthur Bla—

Next thing I know, the roof of the lighthouse shifts open, filling the room with wind and fast droplets of rain that spill onto my head.

Arthur Blac—why can't I remember his name?

Somewhere in the distance, I hear someone say, "You forgot to give her a talisman!"

"Not necessary," Elodie says. "When the lion fawns upon the lamb, the lamb will never cease to follow him."

Jago laughs, but I'm not sure why. I don't know what any of that means, so I focus on the Gray Wolf logo hovering before me…something about alchemy…

Alchemy Black—No!

My lids feel droopy, but my feet have grown wings.

I'm dancing! I sing. *I'm floating!*

All around me, the wind funnels down from the sky and spins like a cyclone.

I want to tell Elodie to make it stop.

I want to shout the news to the rooftops: I've remembered the name, it's Braxton Bla—

No! It's Arthur Black—

A bright and terrible light fills up the sky. A horrible crack sounds overhead. And I dream a wonderful dream of clocks melting down walls, a torch singer wearing a crown of antlers, and a boy with eyes like the sea...

I'm floating—I'm really truly flying, and it's—

"It's really happening!" I whisper, as Elodie presses hard on my wrist.

65

In my dream, a beautiful boy stands before me. His mouth is moving, but I can't hear the words.

Still, none of that matters. Everything will be okay. And I know this, because Elodie has promised as much.

"Tell me what you see?" she whispers.

I tell her a story about boys in slinky dresses and time melting down walls.

"Tell me more about the boy," she urges. "The one standing before you."

I turn my attention away from Elodie and back to him. "He wears a mask, but I can tell that he's beautiful. And he's offering me a drink. A green drink."

"Do you accept it?"

I frown, trying to decide.

"No," I tell her. "But it doesn't matter. It was never about the drink."

"How can you be sure?" she asks.

"Because I've dreamed this dream before. It's about the song—the one the torch singer sings—the same one we sang in your car. It's some sort of lullaby for the mind. Also, the clocks. It has something to do with hands that spin backward."

"And now?" she asks. "Knowing everything you now know, do you leave the club and find your way home?"

I fall silent.

"Natasha?"

From somewhere far away, I'm aware of Elodie softly shaking my shoulder.

"Do you stay, or do you leave? Answer me, please."

All around me, people are laughing, dancing, while waiters wander about with drink trays expertly balanced on their palms, the boys in slinky black dresses, the girls in tuxedos.

The beautiful boy offers me a glass of cut crystal, its contents a pale shimmering green.

"It's called the Green Fairy." He clinks his rim against mine. "To new beginnings," he says, his voice rising over the noise.

I watch him drain his glass. Elodie pushes me to decide.

"Natasha, what are you doing? What are you seeing?"

"Is she okay?" another voice asks. The accent is Spanish, though it belongs to a voice from the future. It has no place here.

"I'm riding the wind!" I'm back in Elodie's car. The top is down, my face pressed to the sky.

But now the beautiful boy is back. He leans toward me, lips just inches from mine.

"Natasha, where are you? What is happening?" She wants to know, but I'm too busy watching. This is the part I missed the last time I dreamed it.

The boy moves closer. He calls me *darling*, lifts me into his arms, and carries me through a crowded dance floor. He walks right through a swaying couple, and I watch in awe as they pixelate and fade from view. Next thing I know, we're in a dim room where I watch Elodie toss my backpack to the ground.

"Told you," she says, watching as he lowers me onto a couch. My body limp, my mind caught in a dream I've never dreamed.

She tips on her toes, tries to kiss the boy, but he pushes her away.

"Where are you?" Elodie prompts.

Time has gone missing and I'm desperate to find it. But I

catch only glimpses of arrangements being made, two voices bickering, as I lie on the couch, my mind lost in a maze I can't find my way out of.

"Come on, Nat. You can do this—tell me what you see."

I'm climbing out of her car. We carpooled to school, but I'm still wearing the same dress I wore to the club.

She hands me a bag, tells me to dump all the contents into my locker, then go to my English class and sit at my desk.

Her final instruction: *At precisely nine thirty-eight, I command you to wake.*

"Nat, what happened—where are you?"

I swallow. My lips are so parched, my throat dry. "You set me up," I tell her, but we already know that.

"Does that mean you stayed—a second time?"

"Told you she would," the Spanish accent says.

"No you didn't," Elodie snaps.

I'm back in the club, Arcana, it's called.

I pull the Wheel of Fortune card.

I laugh at my grave.

A beautiful boy in a mask offers me a Green Fairy.

"It was never about the drink," I say.

"Even so, would you do it again? Knowing what you know— would you stay?"

I think of Mason, and immediately feel an ache deep in my belly. I miss his elaborate outfits, his sarcastic humor. I miss making fun of the snooty spin-class moms, and playing a round of Anywhere but Here.

I think of my mom, and a sob threatens to cave in my chest.

"Would you do it again—or would you leave?"

I watch the boy drain his glass.

"I would stay," I tell her.

The moment I say it, the dream disappears, and I feel myself falling through space.

66

I wake to the sound of buzzing.

Really loud buzzing that's soon followed by pounding.

A moment later, the room floods with light.

"Tasha!"

A whispered voice.

A hand on my shoulder.

A face looming so close to mine.

"What happened? Are you okay?"

I flip onto my belly and bury my face in a soft feathered pillow, but the voice sounds again. "Tasha, please—look at me."

Inside my head, a storm rages. I inhale a ragged breath and will it to pass.

"I left a ton of messages and—"

With a sigh, I roll onto my back and inch up the headboard, as Braxton takes in the state of my matted hair, the dress I was wearing last night that I apparently slept in.

"Aw shit," he whispers, and draws me tightly to him. "I can't believe she's still doing this."

I pull back, run a finger under each eye, and stare in dismay when it comes away streaked with mascara.

"You knew, and you didn't warn me?" My voice is a rasp, my throat so parched, Braxton immediately reaches for the glass of water I keep by my bed and hands it to me.

"She swore she was done with all that. I should've known

better than to believe her."

I look beyond the drapes he must've opened. Outside, it's raining.

I look inside my head and replay the reel of Braxton and Elodie bickering over broken promises, bitter memories, things that happened long before me, while I lay on the couch, my fate in their hands.

But that was true only the first time. Because last night, the choice was mine, and I still ended up here. Strangely, despite everything that's happened, I know I'd make the same choice again.

I return the glass to my bedside table and train my focus on him. Carefully noting the hint of shadow that swoops under each eye, the tight pinch that pulls at the corners of his mouth. And even though I take my time to study his face, I still can't determine if it's worry or guilt that's got him looking this way.

"You didn't Trip, if that's what you're thinking," he says. "Arthur stopped using the lighthouse ages ago. It's outdated technology."

"Looked pretty high tech to me." I tear my gaze away and turn toward the window, tracking the long ribbons of rain as they stream down the panes.

"Maybe in the outside world, which is totally obsolete," Braxton says. "But this place, with its natural elements combined with Arthur's genius, is a century ahead, at least."

"What are you saying?" Returning to him, I gather my knees to my chest and wrap my arms around them, as though I need to fend off whatever comes next, even though I'm the one who asked.

"In short, Gray Wolf Island is a natural wormhole that acts as a portal to the past." He speaks cleanly, plainly, and while it makes sense on the surface, my mind is in a tangle trying to process his words. "But, in order to securely harness that energy,

Arthur developed an advanced technology that not only keeps the wormhole open long enough for a safe departure and return, but also allows him to direct it toward specific moments in time."

"And the lighthouse?"

"It's where the phenomenon was first discovered when all the lighthouse keepers went missing."

"Missing?" My voice rises with alarm, as the horrifying thought spins through my head: *Is that what would've happened to me if I'd chosen to leave?*

67

"The lighthouse keepers disappeared without a trace," Braxton says. "And they were eventually ruled as a series of suicides. The local jurisdiction claimed they must've jumped from the windows and let the sea take them. Truth is, they were lost in the time storm."

I stare speechless. I have no idea what to say.

"That was all long ago. But it's one of the reasons Arthur was able to purchase the rock for so cheap. Between the disappearances and the wind, no one wanted anything to do with it, so they were happy to let Arthur take ownership. Since the lighthouse was the only existing structure at the time, he used it for his earliest experiments. But after building the gilded cage, as you call it, he deactivated the whole thing and moved on."

"But they were pushing buttons, lights were flashing, and the roof slid open—" I remember the feel of rain on my head, but when I touch my hair now, I discover it's dried into a halo of frizz.

"All special effects," Braxton assures me. "The lighthouse was unused until Elodie discovered it and decided to use it for her hazing headquarters…among other things."

I remember the piles of cushions, candles, blankets, and quickly avert my gaze.

"Just to be clear, you didn't go anywhere. Elodie just

hypnotized you."

"But she said I had a choice."

"It's her way of testing your loyalty to the academy and what we do here. Technically, you couldn't undo the choice since you weren't Tripping. Also, you can't return to an earlier version of yourself. It's called crossing your own timeline, and trust me, it leads nowhere good."

"But what if I chose not to stay—what would've happened to me?"

I remember the ruthless way Elodie shoved the bag over my head. How much more is she capable of?

Braxton shrugs. "No one's ever made that choice. Probably because you end up here only if there's nothing worth going back to."

I think about missing Mason, my mom. And yet, it wasn't enough.

"I saw stuff. Stuff I missed the first time."

Braxton inhales a sharp breath, and in that instant, I know that he knows I'm referring to what happened between Elodie and him.

"Hypnosis often reveals that which is kept hidden," he says. "The first time you experienced it, you were in a trance state under Elodie's direction. But just because you lacked immediate recall doesn't mean your mind failed to record it."

A few silent beats pass between us. I break it when I say, "They said something about a talisman." My gaze finds his. "Also, something about lions fawning over lambs and the lambs following."

Braxton sighs and shakes his head. "The quote is Shakespeare, from *Henry VI*."

"So, Elodie thinks she's the lion and I'm the lamb?" I flinch at the sting of truth. I certainly fell for her fawning back at our old school.

"She thinks that about everyone," Braxton says, drawing me away from my thoughts. "As for a talisman, it's a sort of good luck charm you bring along when you Trip. It helps you remember who you really are, and where and when you belong. It's personal to everyone. But it must be either really small and not easily detected, something that would be suitable to the time, or both."

"You mean, without the talisman there's a chance I might not have woken up from the dream?"

"No." He slides a hand up my calf, unaware of the trail of shivers he's left in his wake as his thumb comes to rest on my knee. "If she'd given you a talisman, it would've been nothing more than a show of meaningless pageantry. As for not waking up, I never would've let that happen. I would've found you. I would've figured it out. But Natasha, this is exactly why you need to keep your tablet with you at all times."

My tablet. In the distance, I hear it buzzing again. When I get up to retrieve it, I find a block of messages from Braxton, each one expressing increasing degrees of worry. Once those are cleared, the message of the day pops onto the screen:

> *We know what we are,*
> *but know not what we may be.*
> —William Shakespeare, *Hamlet*

Braxton comes up behind me, the hard angles of his body seamlessly conforming to the soft curves of mine. Then he tucks his arms around my waist and buries his face at the back of my neck. The nearness of him, the scorching warmth of his touch, the cool wisp of his breath on my nape, sparks an ache so deep, it takes all my resolve to suppress it.

"Don't let on that you know." I whisper the words into his shoulder, then reluctantly untangle myself from his embrace and turn to face him. "I don't want them thinking I'm tattling. I may have passed their messed-up trust exercise, but that doesn't mean they actually trust me."

Braxton nods, then pulls me back to him, his fingers tracing a gentle curving line along the hollow of my cheek. Just the sight of his lids falling, his lips angling toward me, has me longing to silence my sensible side and listen to the more decadent needs of my body.

Unlike my brain, it always knows what it wants, and right now, it wants Braxton. And going by the glazed look in his eyes, he's meeting me match for match.

Still, as reckless and self-indulgent as I can sometimes be, my pragmatic side insists on being heard. Which explains why I find myself placing a hand on Braxton's chest to keep him from coming any closer.

"Everything okay?" he asks, confused by the mixed signals I'm giving—the needy heat of the hand that keeps him at bay, and the determined look on my face.

"I've been thinking…" I say, watching as the flame in Braxton's gaze is instantly doused by a torrent of dread. "Maybe…we should just…" I bite down on my lip, hardly able to believe what I'm about to do next. "Maybe we should just sort of…cool it down…way down. At least for a while…"

In an instant, Braxton's fingers fall from my waist, and I'm reminded of the way he and Elodie bickered back at the club while I lay in a trance on the couch, and how angry she was when he pushed her away. He's over her. That much is clear. But Elodie is not over him. And if I have any hope of becoming a Blue and cementing my place here, then I can't risk alienating her any more than I already have.

Also, if I'm being honest, I'm confused by my feelings for Braxton. I mean, my entire world was just flipped upside down. Everyone I knew, and most of what I believed, has been ripped right out from under me, only to be replaced with a slew of new faces and a shocking list of possibilities that I've barely had a chance to process, much less adapt to.

And while I really like kissing him, and while there's an undeniable twinge in my belly and skip of my heartbeat whenever he's near, I'm not sure if that means I have feelings for him; if I've fooled myself into thinking I like him to get back at Elodie; or if he's just a beautiful, sexy boy I kiss in an effort to not feel so lonely.

And until I can manage to sort that all out, I think it's better for both of us to just leave last night in the past.

To Braxton, I say, "For now, I think it's better if I limit my focus to finding my way here at Gray Wolf and learning everything I can, as quickly as I can, so I can make Blue. I can't afford to be distracted by anything else. So…I'm hoping we can be…friends?"

Braxton's eyes graze over me, and while he looks a bit crestfallen, he soon nods in agreement. "Just know, I'm always here for you, Tasha," he says. "Oh, and I left you a tray." He hooks a thumb over his shoulder to where a silver tray with coffee and pastries sits on the table before the velvet settee.

The gesture is so kind, so caring, I have to fight the urge to take back everything I just said, grab hold of his arm, and drag him over to my bed so he can make my body shatter in all the ways I've imagined.

But of course I don't do any of that. I need to stay focused, cement my place here. Once that's done, then maybe I'll have a better grip on exactly what it is that I'm feeling.

As soon as he's gone, I pour some coffee into a pretty porcelain mug, pop a piece of almond croissant into my mouth, and head into the bathroom.

When I emerge, I find a stack of yellow sweatshirts neatly stacked on the shelf where the green ones once were.

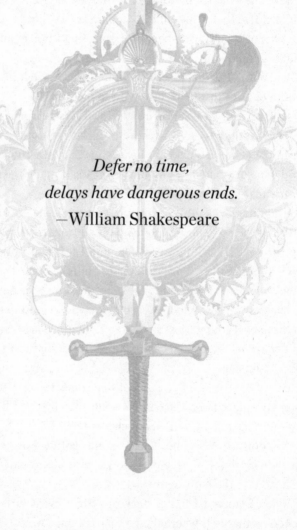

Defer no time,
delays have dangerous ends.
—William Shakespeare

68

The first thing I notice about life as a Yellow is it's not all that different from life as a Green.

And, since there are no other Yellows, and since Braxton and I have been on pause for the last four weeks, mealtimes are especially lonely. Watching the Blues with their heads bent together, laughing and talking, makes me feel like I'm back at my old school—stuck on the periphery, invisible and unseen.

Though time spent after dinner in the Autumn Room gives me a much-needed break. And because of it, for the first time since I arrived, I've made friends. Four to be exact—Song, Jago, Oliver, and Finn. Or maybe five, if you count Elodie which, while we've technically called a truce and agreed to get along, I'm not sure I'm ready to label us that.

Still, if someone told me four weeks ago when I first got here that I'd end up hanging out with a group of kids who shoved a bag over my head, tossed me into the back seat of a car, and basically kidnapped me, hypnotized me, then dumped me back in my room to sleep it off, I would've laughed. But, here at Gray Wolf, we're pretty much forced to make the most of what we have.

Which is why I find myself standing outside Elodie's pink door, about to knock, when she beats me to it and ushers me inside.

My first impression: It's like stepping inside a genie's bottle.

Or, at least what I imagine the inside of a genie's bottle would look like.

I guess because we spend so much time in classrooms and designated dining halls, I've never really visited anyone else's room, so I assumed they were all like my own. But Elodie's room is a whole other level.

Not only is it twice the square footage of mine, but the walls are covered in magnificent works of art—old masters hanging alongside spare modern pieces—and yet somehow, she's made it all work.

"Wow," I say as I move about the space, seeing no point in feigning nonchalance. Elodie knows how much I appreciate a good display of exceptional taste.

I move past a velvet settee much like my own, except hers is upholstered in a rich blue velvet. There's an extravagant handblown Venetian glass chandelier hanging overhead, and her collection of side tables are gilded in gold leaf.

Like mine, her bed is also a canopy. But the carvings are more elaborate, and it has intricately embroidered fabrics gathered along the top and draped down the sides. A riot of multi-patterned pillows—florals, zebras, and leopard prints—lay in artfully arranged piles along the silk chaise longue at the foot of the bed. And nearly everywhere I look are displays of crystals, precious trinkets, stacks of rare first edition books, along with large, overstuffed pillows, plush throws, flickering candles, and smoldering incense sticks, lending the space a sort of posh, bohemian royal look.

A fire roars in the hearth, and I move to stand near it, pausing long enough to feel its warmth on my hands before I wander toward the window to gaze out at a spectacular view of the ocean beyond. And there, down in the far left corner, I can just make out the stark white warning of the lighthouse.

I turn to face her. "Nice digs, El."

She pauses, bends a brow, and my belly instantly clenches. Here at Gray Wolf, the use of slang is frowned upon. But when she bursts into laughter, I breathe a sigh of relief and join in.

Like walking arm in arm, dressing for dinner, selecting the correct stemware for the multiple course meals they serve at lunchtime and dinner, and swearing off all forms of modern music, the more you grow accustomed to the old ways, the more you'll be able to blend when you Trip. And if the last four weeks of culture, history, diction, dance, comportment, languages, social customs, swordcraft, equestrian lessons, and etiquette training (which included the proper use of a chamber pot that nearly had me calling it quits) has taught me anything, it's that the ability to blend is everything.

There's so much to remember, and none of it comes naturally. Or at least not for me. It's been a long time since succeeding ranked high on my list of priorities, and, if nothing else, I have Elodie to thank. Because if I continued the way I was going back home, who knows where I might've ended up.

"I'm curious," she says. "Exactly how long have you known? About Tripping, I mean."

My gaze meets hers. And though I know she'll know if I lie, I still take a few beats to come up with the best way to answer without betraying my promise to Braxton.

But I guess I must pause for too long, because Elodie says, "You don't seriously expect me to believe you needed Keane to tell you?" She tilts her head in a way that causes her hair to fall in a cascade of long, silky waves.

I sigh, remembering the day Keane summoned me to his office, and how he leaned across his desk, his face arranged into an almost comically earnest expression, as he proceeded to reveal the truth of what really goes on here at Gray Wolf, while I did my best to act surprised by the news.

"It was a lot like when my mom told me the truth about

Santa." I shrug. "My dad was long gone, and I figured she was just trying to prepare me for the lack of presents left under the tree. So I acted surprised, like I had no idea it'd been them all along, though of course I'd been clued in for years."

Elodie's gaze narrows on mine. "Very poignant," she says. "But you still haven't answered my question. How long before you figured it out?"

"Why does it matter?" I ask, genuinely confused as to why she would care.

"Because I want to know how long you've been faking it," she says.

The moment stretches between us, and I watch as her fingers play at the glimmering golden disk at her neck. It's a charm, with a snake engraved on the front, and though I've never noticed her wearing it before, the way she handles it makes me wonder if it holds some sort of significance.

At the sound of Elodie clearing her throat, I meet her gaze and say, "I figured it out the first day."

She studies me intently, searching for the lie I'm determined to hide. I mean, maybe it's not the full truth, but I did gather all the clues, and I used them to draw my own conclusion. Braxton only confirmed my suspicion.

After what feels like forever, Elodie finally cracks a small smile. "Just so you know—I saw straight through your act. Still, the way you committed to the pretense fills me with hope."

"Hope?" I squint, unsure what she means.

"Considering what we do here, perfecting the art of deception is probably the most important skill you can have."

My head grows woozy, like all the oxygen's been sucked right out of the room.

Well, that explains just about everything I know about her.

My gaze returns to the slithering serpent on the medallion she wears. Snakes are known for shedding their skin, emerging unscathed and brand new. But then I also remember what Song said about venomous snakes—how she used them as a sort of metaphor for dealing with Elodie.

While I'm pretty sure I haven't done much to heed Song's advice, the fact is, I'm still here, in Elodie's room, on a night that's considered kind of a big deal. So, I must've done something right.

After a prolonged beat of silence, my gaze lights on Elodie's, and I say, "And yet, while I managed to fool everyone else, I didn't fool you."

Elodie's eyes flash on mine. "Not to worry." She shrugs. "Few people do." Then swinging her hair over her shoulder, she says, "Now, how about a toast before the others arrive?"

I watch as she crosses the room, plucks an expensive-looking bottle of champagne from a silver ice bucket, and expertly pops the cork.

"This is nothing like the house parties back home," I say, as Elodie pours us each a glass. "The fanciest we ever got was a case of black cherry White Claw."

Elodie scrunches her nose. "You have no idea what that was like for me. Having to slam shots and pretend that I liked it." She shudders and hands me a glass. "Growing up at Gray Wolf, I was raised on the good stuff. You should've seen the way I gagged when Arthur gave me my first sip of beer." When she sees my startled look, she says, "It took a lot of training to learn how to fit in at a modern-day high school."

"I never even thought of that," I say, unable to hide my surprise. "And you made it look so easy. Everyone pretty much worshipped you from the moment you arrived."

All except Mason, of course.

When Elodie turns to me in shock, I realize it's the first truly nice thing I've said to her in the month since I've been here. Still, there's no point in withholding the compliment when we both know it's true.

"Well, after hours of watching TikTok, scrolling through Instagram, and bingeing some really bad reality TV shows, I guess all that research started to kick in." Elodie laughs and raises her flute.

Careful to pinch the stem and keep my pinkie slightly crooked, just like the etiquette instructor taught me, I raise mine as well. This is the first time we've been alone since I arrived on the island, and there's no telling what she might say.

"To your first Trip!" she says.

I start to lift my glass, then pause when I sense she's not done.

"You've come a long way, Natasha Antoinette Clarke, and you're about to go so much further. Way beyond your wildest dreams."

Her lips curl into a wide, knowing grin.

I grin back.

Then, after tipping our glasses toward each other, we drink.

And for a few brief moments, it feels like the old days.

69

Oliver and Finn snuggle against a pile of pillows arranged by the fire.

Song sits perched on one of the silk cushioned chairs.

Jago sprawls across the velvet settee, as Elodie commands the other half, their legs entwined in a way that makes me wonder if she's decided to *get around to him* like she jokingly promised in the lighthouse.

While I occupy an overstuffed purple velvet chair that pairs so perfectly with the green of my robe I feel like a queen, until I catch another look at Elodie's scarlet caftan and the ruby tiara she's perched on her head, and I'm instantly reminded that title is claimed.

I look around the room, my eyes roaming from the fine furnishings, the masterpieces hanging on the walls, to my new group of friends. Everyone looks so glamorous, it's like being in one of those aspirational spreads you find in the September issue of a fashion magazine. Then again, I'd expect nothing less from Elodie's Full Moon/Half Slumber party.

Apparently, the party takes place before every Yellow's first Trip, and it's meant to build team spirit, camaraderie, and calm any fears the new person may have. From what I've seen so far, it basically amounts to a night when everyone piles into Elodie's room dressed in their finest sleepwear, to swill champagne, gorge on tiny little sweet cakes (more properly known as *petit fours*), and recall their fondest memories from their own first Trip, or any Trip, if the first isn't worth sharing. And, since the first few times it fell on a full moon, the name stuck.

While it's fun to hear about the time Finn posed nude for Michelangelo—he kept the sketch, it's framed on the wall of his room, and he promises to show it to me someday soon; and when Song had tea with Queen Victoria at Buckingham Palace; and Oliver's tale of clay pigeon shooting with members of the British monarchy; and Jago's most recent story of a dinner spent in the company of King Ferdinand VII of Spain—everyone unanimously agrees, Elodie has the best story.

"I Tripped back to the sixteenth century," she says, pausing to sip her champagne. "I visited the royal court of King Henry the Eighth."

I set my empty glass on the gilded side table and draw my knees to my chest.

"I forget what he was celebrating, but the drinks were flowing freely, and Henry was quite taken with me."

Finn cups his hands around his mouth and imitates a soundtrack from a vintage porn movie. "*Bow chicka bow wow,*" he sings. And I can't help but wonder if he does that every time he's forced to hear this story, or if it was a bit of spontaneous improv. Either way, it works. Everyone laughs, including Elodie.

"Hell yeah!" She grins and raises her glass to him. "Anyway, where was I?" She presses a finger to her cheek and feigns a coy look. "Oh yes, so, Henry was in serious pursuit. And believe me, this is a man who does not like to hear the word *no*."

They all laugh. But I'm stuck on her use of the present tense. It reminds me of how Braxton spoke about Leonardo da Vinci, as though he's still out there, among the living. And to hear them tell it, and from everything I've learned, he actually is. And yet, I'm still having a hard time fully embracing the idea that for those with the proper knowledge, resources, and tools, the past is as easy to access as the present.

"As Henry and I danced," Elodie continues, "he was starting to get really grabby. Still, I managed to elude him just enough to keep him at bay but still interested. That's the trick with Henry— he wants what he wants, but he lives for the chase."

"C'mon," Jago says, sliding his foot up her leg. "Get to the good stuff, already."

She laughs and playfully pushes him away. Directing her focus to me, she says, "Henry literally chased me around the Palace. It was hilarious, and actually pretty thrilling if I'm going to be honest."

"Ew." Song cringes, settling deeper into her chair. "This is my least favorite of all your stories. Henry's such a disgusting misogynist, never mind all the wives he beheaded. It's just so gross. I still don't know how you went through with it."

Annoyed, Elodie rolls her eyes, then turns toward the rest of us, about to continue her story when Oliver cuts in. Poking Finn on the shoulder, Oliver says, "Would *you* bed Henry, if given the chance?"

Oliver shoots him an exaggerated lascivious look, and sings the porn song to him, which makes everyone laugh.

"Seriously," Oliver says, speaking over the laughter.

Everyone turns their attention to Finn, which doesn't sit well with Elodie. Her story's been hijacked, and she's not one to tolerate that. Or at least not for long.

"Depends," Finn says. "Are we talking about the young Henry, or the decrepit, totally paranoid, murderous Henry with the foul-smelling ulcerated leg—"

"Oh, for fu—it was early in his reign as king," Elodie says, reclaiming the spotlight. "He was young, handsome, tremendously fit, and it was well before Anne Boleyn lost her head. But more importantly, there's something about being in the presence of that kind of power. He commanded the entire kingdom, and it was amazing to see the lengths the members of his court would go to—all of them competing for his favor."

She could just as easily be describing Arthur, but I keep that bit to myself.

"So?" Jago says. "Did you, or didn't you?"

"You haven't heard this story?" I ask, knowing that by delaying Elodie's big reveal even more, I risk bearing the brunt of her wrath.

Jago shakes his head. Elodie clears her throat and climbs atop the velvet settee so that she towers well above us, claiming our attention. "I, Elodie Blue—" She juts her hip to the side and raises her glass. "Do hereby solemnly declare, that I let King Henry the Eighth chase me all the way into his private chambers, where we enjoyed a delightful royal romp. Or three, if I remember correctly. And, if you must know, I showed him who truly wears the crown, thank you very much."

Elodie bows with an exaggerated flourish, as Song makes a gagging face, and Jago leans forward with a newly interested gaze. "So, how was it?" he asks.

Before Elodie can reply, Finn says, "She begged. *Please, sir, I want some more!*" And everyone falls into hysterics, laughing at a joke I don't understand.

When they finally settle, Elodie looks at me and says, "Natasha, you're the only one who hasn't commented. And I know you must have an opinion, or at least a few questions. So, go ahead, say what's on your mind."

I try to imagine what I would've done in her position. It's a moment before it dawns on me that I could easily find myself in a similar circumstance as early as tomorrow. And yet despite all the preparation and classes, despite Braxton giving me an early head's up on what really goes on here at Gray Wolf, it's still outrageous to think that one day soon I might actually find myself modeling for Michelangelo or taking part in anything resembling the types of stories they told.

Still, as hard as it is to wrap my head around the concept of actual time travel, there's another mystery that looms even larger. A single murky detail they insist on glossing over—one that not even Braxton has seen fit to disclose. And, since Elodie opened the door to questions, I figure now's my chance to get some answers.

"While it all sounds really cool and exciting," I say, turning toward Elodie, "I'm not sure I get it. I mean, what's the point?"

In an instant, Elodie's face falls flat.

"I mean, it's not like Arthur's going to all this trouble and expense just so you can sleep with a king, and Finn can get his portrait sketched by a legend. Because, if that's the case, then what about the class in procurement—what was that about?" I glance around the room only to find everyone has retreated into themselves.

Talk about killing a vibe. I pretty much slammed it with an ax, chopped it to bits, doused it in acid, then set fire to the remains.

Elodie squares her gaze on mine, the salacious glow of having bedded a notorious king completely snuffed out. "After we had our fun," she says, her voice tight, "I waited for him to doze off, then I nicked some of his belongings and got the hell out of there as fast as I could."

There it is. The one thing that no one, not even Braxton, has been willing to cop to: Arthur is training us to be time traveling thieves.

I remember my lunch with Arthur when he showed me the ring that once belonged to Edward the Black Prince. And suddenly I realize it was probably stolen from the past, along with every other precious object I've seen around Gray Wolf.

"And your partner?" I ask, voice shaky.

The room falls eerily silent. Elodie sinks back onto the settee, reaches for her glass, then, remembering it's empty, reluctantly settles on me.

"The first Trip is always with a partner. What happened to yours?" I repeat.

Someone gasps, I think it was Song, but I can't be sure because I'm focused on Elodie.

"Natasha—" Jago starts, but Elodie's quick to call him off.

Breathing a resigned sigh, she says, "He's...not a Blue anymore."

"Then what is he?" I ask, wondering if it was maybe Hawke, Keane, or even Braxton.

"Not everyone's cut out for Tripping," she says, her gaze icy cold. "Tomorrow, we'll find out if you are."

The words hang heavy between us, and I watch as Elodie rises, pulls the empty bottle of champagne from the bucket, flips it upside down, and announces, "I pronounce this party officially over."

As Song passes me on her way to the door, she turns briefly to me and says, "I really hope you don't live to regret that."

70

It's the worst possible way to end a party—insulting the host and all the guests simultaneously.

And as I make the short walk to my room, I'm feeling pretty down on myself, when my slab buzzes with a message from Braxton.

Braxton: I need to see you.

Me: I'm in my pajamas.

Braxton: This will take only a minute.

Me: Okay, come to my room.

It's late. I'm tired. I wrecked a perfectly fun night. And I'm worried about tomorrow.

In theory: All good reasons to not want to see Braxton.

In reality: The moment he taps on my door, my heart skips three beats.

"Hey," he says, voice hushed, as I usher him inside and his eyes fill with the sight of me. "Aw, of course." He motions toward my robe. "Elodie's full moon party. How was it?"

Not wanting to share how I single-handedly slaughtered the good vibe, I say, "Did you know Elodie slept with King Henry the Eighth?"

Braxton squints, rakes a hand through his hair. "She's still telling that story?"

"Is it true?"

"Well, there's no one to disprove it, so…"

"So, you weren't her partner on that Trip?"

He shoots me a curious look. "Why would you think that?"

I dismiss it with a wave of my hand and draw him deeper into the room, over to where, with a quick flip of a switch, a fire springs to life in the hearth. "What's up?" I ask, turning my back to the flames.

"Tomorrow's your first Trip."

I nod.

"Are you nervous?"

"Honestly? Extremely. I don't feel ready."

"None of us did." He takes a breath, stares into the flames. And I use the moment to admire the way the light and heat flickers across his face. When he turns back to me and catches me staring, I quickly avert my gaze. "No matter how many times you Trip," he says, "there's still an element of stage fright that never goes away."

"So, it's a performance, then?"

He shrugs. "It helps to look at it that way."

My fingers pick at the sash on my robe, trying to calm some of my nerves over wrecking the party and alienating the very people I need to rely on tomorrow. But it's no use, regret has taken its hold. "Any idea who my partner will be—or even where I'm going?" I ask, my voice landing just short of pleading.

Braxton is quick to shake his head. "That's a bit above my paygrade," he says.

"Do you miss it?" I ask. "Tripping, I mean?"

He shoots me a curious look. "I still Trip," he says, surprising me with his answer. "I go wherever Arthur needs me." He shrugs. "We all do."

I take a moment to absorb that, then indulge in a fleeting fantasy of us traveling together someday—maybe to a party at the Royal Opera House, hosted by Marie Antoinette. Aware of Braxton looking right at me, I turn my burning cheeks toward the flames.

"Listen—" He reaches toward me, his fingers sliding down the length of my sleeve. "I know you don't want to see me, but I've missed you. And I have something for you."

I lift my gaze to find his.

In his eyes, he carries the world.

In his hand, he holds a small, beautifully wrapped package.

"Happy birthday," he says.

71

I gape at the sight of Braxton standing before me, a small, wrapped gift in his hand, as my mind frantically scrambles through the days, wondering if he somehow mixed up the date.

For a place that's so focused on time, it's strange how easy it is to lose track to the point where I'd completely forgotten about my own birthday.

"It's after midnight." Braxton smiles. "You're officially eighteen now. Go ahead, open it."

With trembling hands, I loosen the ribbon and tear away the iridescent wrapping paper to reveal a small black velvet box underneath. I trace a finger over the lid, almost too afraid to open it, and having no idea what to think. Not only has Braxton remembered a day I've overlooked, but he's gone to the trouble of getting me a gift. And from the looks of this box, he clearly overspent.

"The gift is *inside* the box," he teases.

With a quick intake of breath, I flip the lid open and gasp.

"It's your talisman," he explains as I take in the sight. "Traditionally, it's a magickal object that serves as a focal point for intent—for getting what you want. In your case, I infused it with the energy of home. And by that, I mean Gray Wolf, your new home. Anyway, you should always have one with you when you Trip. It also helps if the talisman serves as a visual reminder of a moment from your past. Something to help you remember who you are, when you are, and, in your case I hope, that there's someone back at Gray Wolf waiting for you to return."

My throat swells hot and tight as I run a finger along the finely detailed charm. It's a small golden cage with a lapis moon, the color of Braxton's eyes, and a single star encrusted with diamonds, nestled inside. And right away, I realize it's us—a symbol for our lives inside this gilded cage, and the night of our first kiss under a waxing moon and a sky full of stars—the two of us tucked away inside an all-glass room,

"I designed it," Braxton says. "Then I asked one of the onsite artisans to make it." He steps forward. "May I?" He gestures toward the piece.

I sweep my hair over my shoulder, trying and failing to stifle an involuntary shudder at the nearness of him, the way his body presses toward mine, the brush of his fingers when he fastens the delicate gold chain at my neck.

"It's weird how no on saw fit to tell me I'd need something like this."

Braxton shrugs, positioning the charm to fall at the center of my chest. "You were on the fast track," he says. "They must've overlooked it in the rush to get you up to speed."

"Still," I say. "Makes me wonder what else they might've forgotten."

"You'll do fine," he assures me. "They wouldn't risk sending you if they didn't think you were ready."

My fingers curl around the charm, sliding it back and forth on the chain, as I contemplate what he just said. I really hope that he's right.

"Depending on where you go, you can wear it on a ribbon, or simply carry it in your pocket. All that really matters is that you always bring it with you."

Something about the way he looks at me makes my eyes spark with tears. This boy is truly looking out for me, and I'm so unused to being cared for like this, I ignore the admonishing voice in my head, tuck into his arms, and breathe in his warm heady scent. "Thank you," I tell him. "It's the most beautiful thing anyone's ever given me."

"Arthur's not big on remembering birthdays," Braxton says, the words whispered just north of my ear. "And I didn't want yours to go unnoticed. Also, as your friend, I feel invested in doing whatever it takes to see you safely returned. The talisman will help with that."

As my friend. Right.

The relationship status I've chosen for us that I'm seriously starting to regret.

"I'm sorry," I say, nuzzling deeper into his arms. "I'm sorry for telling you I wanted to be friends only to push you away for so long. Because, the truth is, I've missed you." I swallow hard, knowing I shouldn't have said it. And yet, is there really any point in denying it, when I knew it from the moment he stepped into my room?

The second it's out, Braxton is quick to untangle himself and take a step back. And when my eyes meet his, I'm left with no doubt that the month we spent apart hasn't impacted Braxton the same way it has me.

72

Oh God. Oh no. What have I done?

I have to save this. Find a way to rewind, and let him know, without a doubt, that—

A red hot flame of embarrassment streaks up my neck. And in a desperate bid to fill up the silence, a flurry of words rushes out of me so quickly, I'm not even sure where I'm going.

"What I meant to say is, I've um, I've missed our *friendship*. And spending time in your company. And…" My voice fades. I close my eyes and shake my head.

Spending time in your company? What the actual hell is wrong with me?

There's a hand-knotted antique Persian rug at my feet, and I'd give anything in this moment to sink right through the wool threads, tunnel deep into the earth, and never resurface.

But when I feel the tip of Braxton's index finger pressing against the underside of my chin, I open my eyes to find his beautiful face looming before me. And the way he looks at me, his gaze so warm, kind, and inviting, makes me wonder if I might've misread his earlier reaction.

"I've missed spending time with you, too," he says, voice gravelly and deep. "But I'm here now. In whatever capacity you want me."

Without another word, I pitch onto my toes, press my body to his, and kiss him in a way that reveals all the desire and yearning that's stored up inside me. Because a month without kissing Braxton felt like eternity.

And when he meets the kiss with a craving that surpasses my own, I draw him to my bed, where I pull him down alongside me and revel in the sheer luxury of being reunited with him, touching him, kissing him once again.

I kiss him on his forehead, his cheek, that irresistible bend in his nose, my body thrumming with all the wanting I've held back for so long. And while it's true what I said about missing him, while not a single day has passed without me longing for his touch, I'm also glad for the break. If for no other reason than it allowed me to prove I'm capable of making it here on my own.

Which means Braxton's not just some beautiful boy I kiss to get back at Elodie or ward away loneliness.

Braxton is the only boy I've ever truly wanted to be with.

Our lips push together—wild and breathless. The sort of deep, desperate, tongue searing kisses meant to make up for all the time that we lost.

He rolls onto me then, centering his body over mine, then lays siege to my mouth, my neck, the lobe of my ear. His lips leave a trail of sparks in their wake as I grasp hold of his shoulders and arch my body hard against his.

How many lonely nights did I lull myself to sleep imagining the playful scrape of his teeth at my neck, the heat of his fingers sweeping over my flesh? And I can tell by the urgent roll of his hips, the insistent brush of his thumbs as they skim along the bend of my waist, over my rib cage, before lingering at the curve of my breasts, that he feels exactly the same.

I dip my hands beneath his soft cashmere sweater, my palms skating along the inviting expanse of his skin, drawing a series of leisurely loops at his navel that sets his heart drumming so hard, I can feel it thrashing under his chest.

A deep groan sounds in his throat as we press our foreheads

together, drawing heated breaths into each other as though we are one. "Tasha," he gasps, sounding my name from lips that soon return to a crushing feverish grind against mine, before skimming their way down my throat. "You have no idea how I've missed you," he says.

Between the push and pull of his kiss and the sweet rhythmic circling of our hips, I don't ever want this to end. I only want more. More of us. More of him. But just as I start to unleash the sash on my robe, Braxton pulls my hand away and clasps it firmly in his.

"Tasha, wait. Just—" The words are ragged, conflicted, leaving me to wonder if this is about consent. Because I think I've made it perfectly clear that I am in full agreement with everything that's happening here.

My hands reach for his face, desperate to bring him back to me, but Braxton pulls away until he's sitting fully upright on my bed. "First, there's something I need to tell you," he says.

I nod, needing him to just say it already so we can pick up where we left off.

"You don't have to do this." His eyes bore into mine.

"But I want to," I whisper, blinking at him in confusion. "I want to be with you—" I reach for his hand, shameless in my desire for him. I want everything—all that I can take—all that he's willing to give. And in return—

He shakes his head, runs a hand through his hair. He's clearly upset about something, but I can't imagine what it could be. "Listen," he says. "Aside from your birthday, there's another reason I came here tonight." The warmth in his eyes swiftly dims, becoming a perfect match for his tone. "And I'm afraid I need to say it now, for the simple reason that you may not like what you hear."

73

I look at Braxton, needing to know what could possibly be so important that he stopped us just when things were really getting good.

"You don't have to Trip," he says. "You don't have to go tomorrow. You can stay right here."

It takes a moment to make the transition from an epic make-out session to the improbable words he just spoke. But once I do, I pull my robe tighter around me and flinch back against the headboard where I sit with my arms locked at my knees.

"What the heck does that even mean?" My voice is hoarse, the words coming so fast, they snag in my throat. "What was the point of all that hard work, or even being here at Gray Wolf, if I'm not going to Trip?" I study his face, perplexed as to why he'd even suggest such a thing. "I thought you wanted me to succeed."

"I do," he insists, but a shade has dropped over his eyes, obscuring the truth.

"I don't get it," I cry, all that pent-up passion now rerouted in an entirely different direction. "You know how hard I've worked—all the sacrifices I've made. For an entire month all I did was practice and study and…and now you're asking me to throw all that effort away?"

"That's not what I'm saying. It's—" he starts, but I'm too riled up to let him finish the thought.

"I mean, let's say I did follow your advice and refuse to Trip. How exactly do you think Arthur would react?"

Braxton's shoulders sag as he tilts his head up and stares at the swag of canopy hanging overhead. "My guess is he'd be extremely displeased."

"Then why are you suggesting I do something that will only put me in jeopardy? That night in the Moon Garden, you claimed it wasn't all bad here. In fact, I distinctly remember you using the word *spectacular* to describe life at Gray Wolf. So what's really going on? Why the sudden change of heart?"

He faces me then. Legs crossed, arms resting on his knees, he leans toward me and says, "Because once you Trip, you can never go back to who you were before."

I blink, knowing there must be more.

"You lose something in the process—a sort of naivete, or innocence, or—"

"Innocence?" I frown. "I'm here because I was found guilty, remember?"

"Not that kind of innocence," he says. "Look—there are things about Tripping that are spectacular, yes. But there's also a downside—a darker side—that you won't even notice until you're drawn so deep into Arthur's world, you can't find your way back."

Just like that, the shade has lifted, allowing a glimpse of what's really driving all this. Braxton doesn't just feel guilty for bringing me here—he feels guilty for the person he's become and all that he's done at Arthur's bequest.

But the redemption he's looking for is not mine to give. All I can do is try to relieve him of some of the blame where I'm concerned.

"I know about the stealing," I say.

Braxton's jaw clenches, his spine stiffens, though he's not nearly as surprised as I thought he would be.

"I basically made Elodie admit it, and it pretty much shut down the party."

"And how do you feel now that you know what Arthur really expects?"

I look toward the window, remembering what Mason said about my choice to hang out with Elodie: *Magic always comes with a price.*

He wasn't wrong. There was a price to the magic of hanging with her. Just like there's a price for Arthur supporting my mom while I live in captive luxury here at Gray Wolf.

To Braxton I say, "Honestly, the moral part of me, the part that clearly knows right from wrong, is equally indignant and horrified."

Braxton nods. "And the other part?"

I sigh, busy my hands with my hair, twisting it into a knot before letting it fall. "The other part questions if that's *actually* how I feel or if it's how I *think* I'm supposed to feel thanks to societal expectations and conditioning and…" I finish the thought with a shrug. "I guess I won't really know until I'm put to the test. Because honestly, everything that's happened so far feels like a fantasy, a fever dream, like it's not really real."

"I get how it feels that way," he says. "But Tripping and thieving comes with great risk. Everything you've done here has been leading to this. And you need to know what you're in for, because once you've agreed to it, there's no turning back." When he looks at me, his gaze is tinged by the residue of a thousand deceits he's performed for Arthur—including the taking of me.

I reach for him then, clasping his hands in mine, and we slide our fingers together until we're perfectly intertwined. "You once told me the deal was done the moment I laughed before my grave," I remind him.

He nods, though a flash of pain crosses his face.

"You also told me I needed to try to adapt to this new life."

His mouth presses into a thin, grim line.

"By choosing to Trip, that's what I'm doing. Look, my mom made a choice when she signed me into Arthur's care, and I made a choice when I agreed to come here. And the irony is, now that I've turned eighteen, I technically have the legal agency to leave, but I seriously doubt Arthur would let me. And even if he did, where would I go? Do you honestly think my mom would welcome me back if it meant the end of Arthur's monthly stipend and gifts?" I sigh. "It's an ugly truth, but there's no point denying it. It's as simple as that. So, if stealing from a bunch of rich people from the past is the price I have to pay to ensure my mom is taken care of, then I guess I'm prepared to accept that."

Braxton wears a sad expression that leaves his lids heavy, his mouth weighted. "I get it," he says. "I have a similar story. Most of us do. It's the only way to make peace with what's required of us."

"And besides," I say. "We're stealing from nobles, right?"

Tentatively, Braxton nods, but his fingers begin to loosen on mine.

"Well, aren't those same nobles stealing from the peasants?"

Braxton lets go of my hands and scratches his chin. There's an uneasy edge in his voice when he says, "I'm not sure I get—"

"Aren't they essentially stealing the peasants' labor in order to build and support their own wealth?" I can feel my pulse racing, but that's probably because I'm getting fired up. "I mean, those poor people live in squalor, with no chance of improving their circumstance. While the rich nobles were born into it— they didn't earn anything they have. It's an unfair system, and when I think about it like that, it's hard to feel bad about taking from them."

Braxton releases an audible sigh. "You're not wrong," he

says. "But I just—"

"Look," I cut in, needing for him to hear me, "despite the moral cost of being here, I can't pretend I don't like the person I've become since I arrived. For the first time in a long time, I'm excelling at something. And it's been exciting to discover I have a talent for the sort of things I once would've never considered. The girl you met at Arcana was an apathetic failure, but I'm not that girl anymore."

I hadn't planned on saying all that, and the sudden outpouring has left me with a bit of a tremor in my belly. My gaze lands on Braxton's, hoping he'll understand. And if not, I'll just keep going until he does.

"I never saw you that way," Braxton says. "I—"

"All I'm asking is that you support me," I cut in. "As for everything else, I need to navigate that on my own."

"Tasha, I'm *always* rooting for you." Braxton reaches for me again, his fingers squeezing mine until I can feel the curved base of the gold ring that he wears pushing into my flesh. "I just don't want you to feel compelled to do something you don't want to just because Arthur asks it of you."

"I can hold my own," I tell him, hoping I sound more confident than I feel.

His lips tick up at the sides, but the burden remains in the slope of his shoulders, the weightiness of his being. Hoping to ease his worry, if only for a moment, I pull him closer until my mouth covers his.

The kiss is tender and deep, but before it can really take hold, Braxton is drawing away. "I need to go, and you need to rest." He leaves me with one final sweet press of his lips, then stands to leave.

"Braxton—" I rush to the door before he can leave and pull him back to me. "Thanks," I say. "For remembering my birthday, and the talisman, and...everything."

I rise onto my toes, kiss him on the place where his nose hits a bend, then open the door and watch him go.

When he disappears around the corner, I'm about to duck back inside, when I glance down the hall toward Elodie's room, just in time to see Jago slinking out with his hair disheveled and a satisfied grin on his face.

Looks like Elodie made good on her promise.

74

Apparently, on First Trip day, the usual schedule does not apply.

After I wake to the sound of Beethoven's "Fifth Symphony," a message appears on my slab that a breakfast tray is on the way. When I'm finished eating, I'm to shower and dress—though avoiding the use of scented products or makeup—then head to the front hall, where an escort will be waiting.

A moment later, there's a knock at my door, and I'd be lying if I said I wasn't hoping to find Braxton on the other side, delivering a tray heaped with coffee and croissants I probably won't eat, partly because my stomach's a jumble of nerves, but mostly because my fear of chamber pots runs deep.

Instead, I'm greeted by a boy who I guess is around my age. He has a sharp beak of a face and a deeply hooded gaze that studiously avoids meeting mine.

"Thank you," I say, relieving him of the tray. "I can take it from here." As I watch him nod and scurry off, I can't help but think about all the others like him who quietly move about Gray Wolf—cleaning rooms, delivering dry-cleaning, necessities, and food—all without uttering so much as a single word no matter how much I try to engage them. Where do they come from? What are their backgrounds? Were they brought here to work as domestic staff? Or is this what happens to the Yellows who fail?

As Braxton once told me: *No one is ever sent home for failing.*

If that's the case, then is that where they end up? Because the thought of being forced to clean up after Elodie is enough to harden my resolve to slay this day, no matter the cost.

As promised, there's an electric cart and driver waiting downstairs, and after cruising through numerous hallways and crossing several checkpoints that require us to show our slabs and prove our identities, we arrive at an enormous room that reminds me of the sort of top secret command center you might see in a big budget sci-fi movie.

The room is divided by a large floor-to-ceiling window. On one side, a massive computer panel blinks and hums, as a buzz of Gray Wolf employees hover around. On the other is what can only be described as a launchpad.

It's like getting an up-close look at the future's future.

Though he's hardly the largest figure in the room, Arthur is the first person I see. I guess because he seems to occupy the most space, exhibited by the way the entire room revolves around him. Then again, he is the final word in what happens in this place.

When he sees me, he waves me over, and the crowd that surrounds him quickly disperses. "How are you feeling?" he asks. "Are you well rested, fed?"

I nod to indicate that I'm both those things.

"I know you're probably nervous," he says. "But not to worry, you're in good hands. Jago's first Trip was fairly recently, so he'll understand what you're going through. And of course, Elodie's completed numerous Trips."

Elodie? A wave of nausea rolls through me. My head goes into a spin. I can't think of a worse traveling companion, especially after I blew up her party. And considering how Jago hooked up with Elodie last night, it's obvious where his loyalties will lie.

"Point is," Arthur continues, "you've got two great partners.

Just follow their lead, and all will be well."

I nod. It's the best I can do. Mostly because I'm so nervous, I don't trust my own voice.

"Just before launch," he continues, "it's customary for Roxane to brief you on the list of Gets."

"Gets?" I say, not entirely sure what he means, but Arthur just waves it away.

"There's nothing specific this time, so don't worry about that. For you, I have something much different in mind. Something the others know nothing about."

75

I stare at Arthur, the words he just spoke swirling around in my head.

Something the others know nothing about.

I tell myself it could be harmless, but the force of his tone has me filled with a sense of deeply rooted foreboding.

"It's imperative you keep the task to yourself," Arthur says, studying me so intently, I struggle to breathe. "At first, you may need to play along so as not to raise Elodie's and Jago's suspicions. But, at some point, I expect you to break away long enough to complete your mission on your own, understand?"

I shake my head. "Honestly," I say, "I'm feeling a little lost here."

Arthur's gaze narrows, the fine lines around his mouth deepening in a way that makes my palms go all clammy. "You'll find the instructions secured in the pocket of your gown. It's a bit of a puzzle, I admit. But that's where your skills come in, those both innate and learned."

"Did Jago have to do this?" I ask before I can stop myself.

Arthur regards me for a long, steady beat, and I feel myself shrinking under the intensity. "No," he says. "But then, you have something special that Jago lacks, and I wouldn't consider putting you to the task if I wasn't convinced of your ability to see it through."

I shift my weight nervously, needing Arthur to finally reveal this special quality only he can see. I'd nearly convinced myself that all the stuff about me being the one who would help him achieve his greatest ambition was a bunch of made-up nonsense. But now I can see he's entirely serious. And while it's nice to know that the legendary Arthur Blackstone believes in me, I'm still not sure that it's warranted. Despite the handful of wins I've scored in this place, my swordcraft, language, and equestrian skills have proved marginal at best.

I want to tell him he's wrong about me, but before I can even open my mouth, Arthur says, "Make no mistake, Natasha. For you, this is no ordinary exam. How you perform on this Trip will determine everything that comes your way next. My only expectation is that you succeed. Nothing more, and certainly nothing less."

I swallow past the lump in my throat.

"Now," he says. "Are you ready?" The way he stands before me, like a sprinter at the starting block ready for the pistol to sound, it's clear he's ready for us both to move on.

Wordlessly, I nod, trying to appear more confident than I feel.

He claps a hand on my shoulder and says, "Roxane will take you from here."

I turn to find a woman, probably somewhere in her early thirties, clutching a clipboard. Her straight blond hair hangs just past her shoulders, and she has the sort of sleek polished sheen of a person who grew up with horses, tennis lessons, and yacht parties—a world rife with power and privilege. But her blue eyes are warm and friendly, and her smile instantly puts me at ease.

She starts to lead me away when Arthur calls, "And Natasha—"

I glance back over my shoulder.

"Bon voyage."

He grins in a way that lights up his whole face. And for a fleeting moment, I get a glimpse of the young boy he once was. The one who, one long ago night, looked out at a sky full of stars, said, *What if?* And then actually went looking for answers.

A moment later, he's turned away, and a team of people descend, all clamoring for his attention.

76

Roxane introduces herself and offers her hand. "You must be Natasha," she says. "I'll be directing this particular Trip."

"Directing?" I walk alongside her. The hall is busy, but no one pays any real notice. "You mean like, a movie?" My head fills with images of cameras, and people snapping clapperboards as they call: *Action!* Or, *Cut!*

Roxane laughs. "Well, I did graduate from film school, but this is a bit different, as you'll soon see."

After walking a few silent beats, she turns to me. "You nervous?" she asks.

I start to pretend that I'm not, but figuring she'll easily spot the lie, I say, "Extremely."

"That's perfectly normal," she assures me. "I remember when I was in your shoes, or should I say, in your sweatshirt. My knees were literally shaking with fear."

"You were a Yellow?"

She peers at me sideways. "Right before I became a Blue."

"And you still managed to go on to film school?"

"When it was time for me to retire, Arthur paid for my education. And, since opportunities for female directors are so scarce, I returned to Gray Wolf."

I guess there are other prospects here, outside of being a maid. I can literally feel a wave of relief rolling through me.

"But long before any of that could happen," she continues,

"I had to prove myself. Like you, I didn't have the best start in life. But when I found myself here, I had nothing to lose. So, I embraced the experience and never looked back. This is a place where dreams can come true, as long as you're willing to let go of the old idea of who you think you are and remain open to the person you can become."

She's paraphrasing the Hamlet quote that popped up on my slab the other day: *We know what we are, but know not what we may be.* And the way she stands before me, her warm blue gaze beginning to cool, I get the distinct feeling that as kind as she appears, it would be a terrible mistake to get on her bad side.

She hands me over to Charlotte, who fits me into a gown and shoes before escorting me into another room where my face is powdered, my lips rouged, and my hair twisted and pulled into an elaborate updo. Once the primping is finished, I'm positioned before a mirror, and my eyes fill with a vision of me I don't easily recognize—a me that belongs to another place and time.

My gown is made of a deep blue silk, with a daringly low neckline, a cinched bodice, fitted three-quarter-length sleeves, a long voluminous skirt, and a ridiculous array of bows and lace that serve as more than just decoration; they also make for good hiding places. Strapped to my leg is a small holster that holds the dagger I pray I won't need.

For the last month, I've grown accustomed to the feel of corsets, hoops, cage crinolines, panniers, silk stockings held up by ribbons and ruffled garters, and all the other indignities women were forced to suffer in the pursuit of fashion, beauty, desirability, and upward mobility.

Back then they wore cages to make their bottom halves look enormous. Today we wear Spanx to suck it all in. The pursuit of an impossible aesthetic never ends.

Meanwhile, men just went from short pants to long pants.

But this dress, paired with the towering hair and makeup—

well, it reminds me of how I felt wearing the black dress and designer heels when Elodie gave me a makeover. Back then, gazing into that window, I was looking at an aspirational future version of me. Today, I gaze into a mirror that reflects a vision from a past that was never mine to claim—until now.

"What do you think?" Charlotte asks.

"I like it," I tell her, and when I sneak another look at myself, I realize it's true. "I feel like I'm in a movie." I laugh, but she doesn't return it. Instead, she points to my shoes.

"Not custom." She shrugs. "But soon. And your talisman?"

"Oh!" I rush toward my bag, hardly able to believe I'd nearly forgotten.

When I show her the necklace Braxton designed, she gently rolls it over her palm. "It's beautiful," she says, then goes about removing the gold chain it came with and attaching a velvet ribbon instead. "This is more suitable for the when you are visiting," she explains as she arranges the charm at my neck.

She moves aside, allowing me to take in my reflection again. The blue of the lapis moon manages to pair beautifully with the rich blue hue of my dress. I take it as a good omen and declare myself ready.

"Good luck, Natasha." Charlotte grasps both my hands, and even though she's usually friendly, the sudden burst of warmth still comes as a surprise.

"*Merci beaucoup*," I reply. Having spent the last four weeks working on my accent, I'm hoping I nailed it.

She grins, gestures toward the door, and I try not to dwell on the troubling glint that flashed in her gaze as I make my way out.

77

E lodie is there.

Jago too.

The two of them dressed in period costume and looking like the natural-born king and queen of every kingdom that ever was or ever will be.

But it's Braxton who claims my attention.

His head is lowered in deep conversation with Hawke, Keane, and Roxane, but the moment I arrive, he must sense my presence, because he immediately looks up and his gaze lands on mine. I bow my head and dip into the curtsy I've also been practicing, and he nods and bows in return.

"How do you feel?" Jago asks. "Ready, excited, like you want to hurl your guts out?"

Elodie elbows him in the side. *Hurl your guts out* isn't the kind of thing one says in Arthur's vicinity.

Still, it makes me laugh. And besides, a quick look behind the glass where Arthur currently sits tells me he has other, more important things to occupy his time.

"How about all of the above?"

Jago grins. "It's a perfect summation of how I felt before my first Trip. You do look completely enchanting, though, if I'm allowed to say so?" He shoots a quick glance at Elodie, who groans and runs a critical gaze from my hair to my shoes before coming to rest at my neck.

"I don't remember seeing this in Wardrobe." She reaches toward the talisman, but I stop her from making contact.

"It was a gift." I cradle it protectively between my fingers.

Her gaze shifts between the talisman and me. "A moon and star in a tiny golden cage," she says, her tongue dripping acid. "That's so…adorbs." Her gaze burns on mine, and I'm about to deliver a biting reply, but luckily, Roxane calls me away just in time. I can't afford to take Elodie's bait. Not today.

"Ready for the big reveal?" Roxane pulls an envelope from a folder and hands it to me.

I slip a finger under the red wax seal bearing the Gray Wolf logo and retrieve a square of paper made of the same card stock my first day's schedule was printed on before I was entrusted with a slab. The instructions are as follows:

Your presence is requested!

When: 25-26 February 1745
Where: Palace of Versailles: The Hall of Mirrors
What: The Yew Ball
Why: Celebrating the marriage of Dauphin Louis to Maria Teresa Rafaela of Spain

What is not committed to print are the verbal instructions that we are expected to freely filch from the revelers whatever we deem worthy of taking that's still small enough to smuggle out. Normally, I'm told, there's an actual Get in mind, but considering how this Trip is meant to serve as my final exam in procurement, Arthur wants to see how I handle myself in a real-time experience.

While I give Roxanne my full attention, pretending to soak in every word, my right hand creeps into the pocket where Arthur has left me my own secret set of instructions. My fingers find the edges of two stiff bits of paper.

"Everything clear?" Roxane asks. Not satisfied with a nod, she makes me recite everything I just read.

Luckily, I have a pretty decent memory, so after reciting the details, I add a bit more in a shameless effort to impress her. "It's a party thrown by King Louis the Fifteenth," I say. "It marks the start of his longtime love affair with the future Marquise de Pompadour." Just voicing the words out loud, knowing I'll soon be mingling among that glittering crowd, sends a swarm of prickling chills over my skin.

"Looks like someone's been studying," Roxane quips, though the slight curl of her lips tells me she's pleased. "As I'm sure you know, the Yew Ball is a masked ball." She gestures for Keane to fit an elaborate jeweled mask onto my face.

Outside, it looks like any other fancy masquerade-style mask. Inside, it's lined with some sort of silicone type substance that molds to my features, forming a skintight seal.

"The mask enables you to skip the contacts, since the directions to the portal are embedded inside the mask itself."

"Just don't lose it," Keane says, stepping away to examine the fit.

I remember wearing the contacts during one of the constructs last week when I found myself in a hologram of the Vienna opera house. Despite being surprisingly thin, they still took some getting used to. So I'm glad to forgo them on my first real Trip.

When I'm ready, I join Elodie and Jago on the platform that I've come to think of as the launchpad.

"You have three hours," Roxane says. "That's how long the portal remains open. If you need to leave sooner, Elodie has the clicker."

I look at Elodie, who points to her left earring. Since the device needs to blend into the time period and match the look of whoever's in charge, it's made to look different each time. Still, my stomach sinks at the thought of Elodie being given ultimate control of whether I make it back safely.

"That's three hours," Roxane repeats, as though I could possibly forget. "If you're late…" She pauses. "Well, let's put it this way—don't be." The look that follows is grim. And while it accurately conveys the seriousness of the threat behind her words, I'm annoyed by her refusal to speak the more alarming truth: *if I'm late, I'll be stuck in 1745 forever.*

"Any questions?" she asks.

I shake my head, swallow past a dry lump in my throat.

"Good. And don't worry, you're going to be fine!" Roxane leaves me with an enthusiastic thumbs-up, then she and Keane head for the control room as a thick glass shield rises around Elodie, Jago, and me.

"Ready?" Elodie grasps hold of my hand, as Jago takes the other.

I've spent the last four weeks fully immersed in my studies.

I've forgone weekends at the Gray Wolf spa—haven't so much as peeked at the indoor pool, never mind Halcyon, the onsite nightclub everyone raves about—all in an effort to propel myself up the color wheel.

And now I'm here. Facing the final exam that will ultimately determine whether or not I make Blue.

Of course, I'm not ready.

Not even close.

I can't possibly master a new language and seamlessly blend into a culture totally foreign to my own in just the course of one month.

My stomach plunges to my knees. My heart makes the leap to my throat. Frantically, I look around, searching for Braxton, needing to see his face one last time before I go.

I find him still settled behind the glass in the control room.

And though I can't easily determine his expression, I watch as his finger taps at his chest, reminding me of his gift. Reminding me of who I am, when I am, and the celebration that awaits my return.

I gaze down, set my focus on the blue moon, the glittering star.

"First thing that'll happen," Elodie says. "The lights will begin to flicker and the ground will shake. Once the wind starts, whatever you do, do *not* let go of our hands."

I'm reminded of the tremor I experienced during my lunch with Arthur, when I was sure another Unraveling was underway, but all it really meant was that someone at Gray Wolf was heading out on a Trip. And yet, it still strikes me as strange that Tripping and the Unraveling share the same effects.

Elodie's fingers squeeze mine. I squeeze back. And the next thing I know, my head fills with the scent of sulphur as a huge cloud of vapor billows and expands all around us and a thunderous buzz explodes throughout the room.

With Jago's hand clasped in mine, and Elodie's fingernails digging into my palm, I watch with wide, frightened eyes as a flash of dazzling white light zooms toward the gaseous cloud, freezes on contact, and instantly morphs into a glimmering doorway.

Before I can even make sense of the miracle unfolding before me, the wall drops, gravity fails, we lift high off our heels, and a huge rush of wind propels us through the portal and rockets us right out of this time and back into another.

78

As I gaze around the Hall of Mirrors, I actually pinch myself to make sure I'm not dreaming.

It's so strange to think that my first visit is not as a ticket holder, but rather as a time traveling party crasher to one of Versailles' most famous events.

I mean, just one month ago, I was hanging out at the mall, trying on sunglasses I couldn't afford. And now, I'm in eighteenth-century France, dressed in a resplendent gown, and literally walking through history.

Even though it's happening to me, it's still hard to imagine.

Once I moved past the initial fright, the journey was over in a matter of seconds. And I'm left struck by the irony that it was easier to travel back two hundred seventy-five years in time than it was to cross the violent waters to get to the academy.

Aside from being short of breath and a bit dehydrated (driven by the horror of having to pee in a chamber pot, I've barely had so much as a sip of water all day), the three of us arrive looking as polished and pristine as we did when we left.

"What now?" I run a nervous hand down the voluminous skirt of my dress while taking in the sheer splendor of the space—the massive candelabras and glimmering chandeliers dripping from the painted dome ceiling, the golden sculptures and marble columns lining the walls—one side covered in mirrors, the other with arched windows that overlook the magnificent gardens beyond.

I remember reading how those mirrors this hall is known for came at a steep cost. At the time, such mirrors were made only in Venice, and it's said that just after these were completed, the craftsmen were ordered to be assassinated for the crime of giving away their trade secrets.

The gate that marks the entry to the palace is covered in gold. In just four and a half decades from now, it'll be destroyed in the French Revolution. Nearly three centuries later, it will cost millions to see it restored.

There's a part of me that needs to warn these people of all the turbulence yet to come. That their extravagant lives and disregard for the well-being of others will ultimately lead to their downfall. But it's not my place to interfere and risk changing the course of history.

Still, as I move to join the party that's now in full swing, I can't help but think: *what has my life even become?*

Together, Elodie, Jago, and I shoulder through the throng. Some people are in costume, others in masks and gowns. Though one thing is certain, this palace is the epitome of opulence, with no expense spared on design. And for one fleeting moment, I can't help but think how much Mason would love being here by my side.

"Is that the king?" I gesture toward a man dressed as a yew tree at the other side of the room.

Elodie turns to me. "King Louis is interested in only one thing at the moment," she says, voice filled with scorn. "And her name is Jeanne Antoinette Poison, who, unbeknownst to her, in September of this same year will be officially presented to the court as Madame de Pompadour. Which means it's not our place to get in the way of their affair and risk changing the course of history. Which also means Louis is strictly off-limits. He is merely the host of this party. He is not the reason for this Trip."

I stare at her in disbelief. She makes it sound like I was out to seduce King Louis when all I wanted was to catch a glimpse of a historical royal figure. Still, the need to stay in character requires me to keep my composure.

"You do understand why you're here?" Elodie asks.

I roll my eyes in return. Though the truth is, now that I'm on Palace grounds, the twin demons of stealing from these people, and possibly facing the consequences of getting caught, have become startlingly real. And I find myself desperately craving some reassurance that not only is this actually achievable, but that it's been done multiple times, without fail.

That the train of history continues.

That these rich nobles barely even notice their missing jewels.

That no one gets hurt.

Elodie leans in, takes my hand in hers, and squeezes so tightly, her nails dig into my skin. "Our job is to mingle, blend, flirt if you must, party if you will, pilfer as much as you can, but to never break character and never get caught because, I assure you, we will not bail you out."

Her casual way of describing an illegal act that's commonly known as grand theft makes me realize that procuring jewels for Arthur comes as easily and guiltlessly to her as it was to procure me.

She releases my hand, tugs the bodice of her lavender gown to expose even more of her chest, then turns on her heel and swipes a flute of champagne straight out of a handsome young gentleman's hand. As she scurries away, she pauses long enough to toss a flirtatious grin over her shoulder that encourages the boy to dash off in pursuit. And I'm amazed at how watching her operate in the Hall of Mirrors isn't so different from watching the way she dominated the hallways of high school.

"That sort of behavior works only at a masquerade." Jago

nods after Elodie without the slightest hint of jealousy. "And even then, she's pushing it. But you know Elodie. By the end of the night, she'll have claimed all his jewels, if not his virginity."

I stare after them, take another glance around a room filled with people happily taking full advantage of the sort of anonymity that only comes from wearing a mask. "Not sure you'll find a single virgin in this place," I say.

"Present company included?" Jago leers suggestively, but he does it in such an exaggerated way, I know he's not serious.

"Is that a confession?" I ask, then watch as he throws his head back and breaks into an uproarious laugh.

"Try to enjoy yourself," he whispers, angling his lips to my ear. "It's rare you get to attend the same event twice. It happens, but Arthur would rather our faces not become too familiar and risk triggering a déjà vu, unless it's to his advantage, of course."

"Déjà vu?" It's not that I'm unfamiliar with the term, I've just always thought of it as having the *feeling* of repeating an experience. The possibility of actually reliving a moment more than once never occurred to me.

"Every moment has already been lived," Jago says. "And continues to be lived. Each choice you make causes your life to shoot off in a new direction. But at the moment of decision, all those varying choices and directions are viable—those roads are already paved. The only question is, which road will you take?"

"How do you know all this?" I stare at his handsome masked face, my head struggling to grasp the deeper implication of his words.

"People always underestimate me because of my good looks and charm, but I'm actually quite studied." He surveys the crowd. "Also, a word of warning, the longer you stay, the easier it is to lose track—not just of time, but also of yourself. They don't call it Tripping for nothing." He pulls away then, and though he grins at that last part, he's clearly not joking. "Your talisman is more than just a good luck charm. When your memory fades, it's the only thing left that links you to home."

When my memory fades? What does that even mean?

Braxton said something about using the talisman to remember who and when I am, but I figured he was just exaggerating. But if what Jago says is true, then why did no one see fit to mention that between the classes in equestrian and swordcraft?

"But what about the mask?" I ask. "Won't it remind me?"

"Technology can fail." Jago leans in, kisses the air just north of my cheek, and merges so seamlessly into the crowd, I instantly lose sight of him.

79

It's not until I'm left standing on my own that I realize Elodie and Jago have effectively ditched me. And here I was worried about finding a way to sneak away from them.

I inhale a steadying breath and take a quick survey of the room. What I see leaves me reeling with nerves. The mere thought of navigating this place on my own fills me with the same sort of panic I felt when Elodie ditched me at Arcana. Only difference is, back then I was fully capable of booking a ride home. Here, in 1745 Versailles, I'm pretty much stuck until Elodie decides we're done, or the portal closes, whichever comes first.

I press a hand to the tightly cinched bodice of my dress and try to remind myself that no one here gives two shits about me. To them, I'm just another anonymous masked face among the glittering masses. So, I may as well make a loop around the room and set my focus on what I was sent here to do.

I've barely taken more than a handful of steps when I spot a woman, probably a decade older than me, teetering precariously just a few feet away. Judging by the sway of her heels, and the way her wig sort of wobbles unsteadily on her head, that half empty champagne flute she holds isn't her first.

She's also dripping in so many jewels, there's a good chance she won't even notice if I should happen to relieve her of a few.

I'm in the process of making my first pass to get a better

idea of which pieces to target when she suddenly grasps hold of my arm, and speaks to me in a flurry of French. The two words I manage to catch are: "…votre amulette!" With a shaky hand, she reaches for my talisman. "Where did you find such a treasure? I must have one!" She pulls me toward her, forcing me to place a hand on her shoulder to keep from falling over.

Since we're already in this ridiculously intimate position, I seize the moment to nick a brooch from her gown and a jeweled clip right out of her hair.

"It was a gift. From an admirer," I say, slipping the trinkets into one of the many hidden pockets sewn into my dress, hoping my attempt to speak French is good enough to carry me through.

"Why, it's divine!" she gushes. "You must connect me with your—"

Before she can finish, I've disentangled myself. "You are too kind," I tell her.

"But I really must go!"

I spin on my heels and push into the crowd, hardly able to believe what I've just done. Surely it can't be that easy? Surely someone's bound to come after me.

I sneak a glance over my shoulder, but there are so many people, the woman is now lost among them. And I'm halfway down the hall before I realize I'm still clutching the bracelet I also swiped from her wrist as I was leaving.

From behind my mask, I survey the crowd. When I'm sure no one's looking, I tuck it into a hidden seam in my sleeve where the silk meets the lace.

Only then am I able to breathe at a more normal rate.

There's a terrace off to the right, and I make a beeline straight for it. It's not until I lean against the stone balustrade that the full realization of what I just did comes crashing down on my head.

I committed a crime.

A crime that, if caught, could see me locked up or possibly even killed.

And though part of me is relieved to have gotten away with it and put it behind me, the other part is horrified by just how easy it was to leap across the border of everything I once thought I was, only to land on this new, shadier version of the person I've allowed myself to become.

And yet, as guilty as I feel, there's something about being here, on this night, in this dress, immersed in this long-ago version of Versailles, that somehow helps dull the sting of the crime.

Maybe it's because it feels more like an elaborate stage play than anything real. And maybe that's how the other Trippers make peace with what we do. Maybe the surreal, almost dreamlike quality of these Trips makes it easier to ignore the darker moral implications of the acts we commit on Arthur's behalf.

Besides, now, after working so hard to make it this far, there's really no way to turn back.

Above me, the sky glimmers with stars, and I steal a moment to close my eyes, lift my face, and fill my lungs with a deep inhale of crisp, cool eighteenth-century night.

Once I'm feeling more centered, I slip my fingers into my pocket and search for the clue Arthur promised.

80

My fingers reach around inside my pocket, pushing against the seams, sure I must've missed something.

I check it again, and all the others as well. But these two tarot cards are all that I find.

The Death card and the Hermit card—both from the same sort of vintage deck my father once had.

I study the cards, front and back, looking for a hand-scrawled instruction, message, or clue of some kind, until I finally realize the cards *are* the clue—the puzzle Arthur has tasked me to solve.

With no clear instruction or end goal in mind, the task is impossible. I mean, what exactly does he expect me to find?

I'm tempted to give up on the spot, but the idea of returning to Gray Wolf as a failure, sentenced to scrub Elodie's toilets forever, is all the incentive I need to stay focused.

Use all your skills, Arthur said. *Those both innate and learned.*

What skills? I mean, it's not like I'm some sort of tarot card reading expert, or—

Just then, a flash of memory pops into my head. A hazy vision of my dad leaning over a similar deck races across the screen in my brain. His head bent toward mine, the bottom ring of his circular tattoo peeking out from beneath his rolled-up sleeve, when he said:

It's never about the first glance. It's always about the second

look, the third, and all those that follow. Look deeper—gather all
the elements, and put them together…

Gather all the elements!

By that, he meant the card's numerology, along with the classical elements they represent, such as earth, air, fire, water…

I study the image of the Hermit, trying to remember everything my dad taught me. It's ruled by Earth, and though these ancient cards aren't numbered in the way modern decks are, the journey of the tarot still follows a particular order—a sort of hero's journey meant to imitate the stages of life. And, since numerology mainly deals with single digits, that means the Hermit, being the ninth card in the Major Arcana, shares a numerological link to the Moon card, which is the eighteenth card, since $1 + 8 = 9$.

Though the Death card is governed by Water, and as the thirteenth card in the journey, its digits reduce to four, which is the card of the Emperor.

The Emperor!

My pulse quickens as I take in the splendid royal gardens splayed out before me. With its endless collection of elaborate fountains and pools, it's a literal translation of water and earth. And, since Arthur never does anything randomly, I'm guessing the object he wants me to find—some rare trinket or jewel, something small enough to be smuggled out—must be hidden somewhere within this series of groves that stretch on for miles.

From where I stand now, it's such an impossible task, I'm left to wonder if I'm being set up to fail.

But I can't afford to think like that, can't allow myself to go down that path. I can do this—I *have* to do this. I just need to delve deeper.

With the cards pinched tightly between my fingers, I study the gardens again, straining to remember more details from that long-ago day with my dad. I sift through muddled fragments of memory in search of the crucial threads I desperately need, while also trying to suppress my budding suspicion of why he saw fit to teach me those things in the first place. It's like he knew someday this would happen...

I shake my head, determined to focus on the task at hand. There must be more elements—something I've forgotten...

Let's see, numerology, the classical elements, and...and *astrology*, of course! The Hermit card is linked to—

From somewhere behind me, the beat of heavy footsteps grows near—an ominous thud of thick-soled boots meeting stone that's soon followed by a firm set of fingers seizing my arm.

In a split second, my knees fold out from under me.

The bitter tang of fear spreads across my tongue as I frantically work to silence the scream threatening to blow up my throat.

I need to stay calm.

Need to do whatever it takes to keep my cool and crank up the charm.

But it's no use.

This is it.

My first Trip and I've already been caught.

81

The grip on my arm tightens, and for one, terrible, free-falling moment, I'm sure that I'm done, headed for prison, the guillotine, or some other punishment I can't even fathom.

With my heart practically pounding its way out of my chest, I'm about to let loose on my accuser, pull my dagger, do whatever it takes, when a charming voice says, "My darling, where have you been?"

My first thought is one of surprise that Braxton is here. He's the only one who ever calls me that. Also, the words are spoken in English. But when I turn, I find myself gazing up at a tall, masked boy dressed in a resplendent costume with so many medals secured to his jacket, I wonder if he's military, a royal, or both.

"I'm sure you have me confused with someone else." I start to pull away, but his grip remains firm.

"Forgive me," he says. Seeing my discomfort, he's quick to release me and lift both his hands. "I didn't mean to frighten. Rather, from the first moment I saw you, I found you so captivating, I knew I had to speak with you at once. And I am happy to see I am not proven wrong."

My breath begins to settle. My pulse slows to a normal beat. He's not accusing me of thievery—this is merely an eighteenth-century attempt at a hookup. And, since this is definitely something that wasn't covered in my lessons at Gray Wolf, I must admit, I'm curious to see how it plays out.

"Are you always so forward?" I ask.

"I find it's the quickest, surest path to getting what I want." He grins in such a disarming way, I find myself instantly at ease. When the eyes behind the mask drop to the tarot cards in my hand, I quickly slip them back into my pocket.

The boy moves to stand beside me and gestures toward the night sky. "Do you ever wonder who else might be looking at that same moon—from somewhere clear across the world?"

Or even clear across the centuries. I crane my neck back and take in a star-studded sky adorned by a glowing half-moon.

The moon!

If Arthur is making me search for clues in the tarot, then is it possible this particular moon phase plays a part?

On the surface, it's a ridiculous stretch, but I'm hardly in a position to rule anything out. I mean, why this palace, on this exact night, when there were loads of other large gatherings that took place in Versailles at various times?

My mind scrambles to collect whatever moon trivia I might've absorbed through the years. Something more than just Mason and me obsessing over our monthly horoscopes.

The half-moon is half lit by the sun; half hidden in shadow. It's related to life and death—the rhythm of....*time!*

The Death card is ruled by the moon, and the Hermit card is linked to the moon. It's all got to mean something, but what?

"Tell me," the boy says, drawing me away from my thoughts and back to him, "are you enjoying the ball?"

When I turn to face him, my mind grows so hazy, I have the strangest sensation of looking at him through a very long lens that reaches far across time. I shake my head, try to clear the fog away, then set my focus again.

I was thinking about something before he arrived. Something urgent, hugely important, but I can no longer recall what it was.

I return to the boy, wondering what he might look like under that mask. He's taller than me, not quite six feet, but in the vicinity, and he has the broad shoulders and solid build of someone who's been trained for life on a battlefield. Though the mask obscures half his face, from what I can tell, his nose appears prominent, but he has the sort of strong jaw and square chin that are well able to support it.

I'm not sure if it's the corset restricting my ability to breathe or the growing suspicion that I'm being pursued by someone I might've read about in a history book (had I bothered to read one of my history textbooks), but I'm beginning to understand why so many women were prone to fainting in previous centuries, because I'm starting to feel really woozy.

"The ball?" he repeats, catching me in the act of studying his lips, which are wide and generous and quick with a smile.

"Oh, I'm quite enjoying it," I say, surprised by the ease in which I reply when I'm not actually sure if it's true.

I mean, how did I even get here? Why am I standing on a terrace back in eighteenth-century France?

Am I dreaming? Like, the watch-me-fly sort of lucid dreaming I sometimes do?

Or is this actually real? Or maybe even one of Arthur's holograms?

My mind is so blurry, it's impossible to tell.

My gaze runs the length of the boy, coming to rest on the jeweled ring he wears on his right hand, then farther down to his polished black boots.

"Where are you from?" he asks.

The question catches me off guard. There must be a right way to answer, but I have no idea what that is.

He leans closer, tilts his head in study. "Your accent," he says. "I'm unable to place it."

I gulp. Mentally flounder about for a suitable reply. In the end, I default to smiling coyly. "Anonymous, remember?" I gesture toward my mask.

When he laughs, I'm quick to join in. It's the right choice to make, but I have no idea why.

When he suggests we go back inside and grab some champagne, I can't think of a single reason to refuse.

82

After a glass or two of champagne and a few twirls around the dance floor, the two of us retreat to our own darkened corner.

Aside from the fact that his breath is a thousand times better than just about everyone here, and that he's wisely chosen to forego the usual powdered wig in favor of tying his long golden curls with a strip of black silk, there's something really intriguing about this boy that ventures far beyond my curiosity about how he might've earned those medals he wears.

So, when I find my back against a wall as this masked stranger presses his lips to the spot just under my ear, whispering how he's never seen teeth so white, or smelled any woman so fresh, I can't think of a single reason to resist his advances.

I tip onto my toes, allowing his lips to find mine, as I lean deeper into the shelter of his arms, the warmth of his kiss. And though it's a perfectly nice kiss—I'd even go so far as to say it's a highly skilled kiss—somehow, it feels like the wrong kiss. Like, somewhere out there is another boy I should be kissing instead.

I push a hand against the front of his jacket, my fingers curling around the collection of honors displayed across his chest. *Should I pluck one free and fold it into my palm?*

The thought comes with a jolt. *Why would I even consider such a thing? I mean, wouldn't that be wrong?*

"You captivate me." His lips retreat as he leans his forehead to mine, mask to mask, and traces a finger along the ribbon secured at my neck. "And this, what does it mean—is astronomy one of your interests? Is that why I found you moon gazing outside?"

I look down to see a tiny golden cage pinched between his fingers, and in one horrible tsunami of a wave, the memory of who I am and what I'm doing comes rushing back to me.

This is not my home.

This is not my century.

I'm merely a tourist from another time and place.

Is this what Jago meant when he warned me about losing track of my identity?

Trying to contain my horror at finding myself in this dark corner with a boy I don't even know, I grasp his fingers in mine and return them to his side. "I must go," I tell him. Slipping free of his embrace, I hurry back toward the way I came.

In my chest, my heart thunders. In my head, a hail of thoughts rage through my brain, beginning with my guilt over Braxton, even though it was only one harmless kiss. And besides, is it really my fault if my memory failed?

Only then do I realize, I haven't just lost track of myself, but also of *time*.

Everything you need to know, it's in the mask, Keane said.

I should've been checking. And now, because I got distracted, it's entirely possible I missed my chance to return.

Frantically, I press my finger to the side of my mask. In an instant, a green arrow appears, directing me back to the portal.

The digital clock flashing above tells me I have less than ten minutes until launch. And that's when I realize I failed to secure the Get Arthur tasked me with.

I push through the crowd of drunken nobles, about to break into a run, when the masked boy grabs hold of my arm and pulls me back to him. "When can I see you again?" He is breathless, eager, but no more so than I am.

Every freaking day if you don't let go of me!

To him, I just shake my head and break free.

Nine minutes and twelve seconds.

"Your name!" he calls. "At least—tell me your name!"

I'm running at a full sprint, but the boy is strong, swift, and has no problem keeping up. And for one fleeting moment, I realize I'm caught in the middle of my own messed-up *Pretty Woman* meets *Cinderella* story. While my coach won't turn into a pumpkin, or even a limo, there's a good chance my portal will vanish without me.

And yet, I know better than to let Prince Charming witness my otherworldly departure. Which means, I need to find a way to discourage him from continuing any further.

With only minutes to spare, and a huge task to complete still ahead, I stop, press a hand to his chest and, remembering what Jago said about rarely visiting the same party twice, I say, "Natasha. My name is Natasha."

The boy lifts my hand to his lips. "I am Killian de Luce, and I shall not forget you."

He leans in for a final embrace, and I return it long enough to lift one of those medals from his jacket, only to decide I can't go through with it. He earned them through feats of bravery; they aren't mine to take.

When I pull away, he presents me with a crisp white kerchief with some sort of royal blue monogram stitched across the front.

I shove the handkerchief into one of my pockets and say, "I *have* to go, and you cannot follow me." My tone is stern, and I hope he's smart enough to listen.

"I hope you shall not forget me," he calls, as I press away from the palace and race into the night.

83

I find my way to the nearest garden—one of the many palace gardens that meander for miles. But once I'm there, I have no idea what to do or where to go next.

The time on my mask tells me there's only five minutes and thirty-three seconds until launch. And in a moment of despair, I wonder which is worse—getting stuck at Versailles in the year 1745 or returning to Gray Wolf empty-handed.

Except I'm not entirely empty-handed. I still have the trinkets I lifted from the drunk woman. And though I try to convince myself it's better than nothing, the odds of Arthur seeing it that way are slim to none.

In a last-ditch effort, I pull the tarot cards from my pocket and give them a quick study.

I've got the elements: the Hermit is tied to Earth and the Death card to Water.

I've done the numerology that links the Death card to the Emperor.

What I've forgotten is the astrological connections.

With only four minutes and nine seconds left on the clock, my mind races to assemble the fragments from my dad's long ago tarot lesson. A thread of memory begins to weave a tale in my head, something about how the Hermit was linked to the Roman god Saturn, who was linked to the Titan god Chronos—the god of Time who ate his own children to keep them from usurping his power—just like the painting, *Saturn Devouring His Son*, in the Venetian construct…

And the Death card—the card everyone fears, that's not what it appears, since endings always lead to new beginnings, and…

I turn a quick circle, taking in the resplendent palace grounds that were once a humble hunting lodge. It's the epitome of new beginnings—a dream brought to life by Louis XIV, also known as the—

"Ou allez-vous?" An angry voice shouts from somewhere behind me.

My stomach twists. I freeze long enough to make the translation, then turn to find a man striding toward me.

What he lacks in height, he makes up for in bulk. His worn muslin shirt and frayed breeches strain against his stout barrel of a chest, the visible pop and bulge of his biceps. An unruly mop of black hair obscures a heavy, unshaven face, leaving me with the impression of a jaw softened by jowls, a mean strip of mouth, a generous serving of nose, and a set of heavy-lidded dark eyes that glint with the sort of undeniable authority of someone who knows their way around this labyrinth of gardens and is none too pleased to find me loitering within.

The man continues his approach, his legs slightly bowed, his gait steady. "Where are you going?" he demands in rapid-fire French. Only this time, he speaks even louder.

Nervously, I lick my lips, try to force a reply. But my tongue has turned useless, sitting dead behind a pair of locked jaws and chattering teeth, as every bit of French I ever knew bleeds right out of me.

"I'm—uh…I mean, *je suis*…" I push a smile onto my face, hoping it might serve to disarm him long enough for me to make a quick getaway. But according to the deep furrow of his brow and the searing blister of his gaze, my attempt to charm is a failure.

Next thing I know, he's standing right before me, snatching the tarot cards right out of my hand.

84

"You shouldn't be here," the man says. His expression is menacing, his voice a snarl.

I stand before him, my knees shaking, a scream rising up the back of my throat that I'm quick to swallow right down. I need to stay quiet, keep a clear head. I can't afford to draw any more attention to myself than I already have.

"You've made a terrible mistake." His fingers clamp down on my arm, squeezing tight as a vise, and before I can do anything to try to stop him, he's dragging me clear across the gravel pathway.

I dig in my heels and insist he let go. When that doesn't work, I purposely throw my weight forward and stumble toward the ground, using the momentum to reach for the holster strapped under my gown.

The man mutters under his breath, jerks my arm hard, and forces me back to my feet, only to gape in surprise as I pull my dagger from its sheath.

"Do not make me use this," I hiss, my breath shallow and stunted, my heart thrashing wildly in my chest. I track the flash of shock that crosses his face and Braxton's warning repeats in my head: *If you're going to pull your dagger, you must be willing to use it.*

And while I really hope it won't come to that, I brandish my blade like any other knife-wielding maniac from every slasher movie I've ever seen. A far cry from the sort of elegant moves

Braxton taught me.

The man lifts his calloused hands in surrender and drops the tarot cards to his feet. Though his cunning gaze fixes on mine, daring me to retrieve them.

I glance between the cards and him, weighing my odds. But with only sixteen seconds now left on the clock, I spin on my heel and sprint through the gardens with all that I've got.

In the distance, I spot Jago and Elodie standing in the glowing doorway, hands clasped and ready. To any nearby onlooker, they give the appearance of a young couple who've broken free of the crowd to enjoy a romantic moment.

To my eyes, they look like they've jointly decided to take off without me.

"Wait!" I croak, gasping for air as a flaming spear of pain spirals hot and bright through my side. "Please—don't go! I-I'm almost there!"

It's only when Jago turns, eyes wide with alarm, that I become aware of the rasp of ragged breath, and the crunch of gravel underfoot sounding from somewhere nearby.

The man has given chase, and he's only a few steps away.

Jago extends an arm past the portal and calls for me to hurry.

My lungs about to burst, I push my legs harder, faster. Watching as the green hologram arrow that flickers before me continues to shrink with every step I gain, as the countdown clock just above burns through time as if to say: *sure, you're getting closer, but you're never going to make it.*

00.00.12.

I switch my focus to Elodie, watching her lips draw tight as her fingers reach for the jewel in her ear.

00.00.11.

My left foot kicks up behind me as the right one shoots forward, aiming for solid ground, only to have my heel catch on a jagged bit of rock, knocking my ankle in one direction, while my body bends in another.

I teeter precariously, falling through space with my arms pinwheeling wildly.

A startled cry rings loudly into the night, as my body slams forward, landing hard on my palms. The blow so sudden, it jolts the air clean out of my lungs.

00.00.09.

Wheezing for breath, I stagger forward, desperately clawing my way to the portal. My hand reaches for Jago's, my fingers grazing his, as the man lunges, grabs a fistful of my poufy blue dress, and wrenches me back so abruptly, my neck snaps hard and my vision turns fuzzy.

00.00.07.

Frantically, I peer through the blizzard of tiny white and gray spots now dancing before me like static on an old-time TV. I scramble to my knees, send an arm swinging wildly. In an instant, my ears fill with the sickening sound of shredding silk, a grotesque cracking of bone under flesh that's soon met by a muffled curse when the man realizes my elbow's laid waste to his nose.

"Hurry!" Jago cries, as Elodie stands before me, fingers pinching closer, ready to push the clicker and leave me stranded forever.

00.00.04.

I struggle to my feet and hurl my body forward, clumsily reaching for Jago, only to crash hard into his side, inadvertently dragging the man along with me. The funk of his sharp scent blasts up my nose, as a gush of blood streams off his chin and onto my dress, leaving a grisly crime scene of a mess.

00.00.03.

Jago grasps hold of me, then kicks the man so hard, he doubles over in pain and tumbles right out of the circle of light.

00.00.02.

His face contorted with rage, the man leaps to his feet and charges straight toward us, as Elodie sighs, grabs hold of my hand, and says, "Seriously, Nat? Caught by the groundskeeper?"

And with a derisive shake of her head and a single snap of the clicker, the three of us soar forward in time.

85

B ack when I was a kid and still young enough to get excited about going trick-or-treating on Halloween, I used to drag the night's haul into my room, dump the contents onto my bed, and spend hours sorting through the mountain of sweets.

My return to Gray Wolf isn't so different.

After a quick debriefing where Keane removes our masks and ensures that, despite the gruesome state of my dress, no one was seriously injured—we go about emptying our pockets so Arthur can examine the goods.

While I have no idea what sort of spoils Arthur is used to seeing, the glimmering pile of jewels looks impressive to me. And yet, I can't help but wonder why he cares about any of this.

Arthur is a trillionaire—a man who can literally buy anything he could ever desire, including jewels much grander than these. So why bother sending three kids back in time to collect a pile of nobles' trinkets of no real historical value?

I mean, what does he actually do with these things? Is he purely driven by greed? Or is there something more—something I'm missing?

"Well done," Arthur says, holding up a thick gold ring for inspection. It came from Elodie's stash, and I can't help but notice the way her cheeks flush in response to his praise.

It's strange to see the change in Elodie's behavior whenever Arthur is there. Back when Song revealed that she regards him as a father, I'm not sure I really understood. But watching her now, vying for his approval, it's like a little girl turning cartwheels and begging: *Look at me, Daddy, look!*

It's then that I realize Arthur is Elodie's kryptonite.

But what is Arthur's?

"I hear you handled yourself quite well out there."

I'm so preoccupied by thoughts of Elodie, it's a moment before I recognize Arthur has shifted his focus to me.

"Then again, you had some terrific chrononauts to guide you."

"Chrononauts?" I squint.

"A fancy word for time travelers," Arthur says.

I glance between Elodie and Jago, both studiously working at avoiding my gaze. And when I return to Arthur, I notice the slightest bend in his brow, as though he wants to see if I'll rat them out for ditching me, or if they'll rat me out for being caught, seized, and chased all the way to the portal, putting us all in grave danger.

I know he knows something happened over there. I don't know how, but he definitely—

Suddenly, I realize that much like the clothing I wore in the constructs, Arthur was monitoring my Trip. I guess it makes sense, considering how much he's invested. And yet—just how much did he see?

Was it just the rate of my pulse?

Or does he somehow know about the drinks, the dance, the masked boy who steered me into a dark corner, pushed me against a wall, and trailed his lips down my neck?

And worse, does he already know just how badly I failed at my task?

Or am I being paranoid, seeing conspiracies where they don't really exist?

If there's one thing I know for certain, it's that this is a test.

One that possibly holds even more significance than the Trip I just took. In a place like Gray Wolf, loyalty, or at least the appearance of loyalty, is essential.

"Couldn't have asked for better partners," I say, my lips pulling wide as I flash a grin at Jago and Elodie.

I'll cut Jago a break, considering how he saved me by pulling me into that glowing doorway just seconds before launch.

But Elodie... It was clear she was more than willing to leave me behind.

To Arthur, I add, "They taught me a lot." I keep my expression neutral, my gaze even.

Arthur nods and turns his attention to my own pile of loot, which consists of a bracelet, a hairpin, and a brooch. Compared to Elodie and Jago's haul, it makes for a pretty pathetic display. "Is this all?" He shoots me a meaningful look. I nod, too ashamed to meet his gaze until he says, "And what's this?"

I glance up to find him holding the crumpled handkerchief I'd forgotten all about. Hadn't even realized I'd taken it out of my pocket. "Oh, that—that's nothing." I reach for it, but Arthur has no intention of giving it back, and my hand falls awkwardly to my side.

"Tell me how you came to procure it." He rubs a thumb over the royal blue thread.

"Actually..." I start, cringing under the weight of Elodie and Jago staring at me. "It was...given to me."

"Given to you?" Arthur tilts his head and studies me with renewed interest. Though it's impossible to tell what he's thinking.

As for Elodie, I can practically feel the scorch of her gaze burning straight through the side of my face, but I refuse to meet it. Considering how she's the clear winner of the night, bringing back the biggest pile of loot, I can't understand why she'd bother to care that someone decided to give me a small piece of cloth.

And of course, Jago came in second. With his good looks and charm, I'm sure women and men were practically throwing their jewels at him.

Though the longer this drags on, the more I'm beginning to understand that this contest is not about who procures the most treasure, it's about bringing Arthur something of interest. And this time, for whatever reason, what interests Arthur is a simple white handkerchief.

"This piece —" Elodie plucks another gold ring from her pile. "It came straight from the finger of a Marqui —"

But Arthur isn't interested. With a single wave of his hand, she falls silent.

"You've managed to surprise me," he says, regarding me for a few prolonged beats. "That's not something that happens often. All in all, a good Trip."

I stare at him in disbelief. I was sure that I'd failed — convinced I'd be demoted to working as Elodie's chambermaid. And yet, Arthur looks undeniably, inexplicably pleased.

"It's customary for the Trippers to receive one of their Gets as a reward for their efforts," he tells me. "These Trips put you at great risk, and it's my way of showing how much I appreciate your hard work."

He presents us each with an item he takes from our piles, then motions for Roxane to catalog the rest of the stash.

As I'm walking away, Arthur calls, "Oh, and Natasha —"

I turn.

"I'll schedule a time for us to debrief later. For now, why don't you head over to Medical and get yourself checked. Once you're cleared, the rest of the night is yours to spend as you wish."

86

Aside from a few minor scrapes and bruises, and an ankle that's tender but thankfully not broken or sprained, I return to my room and head straight for the shower, where I lather myself up with the array of scented soaps and bath oils.

If nothing else, my journey back in time has given me a new appreciation for mundane things like running water, indoor plumbing, and mouthwash.

It's funny to think how much I used to love watching romantic historical movies, imagining what it would be like to wear a fancy gown and glittering jewels while being courted by a handsome boy in breeches and a tailcoat. Well, now I know. And the truth is, the people from those long ago times smell really foul.

With the exception of one.

A vision of his wavy golden hair and masked face blooms in my mind. The impression so startling and real, the bar of soap slips from my fingers and lands hard on the drain. As I watch the water gather and swirl all around, a hot spray beating hard on my back, I wonder how memory can be so cruel as to make me forget Braxton when I Trip, while refusing to grant me the same courtesy of erasing the masked boy upon my return.

On my waist, I can feel the ghost of his hand.

There's a place on my neck where his lips continue to haunt.

And I have no idea what to do with any of that.

Do I risk telling Braxton? I mean, he'll understand, having Tripped plenty of times himself. Right?

Or do I lock the memory away in a metaphorical box?

Since Jago and Elodie were off on their own, it's not like anyone saw. And besides, there's really no point in confessing, when I'll clearly never see the boy again.

I remember the way he spoke his name—Killian de Luce.

It sounds as made up as Elodie Blue.

The whole experience feels so surreal. And even though I experienced it firsthand, it's still hard to believe I traveled thousands of miles and over two and a half centuries in less time than it takes to drive from here to the lighthouse.

Though, when I yawn, I realize that the phenomenon of Time Lag is real, so I shut off the taps, reach for a towel, and pad into my dressing room to find my slab buzzing with a message from Braxton.

Braxton: Welcome back. Meet me in my room to celebrate?

Me: ☺

Braxton: See you soon. Directions attached.

I'm tired, hungry, but also well-versed in the restorative power of a pretty dress. I slip into a backless velvet flocked minidress and a pair of jeweled heels. And though I keep my makeup to a minimum and leave my hair long and loose, I take a moment to add the diamond swan clip I took from that woman in Versailles just a few hours earlier.

By the time I arrive at Braxton's door, I'm fully committed to keeping the encounter with Killian to myself. I just can't see the point in confiding. And besides, I'm unwilling to do anything that'll risk wrecking this night.

I take a deep breath, run a hand over my dress, and knock.

A moment later, Elodie opens the door.

87

"Surprise!" Elodie leans against the doorframe with a sharp gaze and a mile-wide grin. "Bet you didn't see this little plot twist coming."

I stand frozen before her. My heart has plummeted to my belly, and I have no idea what to think. Is this some sort of prank? Is this even Braxton's room? And if so, why the hell is Elodie here, looking so at home?

"Stop messing with her already, so we can pop the champagne!" The voice belongs to Jago, and just as I'm about to turn on my heel and leave, he pushes Elodie aside and pulls the door wide.

Inside, I count Oliver, Finn, Song, Roxane, Keane, Hawke, and there, standing before a window that looks out onto an expansive ocean view, I find Braxton.

Dressed in a pair of slim dark jeans, an ivory silk button-down shirt, and a velvet smoking jacket the same shade of blue as his eyes, his expression is murky, but if I had to describe it, I'd say it's equal parts guilty and apologetic, though I guess he never actually said it was a celebration for two.

As I enter, everyone stands and applauds and, deciding it's best to play along, I curtsy before them.

As promised, Jago pops the champagne and hands me a glass, as the rest of them say, "Speech—speech—speech!"

Doing my best impression of an Academy-Award-winning

actress, I press the flute to my chest and gaze out among them. "This is such a wonderful honor!" I gush. "First, I'd like to thank the academy, literally Gray Wolf Academy. Also, my heart swells with gratitude to all of you lovely friends who helped make this possible—whatever the hell *this* actually is. À ta santé!"

I raise my glass and take a sip, watching as they drink along with me.

"Anyone going to tell me what's really going on?" I ask, expecting Elodie to take the lead, since she's the designated leader of everything. But it's Braxton who steps forward.

"Natasha Antoinette Clarke." He stands before me and places a hand on each of my shoulders as though I'm about to be knighted. "Today you've accomplished something truly remarkable. You've taken part in a miracle born of science, knowledge, nature, and the visionary genius that made the dream possible. Today you've achieved what most consider unachievable, and now, after weeks of extensive training and a successful first Trip, we invite you to join our small, elite group of chrononauts. Tasha, welcome to the AAD Club."

He reaches into his pocket and retrieves a gold ring he fits onto the middle finger of my right hand. It's a lot like the ring he often wears, the one he nervously twists whenever he's trying to hold something back. When I glance at everyone else, I see they're wearing the same ring as well.

It's a signet ring. Flat and square on top, it has an engraving across the front that features a crest with the academy emblem, two more symbols I take to represent wind and time, and the profile of a wolf bordering either side. At the bottom are the initials AAD.

"What does AAD stand for?" I ask.

"Arthur's Artful Dodgers!" Finn cries, lifting his glass along with everyone else. "Welcome to the family!"

I look to Braxton in confusion.

"From *Oliver Twist*," he whispers, and I immediately recall reading that book back in ninth grade English class.

It's about an orphan who joins a gang of juvenile pickpockets overseen by a man named Fagin, who sends them out to thieve in exchange for shelter and food.

"Oh my God," I gasp, as the full reality of my life settles upon me. Jago, Elodie, Song, Oliver, Finn, Hawke, Keane, Roxane, Arthur—they really are my new family.

But before the thought can truly take hold, Braxton pulls me into his arms, kisses me just north of my ear, and whispers, "Welcome back. I'm sorry to surprise you with this, but I promise to make it up to you later."

88

Not only are there endless bottles of champagne, but there's also an elaborate cake that Oliver carries from Braxton's kitchen to the den where we've gathered.

It's a small kitchen, but the appliances look modern and new. And I can't help but think how nice it must be to have the freedom to make your own meals. Like Elodie's supersized room, I assume it's one of the perks of advancement.

Once everyone's settled with cake and champagne, I'm told it's customary for that day's Trippers to share a story, funny mishap, or bit of intrigue that happened on their journey.

"It's the true debriefing," Keane jokes, and I wonder what sort of places and times he might've Tripped to.

Jago volunteers to go first, and he tells a story of being propositioned by a drunk nobleman and his wife that has everyone roaring with laughter. Despite his claims that he absolutely, positively did not partake in the thruple, he did manage to rid them of quite a few of their treasures.

Elodie tells a surprisingly tamer tale that involves some light dancing and flirting, but mostly she claims to have used her time at the Yew Ball improving her already expert sleight of hand abilities.

When it's my turn, I can't help but waver. There's so much I'm unwilling to share. My failed secret mission, the terrifying encounter in the garden, being chased all the way to the portal, and the time spent with Killian are at the top of that list.

To my fellow AADs, I finally say, "I was so nervous. My only goal was to lift a few things without getting caught."

A few people groan with disappointment, but thankfully no one calls me out. I lean against Braxton, relieved to have gotten off easily, when Elodie says, "This is no place for holding back. Everyone here has seen it all, and most of us have done it all."

To that, everyone hollers and laughs.

"So, come now. You're talking to a highly sophisticated, extremely savvy, slightly jaded, world-weary bunch. We're family, and your new brothers and sisters happen to be shockproof, so there's no harm in telling us about all the time you spent gazing at the stars with a dashing, well-decorated gentleman on your arm. In fact, if I'm not mistaken, after a few spins about the dance floor, didn't you two retreat to someplace, shall we say, more discreet?"

The room has grown unbearably warm.

Or maybe it's just me.

Still, I'm overcome by the sickening realization that Elodie only appeared to abandon me when, between bouts of pilfering, she apparently spent most of her time spying on me.

She taps the etched crystal champagne flute against her chin and feigns a look of deep contemplation. "Is he perhaps the same gentleman who gave you that handkerchief you brought back?"

Braxton's arm tightens around me, but I'm quick to turn away. I can't bear to look at him. And I certainly can't bear for him to see me.

Surprisingly, it's Song who comes to my rescue. "Oh, leave her alone," she says. "Natasha is one of us now. Besides, we all know you were too busy crawling inside every pair of breeches at that ball to have the slightest clue of what Natasha was up to."

The room falls silent. Like a tennis match, everyone looks

from Elodie to Song.

There's a moment of decision on Elodie's face, and it's anyone's guess if she'll choose to return.

She shoots a bright smile at Song, but her gaze is pure frost. "Perhaps you're right," she says. "Also, I'm starving. Anyone up for dinner in the Winter Room?"

In a matter of moments, the room clears, leaving me, Braxton, and the lingering discomfort of Elodie's accusation weighing heavily between us.

89

"About that—" I lean toward Braxton, desperate to take control of the narrative before his worst thoughts have a chance to spin their own sordid tale. "What Elodie said—"

But Braxton cuts in. "It's okay." He dismisses the topic with a quick wave of his hand. "You don't owe me an explanation. Whatever did or didn't happen, the only thing that matters is that you returned."

I stare at him, more than a little surprised by his reaction. I mean, I guess I should be happy that he's willing to drop it so easily, but there's a stubborn part of me that insists on explaining.

"That's the thing," I say. "Nothing *did* happen." The lie gives me pause. Not only am I not the slightest bit believable, but I've just made it worse. Now that I've gotten myself into this mess, I need to come clean, no matter how much it hurts. "Or at least it's nothing like Elodie made it sound. It's just—that boy, the one she was talking about, well, he kissed me…" I suck in a breath and will myself to go on. "And…and I'm pretty sure I kissed him back. But that's it. Because the second I saw the talisman, my memory of you, and Gray Wolf, and everything else, it all came rushing right back, and—"

"Tasha." Braxton places a finger to my lips, stopping me before I succeed in making it worse. "I've Tripped. I know about the Memory Fade. I've experienced it plenty of times. That's why I gave you the talisman, to help you remember and find your way back. But just so you know, Fade isn't entirely the curse you may think. Losing sight of your identity also helps you fit in. The trick is to not become totally lost. It's a balancing act that takes time to perfect."

I sink against the velvet cushion, grateful to have his support but saddened to think my indiscretion is what prompted it.

"Tell me," he says. "How was it?"

I gaze up at the domed ceiling, taking a moment to find the right words. "Honestly, it was pretty cool." I sneak a guilty look his way. "I mean, aside from the fact that I failed to procure all my Gets."

I remember the look on Arthur's face as he studied the handkerchief, and how, for whatever reason, it made him forget, or at least not care, about my other, more glaring, failure. Then I sneak another look at Braxton, wondering if Arthur gave him a similar assignment. If maybe it's standard Gray Wolf procedure for Arthur to convince each new recruit that they're the one destined to help him fulfill his biggest ambition, only to send them back in time with nothing more to go on than a couple of randomly chosen tarot cards.

But Braxton's expression remains unchanged. He just nods for me to continue.

I run a finger over the crest on the gold ring that now circles my finger. "I think the reality of actually being there, back in 1745 Versailles…" I look at Braxton, letting my hands fall to my sides. "Well, I'm not sure it fully sunk in until it was over. I mean, most the time I was so nervous, so focused on doing the job without getting caught, there wasn't a lot of time to really soak it up. Or at least not for long."

"And now that you're back?" Braxton bends his head to the side as his eyes fix on mine.

My fingers curl around the bedsheet, knowing I owe him the truth but hoping it won't make him judge me. "When I think about where I actually was and all that I saw…" My gaze drifts around the room before returning to him. "Well, it was even better than I thought it would be." I catch the twitch in Braxton's jaw, note the way his eyes narrow ever so slightly. "And the whole experience felt like a dream. It was kind of surreal and pretty amazing."

Braxton lifts his glass and tilts it toward me. "Looks like you're officially Blue now," he says.

"I don't know about *official*." I reach for my glass and trace a nervous finger around the stem. "Last time I checked, my sweatshirts were still Yellow."

"By tomorrow morning, a new stack will be delivered to your room." Braxton trails a hand along my cheek and tucks some loose strands of hair behind my ear. He knows how hard I've worked for this moment, and yet, I can't help but notice his mood is far from celebratory. "And you were okay?" he asks. "Doing what Arthur required?" He lowers his hand to my arm. The pad of his thumb brushes softly over the finger-shaped marks the groundskeeper made.

There's a question in Braxton's gaze that I prefer not to answer. My struggle with that man is not a place I want to revisit.

I tuck my legs underneath me, drain the last of my champagne, and set my flute on the table beside me. "And by that I take it you mean party crashing and nicking jewels from unsuspecting nobles?" My gaze locks on his, suddenly understanding the true reason behind his lack of enthusiasm.

This is about our earlier conversation, when he urged me not to go through with the Trip. How he warned me that I'll come back changed, and not for the better.

Turns out, he was right. I have changed. I've experienced something truly miraculous—one of the best-kept secrets in the world. I took risks, faced danger, and came out triumphant. And, if lifting a few jewels is the price for me to experience that *and* for my mom to be financially secure for the first time in a long time, then I guess I'm willing to pay. Because now that I've made it back safely, I'm eager to see where and when I get to go next.

Excitement is a hard thing to hide. And I guess Braxton must sense mine, because he's quick to say, "Maybe I've been Tripping so long, I forgot how exhilarating it can be."

There's an uneasy slant to his shoulders, a stiffening in his jaw, which leaves me questioning if he truly believes what he said. And yet, I'm so stirred up by reliving the experience, nothing can get to me.

"There were times when I felt like I was caught in a dream within a dream," I tell him. "Like I wasn't fully able to distinguish between fantasy and reality. Though I suppose that's all part of the Fade." When I realize I've inadvertently brought us right back to the subject I'd hoped to avoid, I feel my face flush a thousand shades of red.

"You're an AAD now." Braxton leans toward me and trails a finger along the gold chain, all the way to the talisman that hangs between the swell of my breasts. "Which means, whatever happens when you Trip will not come between us. Unless you want it to, that is."

There's a question in his gaze, but I have one, too.

"Why would I want it to?" I whisper, pulling him closer and threading my arms around his neck.

I'm not sure who initiates the kiss; all I know is once I find myself ensconced in Braxton's arms, I know this is the place I will always return to.

Not Gray Wolf Island, Arthur Blackstone, or even this academy.

But rather to this boy who has eyes like the sea, a charming bit of bend in his nose, and a kiss that's all-consuming.

As I lean deeper into the kiss, I have a fleeting memory of that time in tenth grade when I dated a senior who'd just made varsity quarterback.

As we kissed our way into the back seat of his car, I convinced myself we were in love.

It didn't take long to realize I was wrong.

After that, I guess I gave up on the concept of romance and love, along with everything else, including myself.

But now, here at Gray Wolf, with Braxton, those memories belong to somebody else.

Braxton's face looms before me, his eyes filling with the sight of me. Then he lifts me into his arms and carries me past the roaring hearth to lay me down on his elaborate canopy bed.

Under the muted glow of the flickering flames in his hearth, he kisses me softly, then savagely. The sound of my name drips like honey from his lips as our legs tangle together, and our bodies press so tightly, it's impossible to determine where his ends and mine begins.

And it's in this moment, with Braxton's lips crushing hard against mine, kissing me like his life depends on it, that I vow to never forget how it feels to be so thoroughly adored and revered.

From this day forward, I make a solemn promise to myself that I will never, ever settle for anything less.

As if sensing my thought, Braxton pulls away, cups my face between his palms, and regards me with a gaze full of wonder.

"I'm so glad you're back. I'm so glad you're home," he says, and I know in my heart that it's true.

This boy is my home now, and I am his.

90

I wake to the beat of a hard driving rain thrumming against a nearby window, and the lonesome feel of the cool length of sheets where Braxton's body once was.

With a deeply contented sigh, I climb out of bed, and am just reaching for the silk shirt he wore the night before when he appears in the doorway with freshly brewed coffee, and says, "I definitely prefer you without it."

In an instant, the shirt falls, the mugs are abandoned, and Braxton lures me back to his bed.

He kisses me desperately, hungrily, as though we hadn't spent the whole night doing just that. Kissing until we were drunk with it. Kissing until I fell asleep with my lips pressed to his, secure in the warmth of his arms.

Before Braxton, I didn't even know it was possible to kiss so much for so long and to be satisfied with only that. But being with this boy has blown open a portal to a whole new world, and unlike every other boy who came before, nothing about being with Braxton feels sloppy, rushed, or, worse, like something I'll regret the second it's over.

At some point during all that kissing, we mutually agreed to take things slowly. Take our time to really savor each other, get to know each other. If for no other reason than we both realized that when something is real, there's no need to rush.

Braxton draws away, trails a finger along the line of my jaw to the tip of my chin. "I don't want to leave you," he says.

"Leave me?" I shift onto my elbow to better see him. "To go where?" It's the last thing I expected to hear, and I stare at him wide-eyed, searching for answers. From what I can tell, no one leaves the island except to go on a Trip. But surely, he's not referring to that, since Trips last only a few hours at best.

"The message came in an hour ago. There's a potential new student—Arthur wants me to head out this afternoon."

Potential new student.

Like I once was.

"Is that how I began?" My tone sounds more bitter than intended. "As an unwelcome notice on your slab?"

He closes his eyes for a handful of beats. "Tasha, please." When he opens them again, his gaze pleads with mine.

I turn away, slide my legs over the edge of the bed, but he reaches for me and pulls me back to him.

"Where are you going?" he says. "Are you angry?"

I bite down on my lip. I feel small, upset for reasons I can't begin to identify. But angry? That's too harsh for the circumstances.

Or is it?

I think of the terrible series of events that landed me here, how hard I've had to work just to carve out a place for myself. And while I'm not sure I'd ever wish that on anyone, there's still no denying the fact that in many ways, my life is so much better than I ever dreamed it could be.

Here at Gray Wolf, I have unlimited access to beautiful clothes, jewelry, fancy dinners, a sexy boyfriend, not to mention the opportunity to *time travel*. All of which is amazing, and in a lot of ways, it's like living inside a fairy tale. One where you're never allowed to leave the castle, unless you're on a Trip, and even then, there's still work to perform by way of thieving for Arthur.

"Hey, talk to me." Braxton cradles my face in his hands, presses his lips from my forehead to the tip of my nose. "Tell me what you're thinking. What are you worried about?"

I pull away, lean back against a pile of pillows, and stare hard at the gold ring on my finger, suddenly overcome with the enormity of what it really means, what I've become.

I want to tell him I'm alarmed by how casually he accepts Arthur's orders to go out and fetch a recruit.

I want to tell him it's wrong—that he should flat-out refuse.

But, in the end, I don't say any of those things.

Partly because just yesterday, I went against Braxton's advice and stole a bunch of jewels at Arthur's command, so it's not like I have any real moral high ground to stand on.

But mostly because Braxton has already grasped the look of accusation on my face. Anything I say now would only add salt to the wound.

"I gave up the idea of fighting Arthur long ago," he says, his voice competing with the sound of rain beating against the window and a harsh crack of thunder nearby. And I'm reminded of what Jago said when he warned me about not playing by the rules. *There's no use fighting a fight that's rigged against you.*

But he also talked about never losing sight of your value, because the more they invest, the more reluctant they are to lose you.

Is that what Braxton's doing, increasing his value?

"This is life in the gilded cage." Braxton's gaze is weighted with sadness, and it breaks my heart to know I'm responsible for putting it there. "We do what we're told—and we take our pleasures when and where we can find them." He sighs. "For a long time, I fooled myself into believing it was enough."

His words make me pause. A door has opened, and now I have to decide whether to enter. I inhale a deep breath, and on the exhale I say, "What really happened between you and Elodie?"

91

I watch Braxton's face closely, but all I see is a sudden shift from sadness to pained.

"Please, don't brush it aside," I say, "or tell me not to worry about it. Just answer the question, once and for all. I deserve to know what I'm up against."

His jaw clenches. He slides a hand through his tousle of hair. But he doesn't pull and twist at his signet ring, and I take comfort in that.

"You're not *up against* anything," he finally says. "It ended months ago."

"For you maybe, but I'm not so sure about her."

"Tasha—"

I follow the trajectory of his gaze. Moving from the rich brocades that spill down the sides of his canopy to the collection of large gilt-framed paintings that occupy the far wall. Though I can't easily recall the names of all the artists, the images are painted in the style of the old masters—vivid, highly detailed, and biblical in nature—portraying subjects with faces twisted from both pleasure and pain as they wrestle with the dueling temptations of earthly delights versus spiritual bliss. Though there is one that stands out from the rest.

"*Narcissus*, by Caravaggio," Braxton says. Judging by the way he winces when he catches me studying it, I figure it must be the most revealing piece in this room.

The painting depicts a handsome boy leaning over a pool of water and gazing at his own reflection. Everything surrounding him is dark, effectively shrinking his reality down to his image.

The painting is beautiful, brooding, like Braxton himself. And I can't help but wonder if it serves as a sort of warning, a cautionary tale, of what becomes of those who lose themselves in the vanities of the world.

"Look," Braxton says, his voice drawing me away from his art, his lush, masculine space with its polished woods, worn leathers, and charcoal gray walls. "Here's what you need to know about Elodie—she's loyal only to herself."

"And Arthur?"

He pauses to think. "Maybe. But that's the extent of it. And the truth is, I'm sorry I ever got involved. For her, it was all a big game."

"And for you—did it mean something more?" I inhale a shallow breath, not entirely sure I want to hear his answer.

"No." He's quick to insist, but maybe too quick? "Or at least not in the way you might think. Look, I consider myself a loyal guy, and...I'm really not sure what you want me to say." His hands helplessly flop on his lap.

"What about when you Trip?" I ask. "Are you loyal then, too?"

The air steamrolls right out of him. He falls back against a pile of cushions and stares at the swoop of fabric hanging over our heads. "Are we really going to do this?"

I pull one of the velvet pillows to my chest and pick at the silk fringe that runs along the edge. "I'm just curious how many princesses or countesses you might've slept with." I hold my breath, feeling silly, needy, and embarrassingly small. But last night, I gave him a piece of my heart, and I want to make sure it's safe in his hands.

"Tasha—" He reaches toward me, his fingers landing on the

curve of my hip. "This is a terrible road to travel."

"But you know everything about me! You researched me, watched me, studied me, stalked my social media, left no stone unturned. And meanwhile I know virtually nothing about you."

"You know plenty." He sighs, swipes a hand across his eyes. The conversation is weighing on him.

"I know you've gone out of your way to be kind, but other than the few details you've shared about your past—"

"What is it you want to know?" He rolls into a sitting position and spreads his arms wide. "Now's your chance. Ask me anything."

"How did someone like you end up with someone like Elodie?"

He regards me for a long, sobering moment. "This place," he finally says. "Gray Wolf changes you. And for a long time, it changed me. But now I'm trying to find my way back."

Outside, a loud clap of thunder shakes the whole sky.

Inside, I rid myself of all thoughts of the past and focus on the present, as this beautiful boy pulls me into his arms and silences me with a kiss.

92

H is bathroom is even bigger than mine.

And when we're finished showering, he hands me a pair of navy-blue sweats and a soft gray T-shirt, so I won't have to make the trip back to my room wearing last night's dress.

As soon as his back is turned, I lift the T-shirt to my face, bury my nose in it, and take a deep inhale. The scent that greets me is as clean and fresh as I expected. But it also carries a hint of the spicy warmth I've come to associate only with him. Which is why I've already decided I'll be sleeping in it every night until he returns.

"Not exactly the sort of high fashion you've become accustomed to," he says, tossing a smile over his shoulder. "But it should at least get you back to your room without eliciting raised eyebrows or probing questions."

"A walk of shame?" I laugh. "Here at Gray Wolf? Why would anyone care?" But just after I've said it, I think about Elodie and all the ways she'd use it against me, and I realize it's a bigger, and even kinder, gesture than I first realized. "And the shoes?" I ask. "Got a pair of ladies' size sevens lying about?" I poke around inside his enormous walk-in closet and reach for a pair of black boots covered in at least a century's worth of dust and dirt. "Maybe these?" I shoot Braxton a teasing grin as I dangle the boots before him. "They're clearly too small for you, so maybe they'll fit me?"

Braxton slides a clean pair of jeans from a hanger and turns toward me. When he sees the boots I've chosen as a joke, his face turns gray as a tombstone. Within a matter of seconds, he's crossed the room and snatched them right out of my hand.

"Definitely not these." He makes for the far side of the closet, where he tosses them into the corner. Which, considering how everything in this closet is so deliberately organized and categorized—a place for everything, and everything in its place—it's weird he'd make such a concerted effort to return the boots to a section clearly reserved for various pieces of sporting equipment.

I stare at his back in confusion, feeling like I accidentally summoned some ancient demon that was better left dormant. "It was just a joke," I say, my voice wavering slightly. "I didn't mean—"

"I know." He's quick to wave it away. "It's just, last time I wore those…" He runs a hand over his clean shaven jaw and squints into the past. "Anyway, I guess they remind me of a long-ago event I prefer not to dwell on."

"So why do you keep them?" I ask.

When he faces me, his gaze is haunted by the torment of something known only to him. "Because I can't afford to forget," he says.

I watch as he goes about stepping into his jeans, my gaze catching on the faint circle tattoo in the crook of his arm. "What is that?" I gesture toward the circle within a circle that somehow strikes me as familiar. "What does it mean? I was going to ask you last night, but I guess I got distracted by other things."

I meant that last bit as a joke, or at least an attempt to lighten the vibe. But it seems to have the opposite effect, as I watch Braxton's jaw clench and his shoulders grow stiff. "That's what you call a mistake," he says, voice edged with grit. "A remnant of my younger, more impulsive days."

"It looks unfinished." I start to move toward him, but well before I can reach him, he's grabbing a sweater from a stack and pulling it over his head.

"Most the time I forget I even have it," he says, adjusting the V-neck and pulling at the sleeves. And though I may be imagining it, I get the distinct feeling he's purposely trying to hide the mark from my view.

"Are you aware of how your accent gets really pronounced whenever you're faced with something you'd rather not talk about?" I pull my towel tighter around me, hugging the T-shirt and sweatpants to my chest, as I watch his gaze slowly lift to meet mine.

"Does it?" he says, speaking in such an exaggerated way he sounds like someone straight out of a Dickens' novel, and it gets us both laughing.

"Just another one of your tells, I guess."

There's a visible shift in Braxton's expression, a lowering of the brow, a tightening on either side of his mouth. "And what are some of my others, *pray tell*?" His grin widens at that last bit, and though it's an undeniably dazzling sight, there's a starkness lying behind it.

"I don't think it's in my best interest to reveal that to you," I say, then before he has a chance to react, I go about getting dressed.

I roll the waist of the borrowed sweatpants so they hang at my hips, twist the hem on the T-shirt into a small knot at my back, and slip into last night's heels. When I finish, I turn to find Braxton leaning against a chest of drawers, watching me with a wistful look on his face.

"You're beautiful," he says, his voice scratching hoarse, unused. "And smart, and kind, and so incredibly amazing that sometimes..." He pauses, eyes crinkling at the sides. "Sometimes I can't believe how lucky I am that I met you."

When I search his gaze, I'm certain he means every word. And though I know we're still a really long way from saying the L word—I can't help but wonder if maybe, one day, we'll get there. And, more importantly, if *I'll* get there. I mean, I've never come anywhere close to being in love, so it's kind of hard to imagine.

"I would escort you back to your room," he says. "But I'm already running late."

"My apologies," I say, fluttering my lashes in a flirtatious way. "You know, for making you late." I tilt my head coyly toward the tangle of pillows and bedsheets.

The ploy works. In an instant, Braxton is standing before me, pulling me into his arms. "Darling, you can make me late anytime," he says, then kisses me so deeply, so fully, I find myself already mourning his absence while waiting for his return.

He releases me with a sigh and goes in search of a duffel bag for him and a spare Gray Wolf Academy tote for me, so I won't have to drag my dress through the halls.

I'm about to toss in the diamond swan hair clip, too, when I pause. "Hey," I say, clip in hand. "I have an idea."

"Yeah?" He races around the space, filling his arms with the items he'll need.

"I was thinking, since you're actually venturing out into the world—"

That's all it takes for him to stop, to take one look from me to the jewel in my hand and immediately shake his head.

"But you don't even know what I was going to say!" My stomach sinks with disappointment.

His gaze squares on mine. "You want me to give that to someone. But Tasha, that can never happen. And if this is about your mom, there's nothing to worry about. As long as you remain here, Arthur will look after her."

"It's not for my mom."

"Then who?" His gaze narrows, his brows merge, like he's

trying to determine who he could've possibly missed on the paltry social column of my pathetic high school résumé.

"It's for Mason. I never got to say goodbye."

A hint of recognition flashes across Braxton's face. "Right," he says. "Your best friend and coworker at the vegan café."

"Wow," I say. "You really *did* memorize my file."

Braxton shrugs. "The answer is still no." He turns away and gets back to packing.

"But you don't have to actually visit him." I trail Braxton from his bathroom to his kitchen where he sorts his vitamins into a small plastic container, then back to his bedroom where he tosses them into his bag.

"Good," he says. "Because I won't be anywhere near there."

"All I'm asking is that you mail it. I want to give him a shot at something better. And with this—" I hold up the clip. "Well, he can sell it and put the money toward college."

Braxton pushes down on the small pile of jeans, sweaters, socks, and underwear, then zips his bag shut in one quick stroke. "You want to help your friend?" When he faces me, his gaze is darker than I've ever seen. "Then make peace with the fact that you can never contact him again. Under any circumstance. Understand?"

The words hang heavy between us. I don't like the sound of anything he just said.

Still, I don't want to end it like this. Not after the wonderful night and morning we shared. So I nod agreeably, kiss him passionately, and leave him to finish whatever he needs to do before he heads off island.

But on my way out, I leave the diamond hair clip on the table by the door, along with a short note from me to Mason, and another note with the address where Braxton can send it.

As I make the trip back to my room, I feel confident that Braxton will do the right thing.

93

According to my slab, the day is mine to spend as I want, and I'm not entirely sure what to do with it, since I haven't really taken a day off since I arrived.

In my effort to advance, my weekends were devoted entirely to study. Which means I missed out on movie nights where Arthur screens new releases well before they're open to the public; beach days where everyone heads to the indoor pool that features an actual sandbar and waves you can surf; the game room that supposedly offers all kinds of video games and VR experiences that are generations ahead of what's sold in stores; and even spa time where, according to the treatment menu on my slab, I can book a facial, a massage, or even time in the isolation tank or the cryotherapy booth.

Deciding on a visit to the spa, I let myself into my room, where the first thing I notice is the stack of blue sweatshirts placed on a nearby table. And before I realize what's happening, I've dropped to my knees as a sudden rush of tears spills down my cheeks.

Normally, I'd have wiped them away well before they could track past my nose. But today, I just let them fall, splashing onto the T-shirt Braxton lent me, as I allow myself to really lean into this victory.

This is so much bigger than no longer eating alone. I mean, while it'll be nice to finally put that behind me, the real reason

I'm crying is because it's been so long since I dared myself to succeed, there was a part of me that feared I wasn't up to the task—that winning didn't happen to people like me.

With a shaky hand, I reach for the ivory-colored envelope that's positioned precisely in the center of the stack, slide a finger under the wax seal, and retrieve the note left inside.

There, written in black ink, on Arthur's personal stationery, I read:

Congratulations.
-A.B.

I run a finger over the message as fresh tears roll down my cheeks. Only this time, I'm quick to wipe them away, thankful that I'm here on my own—that no one will ever know just how much this all means to me.

Setting the note aside, I pluck a sweatshirt from the pile, tug it on over my T-shirt, then I get to my feet and head for the nearest mirror.

Before me, I see a girl made Blue, with a beautiful talisman hanging from her neck, a shiny gold ring on her finger, and the flush of a new boyfriend still fresh on her cheeks.

And though my hair is still brown, my eyes still green, and I'm still barely so much as five foot three without heels, it feels like I'm looking at a completely different person from the one I once knew.

The lessons in diction, comportment, dance, and others have left their mark. And though the changes they've brought are undoubtedly for the better, making me much more confident and poised than ever, I can't help but wonder what happens now. I guess I've spent so much focus on becoming a Blue, I never stopped to think of anything more.

I mean, is this it? Do I stay locked up in this gilded cage, Tripping and stealing at Arthur's behest, until someone fresher and newer comes along and I'm sidelined to one of the supporting staff jobs? Will I *ever* be able to leave this place?

Or is Gray Wolf Island destined to become not just my present but also my future?

Arthur's Artful Dodgers. The words trail softly from my lips to the luxurious room beyond—the collection of fine furnishings, the gleaming crystal chandelier, the handwoven rugs, to walls that are surprisingly bare.

Am I expected to steal my own art? Is that how Braxton and Elodie grew their impressive collections?

My gaze finds its way back to my reflection, where it chooses to linger.

As long as I stay here, Arthur will take care of my mom. And when Mason receives the diamond swan hairclip, I'll have the satisfaction of knowing I did what I could to take care of him, too. If this is the price to help the people I love, then I'm willing to pay it. Despite Braxton's warnings, I won't let Gray Wolf change me for the worse.

I pull the sweatshirt back over my head, fold it neatly, and return it to the pile. Then I head into my closet in search of a swimsuit, cover-up, and some flip-flops. Thinking a little time at the spa, followed by a visit to the beach, might do me some good.

I guess because my days here are so tightly scheduled, I haven't really taken time to search through every additional shelf and drawer beyond the ones I've needed most. After finding a beautiful beaded tunic I plan to use as a cover-up, I'm still searching for a bikini to wear to the wave pool when I open the middle drawer in the island that sits at the center of my closet, only to watch as it flies off its tracks and sends a pile of papers flittering like butterfly wings to the floor.

I gaze at the mess of notes at my feet. Considering where they were stashed, clearly whoever put them there intended for them to stay hidden, which only makes me even more curious.

    I kneel on the soft Persian rug and start to sift through them. Then, realizing they're dated, I go about arranging them in order, before I spread them out before me.

2.8— What is this place? Forced to eat alone—the freaking fourth dimensional road!? Someone Get Me the Hell Out of Here!

2.12— Today's inspirational quote: No Mud, No Lotus. Are they kidding me with this shit?

2.19— Goal: Make Blue whatever it takes. I can't stand another day of eating alone.

3.15— I survived the hazing. What the hell is wrong with these people? Why do they just go along with whatever Elodie says? Don't they realize the only power she has is the power they give her? And why the hell did I choose to make the same choice again? Okay, that last part is bullshit. I know exactly why I did it—because what waits for me off island is way worse than what waits for me here.

3.16— Go Team Yellow. ☺←Whatever. What the hell does a girl have to do to make Blue around here?

3.18— Elodie is out to get me. I can't prove it, but I think it has something to do with Braxton inviting me to his table for dinner. He's nice and all, but not what I'm into. Also, I know I'm being watched. And yet, when I mentioned all that to Song, she assured me I'm being paranoid. Just in case, I need to start hiding these notes.

4.2— Song is my only true friend. I think I might be in love with her.

Sometimes I wonder if maybe we're both just lonely, that we never would've hooked up in the outside world. But that world doesn't exist for me anymore. The sooner I forget it, the better.

5.12– Song is holding something back. Whether it's to protect me, or herself, I don't know. Everyone puts up such a good front with their fancy manners and clothes. But I know I can't trust anyone. They're all out for themselves. It's like being a noble at court, our lives revolve around pleasing King Arthur and gaining his favor.

6.28– Time traveling?
Freaking time traveling—like, for real—not just a construct?
Are they freaking kidding me?

6.30– Tomorrow I Trip. I really hope I find my way back.

6.31– Okay, that was awesome. Braxton ditched me for a while—caught him flirting with a smokin'-hot countess (too bad Elodie wasn't around to see that!). But I made it back and I'll admit: I'm kind of excited to do it again!

7.1– Officially Blue!

8.12– It's really not so bad and Arthur is pleased with my efforts. Song and I are in love. Finn and Oliver are my good friends—and that's more than I ever had before, so it's time I stop with these silly sad notes and focus on truly making a life here. Funny how it took longer than I thought to arrive at this point, but shorter than I hoped.

Thirteen notes offering a pretty accurate chronicle of what it's like to live as a newbie at Gray Wolf.

Question is: If she decided it wasn't so bad, then where is she now?

That last note was dated August 12. By September, Elodie arrived at my school, scouting for a recruit.

Am I this girl's replacement? And if so, is that what Song was referring to that night in the lighthouse, when she hinted that the only reason I'm here is because of an unexplained vacancy?

I gather the notes and stuff them back into the envelope. Then, after finding a bikini and flip-flops, I head out to the spa.

But on my way, I stop by the purple door and knock.

94

Song stands in the doorway and squints like a person who's still in the process of waking up and hasn't decided whether to fully commit.

"Hey, Natasha," she says. "What's up?"

She's in her robe, and I don't want to impose, but this is the sort of thing that's probably better said behind a closed door. "Can we talk?" I ask. "Inside?"

After a moment's hesitation, she waves me through, and the first thing I notice is that her room is not as nice as Elodie's but also not as basic as mine.

When she catches me looking at her collection of modern art pieces, she says, "I guess you haven't visited the Vault yet. Don't worry, you will."

"The Vault?" I follow her deeper into her room and take a seat on her leopard upholstered divan.

"Every successful Trip—and by successful, I mean you've either managed to return with a particularly difficult Get, or you've filched something that surprises and delights Arthur—he rewards you with a visit to the Vault, which houses his private collection of art, and where he invites you to choose a piece for your room."

"Are you saying those pieces in Elodie's and Braxton's rooms—they chose them?"

Song folds herself onto a pale pink cushion and nods.

I think about Elodie's collection—it was massive, impressive. A well-balanced mix of modern works and old masters that totally suits her, considering how she has one foot firmly placed in the old world and the other in the current one.

As for Braxton—the art he chose was darker, brooding, epic in both story and scale, and all similar in theme. A collection of contorted bodies and tortured faces that speak to the pain of being a human, striving for a touch of the divine, but constantly falling short.

And then Song—the canvas directly before me encompasses most of the wall.

"Considering your interest in art, you should really enjoy the Vault," she says.

"How do you know I'm interested in art?" All those nights spent in the Autumn Room, I don't remember ever mentioning that. I don't remember saying anything particularly revealing— none of us did. Here at Gray Wolf, if you're not Tripping to a long-ago past, you work to stay grounded in the present.

"It's one of the reasons you're here," she says. "It's one of the reasons we're all here. Arthur has great appreciation for those with an elevated aesthetic."

"I'm not sure my aesthetic is all that elevated," I say. "I arrived here in a baggy hoodie, sneakers, and a dress Elodie chose worn over a pair of sweatpants Braxton loaned me."

"I'm talking about a deep appreciation for beauty. True beauty. The kind of feel-it-to-the-depths-of-your-soul response you get when experiencing a particularly moving work of art that makes you want to climb inside that landscape, the pages of a book, or even the notes of a song, so you can know the work more intimately, maybe even live there for a while. I know you've felt that way, or else you wouldn't be here. It's not just about finding teens who live on the margins, it's more than that. Arthur has no tolerance for anything he considers ordinary.

It's one of the reasons he abhors social media. Most of the big tech guys secretly do. But for Arthur, all those overly curated feeds—he claims it's turning us all into clones. Everyone talks about their personal style and brand, but Arthur refers to it as a Personal Bland."

I laugh.

"Arthur can be funny, actually. It just takes some time to see that side of him. Anyway, if you're going to try to analyze me through my art, I'll save you the trouble and say I like plain, simple, upfront pieces. I get my fill of shadow and mystery just walking these halls."

I take another look at the canvas. I'm not sure I'd call that Jackson Pollock piece *simple*. The well of emotional turmoil required to cover a canvas that large with multiple layers of splatters feels pretty deep to me. But if that's how Song wants to see herself, it's hardly my place to argue.

"Why do I get the feeling this isn't just a friendly visit?" She stretches her arms high overhead, bends to her right, then left, but all the while her gaze remains leveled on mine.

"I found something," I say. "Something I figured you should have."

Her interest clearly piqued, she sweeps her curtain of long, dark hair over her shoulder and leans toward me.

I study her closely as I pass her the envelope, watching for whatever sort of reaction might play across her face before she has a chance to conceal her true feelings. But it's nothing like that. The moment she unfolds the first note, tears begin to spill down her cheeks.

"Where did you find these?" she whispers, as though afraid of being overheard.

"Hidden behind a drawer."

"Did you read them?" Her gaze is accusing at first, but soon softens. "Of course you did. I would've done the same." She sighs. Then, "Her name was Anjou, like the pear." She tries to laugh, but I watch as the small burst of joy quickly fades from her face. "We were together. I loved her. And I miss her every single day."

"What happened?" I ask, watching as Song's long, graceful fingers flip through the pile of notes.

When she doesn't answer, I ask again, but she just wipes her eyes, tucks the envelope away, and settles her gaze on mine.

"Don't tell anyone you found these," she says, her voice tinged with an unspoken warning.

95

"Song, what happened?" I repeat, my stomach clenching as I watch her spine stiffen as she cinches her sash tightly around her. The way the heavy, embroidered robe hangs on her slim frame makes her appear simultaneously regal and fragile. Though the steeliness of her gaze, and the firm pinch of her rose-tinted lips indicate my welcome is close to being over.

"Promise me you won't tell anyone," she pleads.

I nod. "I promise," I say, my gaze darting around her room once more before landing on a small, leather-bound book lying on the table beside her. The sight of it is so unexpected, I can't help but do a double take.

I mean, I could be wrong, but at first glance, that book looks just like the object I saw in the Unraveling.

The one carried by the girl who disappeared and reappeared in the maze below my window on my first day on this rock.

The maze that doesn't actually exist in this modern-day version of Gray Wolf, though surely it once did, or else I wouldn't have seen it.

There's a symbol engraved on the cover. *Is it a pentagram or some other sigil?* From where I sit now, it's impossible to make out.

I start to lift off my seat, hoping to get a better look, when Song says, "A word of advice?"

I pause in mid-stand, then settle back onto the cushion.

"You need to be more careful," she says.

"I'm...not sure what you mean." I lean toward her, eager to hear more, even though I'm pretty sure I'm not going to like what she tells me.

Her shoulders go slack. She presses a hand to her chest, fingers seeking comfort from the aquamarine talisman that hangs from her neck. "It's like, you work so hard to make Blue," she says, voice quietly wistful. "Mostly because it's so lonely being a Green or a Yellow. But then, even once you've managed to reach the goal, become an AAD, and make friends with people who swear to have your back, you can still disappear without a trace, and not a single one of those people will go looking for you."

"Is that..." My mouth has gone so dry, I'm forced to clear my throat and start again. "Song—is that what happened to Anjou? Did she just...disappear?"

96

"According to Roxane, Anjou asked to go home." Song's gaze lights on mine. Her lip is a snarl, but there are tears clouding her eyes. "*Home*." She shakes her head. "Am I seriously expected to believe that?"

"So…it's not at all possible that it might be true?"

Song closes her eyes, lets a few silent beats pass, before she says, "Does that sound even remotely possible to you? Do you actually believe Arthur would willingly let any of us leave?"

"I don't know," I say. "I mean, didn't Roxane go away for film school?"

"Is that what she told you?" Song rolls her eyes. "Look, there's a reason this place is so off the grid. It's because Arthur can't afford for anyone outside of Gray Wolf to know what really goes on here. Can you imagine if the outside world learned that time travel is real? It would upset the balance of everything. The result would be chaos. Not to mention all those who'd try to abuse it."

I heave a deep sigh. It's something I've tried not to think about—the huge glaring secret Arthur has tasked us with keeping. To Song, I say, "And how can we be sure *Arthur's* not trying to abuse it?"

Song looks at me in alarm, as though I've just put a voice to something that's strictly forbidden.

"I mean, there's got to be more to all this than just stealing jewelry and art—"

Song cuts me off before I can finish. "If there is, I've yet to see it. Arthur is guilty of being a hoarder of history, but I've never seen anything to make me believe he's out to change the course of it." She waves a hand in dismissal. And even though I don't fully buy it, I know better than to push it. "Anyway," she says. "When it comes to being at Gray Wolf, no one goes home. We're all lifers. Well, at least the lucky ones are. The ones who don't disappear."

"*Disappear?*" The word leaps from my tongue, and I'm glad I'm already sitting because my legs have gone so shaky, I doubt they'd be able to hold me.

It reminds me of what Elodie said: *With any luck, you're going to be here with us for a very long time.*

At the time, I had no idea what she meant. I'm pretty sure I still don't.

Before me, Song just shrugs. And while she doesn't strike me as being particularly open to questions, in a tentative voice I ask one anyway. "But exactly *how* did Anjou disappear? Because from what I can tell, there's no viable way off this rock. Or at least not without Arthur's consent."

Song shrugs. "She disappeared the same way most of them do—" Her brown eyes fix on mine in a way that causes my belly to churn. "She went on a Trip and never returned."

A sudden chill spreads through my body, as I imagine Anjou stuck somewhere in a time in which she doesn't belong. Then I remember how close I came to getting stuck in 1745 Versailles, and my spine turns to ice.

It can happen so easily. Too easily.

"Still, there must be something we can do—" I start, my voice fading when I realize that no one is going to do anything except look the other way. Just like when Elodie's Tripping partner failed to return, and now Anjou, and who knows how many others.

"I don't even know where they sent her. Nobody does except the people working the control room, and believe me, I've tried to find out and they're not talking."

There's a hollowed-out pit forming deep in my gut. I haven't felt this hopeless, or this scared, since the first night I arrived.

"I'm sorry," I say, cringing at how inadequate it sounds, but not knowing what else I can possibly offer. My hands twist together as my gaze nervously flounders about the room before coming to rest on the leather-bound book. "Can—can I take a look at that?" I ask, motioning toward it.

Song tilts her head to the side, her gaze roaming the length of me, as though trying to determine whether or not she can trust me. "Some other time," she says. Then, from out of nowhere she adds, "Just so you know, magick has always been the currency of the oppressed." With a solemn smile, she stands, signaling the end of our conversation. "I'm serious about that promise," she says, as I rise to my feet, hoping my shaky legs will carry me as far as the door. "You can't tell anyone about what you found, or anything else I just told you."

"You have my word," I say, noting the way her hand hovers over the keypad as though she's not quite ready to let me go.

I try to sneak a glance past her shoulder, hoping to get another look at the book. But the way Song shifts makes me wonder if she's purposely trying to block it from view.

"And that includes Braxton," she says, her dark eyes blazing on mine.

I squint at Song, unsure what she's getting at.

"I don't want you mentioning any of this to him."

"Okay." I shrug. "I mean, I'm not sure why he'd care, but—"

"But you don't really know Braxton, do you?" There's a quiver in her jaw that stands in stark contrast to the stubborn tilt of her chin, and the sight of it only fuels my unease.

I glance between the door and her. I'm really starting to regret having come here.

"In fact, you don't really know anyone here. You haven't been around long enough to hear all the stories."

Stories? What stories?

To Song, I say, "Maybe you could tell me one?"

She purses her lips, as though trying to decide. After a moment, she says, "We'll talk later. Soon, okay? There is something I want to tell you. But not today."

"You know where to find me." I shrug.

That is, if I don't disappear.

Song pushes her thumb to the keypad, and a second later the door springs open. I'm halfway down the hall when she calls after me. I turn, a look of trepidation worn plain on my face. But she just smiles sadly and says, "Thanks."

97

The next week passes by in a blur.

The days are busy with the usual routine of classes and mealtimes spent with my fellow Blues, but with Braxton still gone, the nights are unbearably long.

I miss the heat of his kiss, the sound of my name whispered from his lips.

I miss the comfort of his arms banded snugly around me, the feel of his body pressing hard against mine.

And I have no idea when he'll be back, when we'll be able to resume that part of our life.

When a Chopin piece blares from my slab, I can't help but groan. The long slog back from the Autumn Room where I transition from laughing with friends to the tomblike quiet of my own room is when the loneliness really sets in.

Except tonight doesn't unfold in the usual way. Because just as we're spilling out the door and into the hall, my slab buzzes with a new message, and I'm surprised to find it's from Arthur.

AB: A surprise awaits. Follow the arrow.

Normally, a surprise is considered a good thing. But a surprise with Arthur attached makes me wonder if he's finally getting around to the debriefing he mentioned after my Trip. And if he is, I have no idea what to expect.

"You coming?" Oliver hangs back as Song, Finn, Jago, and Elodie continue toward our rooms.

I shake my head and proceed to where Arthur sits in one of those small electric carts that zoom around the outer reaches of this place.

He motions for me to take the seat beside him, then navigates a complex series of hallways in a state of complete and utter silence that leaves me so anxious, by the time he parks and leads me to a bank of elevators, my knees are literally shaking.

"You're nervous." He shoots me a look of amusement and ushers me into the elevator car where we quickly descend deep into the bowels of the academy.

When the panels slide open, we head down a short, dimly lit hall. At the end, he pauses before a brushed metal door, where he looks at me with a gaze glinting with something known only to him. "Ready?" he asks.

The best I can do is shrug. The threat of hyperventilating overrides any curiosity I can drum up.

"Welcome to the Vault!" With a push of a button, the thick steel door opens to a sight so wondrous, my jaw literally drops. "Go on, have a look—feast your eyes!" He grins. "There's nothing like your first visit."

To put it simply, it's a museum to end all museums. An enormous, climate-controlled storeroom filled with the most wondrous, important, impactful paintings, sculptures, jewels, letters, trinkets, artifacts, historical objects, and mementos the world has ever known. And as I struggle to take it all in, I have the terrible sinking feeling that all these wonders before me are real. And that it's people like me—the Trippers, the chrononauts—who are responsible for putting them here.

Suddenly, I understand that all the beautiful works I've seen around Gray Wolf aren't the products of the skilled team of forgers and craftsmen Arthur keeps on staff. No, their job is to copy the greatest works of art, which the Trippers then exchange for the real ones.

"I can tell by the look on your face that you understand what this is really about." Arthurs's voice echoes throughout the high-ceilinged room.

I nod. It's all I can do. I mean, what's the proper response when one reveals that it's the museums that house all the fakes? The real art is here.

"You're shaken," he says, without a trace of judgment. "It's shocking, I know. But what you need to understand is that modern society doesn't deserve these great works. Why should a masterpiece like the *Mona Lisa* be reduced to mere background fodder for hordes of narcissistic selfie takers? It's absolute blasphemy to treat her with such disrespect! How often have you stood before a great work, only to hear some boorish tourist announce to the room at large, "*I could paint that!*"

Arthur pronounces "tourist" in the same cringey tone as a church lady whispering a profanity she overheard.

He reels on me then, those obsidian eyes sparking in a way I've never seen. "*No!* I want to tell them—you *couldn't* paint that, write that, design that, build that, compose that, or film that. And, more importantly, you *didn't* do any of those things. Not because you lack the time, as you claim, but because you lack the genius, the inspiration, the courage, the curiosity, the generosity of spirit, and the creative drive required to create a thing of beauty. You've never peered deep into your soul and asked the sort of questions required for such an act."

He pauses, allowing enough space for the words to properly land. "When society turns its back on true artistry for the pursuit of banality, then no, they don't get to visit Leonardo's masterpiece just because they happen to be vacationing near the Louvre and want to check it off a bucket list. Leonardo da Vinci did not labor so that his work could be viewed through the glazed eyes of an unruly tour group less interested in truly *seeing* it than posting to their social media feeds so everyone will know they *have seen* it. Leonardo created because it allowed him to touch the divine, and when we view his works properly, we get a glimpse of that, too."

I swear his eyes are misted with tears, but he does nothing to hide it. He's not the least bit ashamed. This is a man with a passion for beauty like I've never seen. And while I know it's wrong to rob the world of these treasures, in a strange way, I also understand Arthur's point. To love something so deeply can make you fiercely, obsessively protective.

"And now—" He places a hand on my shoulder and steers me deeper into the space. "I get to indulge a favorite moment of mine, when I watch one of my students choose a painting to hang in their room."

I respond with a look of stunned silence, prompting Arthur to say, "I assumed you'd heard about these visits to the Vault."

"I have," I tell him. "I just…"

"You don't think you deserve a reward," he says. As usual, his laser-sharp vision cuts right through me.

"I didn't solve the puzzle." I shrug. "I was right on the verge, but then—" When I look at him, I find his gaze locked on mine, and my mouth goes so dry, I struggle to finish the thought. "Well, then I ran out of time."

"And the cards?" he asks. "I noticed they didn't make the trip back."

"I was confronted and…" I inhale a shaky breath, stare down at my feet. "I lost them."

Arthur looms before me, examining me with such white hot intensity, I feel as though I'm about to ignite under the glare of his lens. "Come," he finally says, breaking the silence. "I want to show you something."

98

Arthur leads me past infinite rows of magnificent works by Picasso, Van Gogh, Matisse, O'Keefe, Botticelli, Kahlo, Michelangelo, Rembrandt, Velázquez, and more, then stops before another door that blends into the back wall so seamlessly, it's impossible to distinguish it until I'm standing directly in front of it.

"Few at Gray Wolf have seen what I'm about to show you," he says. "And certainly, none of the Blues. Before we proceed, you must promise not to breathe a word of this to anyone."

In the short time I've been in the Vault, I've glimpsed so many masterworks, it makes my head spin. So, what could he possibly be hiding beyond this secret door?

Still, I give him my word, then watch as the door opens, the overhead lights blink on, and Arthur leads me to a glass display case positioned in the center of the room. "I present to you, my most prized possession in this entire collection—the Antikythera Mechanism."

He turns to me, as though expecting me to…I don't know, applaud? Jump up and down and shout out in glee?

Instead, I stand awkwardly in place, glancing between him and some ancient scraps of time-worn metal, wondering what it is that I'm missing.

"So…" I steal a moment to rummage through my brain, searching for the sort of response that'll work to convey the appropriate amount of interest, while also concealing my current state of confusion. "It's the, uh…original, then? Which means, somewhere out there, there's a…fake?"

The creases in Arthur's forehead deepen, and for a man whose face rarely reveals what he's thinking, his disappointment is worn plain to see. "I thought for sure you'd recognize it," he says.

I move closer, screwing up my face and squinting, but all I see is an old pile of—

Before I can even register what's happening, my hand instinctively shoots for the display case, fingers pressing against the glass, causing small half domes of fog to bloom around the pointed tips of my nails. Like a video set on time-lapse, I watch in astonishment as this ancient fragment of metal miraculously restores itself to its original glory.

Its case is made of a finely oiled wood.

The mechanism inside gleams with golden dials and knobs, a set of inscriptions I can't decipher, and an assortment of stones and jewels that stand in for various planets and stars.

The restoration is so extraordinary, so exquisite in its craftsmanship and design, I can't help but gasp at the sight.

But even more startling are all the memories the vision unearths. Like stumbling upon an old family album, my mind eagerly flips through a collection of faded pictures of long-forgotten afternoons spent with my dad.

The two of us sitting cross-legged, leaning over a heap of objects spread across a soft braided rug as he patiently teaches me how to reassemble the Antikythera Mechanism he keeps locked away in a drawer.

And how sometimes he'd hide the pieces around the house, then task me with using clues from the tarot cards to discover where they were…

His was a copy, of course, made of cheap plastics and

dented bits of metal. But next to my prized set of model horses, it ranked right up there among my favorite diversions. Possibly because the only times I was allowed to play with it were when my mom was away. On those days, before her car had even pulled out of the drive, I'd start begging my dad to take the secret puzzle out of hiding.

Though I can't remember him ever saying no, I can clearly recall the look of sadness he wore as he watched me reassemble, then disassemble the various parts.

In the movie screen in my mind, I view a clip of the unmistakable glint of sorrow clouding his gaze, as my dad held up a gleaming gold ball and said, "Tell me about this piece—tell me everything you know about the—"

From somewhere nearby, the gravelly scratch of a throat being cleared yanks me out of the reverie and back to reality.

In an instant, the vision is gone.

The memory of my dad recedes.

And I'm left staring at an archaic piece of metal behind a thick sheet of glass.

Too late, I remember Arthur is watching me.

99

"Everything okay?" Arthur tilts his head in study.

The way he regards me, with his brows drawn together, it's clear that he's onto me. Still, I just nod and mumble vaguely about having felt momentarily dizzy.

Right away, I know he's not buying it. But thankfully, for whatever reason, he's quick to move on. "The Antikythera Mechanism is the first ever analog computer," he says. "It was used to accurately predict astronomical positions and eclipses decades in advance. After being lost at sea for over two thousand years, it was discovered in an old shipwreck near Antikythera Island in Greece, which is how it came by its name."

I glance between Arthur and the artifact. I know about its history. One long ago day, my dad told me. Still, I'm not sure why out of everything here, it manages to claim the top spot on Arthurs's list of favorites. I mean, sure, it's extraordinary in its original form. But here, in its current condition, it's not all that impressive.

"Many of its pieces are still missing," he continues. "Metal gearwheels, stones that stood in for the various planets, rotating dials—all of which are vital to its function. Though unfortunately, they've remained hidden for centuries."

I think of all the skilled artisans and craftsmen Arthur keeps on staff. The solution to his problem is obvious. "Why not just replicate those parts?" I ask.

He dismisses the idea with a wave of his hand. "We've tried, but none of it can be duplicated. Only the genuine articles will do." Wearing a look of deep contemplation, he shifts his focus to me. "It's my dream to see it restored to its original form. And that's where you come in. You're going to find those pieces and bring them to me. You're the only one who can."

It takes a moment for the statement to register, but once it does, my stomach begins a slow churn as my entire body breaks out in a cold, clammy sweat. "This—what you mentioned at lunch—this is your greatest ambition." I pause long enough to clock his reaction. As usual, his face reveals nothing, but I know I'm not wrong. "Still, you can't be serious!" I say, only to regret it the second it's out. No one talks to Arthur Blackstone like that. But, since there's no taking it back, I rush to explain. "What I mean is—"

I don't get far before he holds up his hand to stop me from making it worse. "I am entirely serious. And I have no doubt you'll succeed. But for now, I want to hear more about this person who confronted you at Versailles."

Unsure what this has to do with anything, I nonetheless give him the rundown on the groundskeeper and how close I came to missing the window when he attacked me. But by the time I finish recounting my story, Arthur looks surprisingly pleased. "And this is why you believe you failed?"

I stare at him, struggling to comprehend what he means. "Well, I didn't procure the Get, and …"

"But you didn't even know what the Get was, did you?"

He's not wrong, though I'm willing to bet it was one of the missing pieces belonging to this ancient computer.

"Going by your encounter, I'd say you came much closer to retrieving it than you think."

He studies me for a long, intense beat, and not knowing what else to do, I return my attention to the Antikythera. "I guess I don't understand why this is so important to you," I say. "There's got to be more accurate ways of charting the stars. Is there something I'm missing?"

Arthur offers an indulgent smile, the kind normally reserved for favored pets and small children. "As it turns out, there is far more to the Antikythera Mechanism than the scholars who've studied it can even begin to comprehend. Within it lies a great power. To put it simply, it is the means for everything the world has the potential to be. Though unfortunately, ever since its inception, there's been a group of short-sighted fools, like the man you ran into at Versailles, who are committed to halting its promise. It's why so many of its parts have been hidden."

Another look at the ancient scrap of metal leaves me to conclude that Arthur must be extremely bored. I mean, what else is a trillionaire to do after traveling through time to procure all the world's greatest treasures? Instead of taking up golf like every other old rich guy, he's set his sights on completing the ultimate puzzle, and now he's looking to me to handle the grunt work and collect all the pieces so he can claim all the glory.

To Arthur, I say, "Why Versailles? Why not just travel back two thousand years and snatch the mechanism while it's still in one piece?"

An amused look crosses his face. "Because time travel uses an enormous amount of power, and the further one travels, the more power is required. I like to use the rubber band analogy—if you stretch it too far, it'll snap. As of now, we're not yet able to travel back safely more than eight hundred years without snapping. Or, in our case, vanishing. We're working to resolve that, of course. But at this point, the solution is still a ways off."

I'm pretty sure I check out the second he says "vanishing."

100

Arthur's dark eyes narrow on mine. "My team of Blues are an immensely talented crew," he says, drawing me away from a fear I'd prefer not to imagine. "And yet, out of all of them, you're the one I'm counting on to see this thing through. And this—" He reaches into a drawer built into the display case to retrieve what looks like an old piece of parchment. "This will help you locate those hidden pieces."

I peer at a detailed drawing of oceans and continents, with an array of random symbols scattered about, though I sense there's nothing random about them.

"What you're looking at is no ordinary map," Arthur says. "It is *the* map—the same one Christopher Columbus used on his journey across the Atlantic. It was created by Henricus Martellus, a German cartographer, back in 1491. The symbols you see serve as signposts to finding the missing pieces I seek. The map also contains hidden texts we're still working to decipher. So far, they remain mostly illegible."

While the map is undeniably impressive, I'm not sure what Arthur expects me to do. As a member of Generation GPS, I don't even know how to read it, and I have no problem telling him as much.

Undeterred, he says, "But you understand the symbols, don't you? Just have a look and tell me what you see. Though limit your focus to France, please."

I take a moment to study that section of the map. Somewhere outside of Paris, I find the ancient tarot symbol for the Death card and, since I already deciphered that back at the Yew Ball, the words are easily summoned.

"The Death card, which can refer to both endings and new beginnings, shares a numerological connection to the Emperor card, which, I assume is connected to Versailles—not only because it's the royal residence but because it is a symbol of new beginnings. Also, its element is water." I pause to look at Arthur. He's clearly interested, so I continue. "The symbol for the Hermit card"—I motion toward the detailed image etched onto the parchment—"shares an astrological link to Saturn, which is linked to the Titan god Chronos, who is known as the god of time. And, since its element is earth, I assume the object you're looking for is hidden in the gardens somewhere."

"Extraordinary." Arthur breathes, his gaze riveted on me.

"I also assume you already know all this. I mean, isn't that why you sent me there in the first place?"

Arthur nods, and is quick to say, "And yet, it pains me to admit how long it took to connect all the dots. Unfortunately, we've experienced several false leads that have served to greatly delay any progress. May I ask who taught you all this?"

My dad. Over the course of a handful of afternoons, my dad taught me things that didn't make any sense. And for some odd reason, after lying dormant for years, buried deep inside the graveyard of my mind, all those memories are now rising to the surface, like hollow-eyed ghosts refusing to be forgotten.

To Arthur, I just shrug. Thankfully, he doesn't push me for more, though I do have something to say.

"But if you know all this, then what do you need me for?" It's the question I've been wondering all along. Arthur always hints about my having some kind of gift. But whatever that is, he's yet to share it with me.

The look Arthur gives me is unexpectedly candid. "Because out of everyone here," he says, "you're the one best suited to find it. You have exactly the sort of vision I need to see this thing through."

"I'm not sure—" I start, but Arthur raises a hand to stop me.

"You don't need to be sure about anything," he says. "Leave that to me. All I'm asking is that you trust what you see. I think we both know your vision has far more reach than you're willing to admit."

I stand silently before him, barely able to breathe, much less speak. Yet somehow, I manage to say, "Can I take that?" I gesture toward the map.

Arthur replies with a curt shake of his head. "I've already made that mistake. It was a copy, of course, but it never made its way back. But have another look if you please."

I wave it off. I've seen all that I need to. Though there is one glaring detail Arthur's left out. "Are you going to tell me what sort of piece I'm looking for? Is it a gem—a scrap of metal—a piece of the missing cabinet?"

Arthur, about to tuck the map back into its drawer, suddenly freezes. "How did you know about the missing cabinet?" he asks.

101

I stand before Arthur, stomach clenching, pulse jittering, as the full impact of my mistake comes reeling back toward me.

I mentioned the cabinet! And now he knows about the Unraveling and my ability to see glimpses of the past.

Or maybe he already knew about that.

Maybe that's exactly what he meant when he said that bit about my vision having far more reach than I'm willing to admit.

I swallow past the lump in my throat and force the words from my tongue. "Y-you mentioned it," I stammer. "You—"

"No," Arthur says, gaze brightening. "I most certainly didn't." He turns away and tucks the map back into its drawer. When he returns to me, he says, "I trust you'll know the object I seek when you see it."

I'm not entirely sure I agree but, since there's obviously no point in trying to persuade him, I ask him the other question I've been wondering. "Let's say I do manage to find the missing piece, and eventually, all the other pieces as well—what then? I mean, you said the Antikythera Mechanism is the means to everything the world has the potential to be, but I'm not sure I understand. What exactly do you plan to do with it once it's fully restored?"

For one fleeting moment, Arthur's expression takes on a dreamy, faraway look.

When he finds me again, his gaze burns as bright as I've ever seen. "Why, I'm going to remake the world," he says, as though stating something glaringly obvious.

A silence stretches between us, and I remember my conversation with Song, and how convinced she was that Arthur had no intention of messing with the course of history, and then, the night I arrived, when Braxton told me that Arthur was a collector of beauty. And I can't help but wonder if maybe Arthur has set his sights on something between these two things.

Maybe after curating a personal collection of the most vaulted pieces of art through the ages, he's now turned his eye to curating the world itself.

But he can't actually believe he can do such a thing.

Before I can ask him to elaborate, he says, "Now come. Time to choose a piece for your room."

Despite everything that just happened, despite the uneasy twitch in my belly, the thought of one day owning one of these glorious pieces of art makes me as excited as a kid on Christmas Day—one who lives in a house where Santa always shows up and does not disappoint.

Arthur ushers me out of the secret room, and over to a display case featuring a glittering tiara. "A sapphire and diamond coronet Prince Albert designed for Queen Victoria in 1840." He gestures proudly. "Theirs was quite a love story, and this is a symbol of their devotion. What do you think? It's yours if you want it."

I imagine the look on Elodie's face when I show up for dinner in the Winter Room with the crown informally perched on my head. She would totally freak, and that alone is enough to tempt me. Though in the end, I decide against it. A relic of someone else's love story doesn't hold much interest for me.

We head for the section where Arthur stores the more important pieces of art. "How do you emulate the pigments and the materials for the forgeries?" I ask. "There must be experts who are trained to spot the difference?"

"Experts." Arthur scoffs. "Yes, I suppose there are no shortage of *experts* in the art world, but we've managed to fool them all, thanks to the Reds."

I turn to him. "Reds?" Though just after I say it, I realize he's referring to the color of a sweatshirt, like the Greens, Yellows, or Blues. Apparently, there's a whole other category I didn't even realize existed, and I wonder if that might be the next goal to shoot for.

"The Reds tend to keep to themselves. Also, their Trips last much longer. Sometimes they travel as benefactors, commissioning pieces, paying for supplies, that sort of thing. Other times they procure pigments, brushes, canvases, and other tools for our Gray Wolf artisans to use."

I turn to Arthur, torn between complete awe and utter horror at what he's accomplished. "You've thought of everything, haven't you?" I say, then immediately worry I might've spoken out of turn, crossed an invisible boundary by acting too familiar.

But Arthur, proud of his iconoclast status, just grins. "Yes," he says. "I have. And just so you don't get the wrong impression and assume I'm motivated solely by greed, aside from the assigned Gets and the trinkets I allow you to keep, everything else is returned to the timeline in which it was taken and distributed among the poor."

I'm pretty sure my jaw has just landed on the floor as I stare wide-eyed at Arthur. His ability to surprise never ceases to amaze me.

"I've always been one to root for the underdog." His face creases into a close-mouthed grin. "Which is why I try to redistribute the wealth when I can."

"Ohmygosh," I say. "You're Robin Hood." I watch as he tips back his head and lets out a deep-bellied laugh.

"Better to be known as that than Dickens's Fagin," he says

with a wink.

I return to the art, and after serious consideration, I'm about to reach for Boticelli's *Primavera* simply because it's always struck me as joyous and happy, and I could use a little of that. But then I detour in an entirely different direction when I catch a glimpse of a well-known piece from the surrealism school—a picture of a stark landscape and clocks melting. Like the *Mona Lisa*, it also has a river running in the background.

Salvador Dalí's most famous work: *The Persistence of Memory.*

"Interesting choice," Arthur says, and I realize that part of the reason he enjoys bringing us here is so he can analyze our picks and glean something about us that we may have tried to keep hidden. "Dalí claims they're not actually clocks, but rather bits of camembert melting in the sun. What do you think?"

"I think Dalí might've hated art critics."

We both laugh, but I'm self-consciously aware of Arthur's continued study of me.

I wonder if he'll think my choosing this was glaringly on the nose, seeing as how the image relates to time, Einstein's theory of relativity, and the end of the idea of a fixed cosmic order. Ultimately, it doesn't matter what Arthur thinks of my choice, though. For me, having this piece in my room feels like a necessity.

Much like Braxton choosing *Narcissus*, if I can look at this painting every morning when I wake up and every night before I go to sleep, then maybe I can manage to hang on to the memory of what happened that night at Arcana—maybe it'll help me remember there's a whole other world outside these walls.

Because the longer I stay here at Gray Wolf, the more I've come to suspect that Memory Fade doesn't just happen while Tripping—it happens here, too.

The heady combination of extreme comfort and luxury,

combined with the monotony of routine, makes the days blend so seamlessly, it's easy to forget which world I truly belong in.

And that's what scares me the most.

By the time I get back to my room, I find a folded note slipped under my door.

Sorry I've been kinda distant. I have an early morning Trip tomorrow, but let's talk later when I return.

I'm ready to tell you now.

Song

102

oday's inspirational quote feels like it was chosen just for me.

No great artist ever sees things as they really are.
If he did, he would cease to be an artist. —Oscar Wilde

After an hour of French class, I'm just about to head over to the Spring Room for break, when I receive a message on my slab.

Keane: An escort is outside. You are scheduled to Trip

I stare at the screen, unsure if that flicker in my belly is born of excitement or nerves, though after my discussion with Arthur, when he revealed his true expectations for me, I'm guessing it's the latter.

The feeling grows even more pronounced when I realize this will probably be my first solo trip. A final-final exam of sorts. Though, all things considered, I was pretty much solo on my last Trip, too.

Still, being dropped in a foreign place and time, with only myself to rely on, fills me with dread.

I sling my tote over my shoulder and head into the hall to find Roxane standing outside the door of the control center.

Her smile is more efficient than friendly, and as I follow her lead, I can't help but wonder if she really did lie about going to film school like Song told me. And if she lied about that, what else is she capable of lying about?

When she hands me off to Hair and Wardrobe, I ask where and when I'll be Tripping. But in that clipped way she has, she just tells me to relax and assures me I'll be briefed soon enough.

I greet Charlotte like an old friend and settle in for a long session of primping, where a team of people buff my nails, powder my face, rouge my lips and cheeks, twist my hair into a complicated updo with curled bits hanging down past my shoulders, and spritz my décolletage with the same perfume I wore last time.

"No wonder women had so little power," I say. "They spent half their lives getting dressed and undressed. And look at all the help they required." I sneak a glance at Charlotte, but she remains focused on her task.

When she's finished, Charlotte shows me my gown, and I'm disappointed to find it's an exact duplicate of the same blue dress I wore last time. I was hoping to at least mix it up, add a little variety.

"Isn't there another dress I can wear?"

Charlotte shakes her head and cinches the corset so tightly, I gasp.

When she adds the pannier, I audibly groan. They're designed to add an extra foot or two to the width of my hips and they're incredibly awkward to maneuver in.

"We used to take up so much space, but we had no authority," I say. "Now, it's like the more authority we gain, the more we're required to shrink. Why do we agree to this nonsense?"

Charlotte busies her hands with adjusting the side hoops. "Consider yourself lucky," she says. "Ours were made of whalebone or cane. Yours is crafted of a much lighter steel developed by Arthur. Besides, they can come in much handier than you might think." She smooths a hand down the right side and shoots me a look I can't read.

I guess I'm too focused on her use of the word *ours* to

even begin to guess what additional uses a pannier might offer. With her nimble hands and soft, lineless skin, she looks to be somewhere in her twenties, thirty at the most. "No way you're old enough to have ever worn one of these monsters yourself," I say.

Her cheeks flush, and she's quick to turn away as she reaches for the gown. "I'm referring to my ancestors." Her face dips into an uncharacteristic frown, then she proceeds to remind me where the hidden pockets are located. The shoes are also duplicates of the ones I wore before, and when I look at her, she beats me to it. "Next time custom," she says.

"Promise?"

At first, she appears startled, but when she catches my grin, she's quick to return it.

After she transfers my talisman from the gold chain to the black velvet ribbon she's fastened at my neck, she steers me toward the mirror, where the reflection that greets me is pretty much identical to the one last time I Tripped.

When I head out to the launchpad, Roxane hands me an envelope containing a square of paper that states:

Your presence is requested!

When: 25-26 February 1745
Where: Palace of Versailles: The Hall of Mirrors
What: The Yew Ball
Why: Celebrating the marriage of Dauphin Louis to Maria Teresa Rafaela of Spain

After my visit to the Vault, I'm not surprised Arthur's returning me to Versailles.

But why on earth would he send me back to the exact same party?

103

I look between the square of paper and Roxane. "There must be a mistake," I say.

"I'm certain there isn't," she snaps. Then, also like last time, she snatches the paper right out of my hand and makes me repeat what I read.

"You will be Tripping alone," she tells me, confirming what I already guessed. "You have two hours."

"That's an hour less than before!" It comes out like a whine, but I don't even care. I barely made it back to the portal the last time, and this Trip I can't rely on Jago to pull me inside.

"You have the right to refuse," Roxane says. "But if you do, that's it for your life as a Blue." Her gaze meets mine. We both know that's not a choice I'm willing to make.

"How does this work?" I ask. "Going back to the same place and time?"

I mean, of course I studied the concept of past, present, and future all existing at once. Reducing the Yew Ball to a sort of echo of time that repeatedly sounds. But what happens when I run into the drunken lady whose jewels I stole?

Will she still have the diamond swan hair clip—and if so, does that mean the gift I left for Braxton to get to Mason somehow disappears?

Or does my small act of thievery during one visit result in the absence of the thing in the next?

It's enough to make my head spin.

"The Yew Ball exists as a moment in time that you will revisit," Roxane says. "I'm sure you've already covered that in class."

Not wanting to antagonize her any more than I have, I just nod.

"That said, you cannot travel back to a time where you already exist, which is also known as crossing your own timeline—"

"Because the duality of existence results in nonexistence!" I gasp, suddenly recalling what my dad once quoted to me when he tried to explain how the universe is in a constant state of flux and change, and how because of that, nothing ever remains the same.

You cannot enter the same river twice, for it's not the same river and he's not the same man.

But why would my dad even think to say such a thing, much less quote Heraclitus to the nine-year-old version of me?

And why is it that ever since I arrived at Gray Wolf, long-dormant memories of my father, along with multiple references to that old Greek philosopher, keep popping up at every turn?

When I look to Roxane, I find her staring at me with great interest. "Because of that, we've scheduled you to arrive two hours earlier than last time. And, Natasha, whatever you do, do not miss the ride home. The best-case scenario would be you get stuck in 1745. The worst—" She shoots me a meaningful look, and we both know there's no need to voice it.

The worst-case scenario would mean I risk nonexistence.

104

Instead of the usual F given at a normal academy, nonexistence is the Gray Wolf version of failing an exam.

"Okaaay…" I say, unable to fully wrap my brain around the concept, though it's probably better that way. "And the Get?"

"Arthur wants you to bring him something beautiful, extraordinary, and one of a kind. I expect you know what that means?"

Inwardly, I heave a deep sigh. I know exactly what that means. Well, kind of.

Outwardly, I just nod.

"Also, this." She hands me a plain brown envelope. Inside, I find the handkerchief the masked boy gave me during my last visit.

"I—I don't understand." I stare at the handkerchief Arthur was so taken with. "Am I supposed to return it?"

"In a way." She pauses for a breath, while I brace for whatever comes next. "Arthur would like you to locate the boy who gave you the handkerchief and bring him back to Gray Wolf."

I stand before her, knowing I heard correctly, but sure that can't be what she actually meant.

"You want me to bring back *a person*?"

She bobs her head in a brisk, perfunctory way, not a trace of emotion to be found on her face.

"You want me to kidnap someone from another time and

place and bring him here?"

Again with the nod. Only this time, her annoyance is beginning to show.

"Killian," I say. "His name is Killian de Luce. A boy I met at a party that took place over two hundred and fifty years ago and you want me to—"

"Natasha, I think I've made myself clear. This is your assignment. Do you, or do you not, accept the terms?"

I gaze at the control room, where a team of people hurry about, each focused on their individual tasks. Then I stare down at the handkerchief. The fabric is clean and soft. And for the first time since Killian gave it to me, begging me not to forget him, I see his initials are embroidered in royal blue thread. Arthur saw those initials, too, which is why he's assigned me the task of bringing him back.

But who the hell is this person who's managed to catch Arthur's interest?

Once again, I find myself wishing I'd taken the time to read a little more history. Though, in my defense, I was sure I'd never see the boy again.

Wasn't it Jago who told me: *It's rare you get to attend the same event twice. It happens, but Arthur would rather our faces not become too familiar and risk triggering a déjà vu, unless it's to his advantage, of course.*

Well, this is clearly to Arthur's advantage.

Not only does he think I'm close to finding the missing piece to his prized Antikythera Mechanism, but he's counting on me to find Killian as well. And while I guess it's possible in theory, there's just as good a chance that one small shift in events will ensure I never manage to find him. And what then?

What becomes of me when—*if*—I return without Arthur's Gets?

"We need to get you masked and ready."

The sound of Roxane's terse voice yanks me away from my thoughts and back to where I now stand in this big puffy gown, dreading my future as equally as this Trip to the past.

"Tell me," she says. "Do you accept your assignment?"

I fold the handkerchief into a small square and tuck it inside a hidden compartment where the bodice of my dress meets the skirt.

"I'm in," I tell her, turning to find Elodie standing beside Keane, holding my mask in her hand.

105

The sight of Elodie handling the tool I'll need to rely on to direct me back to the portal on time is enough to make my heart skip three beats before stopping completely.

"What're you doing?" I cry, wishing I'd taken a moment to collect myself before I opened my mouth and basically announced how nervous this makes me. But now that it's out there, it's not like I can reel it back in.

"Keane is showing me how to program one of these. I've always been so curious, and he's letting me act as his intern today."

Elodie's gaze locks on mine, and my vision blurs until all I can see is the image of her inside the portal with Jago—the taunting slant of her lips as she watched me run toward her, the way her fingers toyed with the clicker that could've left me trapped in the past forever.

"You didn't sabotage it, did you?"

She rolls her eyes and hands the mask to Keane so he can go about fitting me. "Why on earth would you think such a thing?" She's trying for an air of childlike innocence, but it's not a good fit.

"This is your first solo, so let's go over a few things." Keane stands back to inspect me. "You've got your talisman?"

I tap a finger to the charm at my neck.

"You've got your list of Gets?"

I nod in response.

"Then here's your clicker." He hands me a beautiful white gold and sapphire ring I slide onto my finger. When he instructs me to tap the gem, I notice how the stone gives ever so slightly as it glows from within. "That's only if you need to get out of there early. And it works only when you're standing inside the portal, so don't worry about accidentally clicking it and getting locked out."

I nod again.

"Okay then," he says. "Have a good Trip. And Natasha…" He pauses as though there's something more he wants to add, but in the end, he settles for, "Bonne chance!"

The last thing I see before launch is the curl of Elodie's lips tipping up at the sides, and the murky glint in her eyes as she waves goodbye.

106

When I arrive in the gardens, I cast a nervous glance in the direction of the palace, painfully aware of just how quickly the seconds tick past.

Like grains of sand spilling to the bottom of an hourglass, the countdown is on, leaving me with less than two hours to obtain Arthur's hidden treasure and one masked boy who I'm expected to find in a crowd that's reputed to be over ten thousand strong.

It's a classic needle in a haystack situation with a ticking time clock attached. And if I'm unfortunate enough to miss the return trip and cross my own timeline, annihilation will be the price for my failure.

I will simply blink out of the world as though I never existed.

In the distance, the view of Versailles glowing under a sky full of stars makes for a breathtaking sight. And I can't help but wonder if this is what King Louis XIV had in mind when he gazed upon the former hunting lodge set deep in the forest and dreamed of the sort of splendor it would one day become under his guidance.

How would he feel to see it on this night, at a party hosted by his great-grandson?

What would he think about the palace's ultimate future as a tourist attraction, with an orange juice kiosk parked beside the Mirror Fountain, and a shop that sells postcards, guidebooks, and other themed tchotchkes squeezed inside the former Royal Chapel?

I drag my gaze away and focus on the task set before me. Shortly after my visit to the Vault, I started researching everything I could find on the gardens of Versailles, only to discover they're far more extensive than I initially thought.

And yet, there was one section that stood out among the rest.

One particular fountain that, if I'm right about the symbols on Columbus's map, should lead me straight to the Antikythera Mechanism's missing piece that Arthur has tasked me to find.

But before I can begin, I need to figure out just exactly where I am so I can determine which way to head next.

There's a sculpture beside me of a beautiful woman holding a mask in one hand, while a fox crouches beside her, and I instantly recognize it from a book I found on a shelf of rare first editions in the Gray Wolf library. As I continue to stare at the white marble form, the facts as I remember them unspool in my brain like a breaking news ribbon on cable TV.

The mask symbolizes flattery.

The fox, cunning.

The sculpture was executed in 1685 by Louis Leconte, as per a design by Mignard.

The title he gave it: *Deceit*.

On the screen in my mind, I replay the clip of Elodie handing over my mask—then zoom in for a tight shot of the forced expression of innocence that didn't quite fit. And for a fleeting moment, I wonder if this is her doing—if she's sending a message, trying to mess with my head.

But, just as quickly, I realize how foolish that is. According to Arthur, Elodie doesn't know about the Antikythera Mechanism, much less the Get he expects me to find.

Sure, she may have been messing around with my mask, but I seriously doubt she has any control over where I ultimately land.

And yet, I can't let go of the thought that the sculpture holds a message I can't afford to ignore.

In a moment of panic, I tap the side of my mask, testing to see if it works. Instead of a green arrow directing me to the portal, I see two projected circles shaped like a target, confirming my current location inside its borders, and my shoulders go slack with relief.

While it's nice to know Elodie hasn't rigged my only reliable means of finding my way back to Gray Wolf, I am horrified to discover I've gotten so sidetracked by nonsense that a full six minutes have already passed.

Or is that what Elodie intended all along?

Was landing me next to *Deceit* an attempt to make me suspicious enough that—

I shake my head. I have to stop thinking like this. There's literally no time to waste.

But before I move on, I return to the statue again.

In addition to its symbolism, I also read that *Deceit* is the first sculpture on the north side of the *Allée Royale*. Which means, technically, I don't have all that far to go to reach my desired destination, or at least not on paper.

I exhale an audible sigh of relief and scold my still-wobbling knees to calm the hell down. I have a job to perform. An exam to ace. A sexy boyfriend to return to. Never mind the ultimate threat hanging over my head of my own existential demise.

And yet, despite my efforts to banish all thoughts of Elodie to a land far, far away, that statue continues to nag like an annoying kid kicking the back of a seat on an airplane.

I mean, maybe I've got it all wrong.

Maybe I'm acting paranoid, which caused me to misread all the signs.

Maybe Elodie really is responsible, but rather than intending it as a threat, she meant it as an inside joke—a nodding wink, a knowing roll of the eyes from one female to another.

A tangible reminder to not get too carried away by the grandeur of this place and time.

To never allow myself to forget that as exciting as it may seem, back here in 1745 it was perfectly acceptable to portray *Deceit* as a woman — as though history's long list of Judases and Brutuses were some sort of anomaly.

I skirt my way down the Allée Royale, before crossing over to the collection of Four Seasons fountains, where I go in search of the *Fontaine de Saturne,* an allegory of winter that, according to the book, is located on the Allée de l'Hiver which, according to my rudimentary grasp of French, makes sense.

Between these stiff, ill-fitting shoes and the ungainly pannier that makes it hard to move quickly with any semblance of grace, I forge an awkward shuffle toward my destination, intent on moving purposely, without attracting any unwanted attention, all the while wishing there was a horse grazing nearby so I could finally put all those equestrian lessons to use and gallop the rest of the way.

Though the main event is happening inside the palace, the grounds are far from empty. So I do my best to keep my head down until I reach an area where no one has ventured, then I break into an all-out, gut-busting run.

When I pass the Girandole Grove, an area easily recognizable from the alcove of trelliswork that surrounds it, I push my legs harder, faster.

When I hear the steady drumbeat of gushing water, I know it shouldn't be too much longer.

After skirting around a towering wall of hedges, the Fountain of Saturn pops into view, and I pause long enough to clutch at my knees, steady my breath, and ask the obvious question: *Now what?*

107

I stare at the fountain, wondering if maybe this isn't the best plan after all.

I mean, am I really supposed to wade through the basin to lay claim to some mysterious bauble, and then storm the palace with frizzy hair and a drenched gown in hopes of charming some boy I don't even know into traveling into the future?

What is Arthur thinking?

What am I thinking to agree to such a thing?

From the moment I pegged the fountain as the location, I should've taken the time to come up with a much better strategy.

Still, it's not like I can just trot on over to the Hall of Mirrors, find Killian, and instruct him to chill by the portal while I take a midnight dip with Saturn and friends. So I do the only thing I can do—I stand at the edge of the fountain and conduct a quick review of everything I remember from my studies.

The fountain was created by Girardon in 1677, and it features the Roman god Saturn, also known as the god of time, sitting on a bed of shells, surrounded by cupids, as he leans against a sack that he thinks contains Jupiter, the son he wished to kill, when in fact, the child has been replaced by a stone.

A quick scan reveals everything I expected to see is laid out before me exactly as the book claimed it would be, and a wave of relief washes through me. *All right, then. So far so good.*

I guess because over the years, so many components of this

garden have been remodeled or relocated, Arthur chose to send me here now, in hopes that the treasure he seeks has not been disturbed.

Not to mention, of course, the matter of Killian—which makes for a sort of two-for-one, if you will.

As I slink toward the rim and peer past the towering spouts to the gleaming bronze sculpture that sits at the center, there's a rapid fluttering in my chest that I instantly recognize as the relief that comes from being right—of knowing with absolute certainty that somewhere within this mythological tableau is the prize I seek. All that's left now is to claim it.

But first, I'll have to brave the rocketing geysers launching from the mouth of the sack, along with the other eight jets scattered around it.

After kicking off my shoes and removing my stockings and the holster strapped to my thigh, I grab my skirts in one hand, ease my legs over the edge, and step inside a pool so frigid, I fight to stifle a cry as the icy cold water slices straight through my flesh, all the way down to my bones. Still, I force myself onward, splashing toward the island, where I place my free hand on a cherub's bare butt and use the leverage to pull myself up.

My first thought is maybe the Get is hidden among the assortment of seashells. Though it's as good a place as any to look, after a good bit of crawling around, looking for something, anything, that appears even slightly out of place, I'm coming up zero. And between the soaked state of this dress and the freezing night temperatures causing my teeth to chatter and my toes to turn blue, it's becoming glaringly obvious that I need to find this thing soon. Otherwise, before I can even get to annihilation, I'll be dead of hypothermia.

A quick tap of my mask informs me a total of twenty-seven minutes have passed, and for the first time since I arrived, I wonder if maybe I celebrated too soon—maybe I've somehow misinterpreted the clues.

I mean, what if the Get has nothing to do with this fountain? What if—

I force the doubt from my head and try again. Figuring I should attempt a more search-and-rescue-style approach and comb the terrain in a methodical grid, I brace myself against one of the cherubs and focus on the bits to my right. This time, when my gaze lights on a cherub with his hand grasping toward Saturn's wing, something about that chubby little hand, combined with the tormented look on Saturn's face, reminds me of my second day at Gray Wolf when Arthur tasked me with procuring a ruby during the fancy Venetian hologram party.

There, on the wall, hanging beside Goya's version of Saturn making a meal of his son, was an old masterwork of Heraclitus and Democritus that ultimately led me straight to the prize.

In the painting, Heraclitus wore an agonized expression, much like the look on Saturn's face in the sculpture before me. While Democritus, appearing far more gleeful, pointed directly at the clue I needed, just like this curly-haired cherub points to the space beneath Saturn's wing.

A rush of air licks out of my body as it suddenly occurs to me that ever since my first day at Gray Wolf, Arthur's been leading me down a winding trail of breadcrumbs that's been steering me here all along—right to this bronzed swoop of feathers belonging to the god of time himself.

And much like in the construct, when, for a fleeting moment I caught a glimpse beneath the golden shell of Elodie's locket to the shiny jewel nestled within, as I follow the tip of the cherub's pointing finger, I'm struck by a brilliant yellow light that wasn't there a moment ago but now shines as bright as the sun.

The sun!

In an instant, a vision blooms in my head, and I can see it as clearly now as I did way back then.

I'm back home. Back to my nine-year-old self, with my dad sitting before me, his gaze glinting with an unnamable sorrow as he holds up a piece of a once-favored toy I now recognize as a replica of the Antikythera Mechanism. "Tell me about this piece," he says, holding the shiny golden ball before me. "Tell me everything you know about the sun."

A kaleidoscope of butterflies takes flight in my belly, and in a wild burst of elation, I thrust my hand toward it, only to be left grasping at nothing when it vanishes into thin air.

108

I fall back on my heels, wondering if the cold has somehow gone to my head.

If I've become as desperate as a wanderer lost in the desert who starts seeing mirages beyond every sand dune.

But it can't be. Deep in my gut, I know I'm onto something. Because that night back at Gray Wolf, when Arthur took me to the Vault, I had a vision of the original version of the Antikythera Mechanism, I got to see how it looked before it was dismantled and lost, and I know in my bones, all the way down to my frozen blue toes, that the sun is the key to solving this mystery. And that, for whatever reason, my dad has prepared me for this moment.

Is it possible he was somehow working with Arthur?

I force the thought from my mind and focus on things I know for a fact. All the pieces are falling into place, and every one of them leads back to *le soleil.*

Fact: King Louis XIV was known as the Sun King.

The arrangement of this garden, from the Great Axis that starts at the chateau, then leads west past the *Bassin de Latone* all the way to the *Bassin d'Apollon,* runs in a straight line from east to west—*parallel to the daily journey of the sun.*

Both the Visconti Sforza deck and the modern day tarot deck depict the Sun card using the image of both a cherub and the sun.

On the Sforza deck, the one Arthur and my dad both relied on, the cherub is even holding the sun aloft in its hands.

Also, the Sun card in tarot falls in the nineteenth position.

In numerological terms, $1 + 9 = 10$. And of course, reduced even further, $1 + 0 = 1$.

The Wheel of Fortune card I pulled back at Arcana that began this whole journey is number ten in the Major Arcana, which reduces to one.

While the Magician, the card I associated with Arthur, is number one.

Are these links a coincidence?

Or am I overthinking, seeing connections where they don't really exist?

Either way, I need to find out.

I clamber closer to Saturn's wing and stare at the place where I'm sure I saw the light emanate, but all it reveals now is blank space.

I shoot a look over my shoulder, as though willing the cherub to give up the goods.

Then I return to Saturn, a dude who was so afraid of losing his power, he ate his own kids.

"C'mon," I say, under my breath. "I know you're hiding it. I know—" A flash of something bright and quick catches at the corner of my eye, and I thrust my hand toward it once more, gaping in astonishment as a small golden ball appears from out of nowhere.

This is it.

I know in my gut that it's true.

This ancient sphere of gold is the missing piece to the Antikythera Mechanism that's meant to stand in for the sun.

I curl my fingers around the smooth, shiny surface and give it a yank. When it doesn't come away as easily as I'd hoped, I bend into a crouch, wedge my feet hard against Saturn's butt, tighten my grip, and use the full force of my weight to heave my body back so hard, the sphere comes loose in my hand.

My first thought is one of triumph at having succeeded where others failed.

My second thought is unmitigated horror at discovering the momentum I'd created to pull the sun free is now working against me, causing my head to snap up toward the stars as the seat of my gown careens along the slippery slope of Saturn's outstretched leg, before crashing my hip against the cherub's shoulder where I'm catapulted into the sky, arms helplessly flailing, legs splaying over my head, spinning me backward until I'm somersaulting right over the edge.

I land with a splash.

A gush of disgusting fountain water spills into my mouth, while my feet scramble beneath me, searching for purchase, struggling to determine which way is up.

When I break, when my face splits the surface, leaving me retching and gagging and struggling to purge all the water from my lungs and replace it with air, I realize my right fist is still tight, but I'm too afraid to look inside.

You can do this. My heart thrashes wildly in my chest. *You need to do this.*

Slowly, I force myself to uncurl one trembling finger at a time, convinced that I lost it in the fall, only to gasp in wonder when I find the sun—an ancient artifact over two thousand years old—rolling gently across the lines of my palm.

That rush of adrenaline that kept me going until now gusts right out of me, reminding me again just how damn cold this water is. With one task down and another to go, I quickly shuffle toward the edge, climb over the rim, and have just stepped onto dry land when the sky collapses, the ground caves in, and the entire world crumbles around me.

109

The world as I know it is gone.

Disappeared.

Evanesced in a poof as though it never was here.

Only to be replaced by a strange and ancient dreamscape consisting of the same garden elements, the same fountain, but according to the hazy, sepia tones through which I now view it, this is a much earlier age.

Like all the other Unravelings that came before, I'm a hostage to this drama, an audience of one, forced to watch the play unfold until the final curtain is dropped.

This time, a young boy is the star. His face is obscured by a cascade of dark ruffles that bend past his shoulders in the sort of effortless tousle the girls at my old school would literally die for. His sweater is hand-knit of lumpy brown wool with awkwardly drooping sleeves and a complicated network of scars left from multiple mendings. The pants he wears are at least one size too big, left to hang from a twig of a frame made of jutting elbows and knobs for knees. But what he lacks in bulk, he makes up for in agility and speed, and I watch in astonishment as he steals through the night, his steps quick and sure as a cheetah unleashed.

Though as purposeful as he looks, he's not without fear. I know this by the quickening beat of his heart that is somehow, inexplicably, accessible to my ears.

There's a sheen of sweat on his brow dripping steadily into his eye, and I can feel the salty sting of it as though it's spilled into mine.

When a gut-wrenching wave of nausea rolls through me, I watch in amazement as I clasp a hand to my belly at the exact moment the boy does the same.

Together, we unlock our knees, take several deep breaths, and make a slow count of *un, deux, trois*…until the misery has passed. And I know without question, I'm no longer just an observer. Like gazing into a fun-house mirror, I'm now part of this dream.

Driven by equal measures of determination and trepidation, the boy clambers over the edge of the newly completed fountain and cuts a quick path through the water, barely registering the icy spray that bites through his worn clothes and into his skin—*our* skin. Then he leaps onto the island like I did, crawls past the cherub, and just before hiding the golden ball beneath Saturn's wing—the same golden ball now gripped in my hand—he bends his head, shuts his eyes tightly, and infuses the object with the story now unfolding all around me.

Within the clammy confines of my palm, the sun begins a steady heat and thrum. The intensity of the vibration increasing so rapidly, it jumps in my hand, forcing me to struggle to hang on.

This is no ordinary Unraveling.

This is a message—a sort of energetic telegram the boy intended solely for me.

There's a name for this sort of phenomenon—a term once used by my dad when he tried to teach me about the energy field infused within objects and how to access that power…

Psychometry.

As soon as I land on the word, it's superseded by the boy's message, which spews forth in a rush.

Something about another sun he's tucked away in an ancient royal crypt… It's a decoy… A trap… Two suns were needed because there's so much at stake…

I scramble to match the words to the vision, but it all flows so quickly, it soon overwhelms me.

I force my eyes shut, telling myself it will help me connect, delve even deeper. But the churning revolt in my gut calls me out on the lie, and the next thing I know, the trapdoor of memory bangs open as a deluge of forgotten teachings and truths, things I've managed to suppress all this time, comes slamming back toward me.

My dad knew this moment would come.

He tried to teach me, prepare me, but I'd stubbornly looked away and channeled my effort into forgetting.

Falsely believing that by turning my back on him and all that he taught me, by denying his existence, I could also deny the grief his absence had made.

But now he's here—a shimmering vision of the dad I've secretly missed for so many years. He looks strong. Fit. With a flop of brown hair, a quirk of a smile, a narrow pinch of nose, and eyes just like mine. The sight of him is enough to make my heart splinter into a million unmendable shards.

And yet, my heart also reminds me that he's not *really* here.

This vision of him is more like a specter of memory sent to warn me that, unlike the scary movies Mason and I used to watch, covering my eyes and refusing to look won't save me from the sort of things he needs me to know.

Needs me to see.

Look! he tells me. *Open your eyes and—*

My eyes snap open just in time to watch the boy slip the golden ball beneath Saturn's wing, where it will remain in secret until I come along.

When the boy turns to leave, I catch a quick glimpse of his face.

What I see leaves my jaw unhinged, my eyes gaping wide, as a startled cry trips from my lips.

I lean into the vision, trying to peer closer and confirm the impossible, when a rough hand clamps down on my arm, jolting me out of the dream and back to the horrifying reality of a harsh voice barking into my ear, "Ou allez-vous?"

110

First thing I notice is his nose isn't broken.

It's then that I realize that also means he has no recollection of our prior meeting.

Because my arrival was timed two hours earlier than my last visit, as far as the groundskeeper is concerned, this is the first time he's seen me.

I shoot him an indignant look, and in a chirp of warbled French, I warn him in no uncertain terms that he cannot speak to me in that tone.

It's only after my show of bravado that I notice my stockings and shoes are draped over his shoulder, and while his left hand holds the golden sphere he must've seized while I was lost in the vision, his right hand wields a dagger I soon recognize as my own. Next thing I know, he's pressing it fast to my throat.

"You take what does not belong to you," he says, his French so rapid, it's a moment before I can translate. He slips the sun into a small leather pouch he wears tied at his waist, then angles the tip of my blade until it nearly pierces my flesh.

The same blade I'd foolishly left on top of my shoes in a misguided attempt to keep the holster from getting wet. A ridiculously rookie move if there ever was one.

"You have no business here," the man whispers bitterly into my ear, as he yanks hard on my wrist and pins my body tightly to his. "And now, you will learn what happens to thieves at this court."

He's barely finished the threat before he starts dragging me away, and though I struggle with all my might to break free, my efforts are wasted. This man holds the unfair advantage of being five times my size and possessing three times my strength.

The soles of my bare feet scrape along the gravel, while the sopping skirts of my gown cling to legs now rendered so numb, they feel as though they belong to somebody else.

When we reach the *Parterre D'eau* and a crowd of gowned and masked revelers turn to stare, I can't believe my good luck, knowing that soon, this will be over.

I mean, yes, my hair is a halo of frizz, and I don't need a mirror to know my dress is a catastrophe, but surely they can see past the tragic exterior to the quality of my carriage, the gleam of my jewels, the requisite trappings of wealth meant to convey my rightful place here.

Surely, once they take note of my well-practiced air of breeding and refinement, the only logical conclusion they can possibly draw is that I'm a poor misunderstood noble who's had the misfortune of running afoul of an irrational groundskeeper, and I require their immediate help.

But as I watch their heads bob together, rouged lips tipping with laughter, I remember that no matter which class I appear to belong in, as a female in this place and time, I am completely devoid of all rights.

To their unseasoned eyes, this angry, indignant groundskeeper must have a good reason for dragging me through the night toward a destination known only to him. Clearly, I must've done something egregious to deserve such treatment. So why would they bother to step in?

The realization slams through me as the truth of my situation kicks in. To them, I'm just another addition to the night's entertainment, along with all the jugglers, acrobats, fire-eaters, and musicians. And if I don't find a way out of this mess, it's just a matter of time before the portal shuts down, I cross my own timeline, and I cease to exist.

Cease. To. Exist.

The idea is terrifying enough, but it can't actually be true—*can it?*

I mean, how can a person just…stop…being?

Just…*vanish* as though they never existed?

A jarring shudder passes through me, and I know it's got less to do with the frigid night air, and everything to do with the tidal wave of nausea now rolling up my belly, leaving me gagging, choking on a bitter stream of bile swirling its way up my throat.

I need to find a way out of here—a way to break free.

I need to—

I thrust my body hard against the groundskeeper, jamming my shoulder into his arm. But he doesn't so much as grunt. He just tightens his grip on my elbow and continues to lug me along.

But my right arm is free, and I lift it toward my mask, my fingers discreetly tapping the side, needing to know just how much time I have left, only to be met with blank space where the green arrow and the countdown clock should appear.

I tap it again, firmer this time, but the result is the same.

No green arrow.

No countdown.

Nothing but blackness in the space where the way out should appear.

111

*N*o, no, no, no, no! It can't be. It's just a glitch—it's just—
On the verge of a full-blown meltdown, I press the side
of my mask again and again. But the result is always the same.

A frantic calculation whirls through my brain as I struggle
to subtract the time I've already burned through, from the two
hours I arrived with, but whatever I come up with is merely a
guess. The only thing I know for certain is that this is no longer
pretend.

No longer some existential brainteaser as I try to determine
just exactly how my annihilation will happen.

Will I poof out of existence in the blink of an eye?

Or will it be a more gradual demise? Losing pieces of myself
bit by bit. Limb by limb, until there's nothing remaining except
the memory held by those who once knew me.

And even then, how long before they move on and forget
all about me?

Defeat threatens to swallow me whole, causing my knees to
fold, my arms to turn useless, as the groundskeeper continues to
lob me along like a rag doll.

As we approach the wide marble steps that lead to the palace,
the lilting harmony of orchestral strains grows increasingly
louder, providing a festive soundtrack to this nightmare that
strikes me as ironically funny. I toss a glance over my shoulder,
eager for one last look of Versailles in all its splendor, when I

spot him—a tall, broad-shouldered, golden-haired boy, with a flute of champagne in one hand and a pretty girl with hair the color of flames on his arm.

But it's just a delusion.

A mirage.

All the proof I need to know that I've finally succumbed to the cold. Having progressed well beyond the shivering stage of hypothermia, I'm now well into the far more alarming state of exhaustion and confusion, soon to be followed by a swift decline in consciousness, where I will flounder until my time is up and I fade into nothing.

Still, I blink just to make sure.

And when I blink a second time, I'm amazed to find the golden-haired boy is still there.

"Killian!" I cry. My voice trilling raspy and desperate into the night, I squirm my fingers into the hidden pocket where the bodice of my gown meets the skirt, fumbling for the handkerchief the boy gave me the last time we met, as the groundskeeper continues hauling me toward whatever godforsaken destination awaits. "Killian de Luce!" I call, even louder this time, my tone ringing frantic and high.

I watch as the boy whips around and peers in my direction. Though it's not lost on me that he remains stubbornly, resolutely in place.

Recognizing this may be my last chance, a shot I can't afford to miss, I desperately fumble for the handkerchief, only to find it's not there.

But that's impossible! I specifically remembered shoving it into that pocket just after Roxanne gave it to me. I search again, but the result is the same, and suddenly, the horrible truth descends in a rush.

The handkerchief is no longer there, because much like with the groundskeeper, I've arrived too soon—well before Killian found me on the terrace outside the Hall of Mirrors.

Which means, he doesn't know me.

Has never kissed me.

Never given me his handkerchief with a vow to not forget me.

And, most importantly, because none of that has yet to occur, he has no good reason to step in and save me.

The groundskeeper continues to drag me, and though I struggle with whatever heat and strength I can muster, my small frame is no match for this angry man's bulk.

With each step forward, my chance of enticing Killian to act on my behalf shrinks smaller and smaller. Soon he'll be lost to me forever. But I can't go down without a fight. I have to at least try.

"Killian," I cry. "Killian de Luce!" Stubbornly, I dig my heels into the earth, tears streaming down my cheeks as the groundskeeper's leathery mitt of a hand clenches so hard, it sends a spasm of pain shooting all the way to my wrist. Still, in one last desperate plea, I look over my shoulder and say, "My name is Natasha! And you know me, you—" The groundskeeper slaps a hand over my mouth and hauls me deeper into the night.

As the image of Killian fades from view, it's quickly replaced by the frigid fingers of fear closing in on my throat, and the haunting face of a boy I don't know.

The one I saw in the vision.

The one with the blazing blue eyes that bore an undeniable resemblance to Braxton.

112

I have no idea how to play this.

This is not one of the stories we covered in AP History. If it was, maybe I would've paid more attention.

It's also not the sort of thing we covered at Gray Wolf, where the focus is on learning to blend so seamlessly, you rise above all suspicion and avoid moments like this.

And yet, despite all the time I spent studying, I still find myself being dragged deep into the bowels of Versailles, where the rooms are devoid of all grandeur, probably because they're reserved for torturing traitors and holding them prisoner.

Realizing it may well turn out to be my last chance to save myself, I cry, "Stop! I—I'm sorry. Um…*je suis désolé!*"

The groundskeeper rakes a disparaging gaze over me, then shoves me hard against a wall as I frantically tap my mask once again, but still nothing appears.

Technology can fail, Jago had warned.

And while it's undoubtedly true, I've got my own theories about what's really going on here.

"Do you know what happens to little thieves like you?" The groundskeeper snarls as he jabs the tip of my dagger to a tender bit of flesh just under my ear.

"I'm so sorry," I whisper, my head ducked in shame.

The groundskeeper leans closer. "Repetez!" he commands, and I know I have no choice but to obey.

Slowly, I lift my chin and center my gaze upon his. "I said, I'm so—"

As he cocks his head to the side and leans toward me, I seize the moment to kick my leg high and jam my knee straight into his groin.

"Sophomore year PE, self-defense module," I spit, watching as a shock wave of pain thunders through him, causing his knees to give way as he crumbles to the ground in a heap.

I crouch down beside him, wishing I could take full advantage of the moment and really savor this victory but, since time is definitely not on my side, I'm quick to reclaim my dagger and pinch the small golden ball from the leather pouch at his waist.

Then I cram my stockings into one of my pockets, bite back a scream of agony as I shove my ravaged feet back into my shoes, and just to make sure he won't be rallying anytime soon, I aim a solid kick to the side of his ribs that sends the air whooshing right out of him. Then I spin on my heel and run like the wind.

I have no idea where I'm going, but seeing as how I can't afford to have any of those nobles who spotted me earlier deciding to break out of their fog of apathy and play the hero by returning me to captivity, it's safer to head the opposite way that I came.

There's a corner up ahead, and though I've no idea what mysteries I might discover on the other side, I'm hoping it will allow me to duck out of sight long enough to get my bearings and find my way back to the portal while I still can. Because when it comes down to it, as much as I dread seeing Arthur's disappointment when he discovers I failed to drag Killian back to Gray Wolf, it's still preferable to shaking hands with my own oblivion.

Because, just like the handkerchief vanished from my pocket, I know I'll also vanish the second I cross my own timeline.

The bottoms of my feet are so battered and raw, every step brings a fresh wave of misery. Still, I race forward, about to swing around the bend, when a man turns the corner and I run smack into his brick of a chest.

He cries out in surprise. Settles me back on my feet. And just when I'm sure that I'm free, his gaze darts from me to the flashing bit of gold in my hand, to the gleaming dagger in my other hand, to the place just past my shoulder where the groundskeeper lies curled in a heap.

Next thing I know, he's locking me inside a cell.

113

I remember watching the *Marie Antoinette* movie with Mason, and how we both swooned over the abundance of glamour and opulence—the wild parties; the bottomless glasses of champagne; the towers of tiny, sweet cakes; the piles of shoes and sparkling jewels; her ridiculous birdcage hairdo.

But never once, during all those multiple viewings, did it ever occur to me that I might end up like her—captured at Versailles and bound for the guillotine.

Though, now that I think about it, I probably have a better chance of being drawn and quartered, hung before a crowd of bloodthirsty onlookers, or maybe even burned at the stake, since I'm not sure they used the guillotine as early as 1745.

Either way, it's just details. Because the fact is, I won't even exist long enough for any of that to happen. I'll be annihilated well before then.

It reminds me of what Oliver said about preferring to lose his head than being locked away in one of these bleak, hopeless boxes. And it makes me wonder if he ever found himself in a situation like this. Or am I the only one who's managed to fail so spectacularly?

And I have failed, in every possible way.

The guard has taken possession of the sun, and Killian de Luce is still out there somewhere, sipping champagne and enjoying the party. While I'm locked in this nightmare of a prison, gagging on the scent of shit, piss, vomit, despair, and other foul things I'd prefer not to identify. All the while keeping a steady eye on my cellmate—a fat, filthy rat with beady red eyes that's greedily feasting on a much smaller rat, a fraction of her size. Going by the smaller rat's lack of fur and pink-toned flesh, I'm guessing it's a baby. Which means the mama rat is cannibalizing one of her pups. I remember reading once that rats are prone to that sort of thing when faced with a shortage of food.

As I watch her make a meal of her offspring, hoping she doesn't try to venture anywhere near me, I'm caught by the irony of how my mom essentially sentenced me to a similar fate. By signing me away to ensure her own survival, I eventually ended up here, trapped in this hell until the clock on the portal runs down.

A fresh wave of nausea rolls through me. An involuntary cry of anguish swells in my chest, robbing me of breath and causing my knees to falter, my legs to give out from under me, as I slump to the ground in a heap of sopping wet finery—voluminous rich silks and exquisite lace trim turned into a soggy, drooping mess— the once jaunty bows now a collection of wilted clumps.

Still, none of this regalia matters anymore.

Even in its glorious state, it wouldn't have spared me from becoming yet another nameless, faceless woman abused, discarded, and forgotten by time.

I wonder if Braxton will miss me.

I wonder if anyone will suspect Elodie.

I knew she could be cruel, but this—this is a whole other level.

Never in my life have I felt so alone. So utterly helpless and lost.

I remember back at Arcana, how arrogant I was when I laughed before my own tombstone.

When I picture my grave marker now, this is what it says:

HERE LIES NATASHA ANTOINETTE CLARKE
DISAPPOINTING DAUGHTER – WORSE FRIEND
SHE DIED AS SHE LIVED:
AN UNCONNECTED, UNTITLED,
UNKNOWN GIRL OF ABSOLUTELY NO CONSEQUENCE
SHE WAS LOST IN A PLACE AND TIME
IN WHICH SHE DID NOT BELONG
AND ULTIMATELY FADED INTO OBLIVION

Never mind that the grave will be empty.

There will be no storybook ending.

No dashing knight astride a shiny steed coming to save me.

No handsome corporate raider to whisk me away in a white limousine.

The only foreseeable outcome is the ultimate fade-out.

I rub my hands briskly over my arms to ward off a shiver and reach for the golden charm at my neck, desperate for some small glimmer of hope—a reminder that somewhere outside these walls, the moon hangs high, stars glitter like diamonds, and a beautiful boy awaits my return...

But my talisman is missing.

No.

No!

In an instant, I'm back on my feet. My heart bangs wildly against the walls of my chest as I frantically claw at my skirts, scour my hands down the front of my bodice and under each breast.

I search every inch of the floor of this cell, kicking at urine-soaked clumps of straw, and hissing at the rat, watching as she edges into the corner, dragging her meal along with her, only to confirm the charm truly is gone.

I must've lost it in the fountain, during my struggle with the groundskeeper, or when I ran into the guard.

And now, without the talisman to serve as a reminder, my memory will soon vanish as well.

I rush to the door, wrap my fingers around the bars, and throw my weight against them, shaking with every ounce of my strength. But they're solid, locked from the outside, and offer no hope for escape.

My eyes flood with tears, causing my vision to blur and my body to sag hopelessly against the filthy, cold iron.

I remember what Braxton said about no one ever being sent home for failing. But now I know that's only because when they do, they end up lost in time, all concept of their home and identity forgotten.

This is what happened to Anjou, and probably Elodie's first Tripping partner.

Who knows how many other Blues have failed to make the return trip to Gray Wolf?

And once I manage to cross my own timeline, what then?

Will I vanish in this world, the modern world, or maybe even both?

And what's more—does it even matter?

In the end, mine will be just another name to add to that long list of failures.

I squeeze my eyes shut and fight back the scream that threatens to burst right out of my chest. I can't afford to forget, and I refuse to let Elodie succeed in her attempt to erase me.

I push away from the bars and begin pacing my cell. With my hands clutching at my skirts, I trudge across bloodstained stones, as I whisper to myself:

My name is Natasha Antoinette Clarke. I am from California. I was born in the new millennium. My last address was Gray Wolf Academy. I have a mom, a best friend named Mason, and a boyfriend named Braxton, and I am one of Arthur Blackstone's Artful Dodgers…

I continue to repeat the most relevant bits of my biography, hoping that by continuing to recite the facts as I know them, I can somehow imprint the story of me onto my brain.

This is not my dress.

These are not my shoes.

And this certainly is not my pannier.

I grasp the metal cage by the side, tempted to rip the annoying thing right off once and for all, when I remember the strange expression Charlotte wore as she ran a hand down the right side and assured me that sometimes they really do come in handy.

With my breath billowing before me in tiny crystallized puffs, I reach a hand under my skirts and locate three loose bits of steel that are thicker, stronger, and not nearly as secure as the others.

After wrenching them free, I rush toward the wall, where I carve my full name into the stone. Hoping that by seeing it there, it'll help me remember who I am, when I am, and where I truly belong.

And failing that, at least I won't vanish without anyone knowing I was once here.

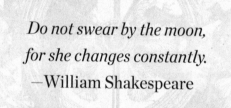

Do not swear by the moon,
for she changes constantly.
—William Shakespeare

114

At the sound of footsteps, I spring into position.

With my back against the wall, I crouch low in the shadows, head bent in submission, hands pressed together as though praying for redemption.

Whoever it is, they're in for a surprise.

I am not the broken girl they're expecting to find.

In my hand I grip three bits of steel I've fastened together and sharpened into a weapon I have every intention of using.

"She still in there?" a gruff male voice calls.

"All yours if you want her," another one replies.

"Hope you didn't start without me." The first voice cracks. "But you can have her when I'm done. If there's anything left, that is." He laughs, a horrible guttural sound that only strengthens my determination to do whatever necessary to find my way out of this hell.

Only problem is, I have no idea where to go once I escape.

The footsteps pause just outside my door.

A face peers through the iron bars.

It's a man I don't recognize, though the fine cut of his clothes leaves me to wonder if maybe he's here to release me. But when I note the salacious leer on his face, I realize he's interested only in what he can take.

A terrible screech of metal grating on metal echoes through the space, and I press the weapon tighter between my palms.

The door creaks open—

I shift my weight from my heels to my toes.

The man enters—

I leap into the air, weapon at the ready.

"*Que diab*—" Before he can finish, the jagged tip is pressed flush to his neck.

"Here's what you're going to do." I maneuver the sharpest part of my hastily crafted blade until it pierces his flesh, leaving no doubt I am not to be messed with. "You're going to keep your mouth shut. You're going to give me that key, then you're going to stay locked inside like an obedient prisoner. And when you're asked what happened, you're going to say you were so drunk that you have no idea how you got here, but you never saw me. *Comprenez-vous?*"

It's a good start, but a second later, he whirls around with such force, it throws me right off, sending me crashing into the wall as an explosion of pain shoots up my arm, the weapon falls from my fingers, and the man kicks it clear across the cell where I can no longer reach it.

I cower before him, my stomach lurching at the sight of his hateful gaze and lecherous grin as his hands busy themselves with unfastening his pants.

"There's nowhere to run," he says. "So you may as well try to enjoy it."

I brace against the wall. My heart thrashing, my knees threatening to crumple beneath me, I use all my best French, hurl a string of profanities I learned from Oliver and Finn, but the man only laughs. And when he goes about dropping his breeches, my body freezes with terror as my mind reels with the realization of the horrifying fate that awaits me.

No. No! There's no way—this cannot be happening. I'm dreaming, caught in a nightmare—I have to wake up, I have to—

With his pants bunched around his knees, I'm amazed at

how he still manages to grab at me, spin me around, and smash me hard against the wall, as he grips either side of my waist.

The ease in which he approaches this violence tells me this is not the first time he's committed such an act. But if I have anything to do with it, it will be his last.

A low grunt sounds from his throat as he grabs the hem of my gown and starts to lift it to my hips. Though he doesn't get very far before a shot of adrenaline races through me, and I spring back to life, jamming my foot into his knee so hard, I hear a satisfying crack.

He howls in pain, arcs an arm toward my head. But with his pants dragging down to his ankles, he struggles for balance.

I steal the moment to duck out from under him and race for the weapon, only to have him reel on me and yank my skirts so hard, I'm pulled right off my feet and drop to the ground.

He's on top of me now. His weight so suffocating, I fight for every ounce of air I can squeeze into my lungs, as his own rancid breath blows hot in my ear, and his fat, greasy fingers tear hard at my dress.

I peer an eye open, seeing the rat in the far corner. She's taken a break from cannibalizing her baby and centered her beady eyes on me as I stretch my arm forward, practically pulling it loose from its socket, but the weapon remains stubbornly out of my reach.

In my ear, the man voices harsh words meant to insult, but I'm way beyond listening and far beyond caring what he has to say.

With a terrible groan, he pulls me up against him, smacks me so hard across the cheek, I can feel the burn of his metal ring branding my skin. And though I continue to struggle, kicking, fighting with everything I've got, he's too heavy, too strong, and with my body caught between the ground and him, my blows bear no effect.

I close my eyes, stifle a tormented cry, when my hair comes loose and one of the many pins and combs that keep the overly complicated updo in place tumbles before me.

I snap my eyes open, my gaze landing on a diamond fan with two sharp prongs.

Are they sharp enough?

Only one way to find out.

The man latches his lips to my ear, tells me to relax and enjoy the inevitable.

Then his fingers grasp at my legs, just as I slam my hand backward and jab the hairpin into his face.

He reels back in shock, and I use the moment to scramble out from under him and race for the weapon.

When I turn, I find him sprawled on the ground, pants twisted around his feet, and a hand clutched to the place just beneath his eye where he yanks the pin free.

A torrent of blood gushes forth. His brow furrows, lips draw tightly together. He's completely enraged.

I inch toward the door. It's wide open and it would be so easy to escape—except that the man still has the key, and he's screaming so loudly now, I'm afraid the guard will hear.

I need to find a way to silence him. Whatever it takes.

He yells at me, calling me a thief, a whore, and a whole lot of other things Finn and Oliver never taught me, but I can assume they're not exactly flattering.

His one good eye wide and crazed, the man struggles to stand and come at me again, but his knee bends the wrong way, sending him reeling back toward the ground.

I rush toward him, weapon at the ready. "Give me the key," I say.

The man spits in my face.

I respond by slamming the blade hard into his neck, tearing away at his silk and lace cravat before hitting his flesh.

With blood oozing from the twin wounds I've made, I shove a ball of lace into his mouth, then yank my stockings from my pocket and use them to tie the man's hands behind his back.

I'm just reaching into his jacket, searching for the key, when he manages to shove his good knee into my gut, nearly knocking the air right out of me.

A storm of rage rushes through me, and I plunge the blade deep into his chest.

I'm about to do it again when a shadow looms over me, and a male voice says, "Stop! You're going to kill him."

115

"**M**aybe he deserves killing!" I snap. With unseeing eyes, I raise the blade again, only to have it snatched right out of my hand.

"It's enough. You've done enough. Trust me, once you've killed, you can never go back."

I look up to find a boy holding my handmade weapon at his side. He's strangely familiar, but the part of his face not hidden by his mask is veiled by shadow.

Retrieving a square of white cotton from his pocket, he offers it to me. "You have blood—" He motions to my cheek and then to my chin.

I make quick work of it, and when I return the square, he stares at the blue embroidery marking the center for so long, you'd think he was seeing it for the very first time.

I turn back to the bloodied man on the floor, and the boy says, "It's not your place to change history. That man has a role to play that surpasses this moment. By killing him, you risk leaving a ripple in time that'll have far-reaching effects."

"That's not my problem." I scoff, torn between wanting to finish the job and the horrible realization of what I've already done, the sort of damage I'm still capable of.

"Let's leave him alive and make sure that it's not." The boy offers his hand, but I brush it aside and find my own way to my feet.

"Who are you?" I ask, taking a deliberate step back. He doesn't appear to mean any harm, but no one's above suspicion anymore. Also, he's acting kind of strange.

He shakes his head. Wipes a hand across his chin. "I found something," he says. "Out there, on the ground." He nods toward a place somewhere beyond the walls of this cell. "I think it belongs to you."

I glance over my shoulder, then back at him, warily watching as he takes a step forward and leans into the light.

His hair is long and golden. His nose prominent, jaw strong. And though the cluster of medals on his jacket, along with the fine cut of his breeches and shine of his polished black boots, suggest he's someone of significance, my attention is claimed by the small golden charm he now holds in the center of his outstretched palm.

It's a gilded cage with a moon and star caught inside.

"Thanks to you, I remember." His voice is merely a whisper. "And now it's time for you to remember, too." He takes another step toward me until there's only a breath of space left spanning between us.

My hand trembles as I reach for the charm, fold my fingers around it, and gasp at the sudden rush of images that swirl through my head like a cyclone.

Braxton.

Gray Wolf.

Arthur.

Elodie.

The portal that's going to close—and my own annihilation, if that happens before I can reach it.

My mind is a tempest of memory.

"My name is Killian de Luce," the boy says. "And I want to help you. Will you let me?" His voice is gentle, kind.

I gaze back with wide, frightened eyes. "Unless you hold

great favor with the king, they'll make you pay for helping me."

He shakes his head. "I don't care about that anymore. I remember who I am now."

"And who's that?" My voice trembles.

"I'm one of you."

Killian extends an arm toward the wall at my back, and at first, I'm not sure what he's getting at.

But when I follow the length of his finger, I find the place where I scratched my name into the rock, along with the initials AAD, in a final bid to hang on to my memories.

"Arthur's Artful Dodgers," he says, as my jaw falls slack with disbelief. "And you're Natasha."

"But that's impossible—" I start, before I realize it's not. I shake my head, begin again. "How long have you been here?" I ask.

"Too long." He sighs, reaches for my hand.

"There's a guard out there," I warn, but Killian shakes his head.

"I took care of him. He's sleeping it off. Still, we need to get out of here before he wakes up."

I start to head out, but then I remember there's one more thing left to do.

"Natasha—whatever you're doing, we don't have time for this!" Killian watches anxiously as I crouch down to where the man lies slumped and bloodied on the floor.

I reach for his hand and snatch the ring right off his finger, same one he clocked me with earlier. And though he's bound and gagged, the uninjured eye that stares back is filled with vivid dreams of revenge.

Once the ring is secured in my pocket, I look back toward the markings I left on the wall, where I publicly declared myself a member of Arthur's Artful Dodgers.

"Should I try to scratch it out?" I ask, but Killian is quick to shake his head.

"Leave it," he says. "You're part of the annals of history now. Don't deprive future historians the fun of deciphering the meaning behind AAD."

He laughs, but I wonder if this slight change in events caused it to already appear in a history book somewhere.

If I ever make it back to the palace in real time, will I find my name etched on these walls?

Something to contemplate at another time, in another place.

I'm about to step out of the cell when Killian stops me. "Your shoe," he says, retrieving the one I must've lost during the struggle and that, according to the bite marks along the heel, the rat was quick to claim as her own. "Also"—he motions toward my face—"you missed a spot. May I?"

My first reaction is to flinch, and the moment he takes note, he's quick to hand over my weapon.

"I want you to feel safe," he says. "But I also want to clean the blood off your face. I mean no offense, but you're a bit of a mess, and it's a whole other world up there. We need to at least try to blend in."

With the blade clutched in my hand, I watch as Killian gently sweeps the handkerchief across the tip of my chin and a spot on my jaw, before slipping it back into his pocket.

"Also—" He points toward my nest of hair that's left in a half-up, half-down tangle of frizz. Removing the rest of the pins, he hands them to me, then coaxes his hands expertly through my hair until it falls in damp waves that tumble over my shoulders.

"Better?" I ask.

"Much better." He grins. "Though I'm afraid there's not much I can do about your dress so, here." He slips free of his frock coat and arranges it over my shoulders.

"Were you a stylist in your past life?" I ask, sinking into the warmth, a welcome respite from the frigid, damp cold that's left me in a permanent state of shaking and numbness.

"I've been many things." He laughs. "But now, I'm soon to be a wanted man, so—"

Without another word, he ushers me out of the cell, and after locking the man inside, Killian and I run for our lives.

116

First thing I see when we reach the end of the hall is the guard who locked me in the cell now slumped on the ground, and the man responsible for putting me there bleeding out from a knife wound.

"What have you done?" I cry, pausing to approach the groundskeeper who, from what I can tell, will soon be dead if he's not already.

"I did what I had to," Killian snaps. "Now come. And hurry. We need to keep moving before someone finds us both here."

I know he's right. There's not even a second to spare. But that small leather pouch is still tied at the groundskeeper's waist, and even if there's only the most miniscule chance that the guard might've returned the golden ball to him, I still need to check.

I bend down beside him. My gaze skimming past the wound in his belly, I focus on the strange round symbol tattooed on the crook of his arm. An intricate series of interlinking circles—a design that's somehow familiar.

I lean closer, wanting to get a better look, when Killian says, "No use mourning the Timekeeper."

I turn to Killian in confusion. "The what?"

But he just shakes his head and says, "You done there?"

I return to the dying man before me, loosen the drawstring of the small leather bag, and sneak a finger inside. Only to exhale in relief when I find the sun has sunk to the bottom.

After stashing the golden ball into one of my pockets, I get to my feet with Killian's help, and together we race toward a spiral stairway.

"How long do we have?" he asks as I rush to keep up.

"I don't know," I whisper. "My mask stopped working just after I arrived."

He glances over his shoulder. "That was no accident," he says, his tone unmistakably cryptic, leaving me to wonder if it's how he ended up stuck here. But there's no time to discuss. We need to keep moving.

"Take my hand and walk quickly," he says. "But don't run until it's safe."

"But we need to get to the portal!" I argue.

"First, we need to get out of here without attracting any undue notice."

I walk alongside him, keeping my eye on the prize—the exit, the garden beyond, and, with any luck, the sculpture of *Deceit* that leads to the doorway that I fiercely hope will stay open long enough for us to reach it.

I had two hours. And the last time I checked, I'd already burned through a good portion of that. Considering the events that unfolded since then, it feels like I've been here for days. If the portal is closed and we're trapped in 1745 with an angry man locked away in a cell, a murdered groundskeeper, and a guard who can awaken at any second, then Killian is doomed, and I'm... Well, I guess it doesn't really matter, since I'll cease to exist.

The thought alone is enough to quicken my pace. I don't care what Killian says, we can't afford any delays. But Killian has other ideas, and the next thing I know, he's lifted me off my feet, swooped me into his arms, and practically swallowed me in his embrace.

"What the hell?" I punch him hard on the shoulder. "I knew

I couldn't trust you! I knew—" I press the blade to his chest, but he doesn't so much as flinch.

"Don't fight me," he says, breathing into my ear. "Or do fight me, but only in a way that looks playful."

"What the fu—"

Next thing I know, he covers my mouth with his, but unlike Jago, Killian doesn't fake the kiss. His lips are gentle, warm, and all too familiar. But unlike the last time we kissed, I'm not in a Fade and I absolutely cannot, will not, play along with his game.

I peek an eye open to see two guards storming toward us. They slow as they pass, taking a moment to scrutinize Killian and me in a way that has me certain they can see right through this facade of a clinch.

Killian clutches me tighter, whispering, "I'm sorry, but please, just go with it for now," then continues to push his lips against mine.

The guards pass, hurrying in the direction we came from, as Killian loosens his grip and starts to pull away, but not before I sink my teeth deep into his bottom lip.

"Good God!" he cries, depositing me back on my feet, and raising both hands in surrender.

"I don't know how long you've been gone—" I glance over my shoulder as I make to flee. "But the rules have changed. You need to ask for consent."

He wipes a hand dramatically over his mouth, as though erasing the kiss from his lips, or maybe he's checking for blood—it's hard to tell. "I needed it to look authentic." He hurries alongside me. "Do you seriously believe the French can't tell the difference? Not to mention there are blood spatters on your dress that my coat can't hide—do you really want them to see that? And, for the record, judging by the way you kissed me back, and how quickly the guards moved on, I'm thinking they weren't the only ones fooled."

I start to argue that I absolutely did *not* kiss him back, when he laughs so hard I realize I played right into his trap.

"Is Natasha your real name?" He peers down at me from behind his mask.

"Isn't Killian yours?"

"It is now," he says. "A lot of us make them up. New life, new identity. That sort of thing."

"I knew Elodie Blue was a fake," I mutter under my breath, but Killian heard me.

"Elodie, huh?" He peers into the distance, whistles softly to himself. But not a sexy whistle, more like a *here-comes-trouble* kinda sound. And I make a note to get to the bottom of that, but later, not now. "It's been a long time since I've heard that name, or even wanted to." Shaking free of the memory, he says, "Do you remember where you left it? The doorway, I mean. Because without the aid of the mask—"

I roll my eyes, annoyed that he's treating me like some kind of amateur. I mean, maybe I am, but I'm not the one who's been stuck here for God knows how long.

The second we're out of the palace, I break into a run. But Killian's legs are much longer, so for him it's more like a jog.

"Up ahead," I gasp, pushing my own legs to pump harder. When we clear a thick grove of hedges cut and manicured into perfectly submissive triangles, I catch sight of the statue marking the location of the portal and double my efforts, taking nothing for granted.

"Deceit?" Killian chases the word with a laugh. Unlike me, he's not at all short of breath. "And let me guess—you think that's a coincidence?"

He laughs even harder, and this time, it's pretty clear it's directed at me.

117

"Y ou sure about this?" I ask as we start to close in on the gap between us and what I hope to be the glimmering doorway I can't actually see. "You sure you want to go back to Gray Wolf?"

"On one condition." He grasps my hand and moves before me, effectively blocking my path.

"You're seriously trying to negotiate?" I huff, pressing a hand against my ridiculously tight bodice and struggling to steady my breath. "I mean, here—now?"

"Considering how I'm on your list of Gets, I think I'm in a position to bargain, don't you?"

"How do you know you're on my list?" I straighten my spine, smooth a hand down the front of my wreck of a gown.

Killian laughs. "Why else did they send you? To filch a gold ring from a duke?"

I roll my eyes and push past him, continuing toward the portal when I realize what he just said, and I whip around to gape at him. "That predator was a *duke*?"

I'm not sure why I'm surprised by the news. In addition to being an asshole, a predator, and a dangerously violent offender, he was totally arrogant and entitled. I frown at the memory, wondering if I've made a mistake by not ending him when I had the chance.

"The Duke de Valentois himself," Killian says, jogging right alongside me. "Though not to worry, I'm sure he had it coming."

"Worry?" I scoff, picking up speed. "I would've finished the job if—"

Killian grasps hold of my elbow, stopping me cold in my tracks. "It wasn't your life to take," he says, his voice earnest.

"And what about the groundskeeper?" I shoot back, watching as Killian cocks his head in confusion. "You didn't have any problem leaving him to bleed out."

Killian runs a hand across his chin. "The *groundskeeper*? Is that what you think he is?" He breaks into a laugh that roars through the night. It grows even louder when I shake my head and push past him again.

"For the record—that man was a *Timekeeper*," Killian says, trailing just behind me. "And trust me, no one is going to miss him. As for the duke, he's managed to make plenty of enemies, and it won't be much longer until one of them finishes what you started. But not until after the duke impregnates his wife, who will then give birth to a daughter, who will ultimately go on to birth several more children, one of whom will make a significant, lasting impact on the world. And that, in a nutshell, is why I stopped you. Think of it like dominoes—you knock one down, you risk losing the whole line. Besides," he says. "Offing dukes is not what you're here for, now is it? There's a reason Arthur told you my name."

"*You* told me your name." I shake my head. *Ugh, what is with this guy?* "Last time I was here, *you* gave me your handkerchief, claiming it was so I wouldn't forget you. But really, you wanted me to show it to Arthur. Which means, you were already awake."

He slips before me, and starts jogging backward, which instantly succeeds in annoying the hell out of me and delaying my progress. *It's like he wants to watch me blink right out of existence.*

"If I gave you the handkerchief then, how could I have given it to you a few moments ago when we were back there?" He lifts an arm, gesturing toward the place where the whole bloody mess went down.

"Because I arrived earlier this Trip and…" I shake my head in frustration and say, "Whatever. None of that matters."

"Then what *does* matter?" he asks, voice betraying a hint of amusement, which serves only to fuel my fury.

"Getting to the portal before it's too late—*obviously!*" I cry. "I mean, exactly what sort of messed-up game are you playing?"

I charge past him, sprinting the rest of the way, until I've finally made it inside what I hope is the glimmering doorway, as Killian remains stubbornly just outside.

"Haven't you ever had something for so long you stopped seeing the meaning behind it?" he says, and before I can reply, he pulls a sword from a sheath at his hip and tosses it onto the ground. "Speaking of, won't be needing that anymore. If you want your claiming of me to look authentic, it's better if I'm unarmed."

"You had a sword?" My eyes flash wide, my voice rising in outrage. "That whole time?"

He laughs, jabs a thumb toward it. "That old thing? That's just my party sword. Much smaller than the one I use in battle. Turns out, it was no match for your shiv."

I roll my eyes, grab him by the arm, and pull until he's finally standing right beside me. And even though I'm really not loving the idea of his company, the relief of having made it in time, with both Gets secured, sends a tsunami of tension rolling right out of me.

"Ready?" I ask, reaching for the sapphire that doubles as a clicker, just about to press it, when Killian stops me.

"What's the rush?" he says.

"Are you joking?" I make a wide gesture. There are revelers everywhere, some of them too close for my comfort. "They can come after us any second, and then what?"

Killian looks around in obvious confusion, then settles on me. "There's no one here," he says. "It's just us."

"Oh, really? What about them—right over there!" I gesture past his shoulder and go on to describe the group of people who've spread a blanket near the *bassin* so they can enjoy a nice picnic on a beautiful spring day. One of them I easily recognize as Marie Antoinette.

Only just after I say it, I realize it's not spring.

It's not daytime.

This is nearly thirty years before Marie becomes queen.

Also, the ground beneath my feet is trembling ever so slightly. The only reasons the lights aren't blinking off is because there is no electricity in 1745.

"Wow." Killian's voice snaps me back to the present, or at least this version of the present. "I didn't see that one coming. Does Arthur know about your gift?" He tilts his head to the side, studying me with renewed interest.

"My...what?" My voice cracks, making me sound as shaky on the outside as I feel on the inside.

"Your ability to see through time."

118

The Unraveling.

I look back to where I saw the tragic French queen enjoying a picnic with friends. She's gone now, all of them are, but much like the girl in the maze my first morning at Gray Wolf, and my parents fighting in the kitchen over a pregnancy test, the memory lingers.

And yet, this is the first time I've peered into the future instead of the past.

Is it because I've traveled into the past only to catch a glimpse of its future?

"I'm not psychic, if that's what you think." I return to Killian. "If I was, I would've known better than to end up here."

"No," Killian says, regarding me carefully. "What you have is entirely different."

"Maybe it was just a distortion of some sort…" My voice fades. We both know that's not at all what it was.

"My advice?" Killian says, his head bent conspiratorially toward mine. "Don't tell anyone what you can do."

"But now you know." I gaze up at him, breath caught in my throat, while I silently admit to a more horrifying truth: *And I'm pretty sure Arthur knows, too. Isn't that why I'm here?*

"And so I do," Killian says. The moment stretches between us, and I'm not sure how to read it. "Before you push that—" He gestures toward the clicker. "I need you to promise me something." I guess I must look wary, because he's quick to add, "Don't forget you owe me. I saved you. Also, I'm the only one who knows your secret."

"You can't be serious!" I balk. "I'm pretty sure I'm the one who made the weapon and beat the shit out of that duke."

"Okay, okay." He flashes his palms in surrender. "So you're not exactly a damsel in distress, but you were in a full-on Fade, so—"

"Get to the point already. What do you want?"

"I want you to pretend that you're returning me to Gray Wolf against my will."

Now I'm confused.

"I want you to promise that when we arrive, you will hold that shiv to my neck, looking like you have every intention of using it. Same way you looked at the duke. Can you do that?"

"Why?"

"I need you to promise."

"Fine. I promise. But at least tell me why, so I'll know who or what it is that I'm up against."

He inclines his head closer. In a grim voice, he says, "Everyone on that rock should be on your radar. Though I'm hoping after everything we just went through, you and I can be friends."

I study him for a long, cool beat. But, since the eyes hold the key, and his are obscured by his mask, it's hard to glean much of anything.

"Why do you want to return if you think it's so awful?" I ask. "I mean, correct me if I'm wrong, but I get the feeling this is not just fear of repercussion after what we did to the duke and the guard."

He leans back, inhales a lungful of air. On the exhale, he bends toward me and says, "Because I'll be the first. No one ever returns once they're lost in the past. Mostly because Arthur never sends anyone to retrieve them. And the fact that you're here leads me to believe he never knew I was lost in the first place, because someone lied and told him I was dead. Still, the plan works only if that person doesn't suspect that I know."

"There's a plan?"

"You really think Arthur created Gray Wolf for the sole purpose of collecting trinkets and art? Everyone in that place has a plan, darlin'. Especially Arthur. And it ain't about that."

The way Killian said that makes me wonder if he knows about the Antikythera and Arthur's plan to remake the world.

But what I say is, "Don't call me darlin'."

"Aw, I see." His lips crack into a grin. "Looks like someone beat me to it."

I roll my eyes. It's a shame he can't see it.

"Who lied—who left you behind? Is this about Elodie?"

Killian looks back toward Versailles, that beautiful jewel of a palace lighting up the night sky. Then he takes my other hand in his and says, "It's about Braxton." Before I can ask him to elaborate, he adds, "And, by the way, you were amazing back there. The way you kicked that duke's ass was truly impressive. Also, for the record, while I apologize for the embrace, especially after everything you suffered with that asshole of a duke, you *did* kiss me back."

Next thing I know, he pushes the sapphire, and we zoom two hundred seventy-five years into the future.

119

The second we land on the launchpad, I punch the blade so hard to Killian's neck, blood begins to bead around the small wound at the tip.

"I said *pretend*," he snarls through gritted teeth.

"That's for the kissing comment," I say. Then loosening my grip only slightly, I add, "This is for pretend."

Killian clears his throat, adopts the posture of a guy who's been dragged through time against his will. But to me, he whispers, "Well, he doesn't change, now does he?"

I turn to find Arthur striding toward us, his gaze darting between Killian and me, but whatever he's thinking is for him to know and for the rest of us to ponder.

"I was beginning to worry." Arthur comes to stand before us. "You were running down the clock. But it looks like your Trip was successful after all."

"Is this what you wanted?" I jab the tip harder, causing Killian to wince.

"Easy, tiger," he mutters under his breath. Relaxing his stance only when Arthur lowers my arm and removes the weapon from my grip.

"I take it you ran into some trouble?" Arthur stops a moment to examine my hastily crafted blade before handing it off to Keane, who's also joined us.

"Nothing I couldn't handle." I smirk at Killian, but he's too smart to respond.

"Are you okay?" Arthur bends his head in study, granting me way more interest than he gave to the weapon. But that probably has more to do with my disheveled appearance than anything else.

The honest answer would be, *I'm not sure.*

Possibly followed by a long list of reminders of how he purposely put me into a dangerous situation, to do a dangerous job, in a time when it was dangerous just to be a female in the world, let alone one accused of committing a crime.

I was assaulted.

Tossed into a cell.

Nearly raped.

And destined to die.

It's the worst thing that's ever happened to me, but I'm in no mood to relive it. For now, I'd rather focus on the triumph, and how with a little ingenuity and a streak of ferocity I never would've guessed at, I managed to survive.

To Arthur, I say. "I'm here, aren't I?"

He motions for Keane to escort Killian into the control room, while Arthur concludes our debriefing.

"He didn't want to come." I watch as Killian refuses to cooperate, forcing Keane to grab him by the arm and forcibly drag him away.

"But you managed to convince him." Arthur offers me a seat, but I prefer standing.

"You going to tell me who he is?" I ask.

"He didn't tell you?"

For a moment, I freeze. Does Arthur know we're only pretending?

Maybe.

Probably.

Arthur knows pretty much everything. But I'm committed

now, so I need to keep going.

"He told me his name is Killian de Luce, but it sounds made-up."

Arthur barks out a laugh, a genuine, wholehearted sound. "And what about you?" he asks. "Are you happy staying as you are?"

I start to reply, but soon recognize the question as being much bigger than I first thought. Arthur's not just referring to my name. He's asking me to choose between the person I've become since my arrival at Gray Wolf versus the future self I've yet to discover.

I remember sitting in that jail cell back home, gazing into a future that offered little hope.

I remember how easily I surrendered my fate, first to Elodie, then Braxton, before ending with Arthur.

I remember watching my mom's face light up at the sight of all that abundance, as my own meager existence was quickly dismantled.

The girl I was then lacked the courage to even try to shape her own destiny. She refused to listen when Mason insisted it wasn't too late to write her own story, choosing instead to believe the lie she told herself, that she didn't have the luxury of deciding her fate.

But according to Jago, the roads were already paved. There were numerous routes to choose from—plenty of ways she could've turned her life around. But she was too apathetic to put in that kind of energy, so she left it for others to make the choice for her.

The girl I once was could never have fought her way out of 1745. She lacked the courage to even attempt such a thing, much less return with the prize.

Twice I've found myself tossed in jail since this whole ordeal began, only the endings were so radically different, it's ridiculous to even try to compare them.

Turns out Braxton is right—once you Trip, you can never go back to who you once were.

But the thing is, I don't want to go back. I like this new version of me.

I'm stronger.

Smarter.

Being at Gray Wolf has sparked a flame inside me that's incinerated my apathy and replaced it such with a burning desire to ascend and succeed that I sometimes find it frightening.

But am I happy staying as I am?

I lift my gaze to meet Arthur's. His, dark and unknowable. Mine, prepared to be entirely open and honest, if only this once.

"No," I say. "This is just the beginning. Though, if it's all the same to you, I'll stick with the name my mom gave me."

120

Arthur grins in a way that's as close to a hug as I suspect we'll ever come. And then I remember I haven't yet surrendered the rest of my Gets.

From one of my hidden pockets, I retrieve the gleaming gold ball.

"The sun!" Arthur's gaze brims with wonder as he cradles the shiny sphere reverently in his palm. Turning to me, he says, "I knew I was right about you."

I remember the fleeting thought I had moments before I claimed it—how the Sun card, the Wheel of Fortune card, and the Magician are all connected. And while I'm still not sure what it means, I know it's more than a coincidence.

I tell Arthur where I found it, about some of the struggle I went through to bring it back to Gray Wolf. Though of course I leave out the part where my own dagger was turned against me, figuring he'd want to hear about that about as much as I want to relive it.

Elodie had referred to that man as a groundskeeper. But Killian spoke with a decided measure of authority when he referred to him as a Timekeeper. Before I can ask what that means, Arthur motions toward the ring I pinched from the duke.

"And that?" he says.

"It belonged to a duke." I'm quick to hand it over, more than happy to rid myself of the reminder of what that man put me through.

And what I nearly did to him in return.

"Is there a story here?" Arthur angles the ring toward the light, as though searching for some mark of significance on an ordinary gold band.

I pull in a sharp breath, not sure I'm ready to share. But when Arthur nods, encouraging me to go on, I realize there are two truths to this story, so I tell him the storybook version I prefer to remember.

"It's a story about a girl who found herself steeped in darkness, sure she was destined to die, only to reach deep into her soul and discover that all the cleverness, courage, and strength she needed to survive already existed inside."

"And the duke?" Arthur asks.

I start to frown, but then remembering the beaten, bloodied, half-blinded state I left him in, I say, "The duke lives on to write his own story. Though I'm sure he'll never forget the day he met me."

Arthur surprises me by reaching for my hand and depositing the ring onto my palm.

"I know there's another side to that tale," he says. "One that's far more painful than the version you told, and for that I am sorry. But I want you to know that your decision to elevate that telling was far wiser than you may realize. Whether it was driven by an attempt to impress me or to make yourself feel better doesn't matter. Because in the end, this ring represents the sort of choice we're all called to make as we narrate our lives through the stories we share with others, but more importantly, the stories we tell ourselves."

He pauses, and I nod for him to continue. There's something about the intensity of his gaze, the seriousness of his demeanor, that leaves me hanging on every word.

"You're the one who decides whether you'll view this ring

as a symbol of all the suffering you experienced, the various ways in which you were victimized—or as the shining beacon of strength you discovered within that ultimately led you to triumph."

A slow smile creeps onto my face. "As the victor, I get to write my own *herstory*?"

Arthur's gaze squares on mine. "We are always writing our own stories—all day, every day. It's the ones you choose to play on repeat that determine your destiny. You alone are the alchemist of the reality you create."

"Amor Fati," I whisper, recalling the phrase often used by my dad. It's about learning to love your fate and making the most out of whatever happens by transforming the undesirable experiences into something meaningful, something better. Though he always said it with a palpable sadness.

I study the shiny golden circle, then fold my fingers around it.

"And Natasha," Arthur says, pulling me away from the memory of my dad. "I'm fully aware of the danger you all face when you Trip. It's why I keep a counselor on staff to help you work through any residual trauma. I'll set up your first appointment for tomorrow. After that, please feel free to go as often as necessary. There's no stigma here. Everyone needs a little help now and then."

I nod, swallow past the lump in my throat, and make my way toward Wardrobe so I can get rid of this dress once and for all when Arthur calls after me.

"Oh, and thanks for bringing Killian back," he says.

I know it's a test.

That if I'm really committed to the ruse, I'll say, *Back? Whatever do you mean—bring him back? Is that to say he was once here?* And a bunch of other nonsense like that.

But I'm too tired for that game. And besides, what would

be the point? We both know that I know. It's foolish to ever try to pull one over on Arthur. So I say nothing.

"I'm thinking this requires another trip to the Vault."

I turn, watching the glee with which he dangles his golden carrot from a very short stick.

"I'm pretty sure Boticelli's *Primavera* is still available."

I take a moment to consider—the painting is so beautiful, so vibrant, and joyful. Then I surprise us both with my response.

"No," I tell him. "That one's no longer for me. What I'd really love is that painting hanging near the front hall. The woman standing in the graveyard, holding the hourglass. *Vanitas*, I think it's called."

Arthur studies me for so long, I start to worry I've tested the boundary of the invisible fence that surrounds him.

"I'll see that it's arranged," he finally says, then turning on his heel, he sets off to debrief Killian as I head for Wardrobe to peel off this costume and apologize to Charlotte for the damaged gown, the rat-chewed shoes, and the three missing pieces of steel.

121

I take great care getting dressed.

My hair is worn wavy and loose, and I add a touch of color to my face by way of eyeliner, mascara, and lip gloss, with a generous wash of peachy-pink blush I swirl across my forehead and cheeks. When I'm finished, I stand before my full-length mirror and smile at the image I see.

The dress I chose is probably better for summer. But while a winter storm rages outside, slamming rain so hard against the windows it rattles the panes, for those of us sheltered inside, we choose the season we wish to live in.

The dress is made of a crisp cool linen the color of grass, with a rich embroidery of spring flowers crafted from an array of pink, purple, and yellow silk threads. It's cut into an empire silhouette, with a low square neckline and puffed elbow-length sleeves that effectively hide the ugly bruises where the groundskeeper dragged me by the arm. Never mind the ones on my waist from when the duke clawed at me.

With a shaky hand, I reach for the mirror, my fingers digging into the frame. And for one horrible, gut-plummeting moment, the memory of the duke's leering face whirls through my head, until all I can see is the sneer of his lips, the degrading gleam in his eyes, as I remember how close he came to…

I shake my head, shake the image away, desperate to replace it with the far more satisfying crack and bend of his knee when

I kicked him—the gash in his face when I left him to bleed...

The duke has taken up enough of my day. And though I know Arthur is right—that it'll take way more than my own resolve to exorcise the memory of him from my mind, there's plenty of time to deal with that tomorrow.

I will not give him this night.

My hand returns to my side. I square my shoulders and straighten my spine. *I'm a Blue now,* I remind myself. And, since clothes are a form of expression—a visible way of broadcasting a mood—by wearing a dress that does nothing to hide the trail of bruises scattered across my legs—I'm hoping to express that I'm fully committed to the life I've made here.

Though my feet have taken a beating, abraded by gravel that's resulted in raw patches of skin, a visit with the nurse saw them carefully salved and bandaged, allowing me to slip on a pair of well-cushioned flats that cause only minimal discomfort.

I add a collection of diamond studs and small hoops to my ears, then stack an assortment of slim jeweled rings onto my fingers.

The duke's ring has been tucked away for another day. And though I can't bear to look at it now, someday, when I'm ready, I'm thinking I might take it to one of the artisans Arthur keeps on staff and see if they can melt down the gold and turn it into something I might actually want to wear.

Taking something ugly and turning it into something beautiful.

Changing the story from victimhood to triumph.

That's the sort of alchemy I've learned at this school.

While I was ridding myself of that eighteenth-century gown, Charlotte moved my talisman from the torn piece of velvet ribbon back to the golden chain that now hangs from my neck.

"You're lucky you found it," she said.

I started to tell her that I didn't find it. That Killian's the one who returned it, but we soon moved on, and the memory was lost.

Only now that I remember, I find myself eager to forget.

I move to stand before the painting now hung on my wall. Who would've thought I'd end up owning an original Salvador Dalí?

In truth, I suppose I don't actually own anything here. In the end, it all belongs to Arthur. The painting is just on loan. For how long was never made clear.

I check my slab again. I've been checking it obsessively since the moment I returned to my room. But still no word from Braxton.

Though there is the inspirational quote of the day:

> *The music is not in the notes,*
> *but in the silence between.*
> —Wolfgang Amadeus Mozart

And below it, a message from Elodie. The real reason I've decided to put so much effort into my look.

Elodie: Party at Halcyon. 8 sharp.

Me: ☺

There's no point in letting on that I know she's responsible for sabotaging my Trip. There's plenty of time for that later.

Better to give the appearance of being friends while I come up with a plan. According to Killian, everyone has one, including Braxton.

Or at least, that's what Killian implied when he blamed him for his extended Trip to 1745, just seconds before we rocketed two and a half centuries forward in time.

Then again, he also accused me of returning his kiss, when I'm certain I didn't.

Also, since Halcyon is open only on weekends, and even then, only Blues or above are allowed entry, this will make for my first visit to the club, and I'm curious to see not only what all the fuss is about, but how Elodie managed to gain access on a day when it's normally closed.

With one last glance in the mirror, I toss my slab into a small bag, add a tube of lip gloss, and let myself out.

Remembering the note she left for me earlier, I pause to knock on Song's door, wondering if she might want to talk, or at least head to the party together. But when she doesn't answer, I figure she's already there and continue along.

122

Turns out, Halcyon occupies an entire wing of its own. And once I've ducked past the heavily lacquered, bright orange doors, I find myself squinting into a dimly lit, cavernous space that requires a few moments for my eyes to adjust.

A soft jazzy tune drifts from hidden speakers as my gaze streaks along a meandering, glittering smear of a room. The dark floors are a ramble of mismatched tables and chairs—the softly curving walls display a gaudy assortment of treasures hailing from so many cultures and ages, it makes for a brash and unruly aesthetic.

"I thought this was a party." My gaze flicks from an amethyst chandelier hanging overhead to the place where Elodie stands behind a green marble-topped bar, silver cocktail shaker in hand. I move to join her, settling onto an empty stool, then I place my bag on the one just beside it.

"It's a party for us," she says, speaking over the rattle as she jiggles the shaker. "We never get to hang out like we used to." She releases the lid from the tumbler, carefully distributes the iridescent red liquid between two large martini glasses, then slides one toward me.

"Cheers!" She grins, raising her glass and taking a slow, thoughtful sip. A moment later, I do the same. "What do you think? And be honest," she says.

I close my eyes, search for just the right word. I settle on two.

"Strange. Sweet," I say. "But I like it. What's in it?"

"Secret recipe." She wiggles her brows and takes another sip. "I've been working on it for ages. Haven't quite mastered it, but I'm close. Maybe that's what I should call it—Strange Sweet. Do you think anyone would order it?"

When she grins, it leaves no doubt that if anyone could make the drink trend, it's her.

"It's good to see you." Her perfectly manicured thumb taps against the stem of her glass as her gaze snags on mine. "I was so worried."

I tip the glass to my lips and observe her from over the wide crystal rim. "Worried? Why?"

She shrugs, blue eyes flashing hot and bright, expertly concealing whatever it is that she's thinking. "The first solo Trip is always the hardest. A lot can go wrong. I'm relieved to see you made it back in one piece."

There's a long, drawn-out pause, as though she's expecting a jog in my memory, the confirmation that her plan almost worked.

Instead, I use the moment to consider the best way to respond to her false show of concern.

I can either take the bait and let on that I know she's the one who tampered with my mask in an effort to not just strand me in the past but knock me right out of existence itself—or I can take another sip of my Strange Sweet drink and act like it was no big thing.

I go with the latter. As my dad used to say: *Act in haste, repent at leisure.* It wasn't until recently that I truly understood what it means.

Then again, it wasn't until recently that I truly understood a lot of my dad's teachings.

To Elodie, I say, "I got my list of Gets and found my way back. Easy-peasy." I grin.

"You have no idea how happy that makes me." Elodie

flutters her impossibly long lashes and presses a theatrical hand to her chest. "That whole time you were gone, I was worried I might've somehow messed up."

"How?" I shift on my stool, rest my forearms against the cool marble slab, curious to hear what sort of excuse she's drummed up.

"Well, I'd never programmed a mask before, and when Keane insisted I learn, I—"

"Keane insisted?" My gaze cuts right through her. That's not at all how I remember it. Mostly because that's not at all how it happened.

"Well, yeah." She shrugs. "They're always trying to get me to take on more responsibility. But I like being a Blue. That's all I want to do." Her head bobs to the side in an almost comical attempt to appear innocent.

I cut her off with a sharp jerk of my hand. I'm over this shit. Exactly how dense does she think I am?

"Anyway—" She grabs the silver shaker in one hand and her martini glass in the other. "I know you won't believe me, but I like having you here. Gray Wolf wouldn't be the same without you." She slinks around the bar and motions for me to join her at some more comfortable-looking chairs set up nearby.

I watch as she settles onto a plush velvet seat, curling one leg beneath her and extending the other to rest on a table with an intricate inlay of pearl and wood that's probably worth more money than my mom used to make in five years.

I know what she's doing. She's trying to remind me just how at ease she is in this world of fine, priceless objects. That she can rest her feet as confidently on this precious artifact as she did on the cheap plastic tables in the school cafeteria.

Elodie never misses a chance to remind me of how she's been here the longest, and of all the various territories she was the first to conquer.

Gray Wolf.

The lighthouse.

The Blues.

Braxton.

But vanquishing is one thing. Whether or not she can hold on to that power remains to be seen.

She tilts her chin toward me, and for one pure, unmasked moment, the facade has dropped and the challenge in her gaze is worn plain to see. She wants the confrontation. She's itching for the fight.

But, since I'm heavy on suspicion and woefully light on proof, I stick with what I learned in my comportment and etiquette class, grab the worn leather chair across from hers, cross my legs primly, and settle in for a much longer game.

123

"What do you make of all this?" Elodie asks. Surrendering to the stand-off between us, she motions around the space, taking obvious pride in being the first to share it with me.

"I think it's a maximalist's dream." I peer at a shield that looks like it came from the time of Viking rule, then over to a marble bust of a head that looks a lot like Julius Caesar.

"It's not a hologram, if that's what you're thinking. Everything you see was brought back by Trippers."

"Seriously?" I take another, more appreciative, look at the madcap collection of strange artifacts and extravagant mishmash of relics.

"You know how Arthur lets you keep a trophy when you return?"

I nod, remembering the diamond swan hair clip that Mason should have by now. And of course, the gold ring I took from the duke.

"After a while, they just sort of started taking up space, so Arthur agreed to let us turn this club into an archive of our own. Then, of course, everyone started getting competitive about the types of things they brought back. And, well, what you see here is the result."

My gaze lands on a human skeleton displayed in a coffin made of glass. Its skull inexplicably encrusted in jewels; the body adorned in a black velvet robe with elaborate gold and silver embroidery trailing down the front. The piece strikes me as simultaneously beautiful and unnerving.

"And Arthur doesn't mind?" My attention lingers on the strange, haunting thing—the jaw embedded with diamonds and rubies, the skull paved with bits of gold and pearls.

"As long as we return with his list of Gets, he's fine with it. And as for that—" She motions toward the coffin. "That's one of Braxton's contributions."

I turn toward Elodie, sure that she's bluffing. Unfortunately, my barefaced show of surprise looks like it only delights her more.

"I thought for sure he would've mentioned it," she says, not even trying to hide the glee behind her reveal—of knowing something about Braxton that he hasn't gotten around to sharing with me. "He's ridiculously proud of his find."

I glance between Elodie and the jewel encrusted skeleton. On the one hand, it's eerie, creepy, and morbid as hell. On the other, knowing Braxton's taste in art, it makes sense.

"It's an old Roman catacomb saint," she explains. "They became controversial, which is why there are so few of them left these days. Of course, Braxton brought this one back from the sixteenth century."

I try to picture him rushing for the portal with this thing strapped to his back. It's impossible to imagine, but who am I to dispute it?

"Now that you're a Blue, you can finally hang here on the weekends. It can get pretty wild, and you wouldn't believe the bands and special guests Arthur brings in." She hooks her thumb toward a stage at the far end of the room. It reminds me of the one I saw in Arcana.

"You mean hologram bands." I return my focus to Elodie, though my mind lingers on the memory of the torch singer and the hypnotic song she sang.

Elodie tips her glass to her lips. "Do I?" She grins coyly. "Anyway, tell me about your Trip. I want to hear all the juicy details."

I uncross my legs, settle deeper into my seat. "It was all pretty standard," I lie. "Though there is something I was wondering…"

She shifts closer to the edge of her cushion and leans toward me. Her face lit with anticipation, as though the moment she's been waiting for has finally arrived. The moment when I accuse her of things of which I have no proof, so she can go running to Arthur, and I can be stripped of Blue status and demoted to work as her maid.

My fingers play at the stem of my drink, my gaze locked on hers. "When you Trip back to times like that, are you ever tempted to smuggle in things like tampons and birth control? You know, to give our bygone sisters some semblance of autonomy over their lives?"

For a moment, Elodie freezes. Then I watch as she breaks into the sort of full-bodied laugh that has her rocking back in her seat so abruptly, she inadvertently splashes her drink down the front of her dress—a slinky sequined slip nearly the same creamy buttermilk shade as her skin.

Between the dress and the way she wears her blond hair coiled high on her head, she looks startlingly similar to the sculpture of *Deceit*, and I can't help but wonder if the look is deliberate, intended to taunt me.

Though it's also entirely possible that, where she's concerned, I've grown so paranoid, everything surrounding her falls under a veil of suspicion.

Elodie continues to laugh as she reaches for a cocktail napkin to sop up the stain on her dress. And while I know it's not the accusation she braced for, I'm glad I managed to amuse her, if for no other reason than it served to lighten the mood.

"Can you even imagine?" she says. "We'd probably be dragged before an all-male council, who'd waste no time accusing us of witchcraft so they could get their rocks off watching us burn at the stake." She shakes her head and tacks on a grimace. "No thanks."

And just like that, the tension between us has vanished. We're friends again. Or, at least on the surface.

And then it dawns on me that maybe the superficial appearance of friendship and loyalty is all Elodie is capable of.

Maybe she's been under Arthur's wing for so long, molded under his hand, forced into playing various roles, and made to compete for his favor, that she has no idea how to be a good friend—has no idea who she really is outside of performing for him.

Is it possible she deserves more of my mercy and less of my mistrust?

"I used to think it would be so cool to live back then." I sigh, deciding to drop my misgivings, at least for a while. "In the movies, they make it look so swoonworthy."

"Sometimes it really is," Elodie says, settling back in her seat, her face overtaken by a soft and dreamy expression. "I've waltzed with handsome princes, ridden in gilded horse-drawn carriages..."

"And bedded King Henry the Eighth," I tease, still not sure I believe it.

"That too." She nods and takes a careful sip of her drink.

"Still, while it is interesting to visit, I think I'm more suited to a world of flushing toilets and blow dryers." I laugh.

"Hear, hear!" Elodie raises her glass, and I do the same. But when she looks at me, the laughter fades, and her expression turns somber. "You want to know the truth?"

She speaks as though everything that came before was a lie—and of course, there's a good chance it was. And that this will be, too.

"From the moment I arrived here at Gray Wolf, I never dreamed of living anywhere else. It's only recently that I've come to understand that not everyone feels the same way."

Her gaze lands on mine, and I get the feeling she wants something from me. Probably a display of gratitude for changing my life.

When I don't respond, she inhales deeply and says, "Are you still angry with me?" She holds her breath puffed in her cheeks. But I delay for so long, she's forced to repeat it. "Are you angry with me for bringing you here?"

If I answer too quickly, she'll never believe me. Elodie, like Arthur, is a hard person to fool.

"No," I finally say. "Not—" I start to say, *Not for that*. But at the last second, I change it to, "Not anymore." And when I meet her gaze, I hope what she sees is the truth.

Because I'm no longer angry with her for bringing me to Gray Wolf.

I'm angry because she tried to sabotage my mask so that I'd never return.

Despite my momentary lapse of pity toward her, I know she's responsible, and someday I'll prove it.

She reaches for the shaker, about to refill our empty glasses, when my slab begins to buzz, and my hand shoots for my bag, sure it's a message from Braxton.

But when I notice Elodie's slab buzzing as well, I figure it must be something else, something not nearly as exciting.

"The new recruit is here." Elodie stands, smooths a hand down the front of her dress. "Arthur wants everyone to meet downstairs."

But all I can think is: *Braxton is back!*

124

Elodie holds the door, then follows me into the hall. I've barely walked more than a few steps when she places a hand on my shoulder to stop me.

"What happened?" She motions toward my chest.

At first, I think maybe I dribbled my drink on my dress, but then I realize she's reaching for my talisman.

"It's dented. Right here."

While I really don't like the sight of her fingers grasping the charm Braxton gave me, I soon realize she's right. There's a place on the front where two of the gold bars appear to curve slightly inward when they didn't before.

I guess it must've happened when I lost it, but I was so happy to have it back, I didn't take the time to examine it.

Elodie peers hard at the jewels nestled inside. "Good thing you didn't lose that star," she says. "It could've so easily slipped through those bars without you even realizing until it was too late." She tilts her head, and the way her gaze latches onto mine causes a prickle of chills to race up my spine.

"Reminds me of that quote from Ovid," she says. "*Beauty is a fragile gift.*"

Her perfect rosebud lips curl up at the sides, and though there're a number of ways I can translate her expression, it's not a trail I'm willing to follow. Right now, I'd rather focus on Braxton—his return to Gray Wolf, to me—and the happy reunion to come.

Without a word, I remove the charm from her fingers, and make for the staircase.

When I see everyone already assembled downstairs, my mind hurtles back in time to the night I arrived.

I remember how I stood awkwardly beside Braxton, simultaneously angry and scared out of my mind.

I remember taking in the odd assortment of wingback chairs swinging from thick silver chains, and the strangers who occupied them, people who are no longer strangers today.

Oliver, Song, Jago, Finn—I tried my best to keep them all straight.

All of them are here now, except Song, who is notably missing.

When Elodie strode into the room with that tiara perched on her head, she was clearly the star of the show.

As she strides in beside me now, I realize her reign is far from over.

Back then, I didn't know what any of it meant.

Why the chairs hung like swings.

Why Elodie was dressed like royalty.

Why everyone was so unsettled by me.

Why I was chosen to live here among them.

But now that I'm one of them, I promise myself that whoever this recruit turns out to be, I will be kinder and more helpful to them than any of these people ever were to me.

I don't care if Blues are expected to keep to themselves—a little more guidance would've been nice. And as far as shoving a bag over someone's head and dragging them off to the lighthouse—it's time for that sadistic tradition to end.

Elodie claims the last vacant chair, leaving me to occupy the pink velvet divan. As I settle onto the cushion, I feel jumpy, twitchy, like there's a swarm of bees building a hive inside my belly, but I chalk it up to excitement over my reunion with Braxton.

I turn to Oliver, who's sitting in the chair beside mine, about to ask if he's seen Song, when he leans toward me and says, "Good to see you made it back."

I'm about to respond when I realize there's more.

"And I see you brought a friend."

His dark eyes flicker toward the staircase, where a tall, gorgeous boy dressed in a loose silk shirt, a pair of soft faded jeans, and velvet slippers makes his way down the steps.

When I catch sight of his golden curls, recently cut to fall just shy of his shoulders, leaving the front bits to casually tumble over his forehead, I realize the boy is Killian.

125

I guess I must've gasped out loud, and not just in my head like I thought, because Oliver laughs. "An appropriate response to that hot piece of smolder," he says. "Just don't let Braxton hear you do that. He and Killian are not exactly what one would call friendly."

It's the first time I've seen Killian without a mask, and it takes a moment to adjust to the sight. The nose that I once thought of as prominent appears less so when taken in with his other features. Still, his is a strong face. The face of ancient Roman coins, of statues molded under Michelangelo's hand. There's a hard, almost brutal quality to the square of his jaw, the thrust of his cheekbones and chin. But his blue eyes are warm and friendly, and his lips are smiling brightly.

"Greetings, old friends." As his gaze bounces among the gathered crowd, I use the moment to study their varied reactions.

Finn swipes a hand through his straw-colored hair, his shoulder nudging Oliver's. The two of them exchange a look that's probably meant to be discreet but falls far short.

Jago just nods. He's clearly too new to have any idea who Killian is.

Elodie shoots a wary look between the two of us, but surprisingly keeps her lips sealed.

"So, this is the new millennium version of you." Killian's gaze drags over me with lazy appreciation, taking a slow, leisurely inventory of my hair, my dress, my bare legs. "I have to say, this century suits you."

When he drops down beside me, I whisper, "Are you sure you want to sit so close? Last time you saw me, I was pressing a blade to your throat."

He laughs in a deep-bellied way, throwing his head back and exposing a strong column of neck with a small puncture mark where I pressed my weapon just a little too hard. Then, settling in closer, he says, "I have been known to hold a grudge. But not toward you. Turns out, I'm saving that up for somebody else."

I sink back against the seat. He sinks back, too, spreading his legs so wide, they take up all his space and a good chunk of mine.

"Another thing that's happened in your absence," I say, knocking my knee hard against his. "Manspread has been banned. In fact, the entire patriarchal system has been put on notice. You have a lot of catching up to do."

In an instant, he corrects himself by crossing one leg over the other, then leans closer to whisper, "Sounds like I missed the revolution. Though I do look forward to you teaching me all about this brave new world I've found myself in." To the room at large, he says, "Tell me, how has everyone been?"

Oliver and Finn merely shrug.

Jago eagerly introduces himself.

As Elodie continues to swing back and forth on her purple wingback throne.

"Okay, so nothing has changed." Killian pulls a sardonic grin. "Except apparently, or at least according to my new friend Natasha here, some rather restrictive courtship rules have been put into place. Though, not to worry, I have every intention of ridding myself of my barbaric ways so that I may once again mix with polite society. Seeing as how Natasha has volunteered to tutor me, it shouldn't take long. Least she could do, really, considering how she dragged me back here against my will."

"Natasha. Dragged *you*. Back here?" It's the first thing Elodie has said since Killian arrived, and there's an audible bite to the words.

Killian regards her with a cool, measured gaze. "Held a bloody knife to my throat. Well, actually it was a shiv that she crafted from her corset, but still."

"Pannier," I correct.

"What?" His eyes squint with amusement.

"Panni—whatever." I frown and dismiss it with a wave of my hand.

Killian leans his head back against the cushion and studies the enormous crystal chandelier hanging above. "Corset, pannier, fancy lace knickers, still a brilliant bit of genius, I'll say. Also, scary as hell to be caught on the killing end of that stick."

He's adopted a cockney accent now, and I get the feeling that he's always playing a role or wearing a mask of some sort. This is a guy with so many personas, I wonder if he's even able to determine the real from the fake.

But then I remember the grim line of his lips, the sharp barb of his tongue, when he named Braxton as the one he suspected of sabotaging his long ago Trip, and I realize that was probably as close to his truth as he'll ever reveal.

"Funny how you conveniently left out that part when I asked about your Trip." Elodie anchors a foot on the floor and uses it to swing her chair back and forth, all the while her gaze shooting daggers at me.

"Did she?" Killian regards me through a sleepy, half-lidded gaze. "Well, that's probably because this one here's too modest to brag." He bumps his shoulder playfully against mine. "Not that you would know anything about that, El. You've never been known for humility, have you?" When he turns that gaze on Elodie, it takes on an entirely different affect.

I'm pretty sure we all suck in a breath, curious to see how

Elodie will respond. Surprisingly, she just rolls her eyes and silently seethes, leaving me to wonder what might've happened between them to make her surrender so easily.

"Well, at least we know people can return," Finn says, eliciting a look of warning from Oliver. "That means there's still hope for Song. Not to mention Anjou," he mutters in a much quieter, but still bitter tone.

"Song is missing?" I say, but Jago speaks up at that exact moment, and his voice easily overpowers mine.

"Did that really happen?" Jago leans forward in his chair and wags a finger between Killian and me.

"You mean, about the shiv?" Killian laughs. "Course it's true! Don't underestimate this one, she's a freakin' beast." Killian slaps a hand on my knee. Then, with a pained expression that's clearly faked, he says, "Aw, damn, did I just break another one of your rules?"

"They're not just *my* rules, they're — " I'm about to really lay into him when Braxton walks into the room.

His gaze darts straight from me, to Killian, to Killian's hand clutching my knee.

But all I can see is the recruit standing directly behind him.

He's terrified, angry, and looking for someone to blame.

In an instant, his eyes settle on me.

And I'm out of my chair, out of my mind, as I cry, "What the hell is Mason doing here?"

126

The scene unfolds the same way it did back when I was the fresh recruit, only this time it feels entirely different, because the recruit is not me, but rather my best friend, Mason.

Also, much like I blamed Elodie, going by the scathing look Mason directs my way, he blames me.

"What have you done?" I say to Braxton as I rush toward my friend.

But Mason is quick to hold up a hand. "Don't," he says, his voice is stiff, his eyes so cold I immediately stop in my tracks. "Don't act like you're blameless. Don't pretend we're still friends."

I stand frozen in place, aware of Jago, Killian, Elodie, Finn, and Oliver practically falling out of their seats to get a better view of the spectacle. But I don't care what they think. All I want to know is how the one person I've really come to care about could do such a horrible thing to the only other person I care about, outside of my mom.

Braxton rakes a hand through his hair, skirts past my gaze, and settles on Killian.

Mason stands before me. His green and gold brocade overcoat drenched with rain, he wears a pair of tall rubber boots, like those the skipper gave me to wear on the boat ride to Gray Wolf, while a pair of blue high-heeled shoes dangle from his fingers. When I notice the state of his raw and bloodied knuckles, I can't help but feel a surge of pride knowing that at least he didn't go down without a fight.

"Mason, please," I say. "I didn't know, I—" But it's no use, my words blow right past him.

As Mason glares at me through mascara-streaked eyes, Arthur appears.

After everyone introduces themselves, Arthur orders Jago to show Mason to his room, then tells everyone to disperse except me.

"Are you going to be okay?" Arthur's obsidian gaze bores right through me.

On the surface, the question is benign. But I know what he's really asking is if I'm going to be a problem.

If I'm going to continue to do things like jumping out of chairs and shouting in outrage.

If I'm going to insist on fighting an event that has already happened—that is completely beyond my ability to change.

And because I don't know the answer, because I haven't had a chance to sort through my feelings and the short list of responses Arthur might approve of, I lift my gaze to his and say, "I was caught off guard. It wasn't what I expected."

With a sharp nod, Arthur turns and motions for me to follow. Other than the click of our shoes on the bowling-alley-style hallway, we walk in silence.

When we reach the end, Arthur stops. "You've done well for yourself here." He turns to face me. "What makes you think Mason won't gain the same benefit as you?"

I start to say because unlike me, Mason has a shot at a future, he has something to lose. Instead, I say, "But what about his grandmother? She loves him and—"

"She signed the papers." Arthur speaks with his usual quiet authority. "And she was happy to do so. Have you ever stopped to consider that maybe it's not quite the act of abandonment you assume?"

I can feel him peering at me, but my face is so flushed with bitterness and rage, I can't afford to meet his gaze until I get ahold of myself.

"You caught a glimpse of your mother expressing her excitement over the prospect of a new car and rain gutters, and you've made that the crux of your story. But what you didn't see was the amount of hand-wringing that led up to that point. The assurances she insisted I give her that you'd be well looked after, well cared for—that I'd provide you the sort of opportunities she could never afford on her own. And so far, I think I've delivered, no?"

I don't know how to respond. Not only because I have no way of knowing if he's speaking the truth, but I also haven't truly determined what it means to be here.

In some ways, many ways, Arthur is right. Coming here is the best thing that ever happened to me, and my life has obviously taken a turn for the better.

And yet, I can't shake the feeling that Gray Wolf has yet to reveal its full self.

That there's more to this place—something far darker, more sinister—than Arthur lets on. And, seeing as how he's counting on me to gather all the missing pieces to the Antikythera Mechanism to get that job done, I can't help but wonder if I've made a terrible mistake by returning from Versailles with the sun.

Back when Arthur told me he wanted to use the completed Antikythera to remake the world, I didn't take him literally.

But now I'm sunk by the terrible feeling that maybe I should have.

127

"Your friend is incredibly bright," Arthur says, leading away from my worst fears and suspicions and back to the present. "He's handsome, loaded with potential, and though he doesn't realize it now, this is a wonderful opportunity for a promising kid with limited resources to forge a better life for himself. You, better than anyone, can help him find his way here."

"I'm not sure Mason wants my help." I wince, unable to shake the pinch of Mason's perfectly drawn red lips, the furious slant of his brow. "It's clear he blames me."

"And who do you blame?"

I sigh. When I arrived, the list was long, but I've since whittled it down to just one—me.

Elodie set me up, my mom signed me away, but *I'm* the one who chose to fail my way out of school and go along for the ride.

"You've had a long day," Arthur says. "Why don't you take some time to relax, and then tomorrow, you can bring a breakfast tray to Mason's room, have a long chat, and see if you can't begin to heal some of those wounds."

I nod. I mean, what else can I do?

Though just as I'm about to leave, I notice the blank spot on the wall directly behind Arthur.

It's the spot where *Vanitas* hung.

Nothing Arthur does is by accident. Even a simple walk down a hall comes with a motive attached.

When he notices me looking, he hooks a thumb over his shoulder and says, "I had it transferred to your room. If you don't like the placement, say the word and it can be moved."

I stare at that blank square on the wall, noticing how the paint is one shade darker than the surrounding area. Then I glance at Arthur, and I feel sick to my stomach.

Though I initially asked for the piece as a reward for all I went through to secure Arthur's Gets, now I can't help but wonder if his agreeing to hand it over has more to do with Mason.

Is Arthur using the painting to distract me from the horror of what he did to my friend?

I swallow past the lump in my throat, lower my gaze to my fancy designer-shod feet, and say, "Thank you." It's all I can say.

He regards me with a hooded gaze. "No reason to thank me. You earned it."

What remains unclear is exactly how I might've *earned* it.

By bringing him one step closer to restoring the Antikythera Mechanism?

By returning Killian to Gray Wolf?

Or by agreeing to help Mason accept this unexpected detour in his life's path?

"Besides," Arthur continues, his brow gathered in a way that renders his gaze into two glimmering shards of obsidian, "as you know, there are still more missing pieces to gather, and you're the only one who can find them. In fact, you might even get to stay a while in this next location. It'll require specialized training, of course, so we'll have to see how that goes. But what do you think about Tripping back to Renaissance Italy for a couple of weeks?"

On the outside, I blink, but otherwise remain motionless before him.

On the inside, my mind is a whirl of possibilities of what

I might do there, all the people I'd meet. I mean, *Renaissance Italy*! The time of Leonardo da Vinci, Michelangelo, Botticelli, Titian, Caravaggio, Raphael, Donatello…there are too many to mention.

"Are you familiar with the painting *Salvator Mundi*?" Arthur asks.

"Th—the *Savior of the World*?" I stammer, my skin pricking with chills when I see Arthur nod.

"And what exactly do you know about it?" he says.

I squint toward the blank square on the wall as I struggle to remember. "I learned about it in art class—it's thought to be a long-lost painting by Leonardo da Vinci that was purchased for less than two thousand dollars, then ultimately sold at auction for over four hundred million."

I blink at Arthur, wondering if he wants me to go back in time and fetch it, so he can be the one to claim the windfall. But, judging by the way Arthur waves a hand in dismissal when I mention the dollar amount, that's not what he cares about.

"And you've seen pictures of this painting? You know what it looks like?"

I shrug. "It's been a while, but I think it's a portrait of Jesus."

"And do you remember what Jesus is holding?"

"I…" I rub my lips together, struggling to summon the image. "One of his hands is…raised?"

"And the other?" Arthur nods for me to hurry and get to the good stuff.

I close my eyes. High school art class feels like a lifetime ago. "A crystal—like, a crystal orb, maybe?"

"And what does that orb remind you of?" he asks. "What does it resemble?"

A flash of memory streaks through my head, and I watch as my dad stands before me, cupping a small crystal ball in his hand. *Tell me about the eighteenth card*, he said.

"The moon." The answer slips past my lips, and when I open my eyes, I find Arthur standing before me, much like my dad in the vision. Except Arthur is grinning, where my dad veered much closer to sad.

"Something to think about," Arthur says, dangling the prospect like catnip. "But please, no mention of this to anyone. For now, get some rest. You've earned that as well."

128

As I head back to my room, I'm so lost in the maze of my tormented thoughts—my horror at seeing Mason at Gray Wolf versus the undeniable thrill of possibly meeting Leonardo da Vinci in person—it's not until I've nearly crashed right into him that I notice Braxton at the end of the hall.

Inside, I feel gutted, like my heart's split in two. Still, I manage to say, "What have you done?" in a voice so accusing, I watch him cringe in response.

"Please," he whispers. "Not here. Come to my room. We can talk privately there." He grasps for my hand, but when he sees me flinch, he's quick to retreat.

"What did you *do*?" I cry, not caring who overhears. "Why did you bring Mason here?"

"Tasha." He closes his eyes. When he opens them again, he peers at me through a shipwrecked gaze. "I'm begging you, please."

I glance down the hall toward my room where, at my request, *Vanitas* now hangs. A painting meant to remind one of the fleetingness of life and the utter worthlessness of directing one's efforts toward amassing worldly pleasures and goods.

A painting that, just by owning it, serves to mock its own message.

A painting I used as a power play that's now destined to haunt me for the rest of my days.

"Fine," I say, reluctantly following. "But don't even think about holding my hand."

When we reach his room, Braxton ushers me inside, sets his duffel on the floor, and heads for the antique bar cart by the window.

"Do you want a drink?" He turns to me. His sweater is rumpled, his hair tangled and wet, and there are twin moons casting deep violet shadows beneath both his eyes. I've never seen him looking so exhausted, so defeated.

I shake my head, preferring to be alert for the interrogation I've planned.

"Do you mind if I have one?" he asks.

I start to shrug when I notice the fresh scrape across the left side of his jaw and immediately remember the sight of Mason's raw and bloodied knuckles.

"Did Mason do that?" I motion toward the spot where Braxton's face took a blow, watching as he absently rubs at the cut like he'd forgotten about it till now.

"Clocked me pretty hard." He winces at the memory. Then, uncorking a crystal decanter, he measures a couple fingers of Scotch into a tumbler, downs it with one elegant toss of his head, then pours himself another, which he chooses to savor.

"Mason's tougher than he looks," I say. "If you're going to dress like that, as a Black kid, at our ignorant school, learning how to fight is a matter of survival. By the end of ninth grade, no one dared mess with him. Until you."

Braxton leans against the wall, regarding me with a gaze so heavy and raw, it's easy to see the toll this Trip has exacted. Which is the only way to explain why he sees fit to open with, "What the hell is Killian doing here and why did he have his hand on your knee?"

I glance longingly toward the door and give serious consideration to leaving. Instead, I say, "You cannot be serious."

He grips the glass so hard, his knuckles turn the color of bone, and I can't help but cringe as I imagine it shattering into a mess of bloody shards.

"How did he get here?" He jabs a thumb toward the door as though Killian is waiting on the other side.

"Maybe," I say, my voice even but tight, "the more important question is—how did he get left behind in the first place?"

Braxton works his jaw, tosses back the drink, then sets the glass aside and collapses onto a worn brown leather couch that looks like it was lifted from some posh young royal's country estate.

"How long has he been back?" He pushes the words through gritted teeth.

I move to stand before him. "You answer mine. I'll answer yours."

The look he gives me is wary.

"What is Mason doing here?" I say.

129

I stand before Braxton, watching as his features soften. The rigid line of his shoulders relaxing, loosening, as he looks past my anger, past his own anger, and allows his eyes to graze over me as though seeing me for the first time since he walked into Gray Wolf and found me sitting with Killian.

"Sit." He pats the cushion beside him. "Please."

Hoping he won't mistake my compliance for surrender, I skirt around a table and join him.

"God, you're so beautiful," he says, his voice low and husky, though he makes no move to touch me, correctly sensing that it wouldn't be welcome. "You have no idea how much I missed you."

His hands lay empty and open on his lap. The sight of him looking so defenseless makes me remember how close I came to never seeing him again, and my heart peels apart in my chest.

And now that he's here, sitting before me, hair dampened from the rain and left to curl in soft waves around his face, his eyes gazing upon me with such palpable longing, I realize how easy it would be to reach out and pull him so close, all our troubles would instantly melt away.

The lure between us is undeniable, but right now, we have more important things to discuss.

I guess he must sense my impatience because he's quick to say, "How did you manage to get the diamond hair clip to Mason?"

"Wait—what?" Now it's my turn to be confused. "Are you saying you didn't send it?"

Braxton shakes his head, presses his lips together so tightly, they fade into the rest of his face. "No." He sighs. "I didn't send it. For exactly the reasons I told you. Which is why I can't figure out how it ended up in his possession."

The way he says *in his possession* makes my stomach lurch. It's the sort of phrase used when someone's been charged with a crime. A moment later, my worst fear is confirmed.

"They found the clip, and he was busted for theft. I was already in place on the East Coast when I received word there was a change of plans."

"Oh God, oh no…" My breath comes too shallow. My pulse thrums too fast. In an instant, the room recedes all around me as I wrap my arms at my waist, guarding against what I know will come next.

"I was sent to California, where I was instructed—"

"To go to my school." I stare at Braxton with wide, frightened eyes. "Oh my God—it really is all my fault!"

"How did you manage to send it?"

I drop my head in despair, my mind straining to find a logical explanation for how this could've happened.

After a few frantic beats, I lift my gaze to meet Braxton's. "I didn't take you seriously. I thought you were being…" I bite down on my lip. I feel like such a fool, but I force myself to keep going. "I don't know, I thought you were just in a hurry and didn't want to be burdened with an extra task. I thought you might change your mind once you finished packing and got yourself sorted. So I left the diamond swan on the small table by your door, along with a note from me to Mason and another piece of paper listing his home address. I figured you'd see it on your way out and…"

"I never saw it."

His words are like an ax chipping away at my heart.

"I rushed out of here not long after you. I was in a hurry to get off island so I could make it to the airport."

"But if you didn't send it, then who?"

Braxton's features grow taut, sharpening at the edges as his eyes narrow to slits. "Who's the first person who springs to mind? Our instincts are usually right."

I close my eyes and sigh. Same person who always springs to mind when it comes to sabotage, trickery, fraud, and deceit. When I look at him, I say, "This is pure Elodie. Mason always disliked her. He never trusted her. And he warned me on multiple occasions that no good would come from my friendship with her. But how'd she get into your room—did you give her access?"

Braxton holds up a hand. "Not even when we were together." He rests his arm along the back of the couch, his fingers straining toward me but not quite reaching. "Then again, she's been here longer than any of us. I'm sure she's found a way to access all sorts of things."

"She managed to access Halcyon on a weeknight, so what's stopping her from getting in here?"

"You went to Halcyon?" Braxton's surprised, but I'm in no mood to discuss it, never mind his disturbing donation to the decor.

I sag against the soft leather cushions, glancing from the unlit hearth to the art-covered walls, then over to Braxton, who wears the same tormented look as those oil-painted subjects.

"She tried to sabotage my Trip," I tell him. "I guess she figured it was a win either way. If I didn't make it back, she'd still find a way to let Mason know I was to blame for wrecking his life. And if I did return, well, then I'd get the pleasure of witnessing Mason's burning hatred firsthand."

The silence spreads between us like a river I fear we'll never bridge.

But then Braxton moves closer and says, "Tasha, I need to know—what exactly was your role in Killian's return?"

He wears his distress on his face, and though I know it will upset him, I say, "I brought him back. Killian was on my list of Gets."

I watch the shift in Braxton's demeanor—the way his body tenses as his gaze retreats inward, rendering him completely inaccessible.

"And where exactly did you find him?" He struggles to keep his tone calm.

"Versailles." I tuck a leg underneath me and pull a needle-point pillow onto my lap. It's a scrappy Union Jack pattern, with frayed edges that look like a dog might've chewed them. For a moment, I wonder if it were once the property of Queen Elizabeth and one of her beloved corgis might've had their way with it, but I abandon the thought just as quickly. "My first solo trip was basically a repeat of the previous one. Arthur made me return to the Yew Ball."

Those shadowed moons under Braxton's eyes have grown deeper, darker. "And why's that?" His voice is hushed, as though he dreads the response that will follow. "Why do you think he chose to send you back?"

I hug the pillow to my chest and force myself to say the words he absolutely does not want to hear. "Because the last time I was there, Killian and I...met."

130

Braxton inhales a ragged breath and looks around the room, his gaze skittering from object to object in an obvious attempt to avoid looking at me.

"I see." He shuts his eyes, scrubs a hand across his face. "Killian was part of your Fade."

"You said you understood—that I wasn't to blame." My voice pitches higher than I would've liked, but I won't allow him to fault me for a phenomenon beyond my control.

"I don't blame you." Finally, his gaze lands on mine. "Truly. I don't. Killian, on the other hand…he's a whole other story."

"But that's the thing," I say. "Killian was caught in the Fade too. He had no idea what time he was from, and—" Too late, I realize waging a defense for Killian is the opposite of what Braxton wants me to do.

I watch as his lips tug down at the sides, hinting at something dark and unknown. "And you know that because…"

I shrug. Toss the Union Jack pillow onto the floor, leaving myself vulnerable and bare, but the choice is his whether to believe me or not. "Look—I don't know what you want me to say. All I know is what I experienced, and it was real to me."

"I'm sure it was." Braxton sighs, his fingers clenching as though grasping for something just out of his reach. "Killian has a gift for convincing people of all sorts of things. Despite what may have happened between you, you don't know him like I do."

I'm getting tired of this. Tired of this cloak-and-dagger rivalry between them that started long before me. Which is probably why I make the mistake of saying, "Well, if it makes you feel any better, I'm pretty sure he feels the same way about you."

"Meaning?" Braxton's sharp gaze cuts right through me.

I breathe an exasperated sigh. The truth is, I don't even know what it means. I don't know what any of this means, other than Killian clearly alluded to something about not trusting Braxton.

And Song did the same when she warned me that I didn't really know Braxton as well as I thought—that I haven't been here long enough to hear all the stories.

Clearly, Song was right about one thing—these halls really are brimming with shadows and mysteries, all of which are unknown to me. Including that book I saw in her room—the one she clearly didn't want me to see—the one I'm pretty sure I saw the girl holding in the Unraveling.

Could the girl have been Song? Or Anjou? Or—

I shake my head and return to Braxton. "Did you know Song is missing?" I say, studying his face, curious to see how he'll react to the news.

I'm about to voice some of my growing suspicions when he mumbles some distracted reply about that being the risk of Tripping. He's clearly so obsessed with thoughts of Killian, he doesn't even bother to drum up a more appropriate, compassionate response.

"Is that how you would've reacted if *I'd* gone missing?" It's a cheap shot, but at least it works to get his attention.

He whips his head around to look at me. "No! Of course not. Just the thought of it—" He rakes a hand through his hair. His eyes glinting with pain. "How could you say such a thing?"

"Killian helped me escape," I tell him.

Braxton won't budge. Won't even listen. His face, like his voice, is pure bitterness when he says, "I'm sure he did."

131

I'm about to say something more, no longer caring how Braxton reacts, when I remember back to my first Trip to Versailles when Killian gave me that handkerchief—how he waved it before me, as he promised he'd never forget me.

If seeing that handkerchief tonight woke him from the Fade, then why didn't it wake him back then?

Or is it possible he was never actually in a Fade?

Did he instantly recognize me as a girl out of time, and after taking advantage of my own Fade, he gave me that embroidered piece of cloth knowing once Arthur saw it, it was just a matter of time before I was sent back to fetch him?

No.

It's impossible.

Surely Killian was in a Fade. I mean, why else would he stay in Versailles for so long?

Unless he was purposely avoiding something at Gray Wolf.

Or, maybe even some*one*, like Braxton?

I remember how Killian hinted about there being more to Gray Wolf than collecting trinkets and art. But I was so incensed by his calling me *darling*, I missed the chance to ask what he meant.

Does he know about the Antikythera? Is that why he was in Versailles? Is that what Arthur referred to back in the Vault when he mentioned the costly mistakes he'd made in an effort to decipher the map? Was Killian that costly mistake?

Also, why did he refer to that man he'd left to bleed out as a *Timekeeper*? I mean, what the hell is that? And if that man is the enemy, then why did he have the same sort of tattoo, in the exact same spot, as my dad?

And what about the vision I saw in the garden? The one left from the boy who'd energetically imprinted the message into the sun. The same wavy-haired boy who bore an alarming resemblance to Braxton.

And why have all these memories of my father's strange esoteric teachings—lessons that've lain dormant for years—suddenly awoken from a near decade's long slumber starting from the moment I arrived at Arcana?

My dad, Arthur, the Timekeeper, Killian, Braxton—what could possibly be the connection?

"What're you thinking?" Braxton slides closer, tentatively rests a hand on my knee. The startling warmth of his touch draws me back to the present, where the two of us sit in this opulent room.

I sigh heavily, releasing the burden of things I don't want to carry. "I'm thinking about everything. And nothing. My thoughts are a puzzle, and not a single piece fits." I press my eyes closed. Wishing I could clear my mind like a fresh coat of primer swept across a used canvas and start all over again.

"Please don't let them divide us," he says. "Arthur, Killian, Elodie—they're out for only themselves. You're the one true thing I have in my life."

When I open my eyes, I find Braxton leaning toward me. His gaze soft, tentative, as though he's no longer sure if his kisses are welcome. And for the first time since I saw him with Mason, I look at him through an unfiltered lens.

Gray Wolf holds so many secrets, but right now, this beautiful boy who sits before me, with a bit of a bend in his nose and eyes like the sea, has gone out of his way to protect me. To be true to me. And I can't say that about anyone else I've met in this place.

I tip my body toward his, slide my hands over his cashmere-covered chest, and entwine my fingers at the nape of his neck.

But when his lips first meet mine, I flash on an image of the duke's hideous, leering mouth, and I instinctively recoil from his touch.

"You okay?" Braxton draws away, gazing at me with such compassion and concern, it sets my heart lurching.

I remember what Arthur said about how I'm the one who decides how to frame my own stories.

Is it denial to focus only on the good stuff?

Or am I just choosing the brighter side of the truth?

Either way, I'm the one who determines what happens next. The duke will have no part in that.

"Yes," I say, returning to Braxton, my lips eagerly tipping toward his. Because I am okay.

Better than okay.

I am triumphant.

And when Braxton's mouth opens for mine, I delve into the kiss, reveling in the sweet burn of his lips, the tenderness of his tongue, the craving of his body pressed fast to mine.

I settle onto him then, opening myself to the unlikely miracle of the two of us having found each other against every odd. Anchoring my knees around either side of his hips, I trace the scrape on his jaw with the tip of my tongue as he groans deep in his throat and nuzzles my neck.

"What happened here?" He draws away, lifts the talisman from my chest. His finger gently pressed to the spot where the gold bars are now dented.

Instinctively, I start to tell him the story of the man who turned my own dagger against me—

Of my mask failing—

Of fighting for my life —

Of losing my talisman and forgetting myself —

Of the rush of memory that came with its return —

Of my strange ability that allows me to see through time —

But in the end, I decide not to share any of that.

There are so many ways I could narrate my story; this is the one that I choose:

"I lost it. Then I found it. And now I'm back here, with you."

Then I pull him so close, his eyes no longer resemble a storm-ridden sea, but rather an endless night sky where the moon shines, a star twinkles, and the world brims with possibility.

END OF BOOK ONE

Turn the page for an exclusive look at one bonus scene from Braxton's point of view...

ARCANA

Braxton

I watch her from the dark side of the mirror.

Watch as she maneuvers through the dimly lit space, the heels she's not used to wearing wobbling unsteadily along the gravel pathway, like an unsteady colt testing its legs. Unlike all the others who've walked the path before, this girl shows no fear.

"Admiring the view?" Elodie asks as she enters the room.

I nod, seeing no use in pretending. The girl is pretty, that much is clear. But unlike most modern-age girls, she doesn't act like she's one selfie away from influencer status—and I find the prospect refreshing.

"I told her you wanted to meet her. Even showed her your picture."

My heart jolts in my chest, but I respond with a shrug. I can't afford to let on to a truth I'm barely willing to admit to myself—that while so far, I've known her only on paper, I've grown quite fond of the girl.

I lean closer to the glass. The girl has just found her way to the trail of broken-eyed baby dolls, and I'm curious to see how she'll react.

"What was it she called you? A face-tuned pixel jaw?" Elodie laughs, a grating, indulgent sound I do my best to ignore. "She didn't believe you were real. *Too dreamy to be true!*" Elodie adopts the tone of a vacuous, empty-headed fool. But I've been watching the girl since Arthur first found her. I've practically memorized the dossier he'd compiled, which means I know with certainty there is nothing vapid about her.

And yet, maybe this girl, this Natasha Antoinette Clarke (though, in my head I've taken to calling her Tasha) is onto something. Not about the dreamy part, of course. But rather the part about not being real. Most days I feel like a ghost, even though I'm not foolish enough to believe in such things.

Mainly, because no one ever really dies.

Death is an illusion, and time nothing more than a flat circle, looping round and round, without end.

"I'm bored," Elodie whines, slinking up from behind me. "And I missed you." She presses her lips to my neck, tries to snake her hand down the front of my pants.

But I'm not having it. Not today. Not ever again. I catch hold of her fingers and promptly move them away.

"You can't be serious." Her tone is equal measures anger and disbelief, but the truth is, I've never been more serious.

In hindsight, I can see our time together for what it was—an act of weakness, or loneliness, or any of the long list of desperate-making vulnerabilities that result from prolonged isolation and lack of meaningful human contact. But now that it's over, it's clear I made a terrible mistake—one I vow to never repeat.

I shirk away from Elodie and move closer to the mirror. Tasha has reached the tombstone, and I watch as she leans forward, tucks her hair behind her ear, and finds her name etched into the white marble grave marker.

This is the most telling part of the whole construct.

The moment that provides a true glimpse into her character

in a way that school records, phone hacking, and social media surveillance never can.

I press a hand to the glass, my gaze narrowing as she notes the date of her death, today. Which is also accurate in its own way.

"Here come the waterworks." Elodie exhales a wearied breath and slumps onto a nearby sofa. "I swear, this is always the worst, most tedious, most predictable part."

Normally, I'd agree. But lately, I find myself dreading every phase of recruiting. Still, I made my choice long ago.

And soon, Tasha will have to make hers.

I'm so lost in the thought, it's a moment before I realize she isn't reacting in any of the ways I've come to expect.

"What the—" Elodie pushes away from the couch and squints through the glass. "Is she actually...*laughing*?"

A smile creeps onto my face. Within an instant I see a green light flash on my tablet. A message from above: *Tasha is a go*.

A moment later, I'm securing a mask to my face. "Pour the drinks and cue the music," I say, racing for the door.

"Where the hell do you think you're going?" Elodie rasps. "You can't go out there now! It's against protocol. It's not—"

But I'm already gone.

Already on my way to changing Tasha's life in a myriad of ways she'll never see coming.

As I make my approach, I become acutely aware of something shifting inside.

There's a quickening in my chest.

A swift flutter of some strange, winged, achingly hopeful thing—like watching a springtime sun triumphantly muscle its way through the clouds after a long bout of rain.

Tasha, of course, won't know any of this. Which is why she'll predictably begin by resenting me.

But maybe I can find a way to turn that around.

Maybe, if I really extend myself, she might actually grow to like me—and someday even forgive me for everything that will soon follow.

And if I can manage to win over a girl like her, then maybe it'll serve as proof that I'm not quite the monster I fear I've become.

Acknowledgments

This is the part where I thank everyone who helped in the making of this book. And while there are a lot of people who contributed their talents and expertise, none of this would be possible without my readers. To those who've been with me from the start, and those who are just now discovering my books—thank you, thank you, thank you from the bottom of my heart. You make this dream possible.

Also, a big sparkly thank you to the entire Entangled team, including but not limited to: Liz Pelletier, Stacy Cantor Abrams, Jessica Turner, Meredith Johnson, Riki Cleveland, Bree Archer, Curtis Svehlak, Nancy Cantor—all of you helped turn my little time travel book into this gorgeous package called STEALING INFINITY, and I am forever grateful.

Another big thank you goes out to my agent and friend, Elizabeth Bewley, this one's for you.

To my family and friends—thank you for the much needed laughs over Zoom and in person. And to Sandy—thank you for reading every draft, helping me grapple with those pesky time travel paradoxes, and cheering me on every step of the way.

Stealing Infinity is a pulse-pounding, romantic time-traveling adventure with a satisfying happy ending. However, the story includes elements that might not be suitable for all readers. A scene of near-rape/sexual assault, violence, and discussions of poverty and a disappearing parent all appear in the novel. Readers who may be sensitive to these elements, please take note.

Let's be friends!

 @EntangledTeen

 @EntangledTeen

 @EntangledTeen

 @EntangledTeen

NEWS bit.ly/TeenNewsletter

entangled teen

an imprint of Entangled Publishing LLC